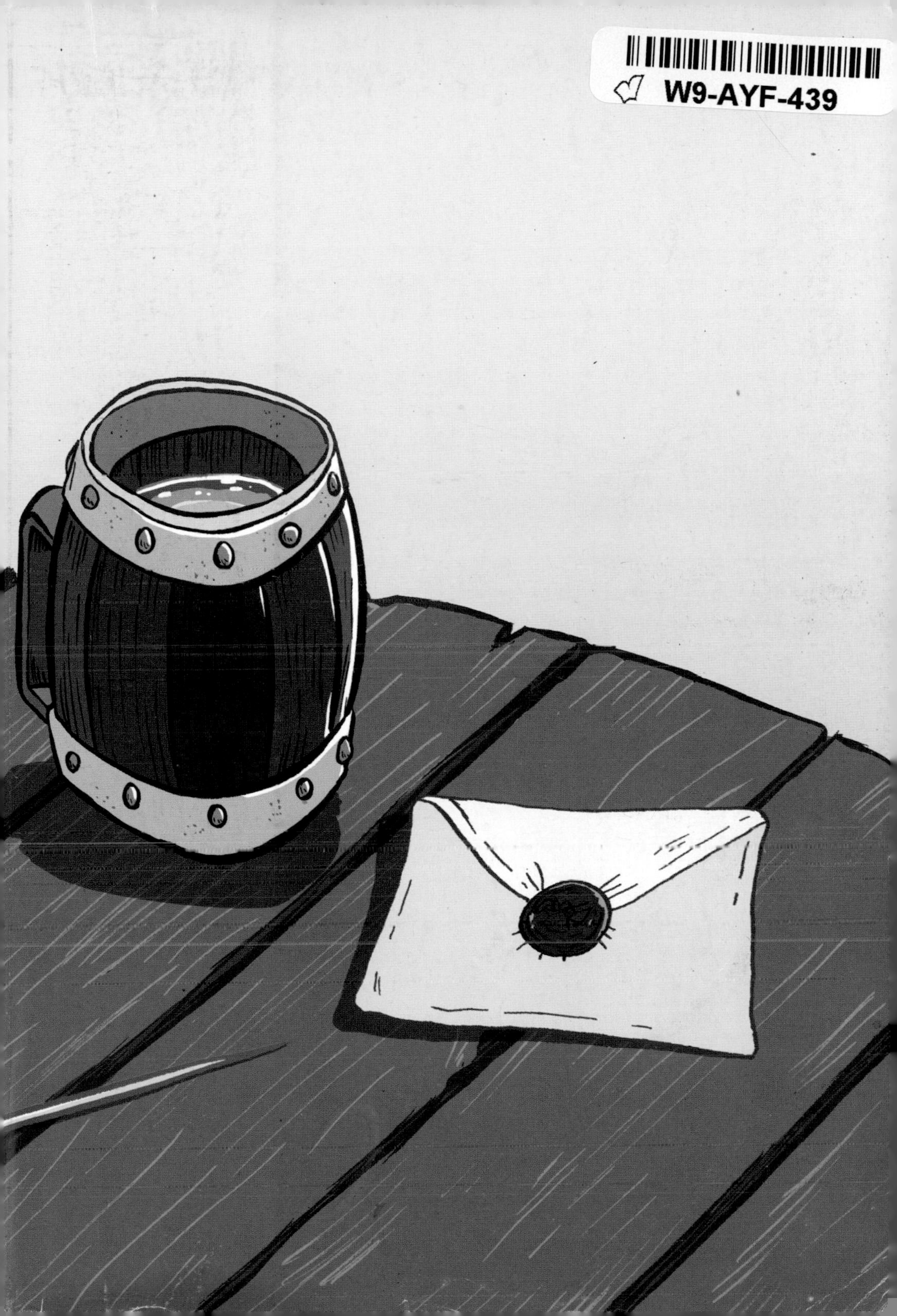

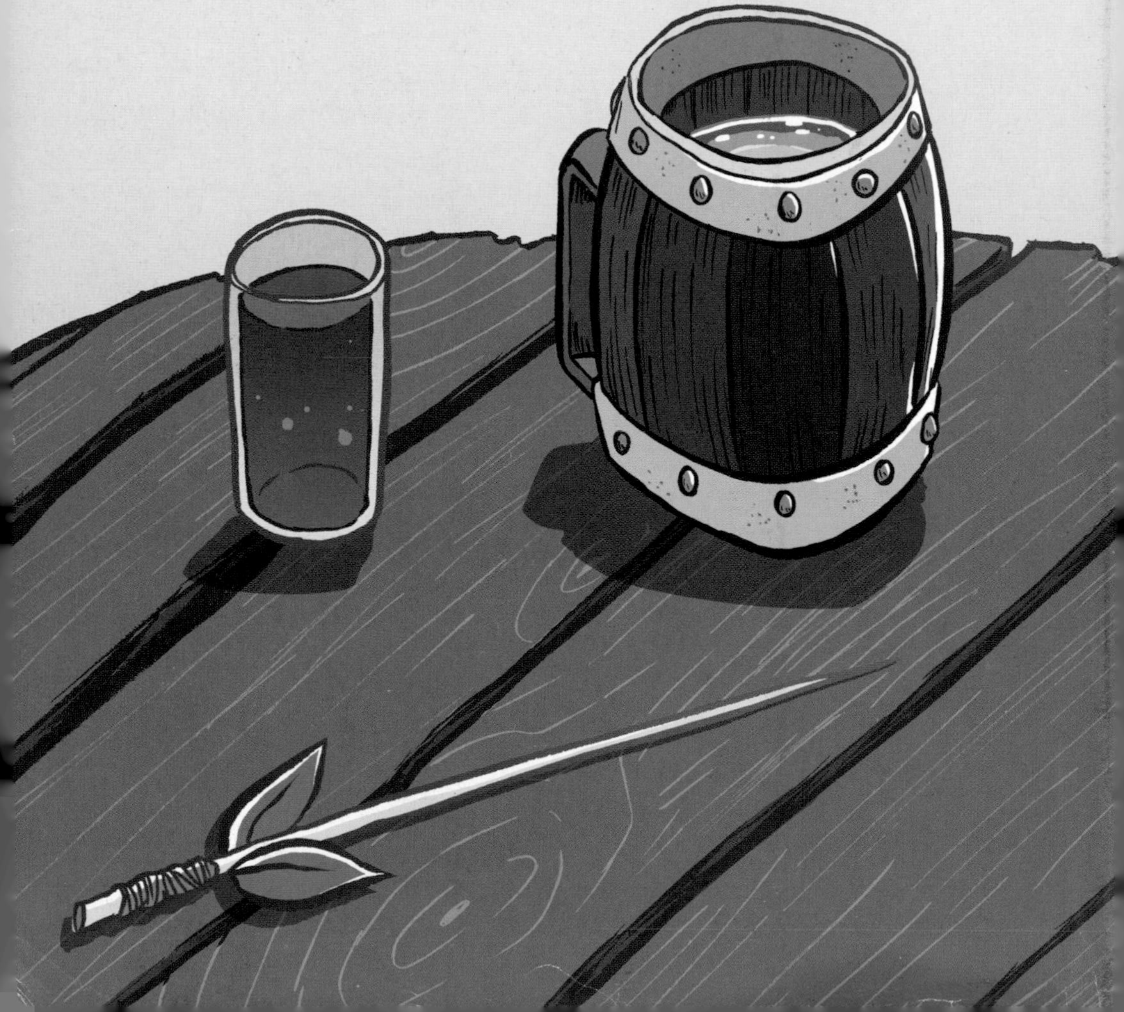

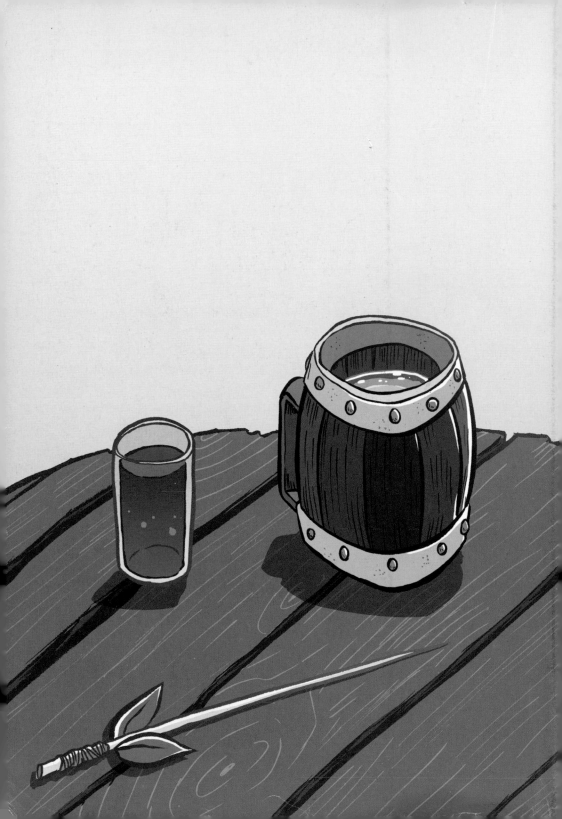

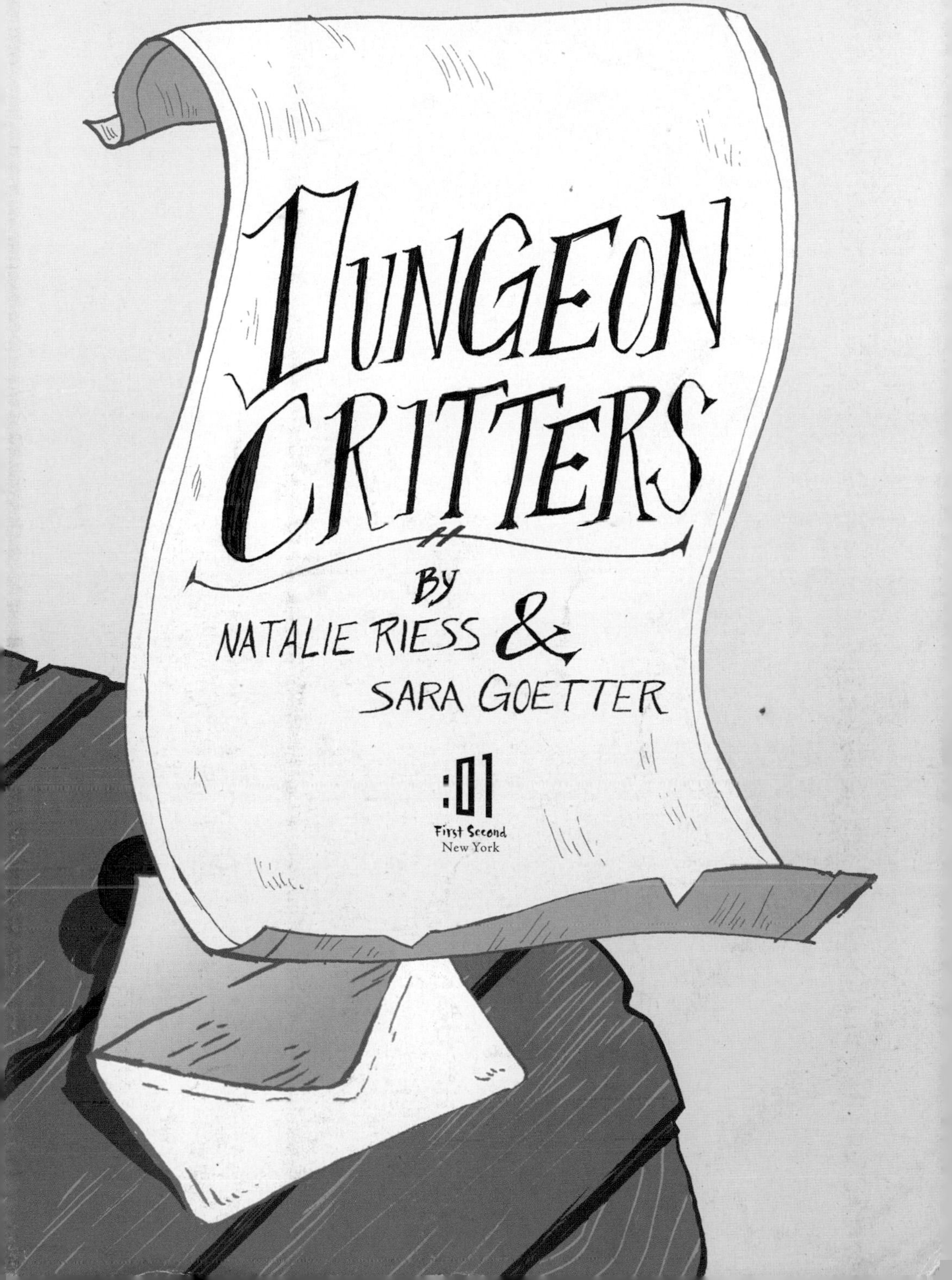
DUNGEON
CRITTERS
BY
NATALIE RIESS &
SARA GOETTER
:01
First Second
New York

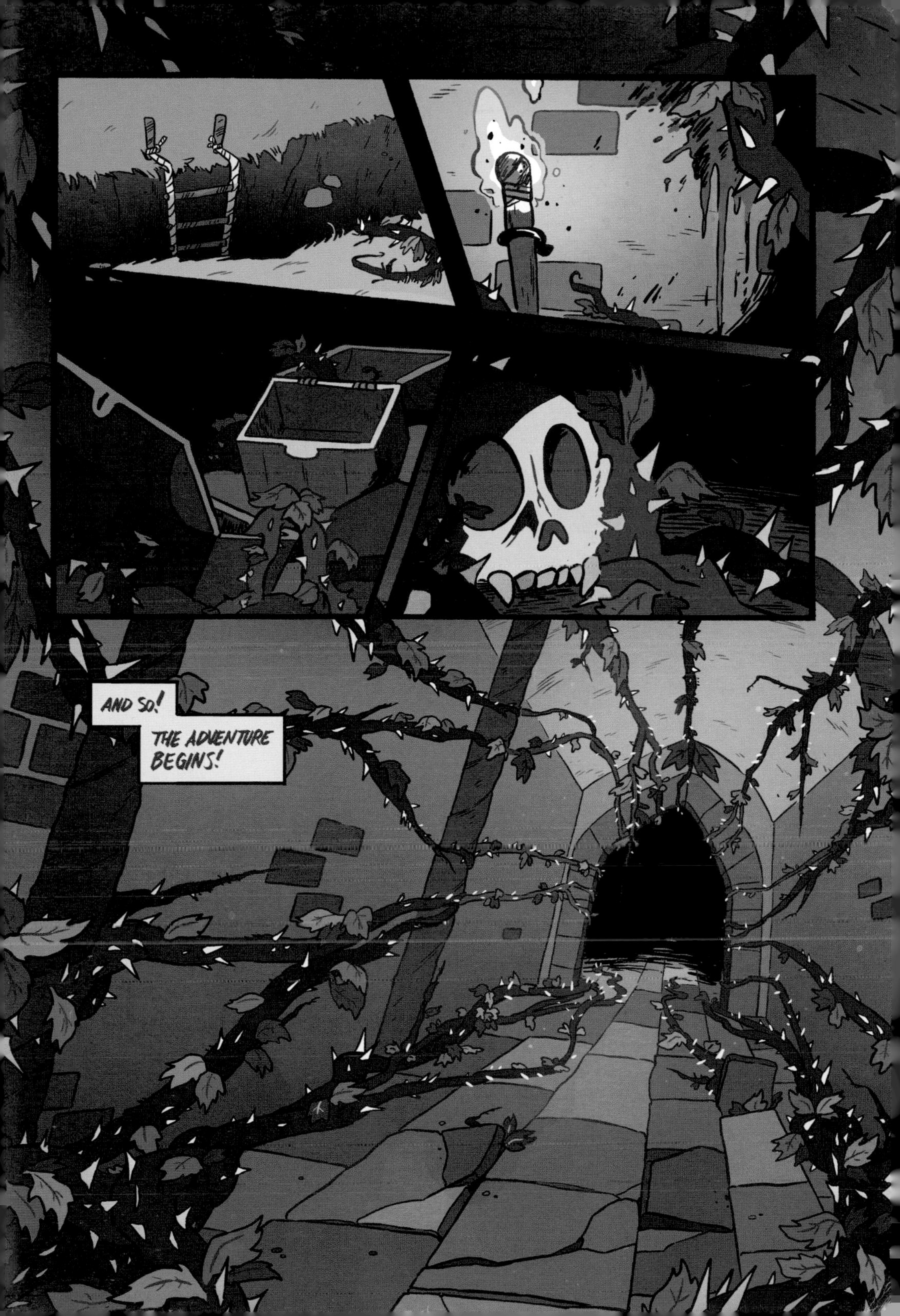
AND SO!
THE ADVENTURE BEGINS!

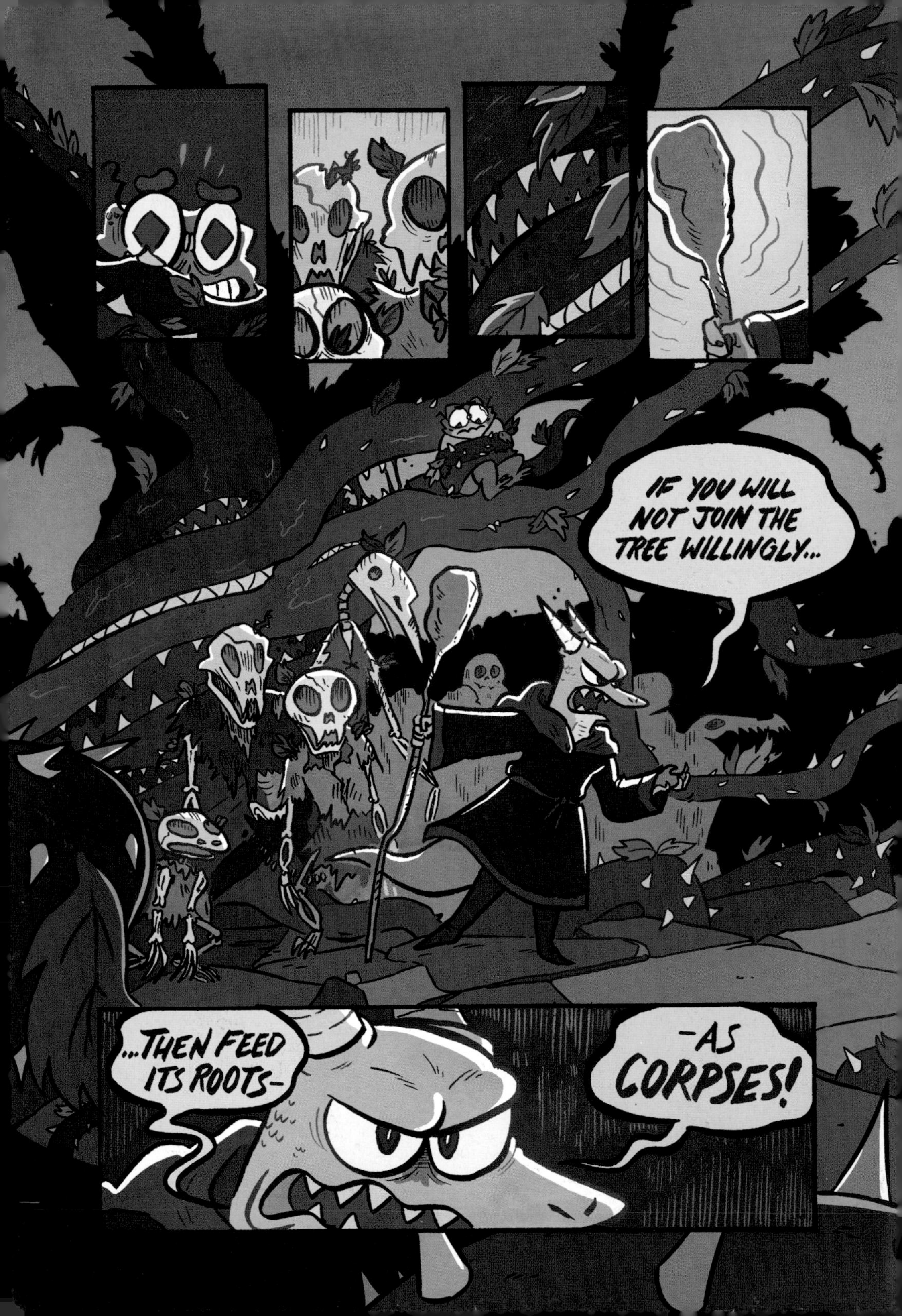
IF YOU WILL NOT JOIN THE TREE WILLINGLY...
...THEN FEED ITS ROOTS-
-AS CORPSES!

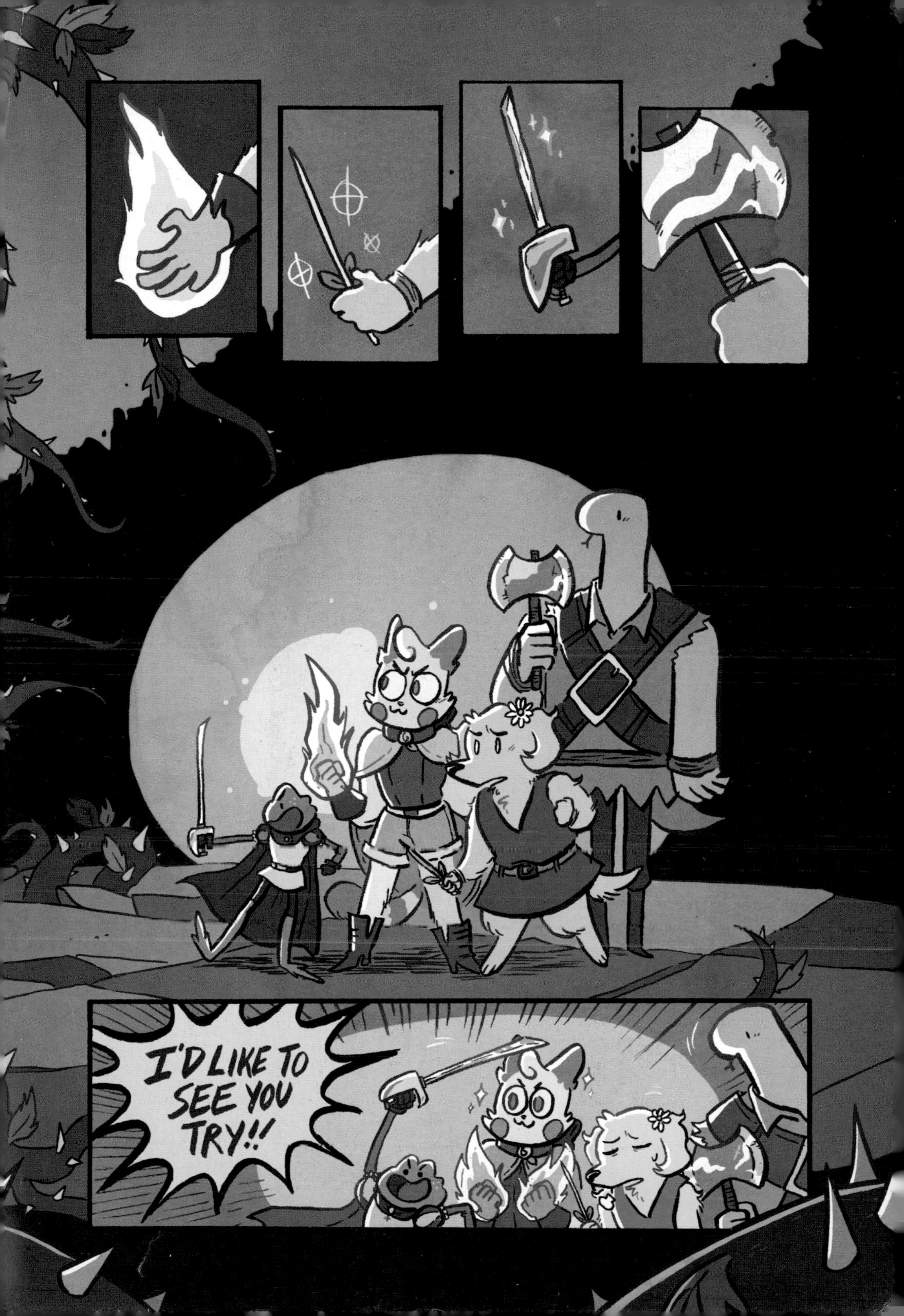
I'D LIKE TO SEE YOU TRY!!

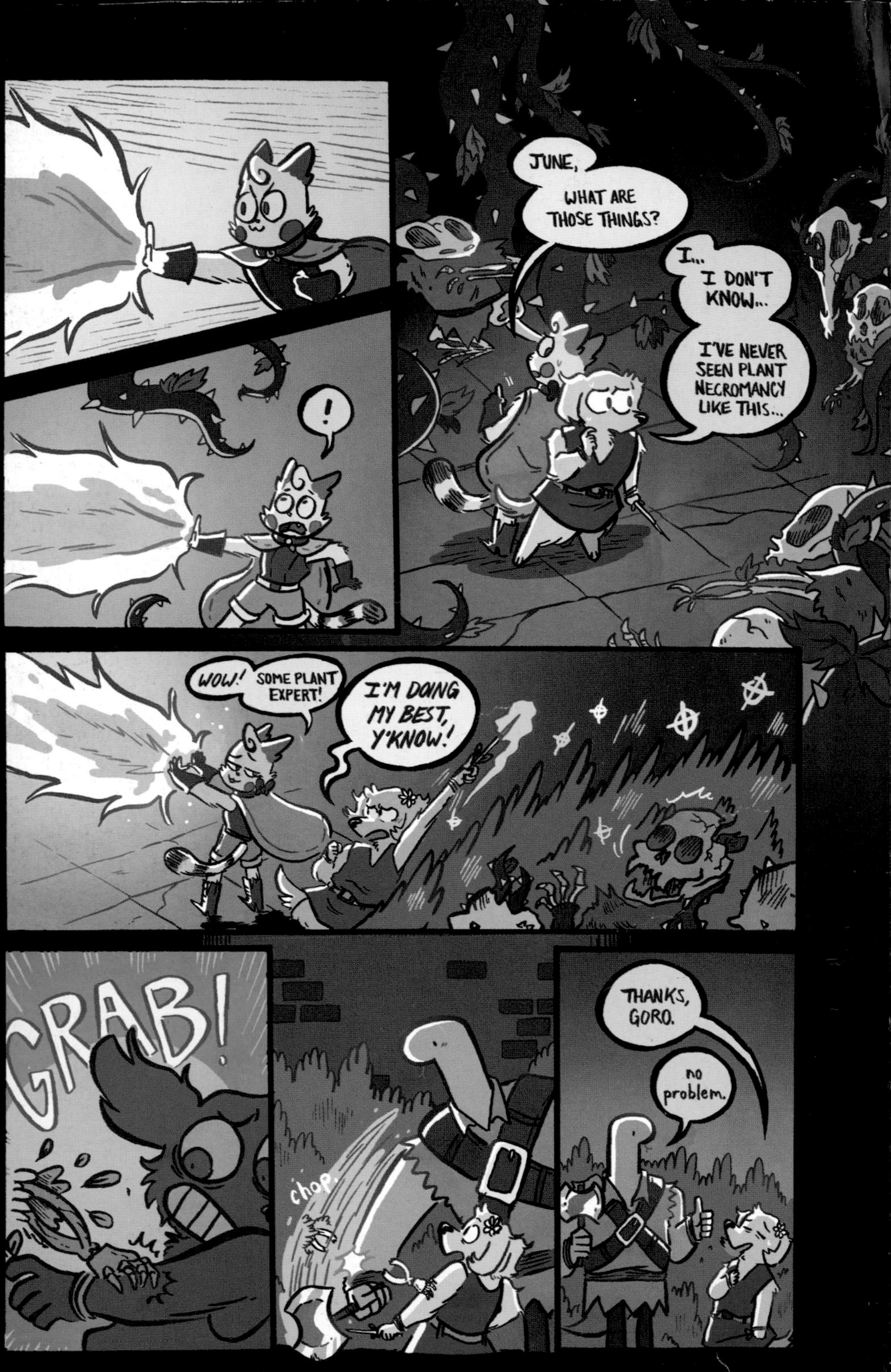

JUNE,
WHAT ARE THOSE THINGS?
!
I...
I DON'T KNOW...
I'VE NEVER SEEN PLANT NECROMANCY LIKE THIS...
WOW!
SOME PLANT EXPERT!
I'M DOING MY BEST, Y'KNOW!
GRAB!
chop.
THANKS, GORO.
no problem.

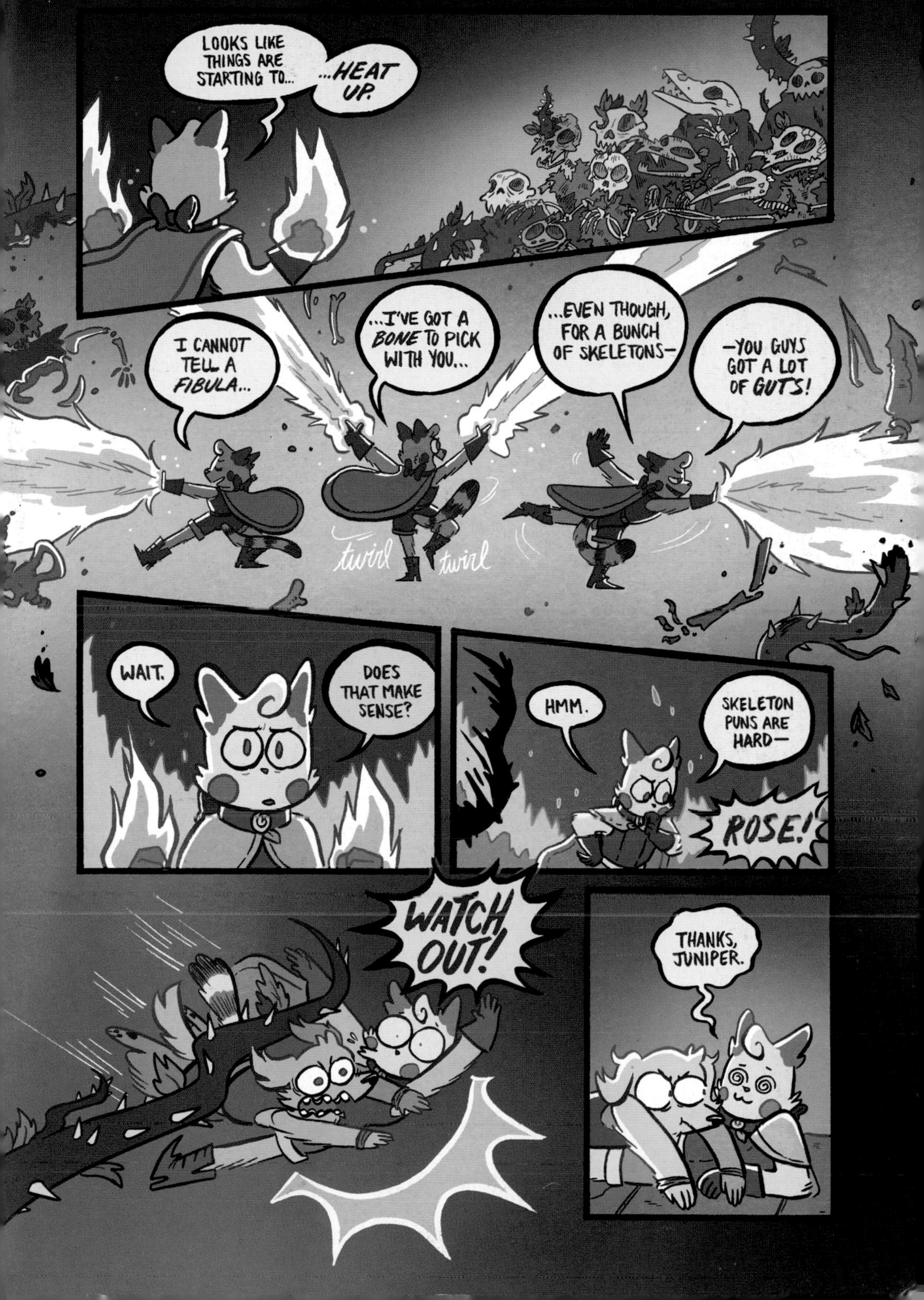
LOOKS LIKE THINGS ARE STARTING TO...
...HEAT UP.
I CANNOT TELL A FIBULA...
...I'VE GOT A BONE TO PICK WITH YOU...
...EVEN THOUGH, FOR A BUNCH OF SKELETONS—
—YOU GUYS GOT A LOT OF GUTS!
twirl
twirl
WAIT.
DOES THAT MAKE SENSE?
HMM.
SKELETON PUNS ARE HARD—
ROSE!
WATCH OUT!
THANKS, JUNIPER.

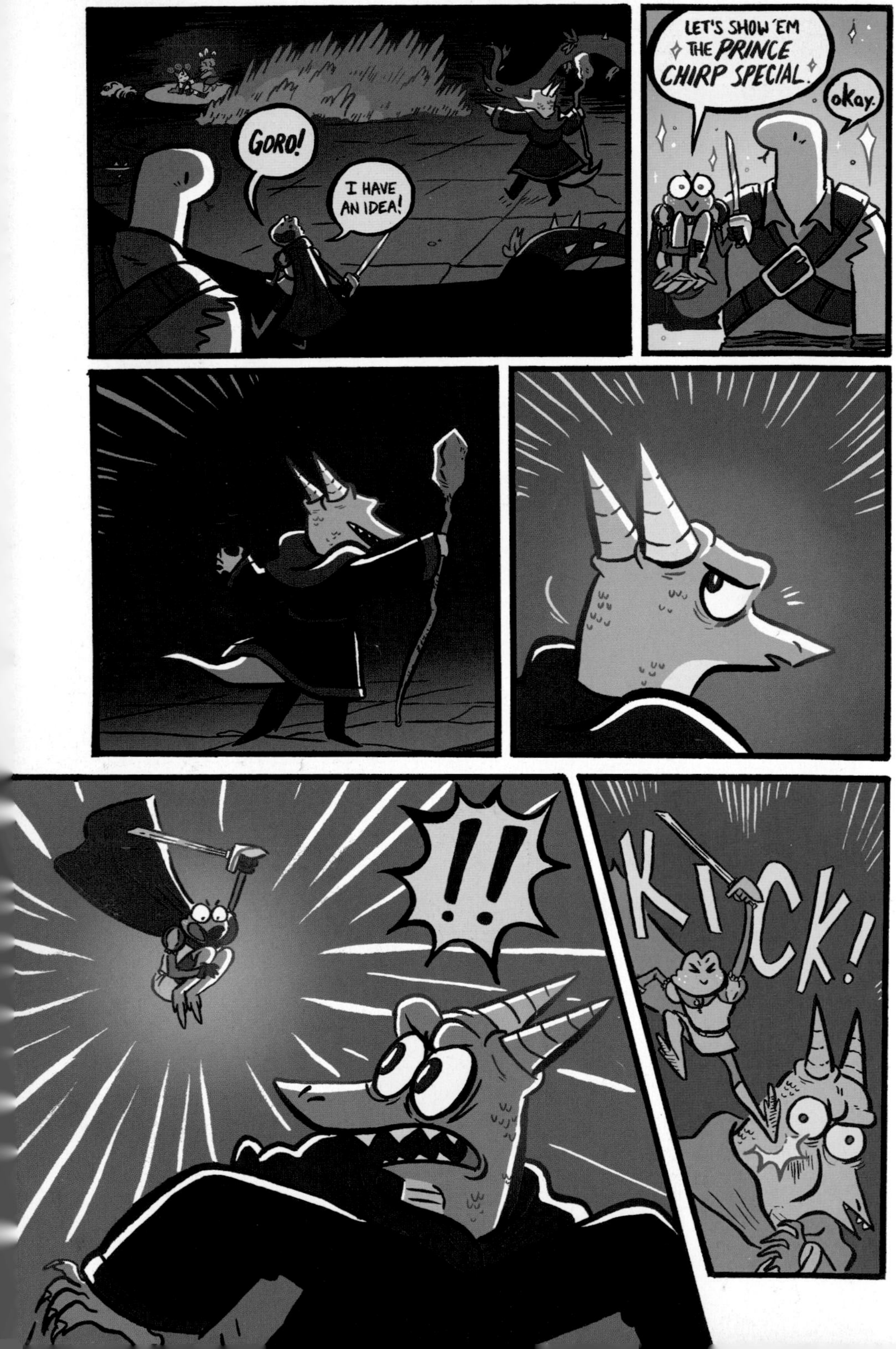
GORO!
I HAVE AN IDEA!
LET'S SHOW 'EM THE PRINCE CHIRP SPECIAL.
okay.
!!
KICK!

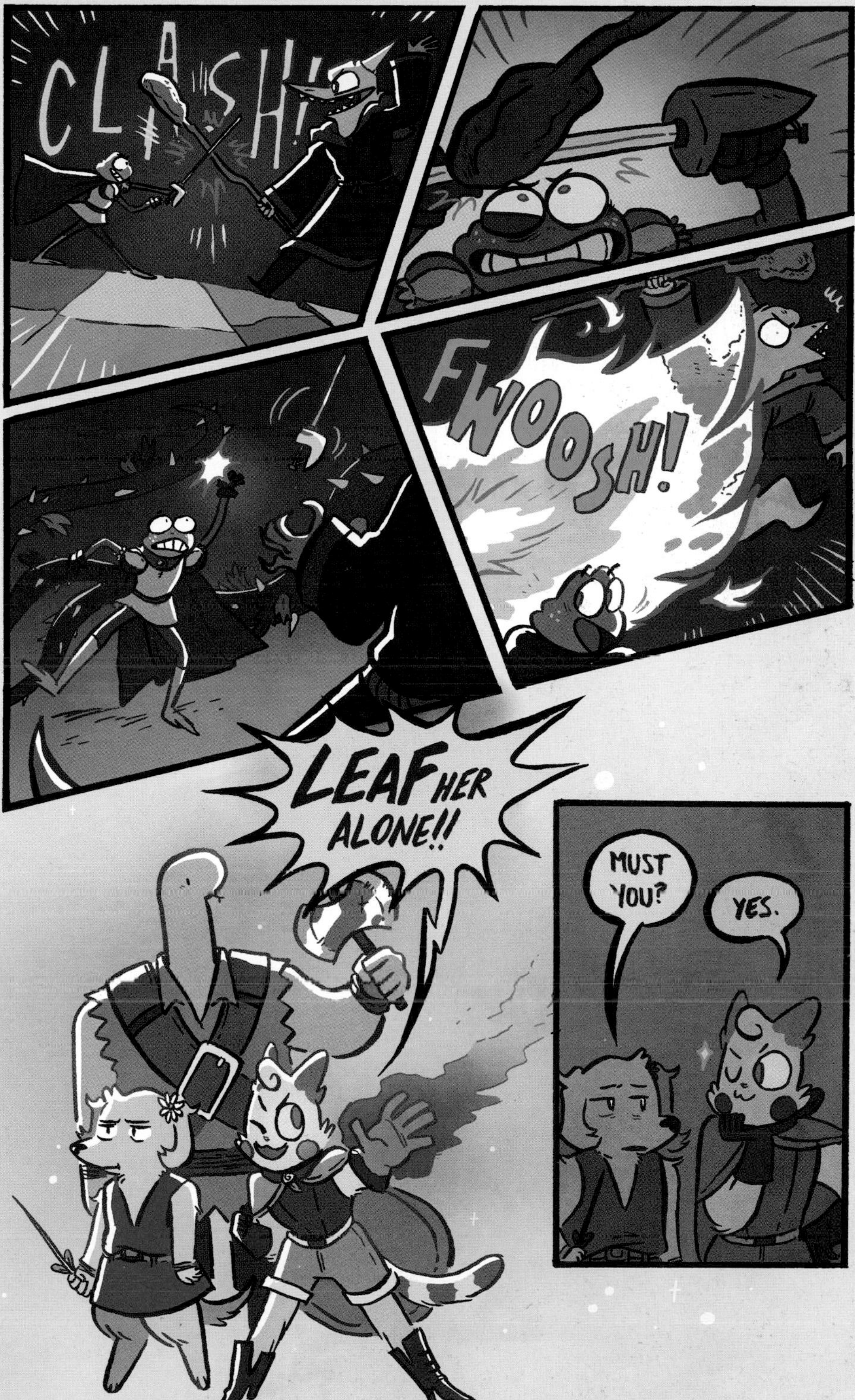
CLASH!
FWOOSH!
LEAF HER ALONE!!
MUST YOU?
YES.

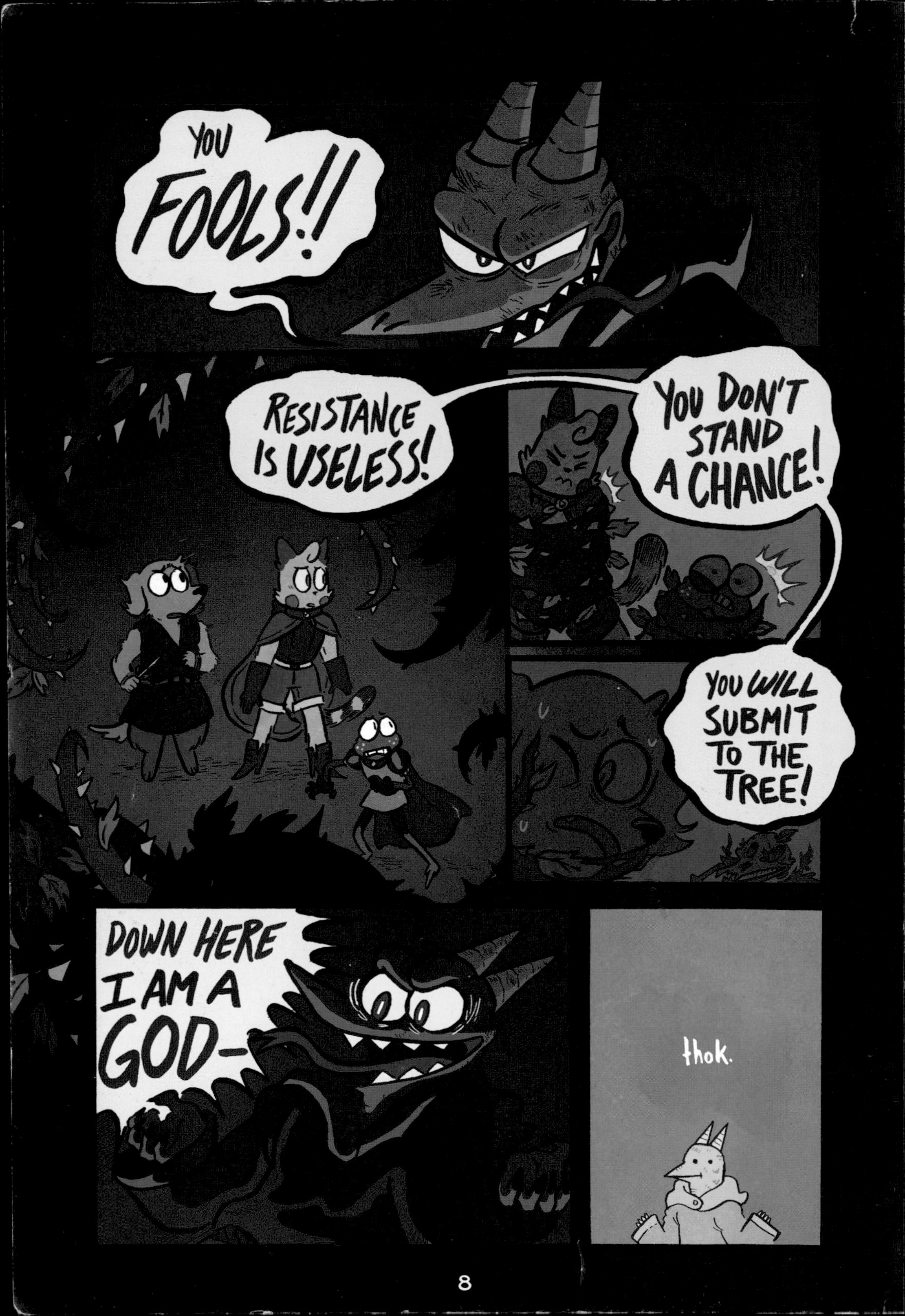
YOU FOOLS!!
RESISTANCE IS USELESS!
YOU DON'T STAND A CHANCE!
YOU WILL SUBMIT TO THE TREE!
DOWN HERE I AM A GOD-
thok.

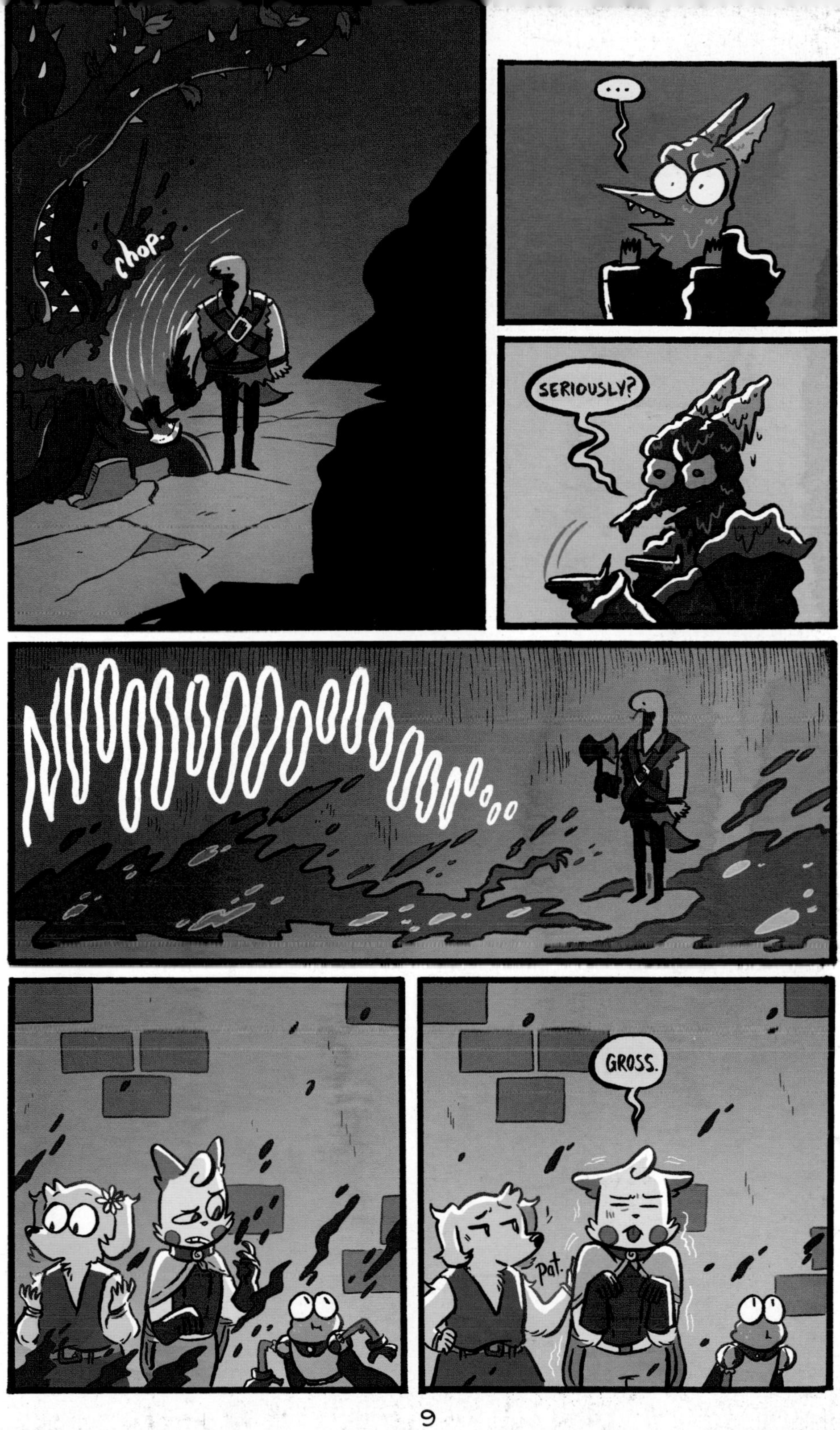
chop.
...
SERIOUSLY?
NOOOOOOOOoooooooooooo
pat.
GROSS.

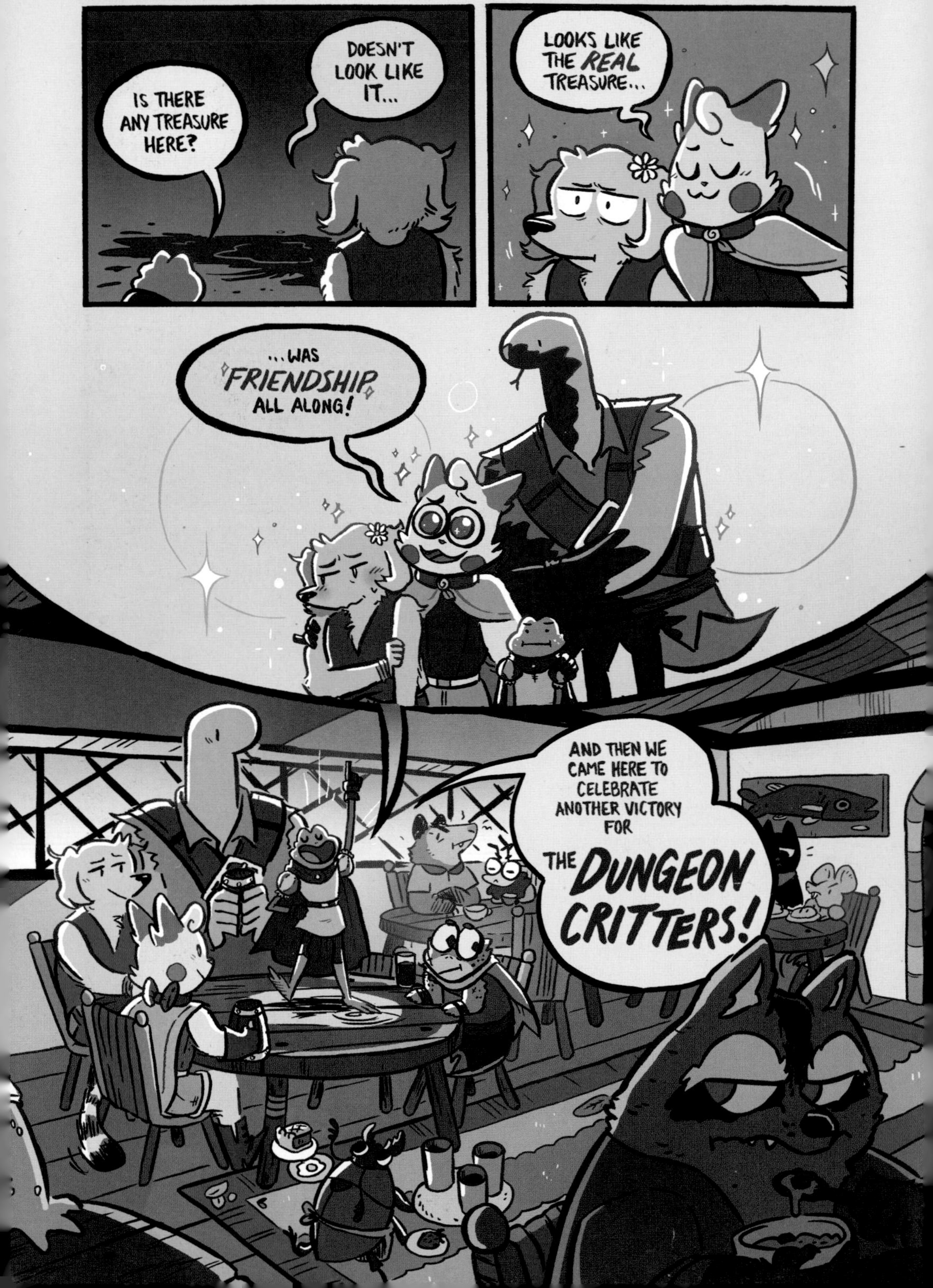
IS THERE ANY TREASURE HERE?
DOESN'T LOOK LIKE IT...
LOOKS LIKE THE REAL TREASURE...
...WAS FRIENDSHIP ALL ALONG!
AND THEN WE CAME HERE TO CELEBRATE ANOTHER VICTORY FOR THE DUNGEON CRITTERS!

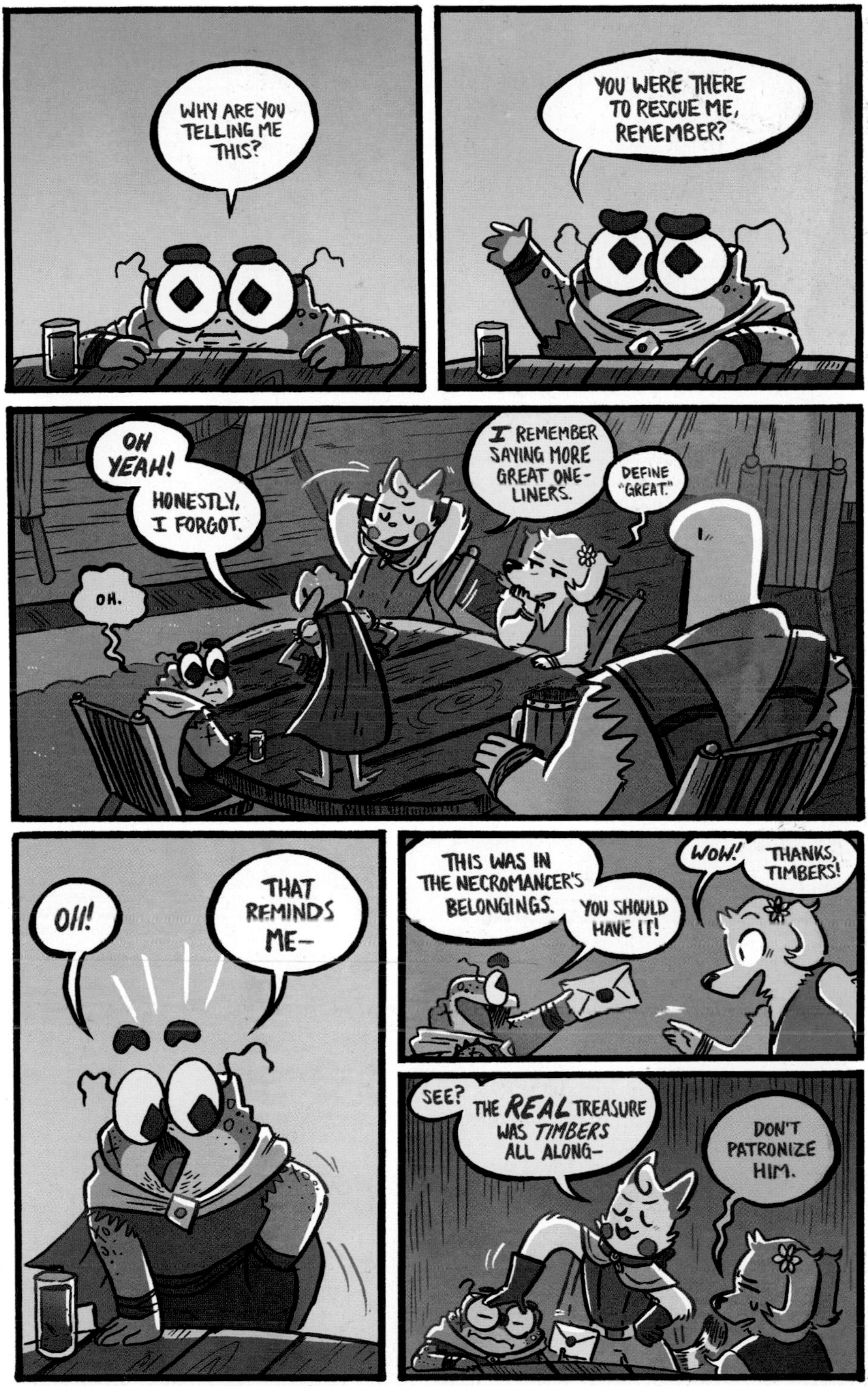
WHY ARE YOU TELLING ME THIS?
YOU WERE THERE TO RESCUE ME, REMEMBER?
OH YEAH!
HONESTLY, I FORGOT.
OH.
I REMEMBER SAYING MORE GREAT ONE-LINERS.
DEFINE "GREAT."
OH!
THAT REMINDS ME—
THIS WAS IN THE NECROMANCER'S BELONGINGS.
YOU SHOULD HAVE IT!
WOW!
THANKS, TIMBERS!
SEE?
THE REAL TREASURE WAS TIMBERS ALL ALONG—
DON'T PATRONIZE HIM.

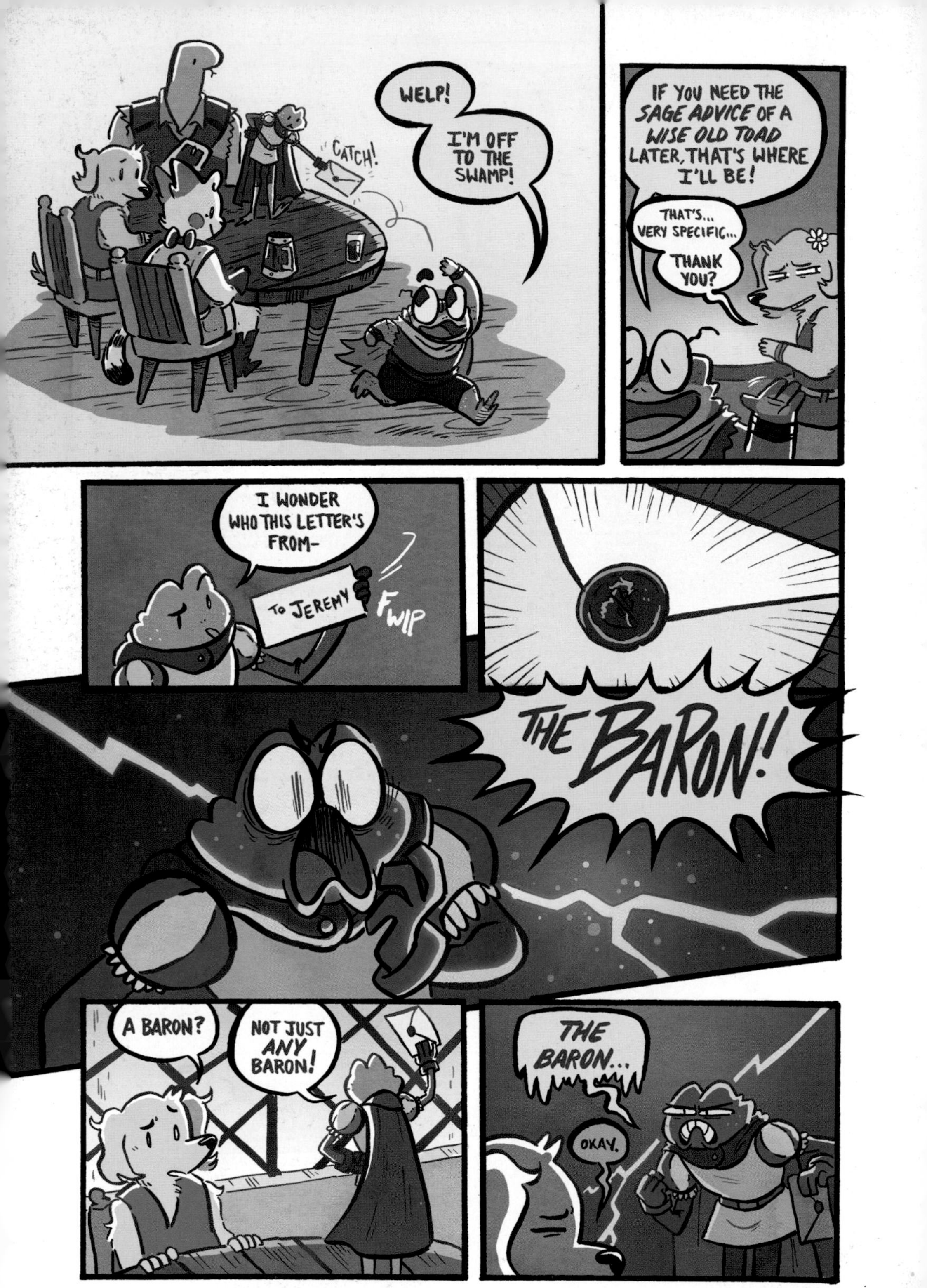
CATCH!
WELP!
I'M OFF TO THE SWAMP!
IF YOU NEED THE SAGE ADVICE OF A WISE OLD TOAD LATER, THAT'S WHERE I'LL BE!
THAT'S... VERY SPECIFIC...
THANK YOU?
I WONDER WHO THIS LETTER'S FROM-
TO JEREMY
FWIP
THE BARON!
A BARON?
NOT JUST ANY BARON!
THE BARON...
OKAY.

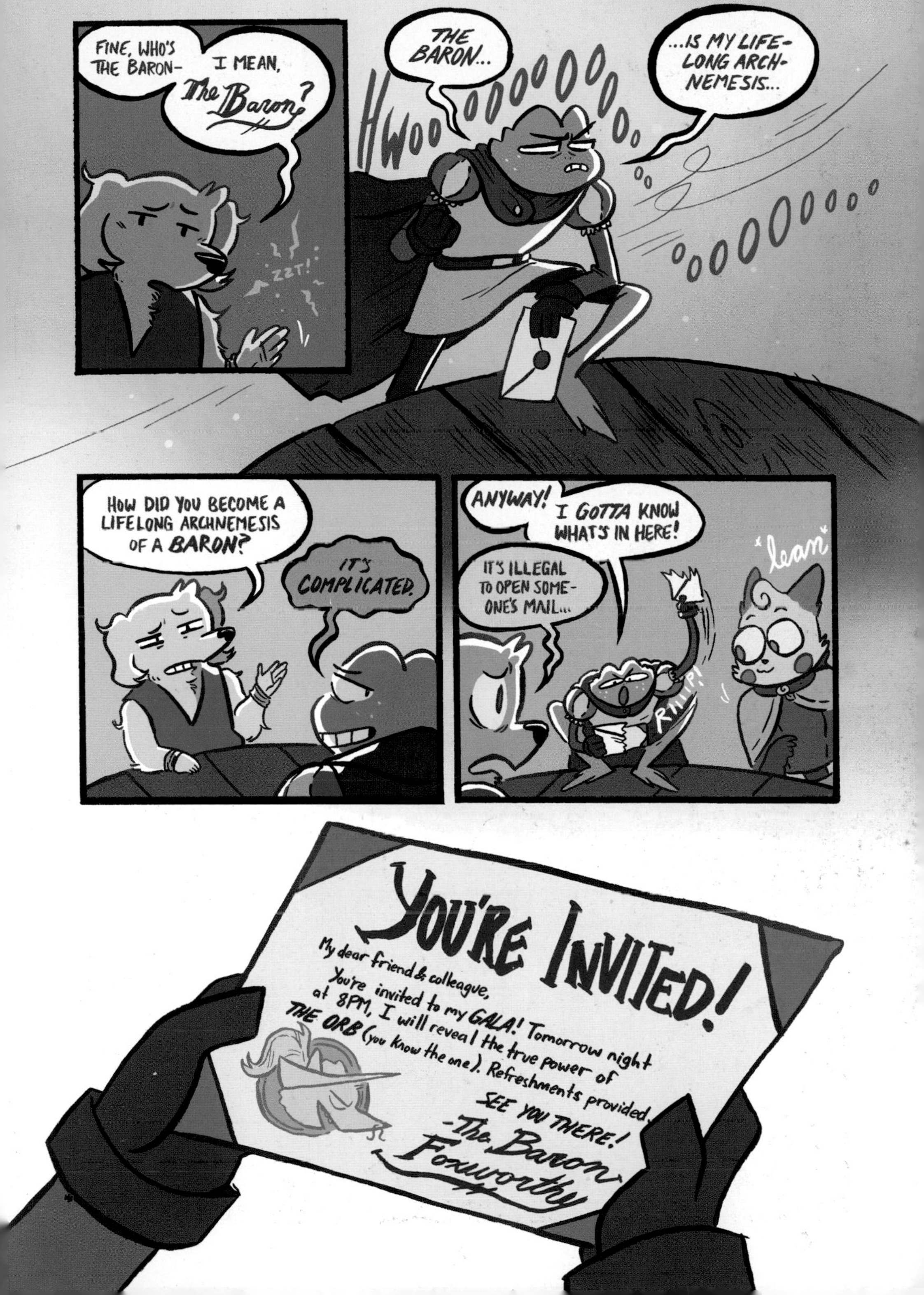

FINE, WHO'S THE BARON-
I MEAN, The Baron?
THE BARON...
HWOOOOOOOOOOOOOO
...IS MY LIFE-LONG ARCH-NEMESIS...
OOOOOOOOOOOO
ZZT!
HOW DID YOU BECOME A LIFELONG ARCHNEMESIS OF A BARON?
IT'S COMPLICATED.
ANYWAY!
I GOTTA KNOW WHAT'S IN HERE!
IT'S ILLEGAL TO OPEN SOME-ONE'S MAIL...
lean
RRIIP!
YOU'RE INVITED!
My dear friend & colleague,
You're invited to my GALA! Tomorrow night at 8PM, I will reveal the true power of THE ORB (you know the one). Refreshments provided.
SEE YOU THERE!
-The Baron Foxworthy

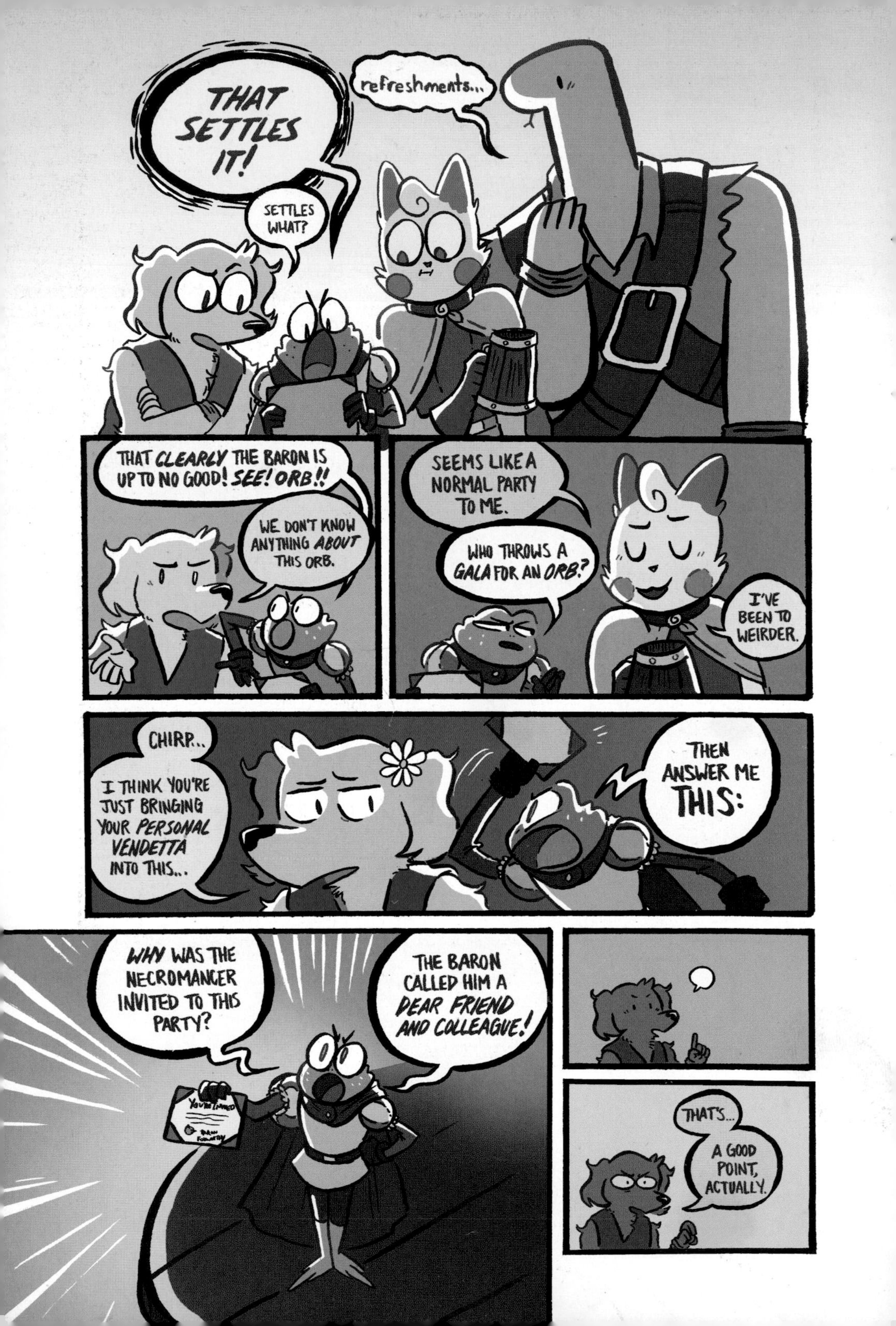

THAT SETTLES IT!
refreshments...
SETTLES WHAT?
THAT CLEARLY THE BARON IS UP TO NO GOOD! SEE! ORB!!
WE DON'T KNOW ANYTHING ABOUT THIS ORB.
SEEMS LIKE A NORMAL PARTY TO ME.
WHO THROWS A GALA FOR AN ORB?
I'VE BEEN TO WEIRDER.
CHIRP...
I THINK YOU'RE JUST BRINGING YOUR PERSONAL VENDETTA INTO THIS...
THEN ANSWER ME THIS:
WHY WAS THE NECROMANCER INVITED TO THIS PARTY?
THE BARON CALLED HIM A DEAR FRIEND AND COLLEAGUE!
THAT'S...
A GOOD POINT, ACTUALLY.

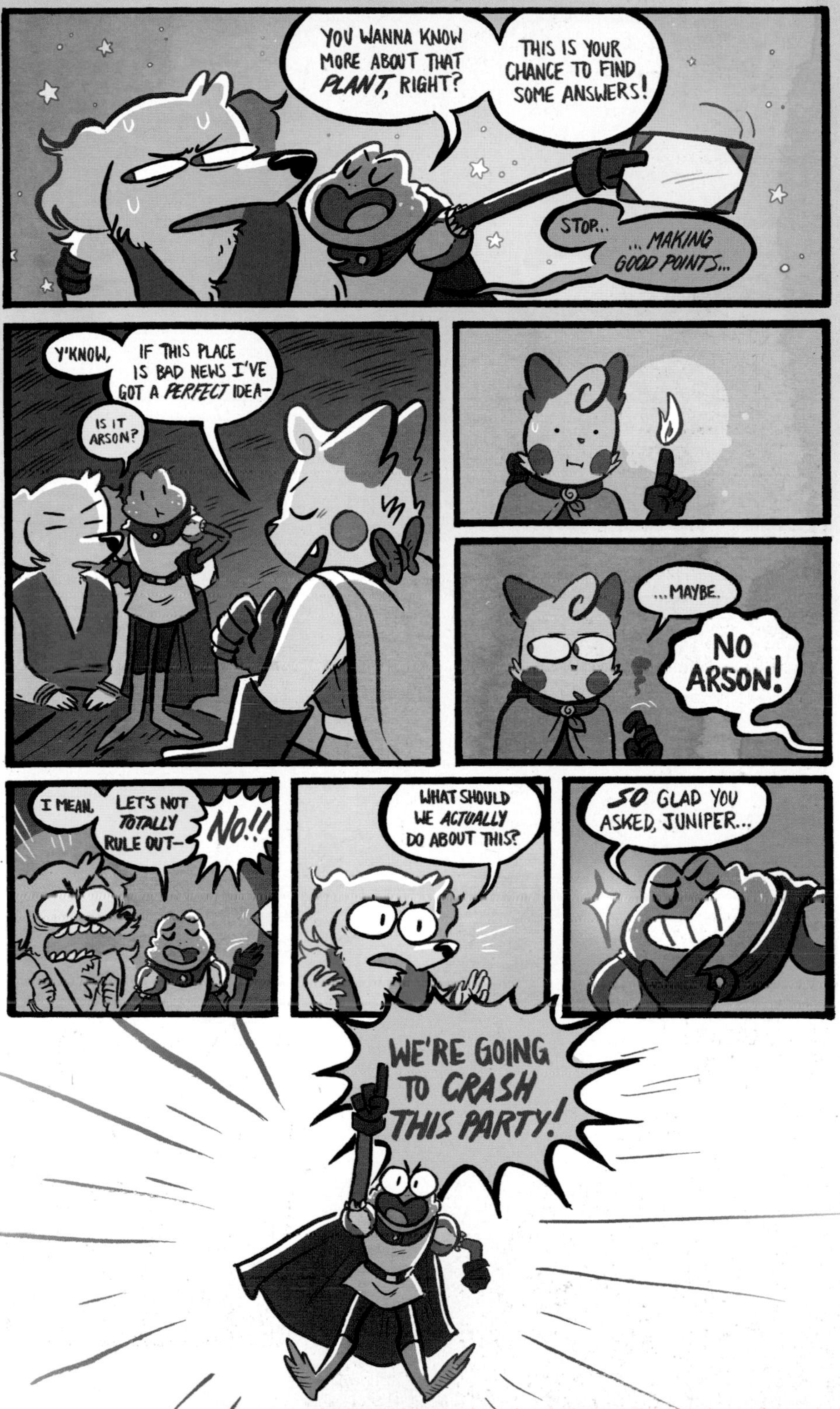
YOU WANNA KNOW MORE ABOUT THAT *PLANT*, RIGHT?
THIS IS YOUR CHANCE TO FIND SOME ANSWERS!
STOP...
... MAKING GOOD POINTS...
Y'KNOW,
IF THIS PLACE IS BAD NEWS I'VE GOT A *PERFECT* IDEA-
IS IT ARSON?
...MAYBE.
NO ARSON!
I MEAN,
LET'S NOT *TOTALLY* RULE OUT-
NO!!
WHAT SHOULD WE *ACTUALLY* DO ABOUT THIS?
SO GLAD YOU ASKED, JUNIPER...
WE'RE GOING TO *CRASH* THIS PARTY!

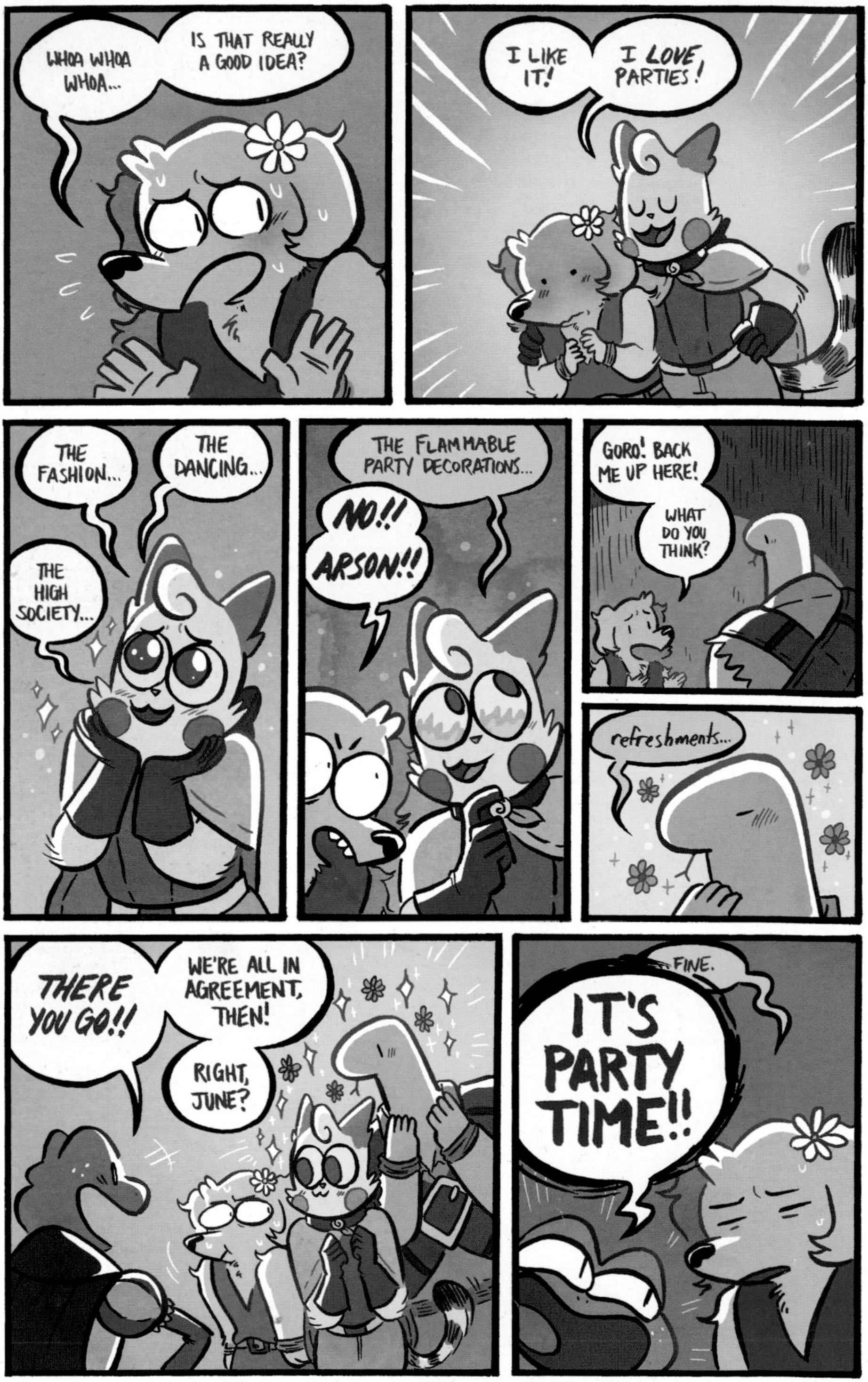

WHOA WHOA WHOA...
IS THAT REALLY A GOOD IDEA?
I LIKE IT!
I LOVE PARTIES!
THE FASHION...
THE DANCING...
THE HIGH SOCIETY...
THE FLAMMABLE PARTY DECORATIONS...
NO!! ARSON!!
GORO! BACK ME UP HERE!
WHAT DO YOU THINK?
refreshments...
THERE YOU GO!!
WE'RE ALL IN AGREEMENT, THEN!
RIGHT, JUNE?
FINE.
IT'S PARTY TIME!!

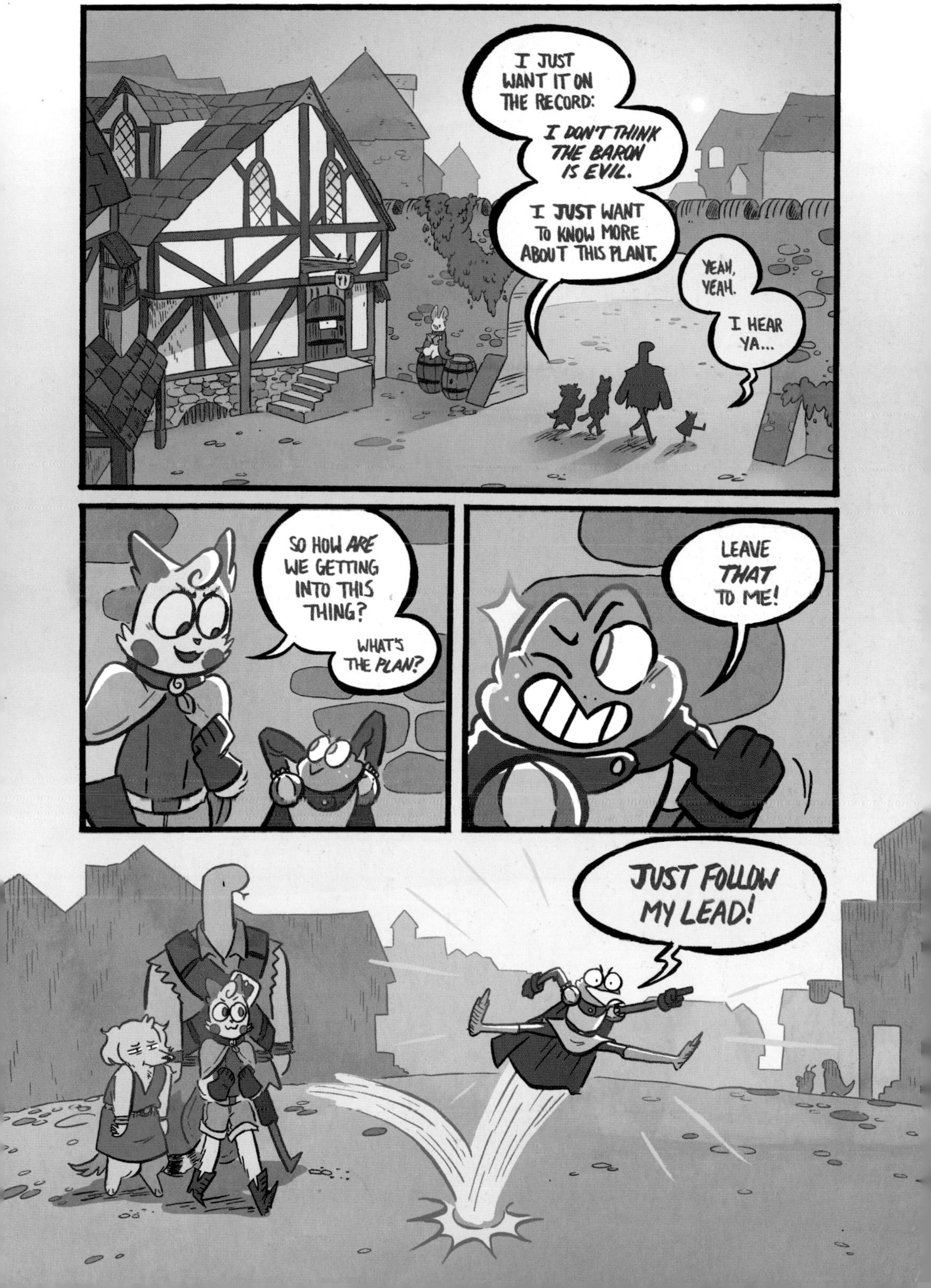
I JUST WANT IT ON THE RECORD:
I DON'T THINK THE BARON IS EVIL.
I JUST WANT TO KNOW MORE ABOUT THIS PLANT.
YEAH, YEAH.
I HEAR YA...
SO HOW ARE WE GETTING INTO THIS THING?
WHAT'S THE PLAN?
LEAVE THAT TO ME!
JUST FOLLOW MY LEAD!

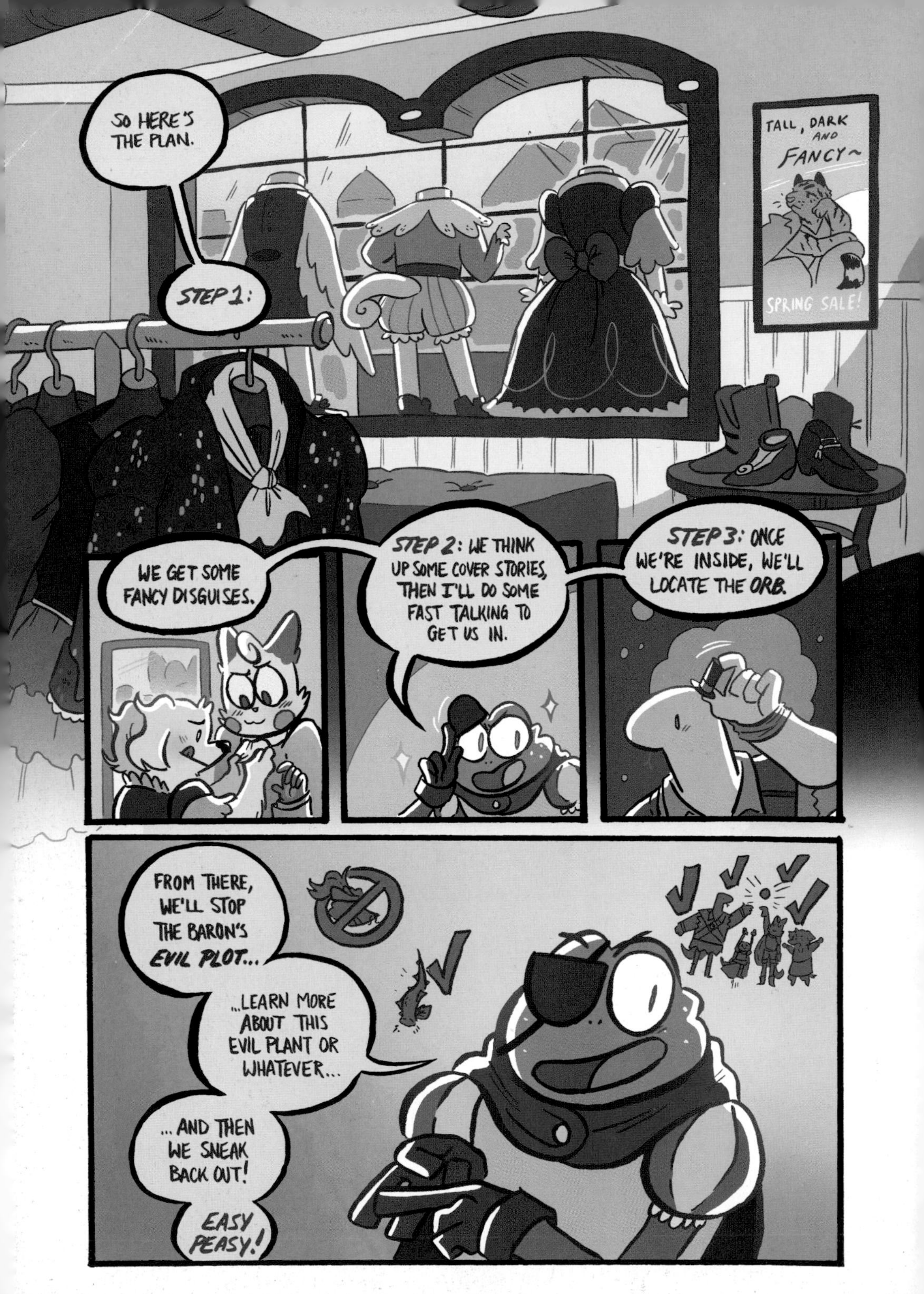
SO HERE'S THE PLAN.
STEP 1:
TALL, DARK AND FANCY~
SPRING SALE!
WE GET SOME FANCY DISGUISES.
STEP 2: WE THINK UP SOME COVER STORIES, THEN I'LL DO SOME FAST TALKING TO GET US IN.
STEP 3: ONCE WE'RE INSIDE, WE'LL LOCATE THE ORB.
FROM THERE, WE'LL STOP THE BARON'S EVIL PLOT...
...LEARN MORE ABOUT THIS EVIL PLANT OR WHATEVER...
...AND THEN WE SNEAK BACK OUT!
EASY PEASY!

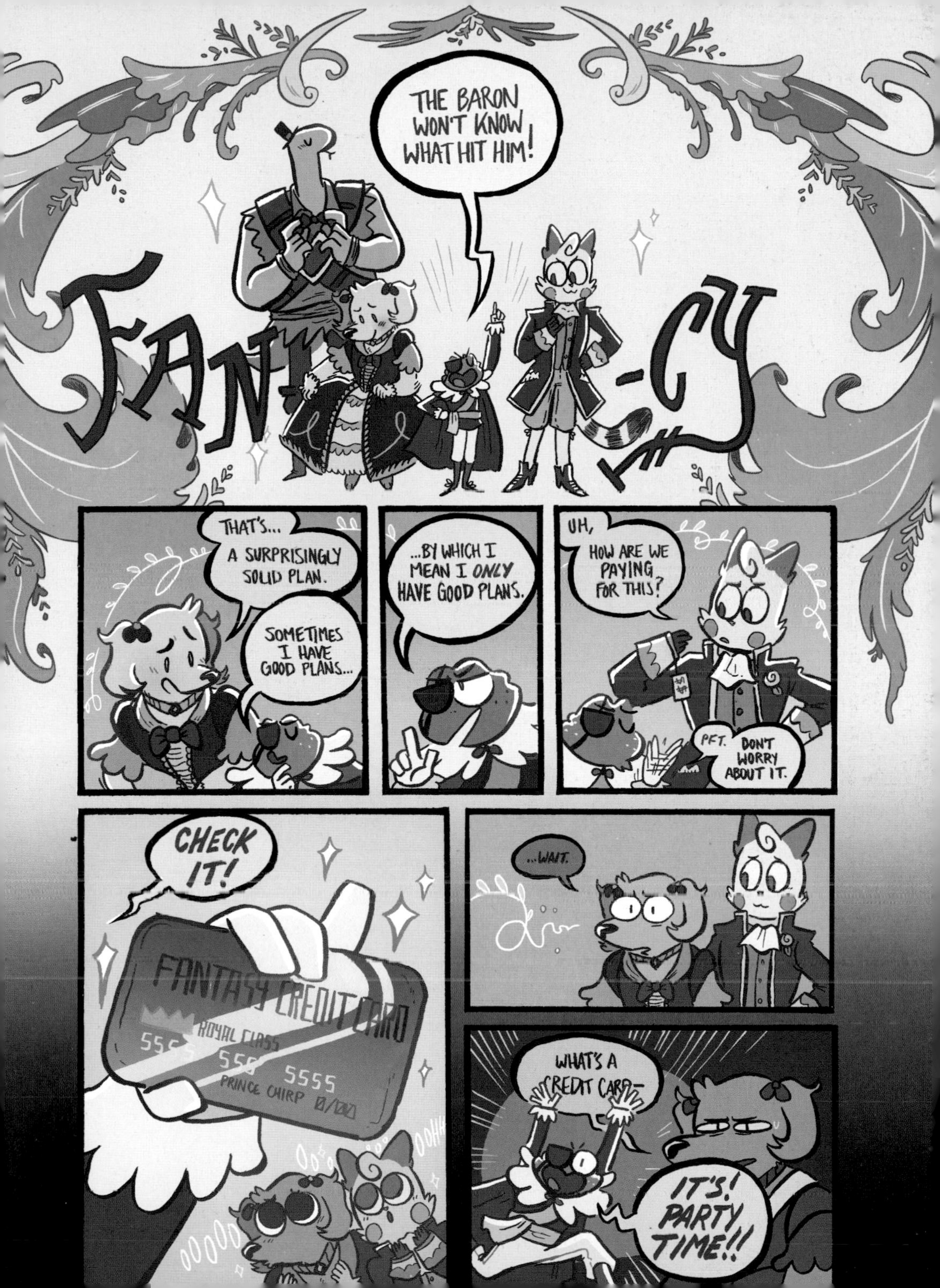
THE BARON WON'T KNOW WHAT HIT HIM!
FAN-CY
THAT'S...
A SURPRISINGLY SOLID PLAN.
SOMETIMES I HAVE GOOD PLANS...
...BY WHICH I MEAN I ONLY HAVE GOOD PLANS.
UH,
HOW ARE WE PAYING FOR THIS?
PFT.
DON'T WORRY ABOUT IT.
CHECK IT!
FANTASY CREDIT CARD
ROYAL CLASS
5555 5555 5555
PRINCE CHIRP
OOHH
...WAIT.
WHAT'S A CREDIT CARD—
IT'S! PARTY TIME!!

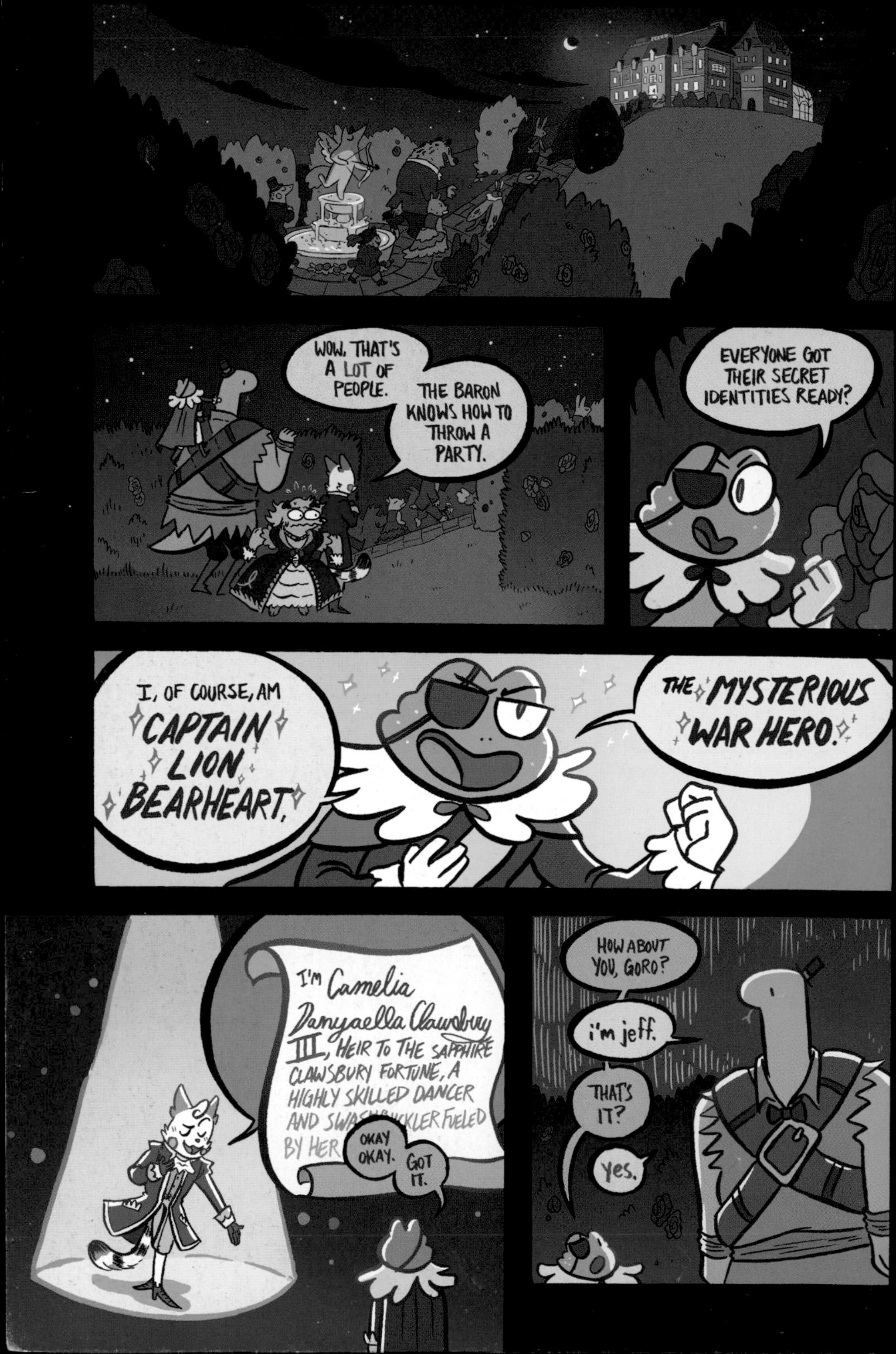
WOW, THAT'S A LOT OF PEOPLE.
THE BARON KNOWS HOW TO THROW A PARTY.
EVERYONE GOT THEIR SECRET IDENTITIES READY?
I, OF COURSE, AM CAPTAIN LION BEARHEART,
THE MYSTERIOUS WAR HERO.
I'M Camelia Danyaella Clawsbury III, HEIR TO THE SAPPHIRE CLAWSBURY FORTUNE, A HIGHLY SKILLED DANCER AND SWASHBUCKLER FUELED BY HER
OKAY OKAY.
GOT IT.
HOW ABOUT YOU, GORO?
i'm jeff.
THAT'S IT?
yes.

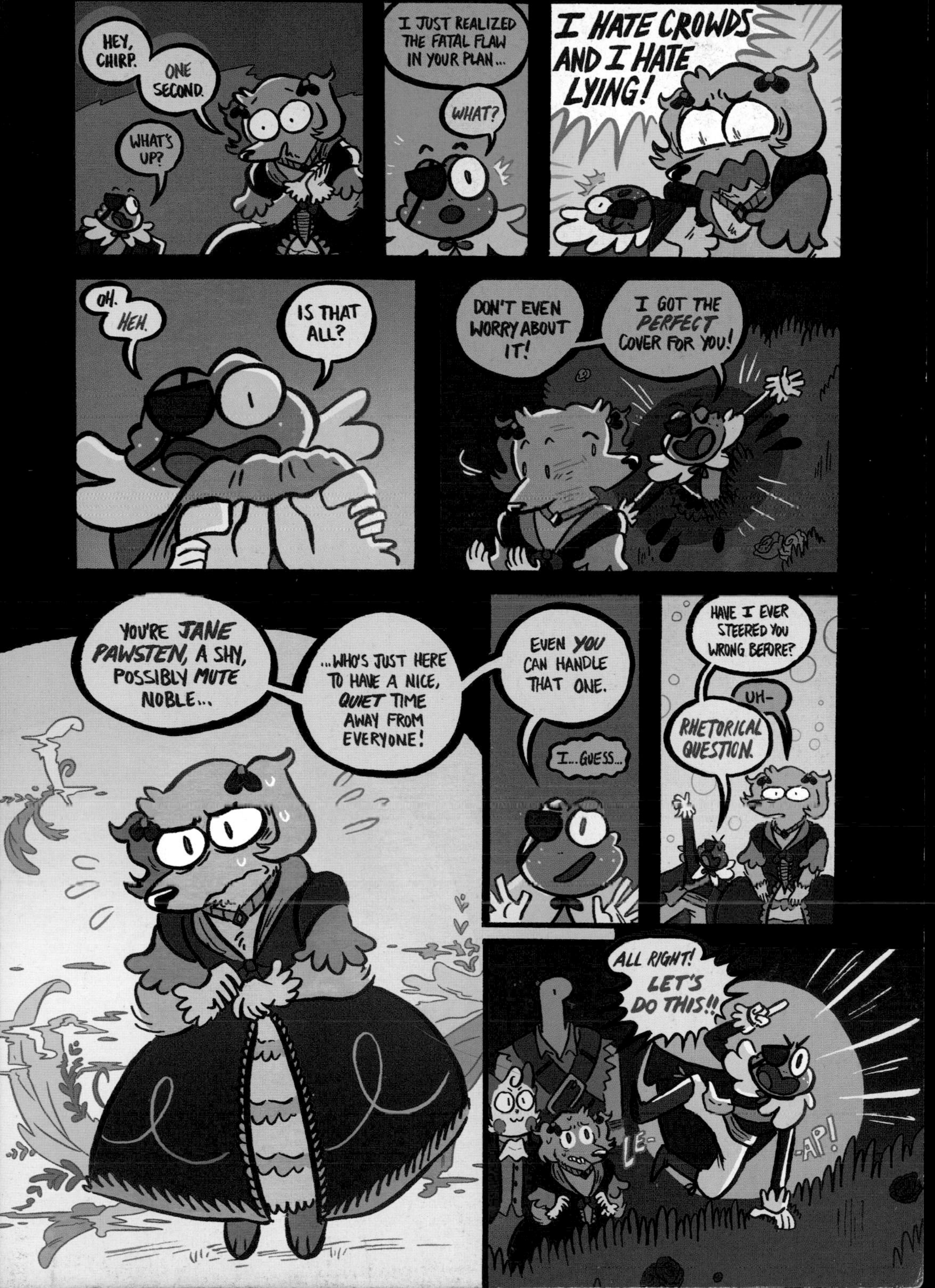
HEY, CHIRP.
ONE SECOND.
WHAT'S UP?
I JUST REALIZED THE FATAL FLAW IN YOUR PLAN...
WHAT?
I HATE CROWDS AND I HATE LYING!
OH. HEH.
IS THAT ALL?
DON'T EVEN WORRY ABOUT IT!
I GOT THE PERFECT COVER FOR YOU!
YOU'RE JANE PAWSTEN, A SHY, POSSIBLY MUTE NOBLE...
...WHO'S JUST HERE TO HAVE A NICE, QUIET TIME AWAY FROM EVERYONE!
EVEN YOU CAN HANDLE THAT ONE.
I...GUESS...
HAVE I EVER STEERED YOU WRONG BEFORE?
UH-
RHETORICAL QUESTION.
ALL RIGHT! LET'S DO THIS!!
LE-
-AP!

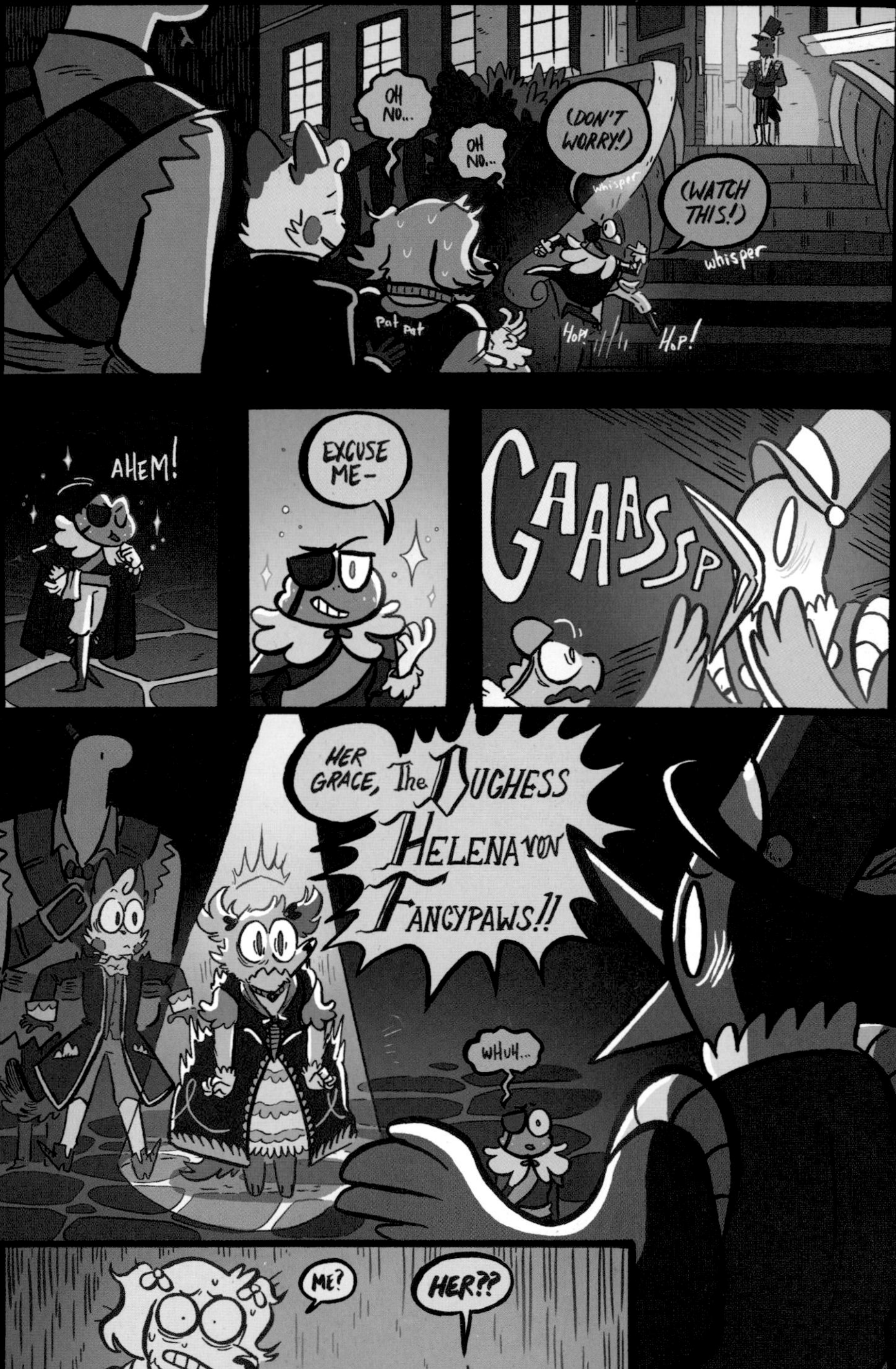

OH NO...
OH NO...
(DON'T WORRY!)
whisper
(WATCH THIS!)
whisper
Pat Pat
HOP!
HOP!
AHEM!
EXCUSE ME-
GAAASSP
HER GRACE, The DUCHESS HELENA VON FANCYPAWS!!
WHUH...
ME?
HER??

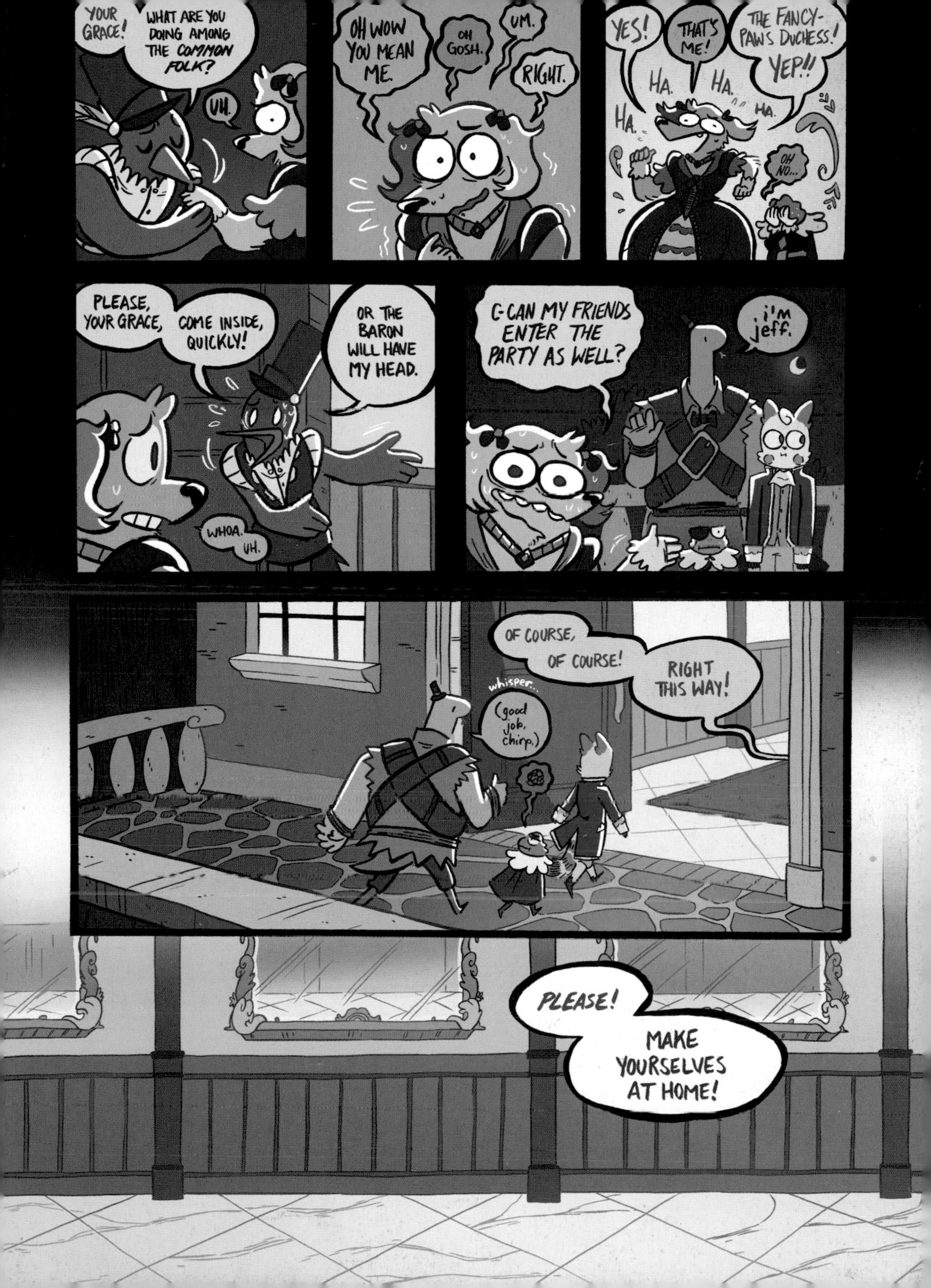
YOUR GRACE!
WHAT ARE YOU DOING AMONG THE COMMON FOLK?
UH.
OH WOW YOU MEAN ME.
OH GOSH.
UM.
RIGHT.
YES!
THAT'S ME!
THE FANCY-PAWS DUCHESS! YEP!!
HA. HA. HA. HA.
OH NO...
PLEASE, YOUR GRACE,
COME INSIDE, QUICKLY!
OR THE BARON WILL HAVE MY HEAD.
WHOA. UH.
C-CAN MY FRIENDS ENTER THE PARTY AS WELL?
i'm jeff.
OF COURSE, OF COURSE!
RIGHT THIS WAY!
whisper...
(good job, chirp.)
PLEASE!
MAKE YOURSELVES AT HOME!

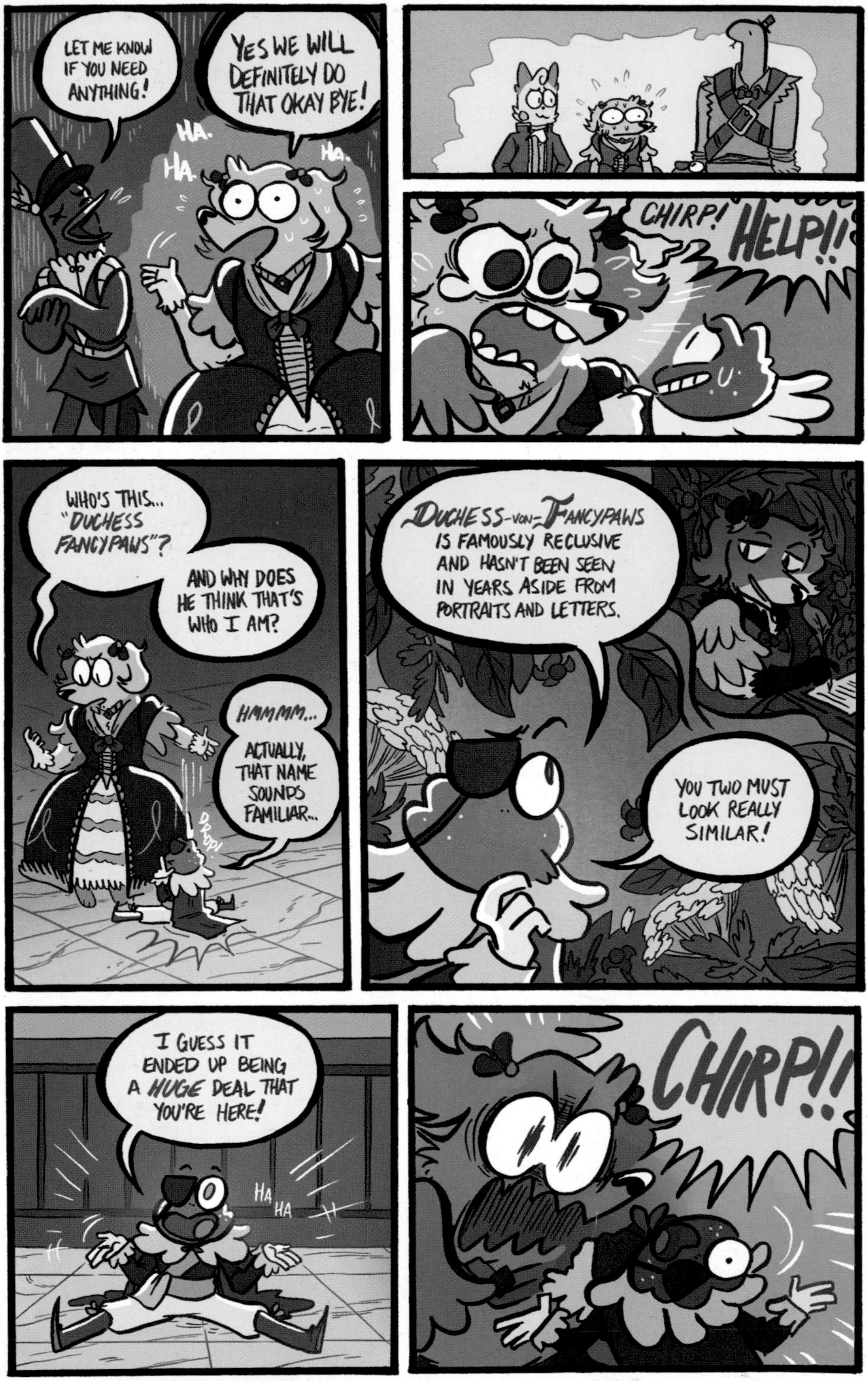
LET ME KNOW IF YOU NEED ANYTHING!
YES WE WILL DEFINITELY DO THAT OKAY BYE!
HA. HA. HA.
CHIRP!
HELP!!
WHO'S THIS... "DUCHESS FANCYPAWS"?
AND WHY DOES HE THINK THAT'S WHO I AM?
HMMMM...
ACTUALLY, THAT NAME SOUNDS FAMILIAR...
DROP!
DUCHESS-VON-FANCYPAWS IS FAMOUSLY RECLUSIVE AND HASN'T BEEN SEEN IN YEARS ASIDE FROM PORTRAITS AND LETTERS.
YOU TWO MUST LOOK REALLY SIMILAR!
I GUESS IT ENDED UP BEING A HUGE DEAL THAT YOU'RE HERE!
HA HA
CHIRP!!

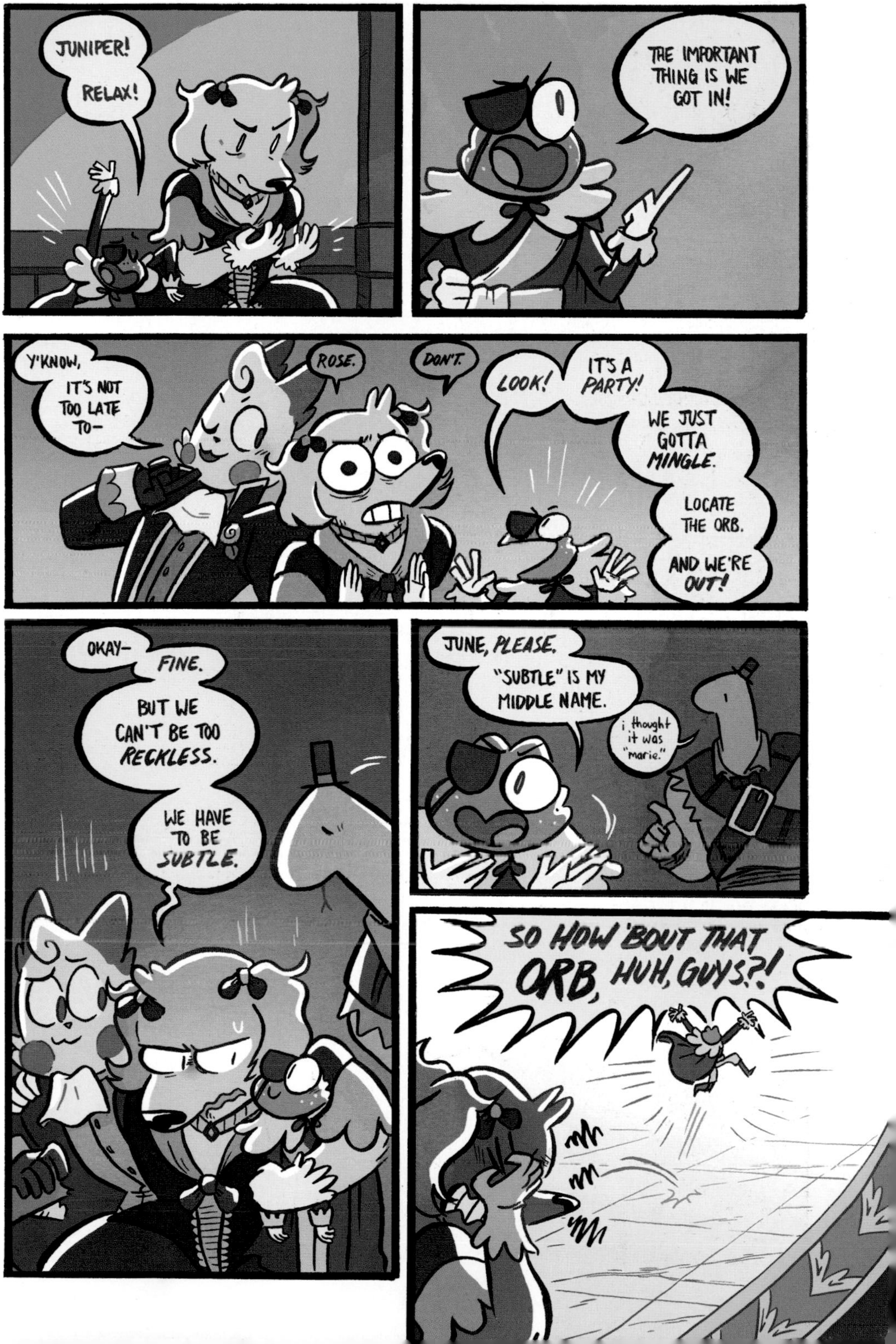
JUNIPER!
RELAX!
THE IMPORTANT THING IS WE GOT IN!
Y'KNOW, IT'S NOT TOO LATE TO—
ROSE.
DON'T.
LOOK!
IT'S A PARTY!
WE JUST GOTTA MINGLE.
LOCATE THE ORB.
AND WE'RE OUT!
OKAY—
FINE.
BUT WE CAN'T BE TOO RECKLESS.
WE HAVE TO BE SUBTLE.
JUNE, PLEASE.
"SUBTLE" IS MY MIDDLE NAME.
i thought it was "marie."
SO HOW 'BOUT THAT ORB, HUH, GUYS?!

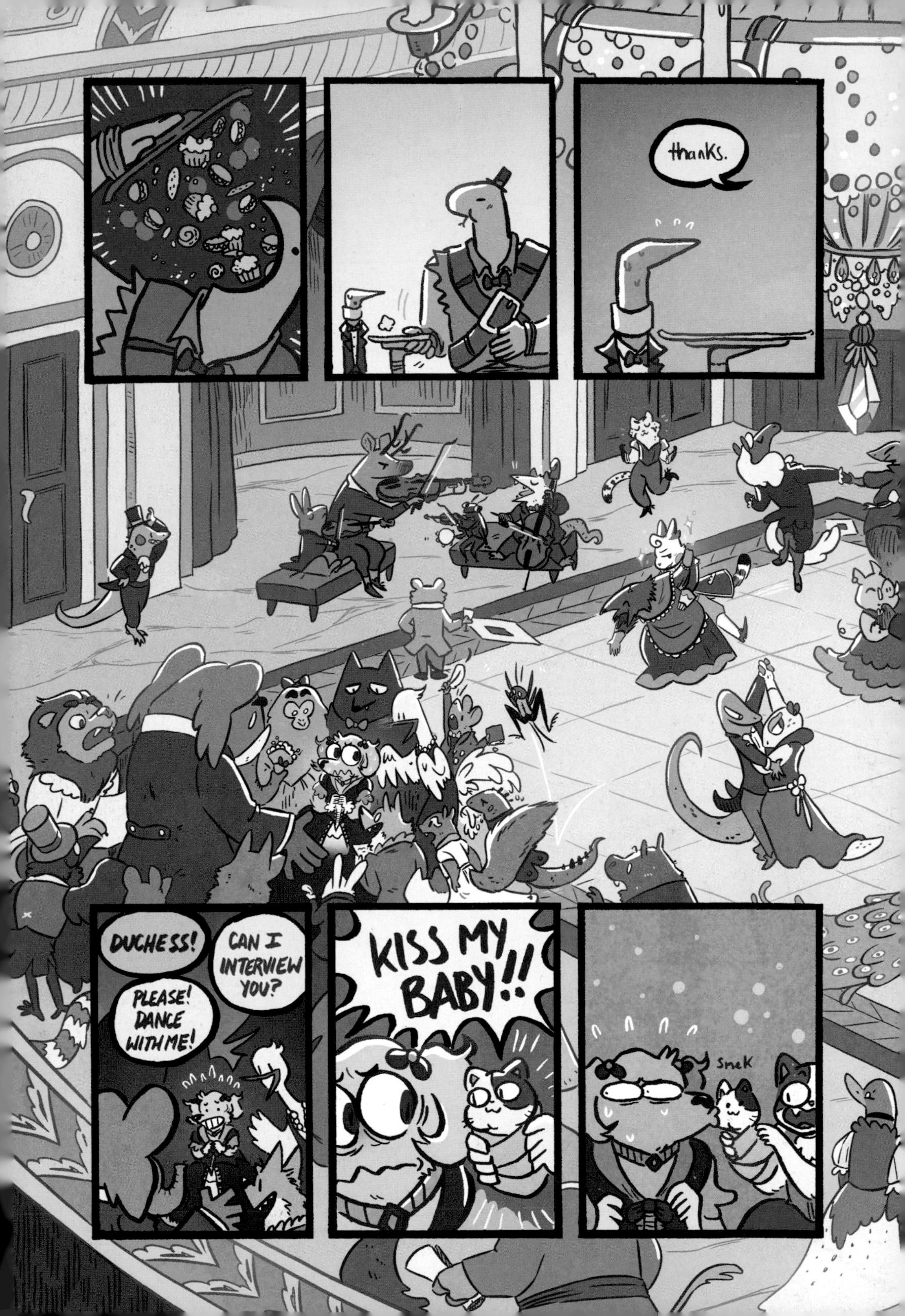

thanks.
DUCHESS!
CAN I INTERVIEW YOU?
PLEASE! DANCE WITH ME!
KISS MY BABY!!
SMCK

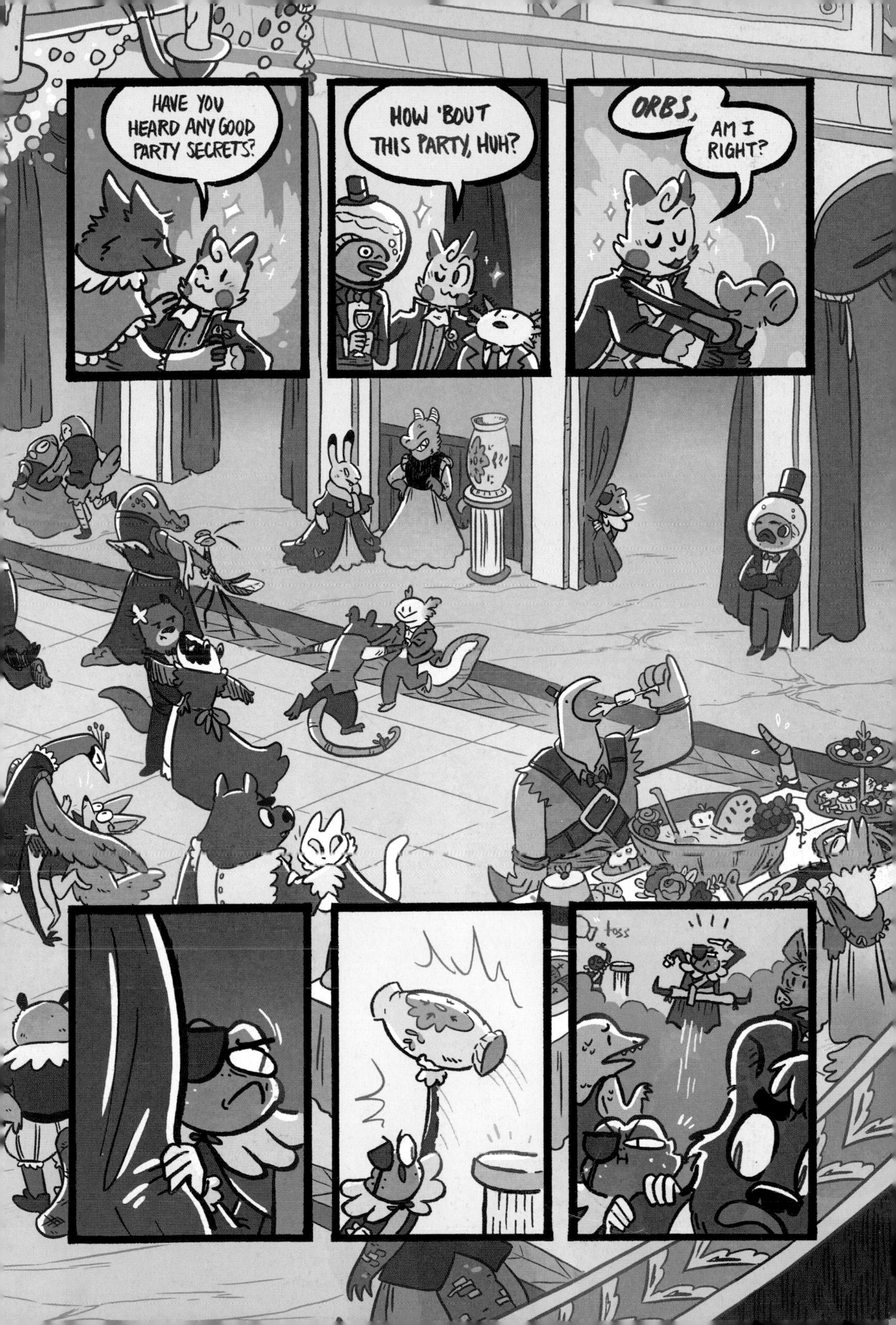
HAVE YOU HEARD ANY GOOD PARTY SECRETS?
HOW 'BOUT THIS PARTY, HUH?
ORBS,
AM I RIGHT?
toss

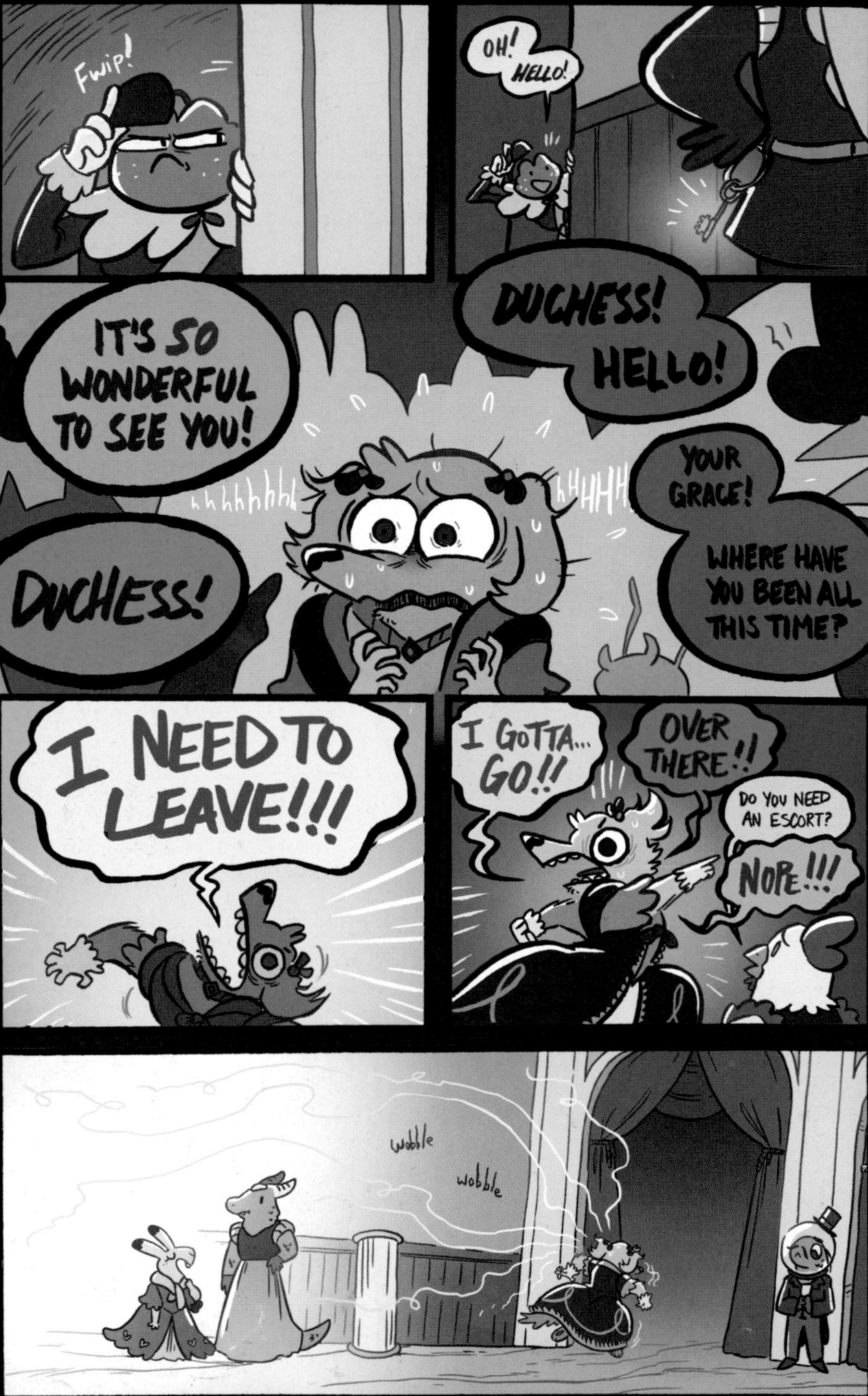
Fwip!
OH!
HELLO!
IT'S SO WONDERFUL TO SEE YOU!
DUCHESS! HELLO!
DUCHESS!
YOUR GRACE!
WHERE HAVE YOU BEEN ALL THIS TIME?
I NEED TO LEAVE!!!
I GOTTA... GO!!
OVER THERE!!
DO YOU NEED AN ESCORT?
NOPE!!!
wobble
wobble

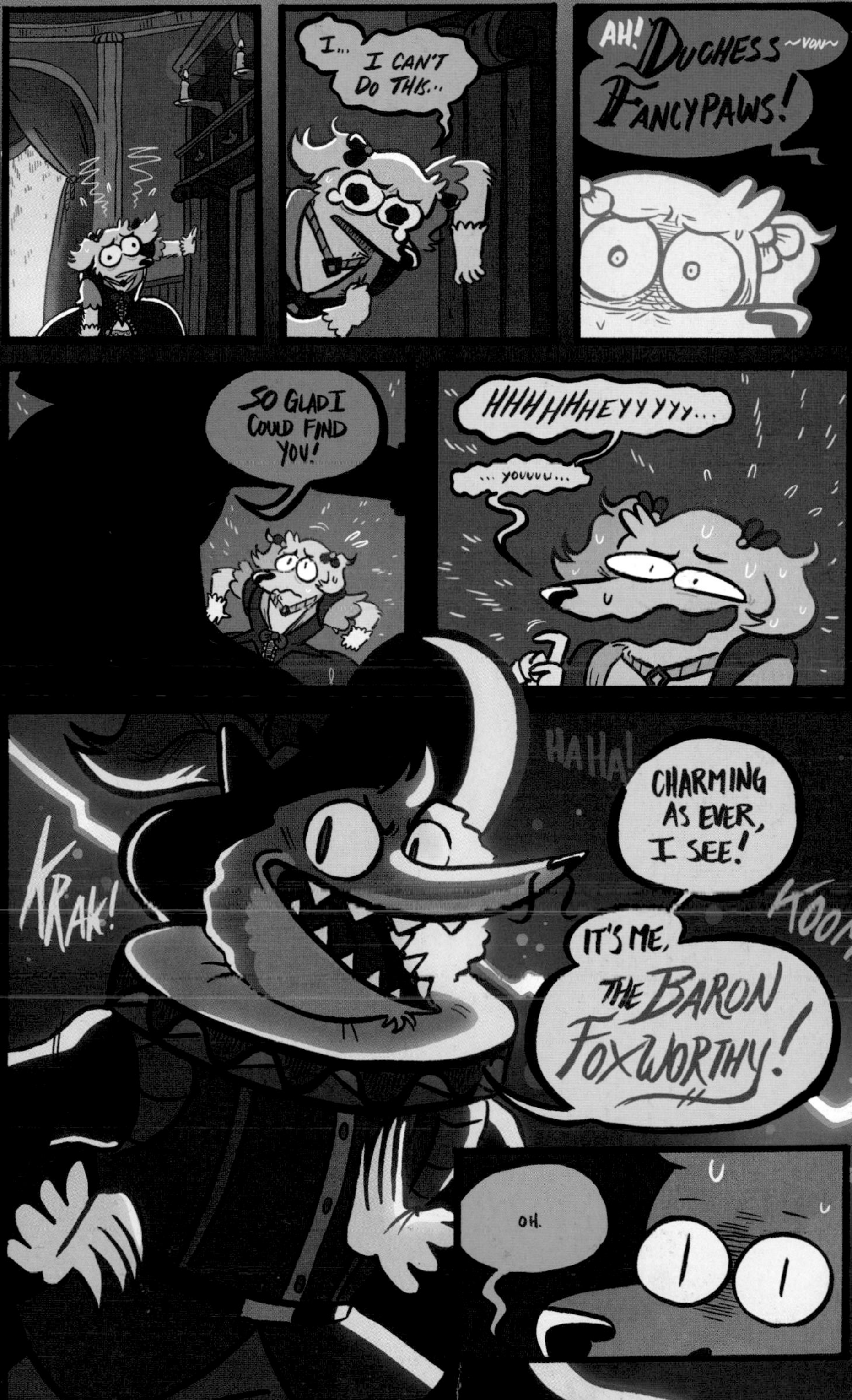

I... I CAN'T DO THIS...
AH! DUCHESS ~VON~ FANCYPAWS!
SO GLAD I COULD FIND YOU!
HHHHHHEYYYYY...
... YOUUUU...
HAHA!
CHARMING AS EVER, I SEE!
KRAK!
KOOM!!!
IT'S ME, THE BARON FOXWORTHY!
OH.

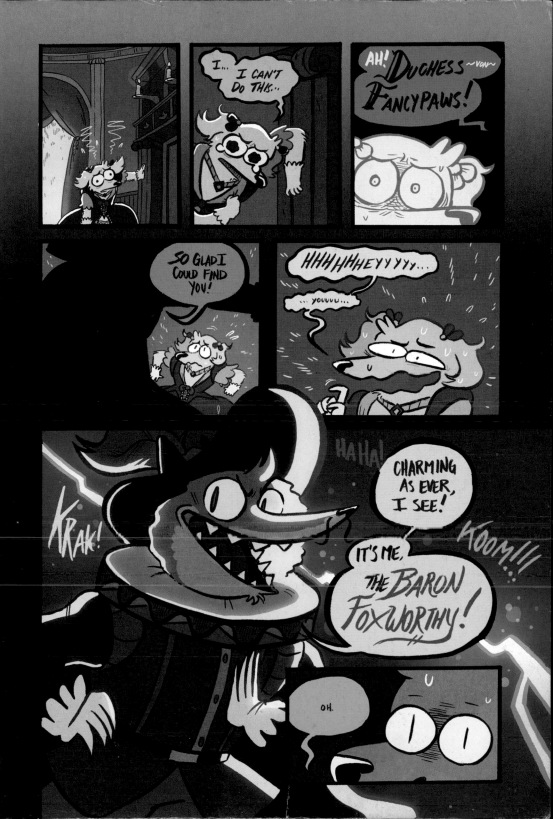

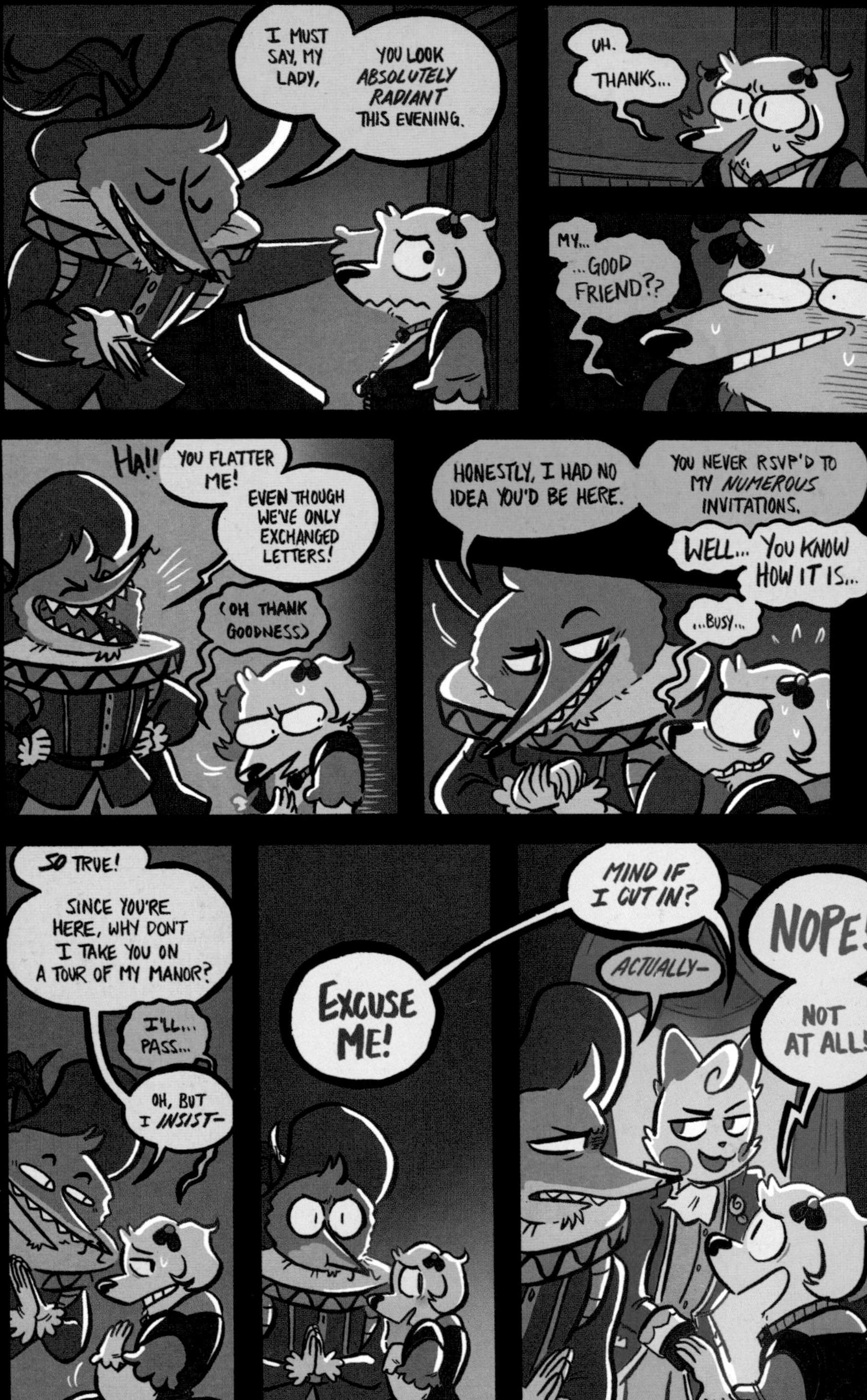
I MUST SAY, MY LADY,
YOU LOOK ABSOLUTELY RADIANT THIS EVENING.
UH. THANKS...
MY... ...GOOD FRIEND??
HA!!
YOU FLATTER ME!
EVEN THOUGH WE'VE ONLY EXCHANGED LETTERS!
(OH THANK GOODNESS)
HONESTLY, I HAD NO IDEA YOU'D BE HERE.
YOU NEVER RSVP'D TO MY NUMEROUS INVITATIONS.
WELL... YOU KNOW HOW IT IS...
...BUSY...
SO TRUE!
SINCE YOU'RE HERE, WHY DON'T I TAKE YOU ON A TOUR OF MY MANOR?
I'LL... PASS...
OH, BUT I INSIST-
EXCUSE ME!
MIND IF I CUT IN?
ACTUALLY-
NOPE!
NOT AT ALL!

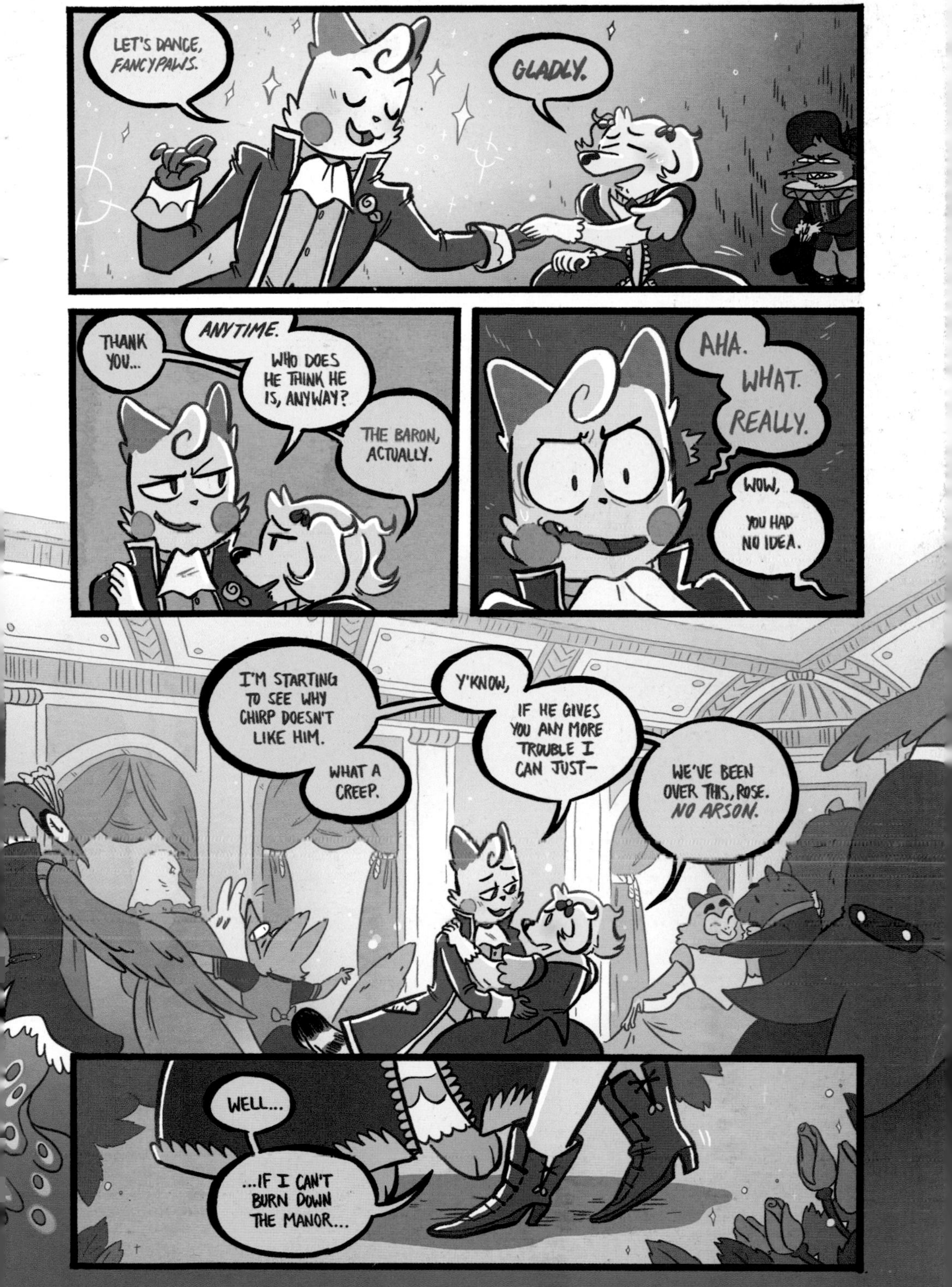

LET'S DANCE, FANCYPAWS.
GLADLY.
THANK YOU...
ANYTIME.
WHO DOES HE THINK HE IS, ANYWAY?
THE BARON, ACTUALLY.
AHA.
WHAT.
REALLY.
WOW,
YOU HAD NO IDEA.
I'M STARTING TO SEE WHY CHIRP DOESN'T LIKE HIM.
WHAT A CREEP.
Y'KNOW,
IF HE GIVES YOU ANY MORE TROUBLE I CAN JUST—
WE'VE BEEN OVER THIS, ROSE. NO ARSON.
WELL...
...IF I CAN'T BURN DOWN THE MANOR...

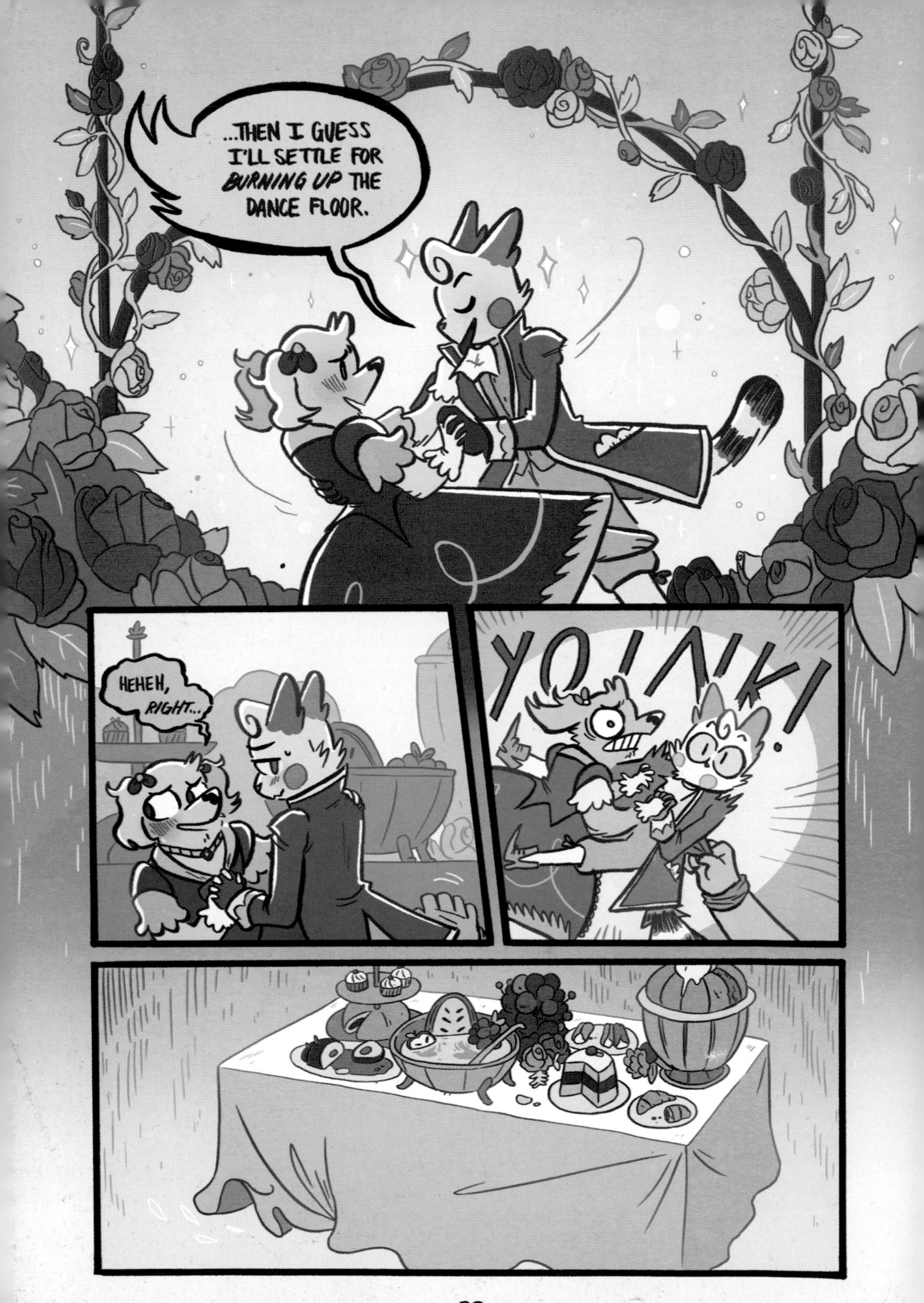

...THEN I GUESS I'LL SETTLE FOR *BURNING UP* THE DANCE FLOOR.
HEHEH, *RIGHT*...
YOINK!

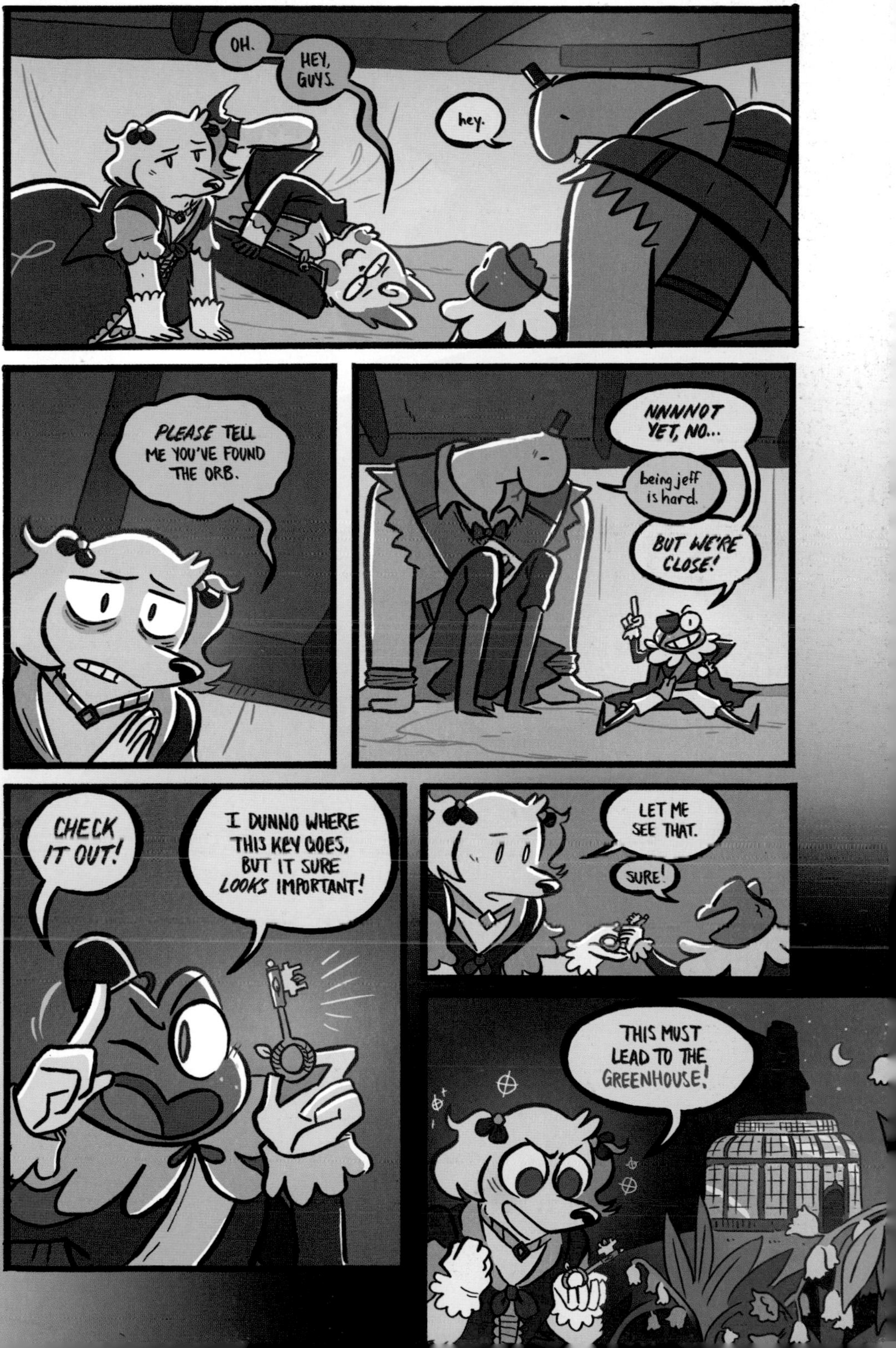
OH.
HEY, GUYS.
hey.
PLEASE TELL ME YOU'VE FOUND THE ORB.
NNNNOT YET, NO...
being jeff is hard.
BUT WE'RE CLOSE!
CHECK IT OUT!
I DUNNO WHERE THIS KEY GOES, BUT IT SURE LOOKS IMPORTANT!
LET ME SEE THAT.
SURE!
THIS MUST LEAD TO THE GREENHOUSE!

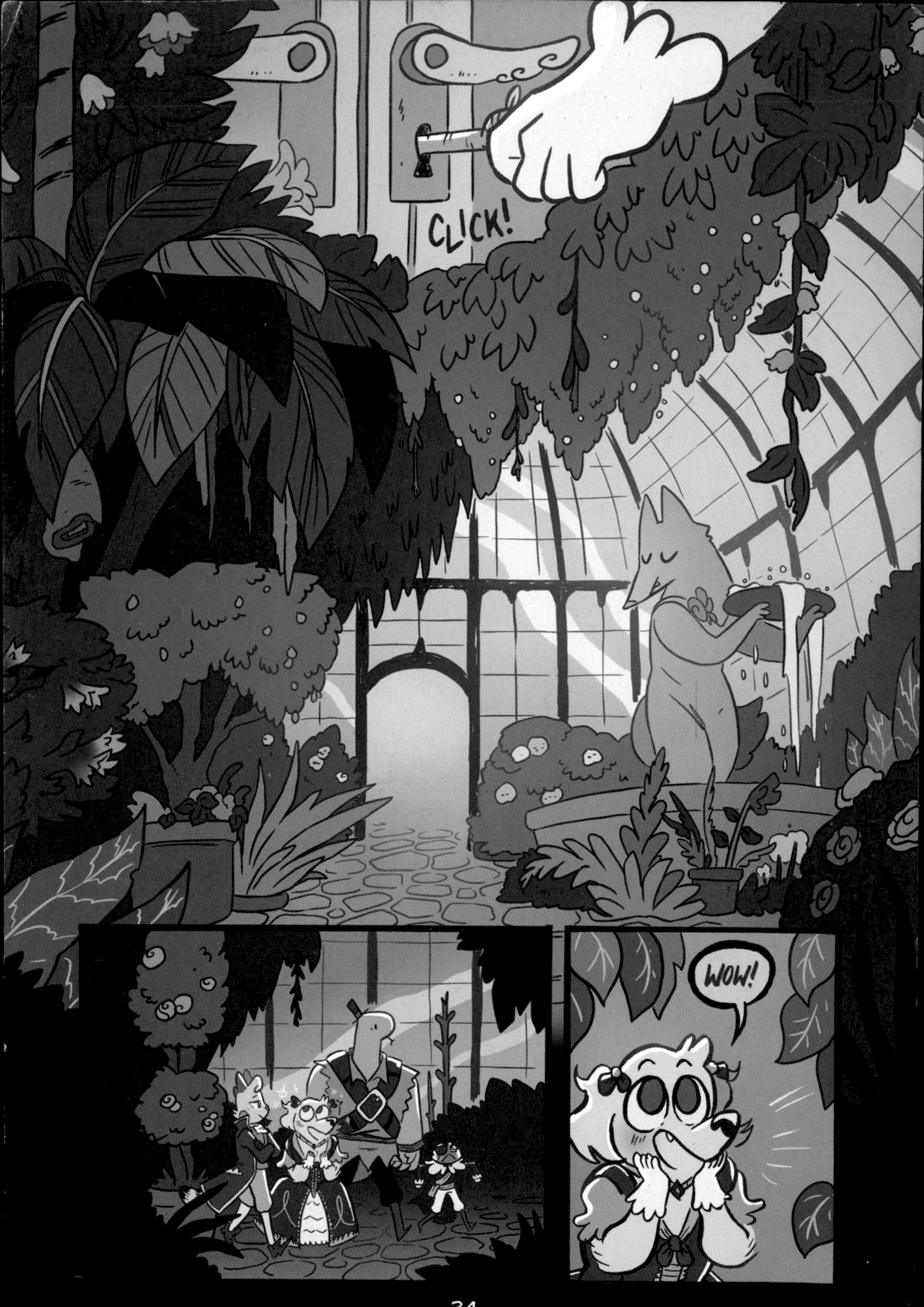
CLICK!
WOW!

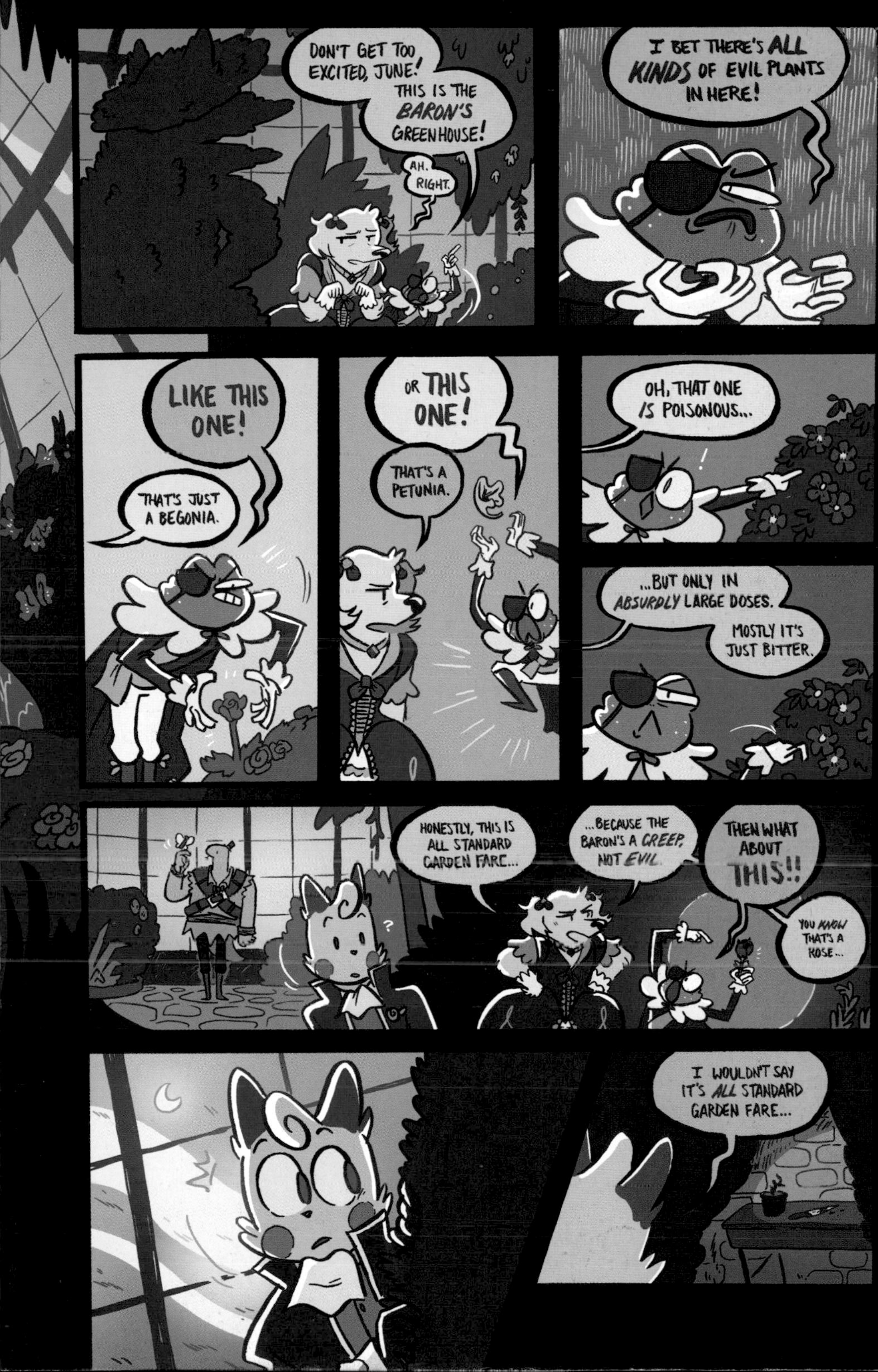
DON'T GET TOO EXCITED, JUNE!
THIS IS THE BARON'S GREENHOUSE!
AH. RIGHT.
I BET THERE'S ALL KINDS OF EVIL PLANTS IN HERE!
LIKE THIS ONE!
THAT'S JUST A BEGONIA.
OR THIS ONE!
THAT'S A PETUNIA.
OH, THAT ONE IS POISONOUS...
...BUT ONLY IN ABSURDLY LARGE DOSES.
MOSTLY IT'S JUST BITTER.
HONESTLY, THIS IS ALL STANDARD GARDEN FARE...
...BECAUSE THE BARON'S A CREEP, NOT EVIL.
THEN WHAT ABOUT THIS!!
YOU KNOW THAT'S A ROSE...
I WOULDN'T SAY IT'S ALL STANDARD GARDEN FARE...

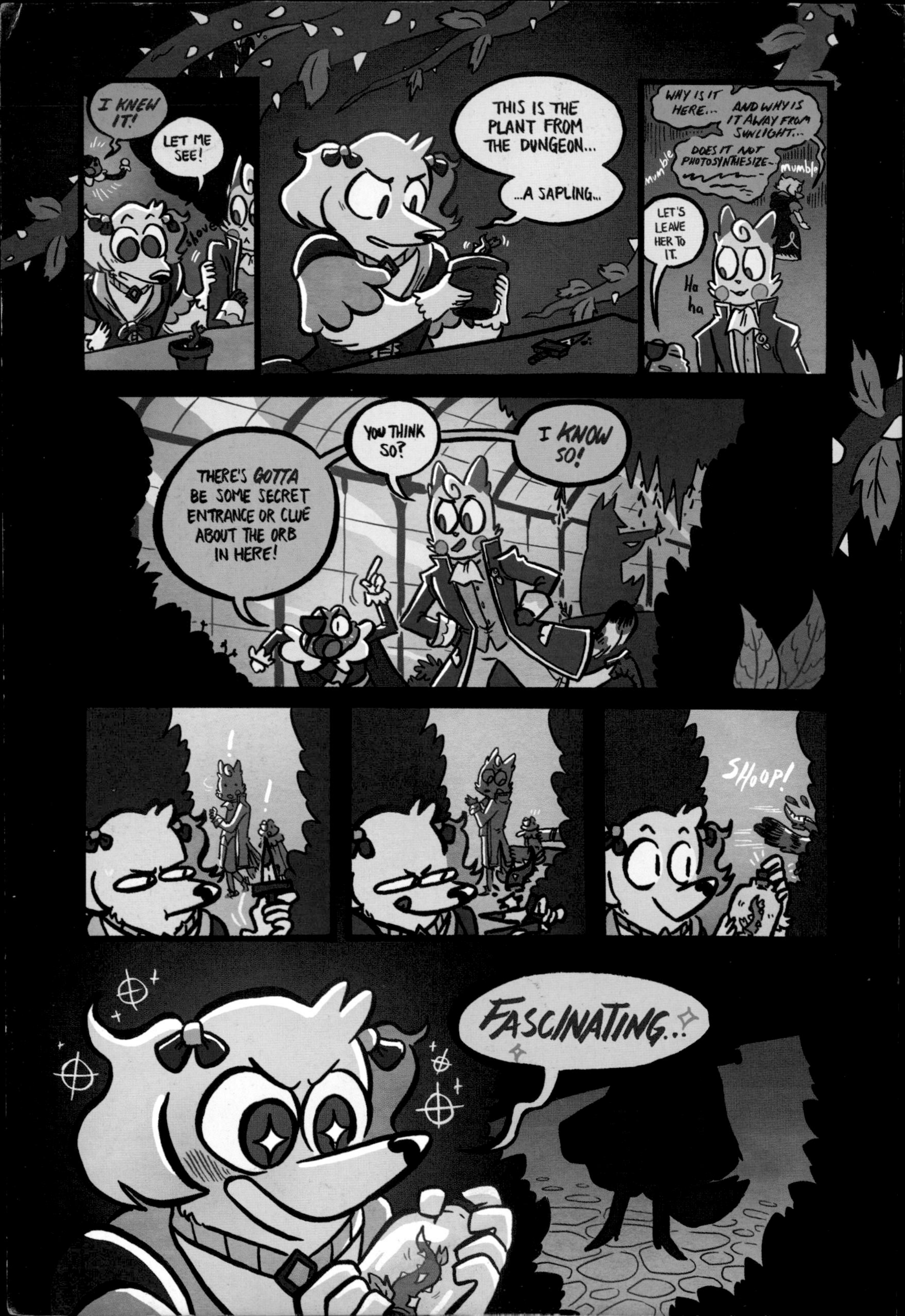
I KNEW IT!
LET ME SEE!
shove
THIS IS THE PLANT FROM THE DUNGEON...
...A SAPLING...
WHY IS IT HERE... AND WHY IS IT AWAY FROM SUNLIGHT...
DOES IT NOT PHOTOSYNTHESIZE~
mumble
mumble
LET'S LEAVE HER TO IT.
Ha ha
THERE'S GOTTA BE SOME SECRET ENTRANCE OR CLUE ABOUT THE ORB IN HERE!
YOU THINK SO?
I KNOW SO!
SHOOP!
FASCINATING..

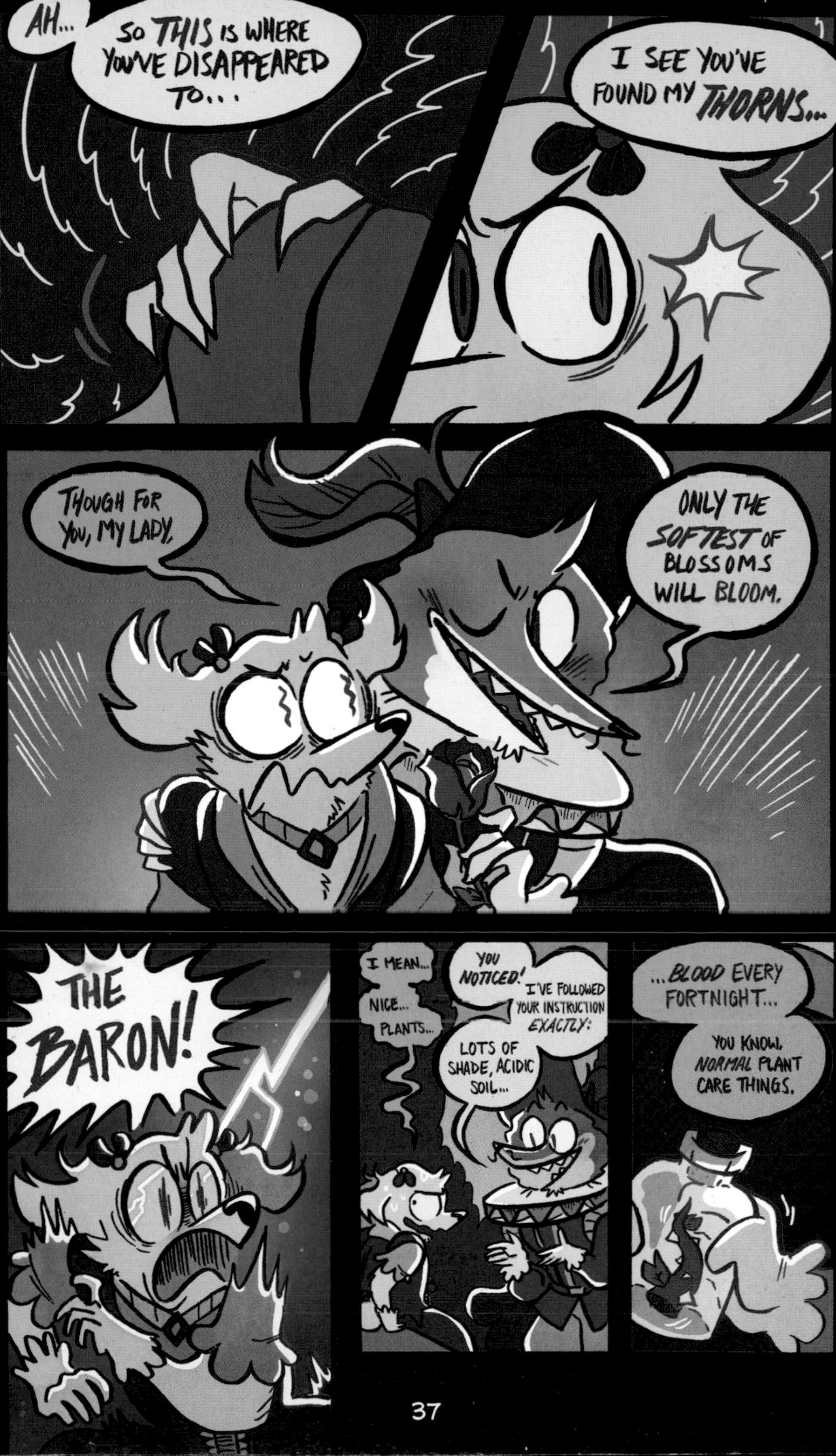
AH...
SO THIS IS WHERE YOU'VE DISAPPEARED TO...
I SEE YOU'VE FOUND MY THORNS...
THOUGH FOR YOU, MY LADY,
ONLY THE SOFTEST OF BLOSSOMS WILL BLOOM.
THE BARON!
I MEAN... NICE... PLANTS...
YOU NOTICED!
I'VE FOLLOWED YOUR INSTRUCTION EXACTLY:
LOTS OF SHADE, ACIDIC SOIL...
...BLOOD EVERY FORTNIGHT...
YOU KNOW, NORMAL PLANT CARE THINGS.

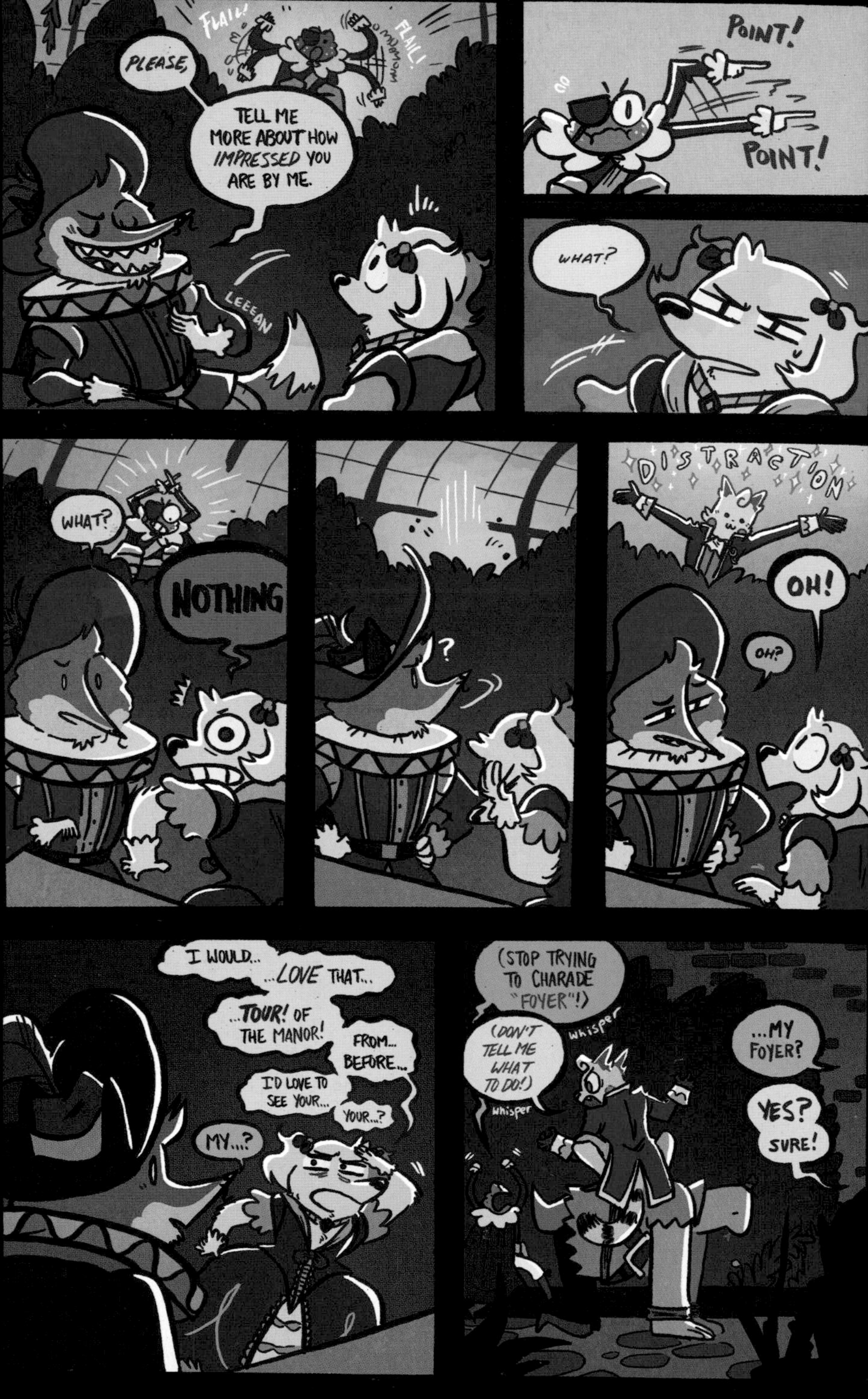
FLAIL!
FLAIL!
PLEASE,
TELL ME MORE ABOUT HOW IMPRESSED YOU ARE BY ME.
LEEEAN
POINT!
POINT!
WHAT?
WHAT?
NOTHING
?
DISTRACTION
OH!
OH?
I WOULD... ...LOVE THAT...
...TOUR! OF THE MANOR!
FROM... BEFORE...
I'D LOVE TO SEE YOUR...
YOUR...?
MY...?
(STOP TRYING TO CHARADE "FOYER"!)
whisper
(DON'T TELL ME WHAT TO DO!)
whisper
...MY FOYER?
YES?
SURE!

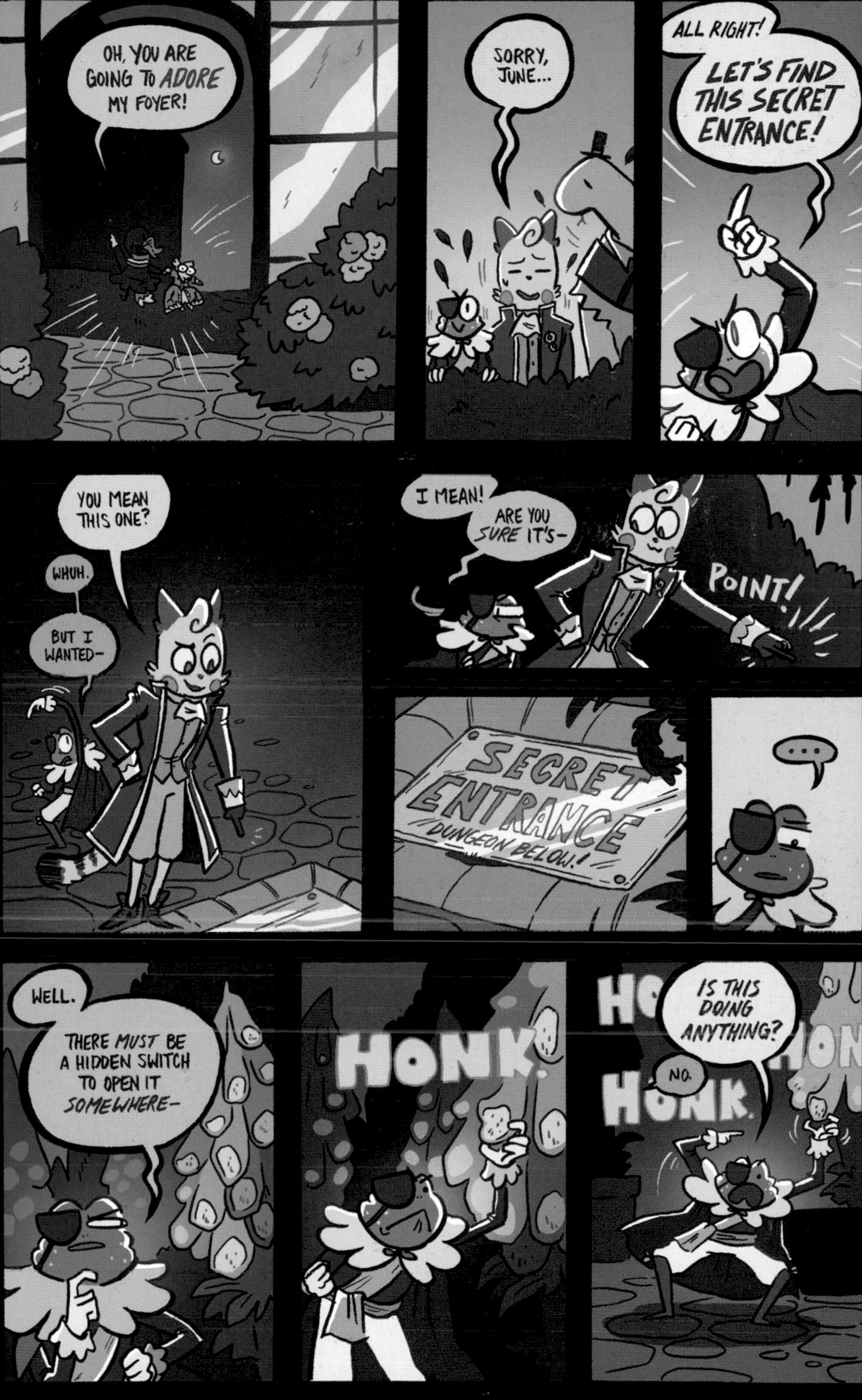

OH, YOU ARE GOING TO ADORE MY FOYER!
SORRY, JUNE...
ALL RIGHT!
LET'S FIND THIS SECRET ENTRANCE!
YOU MEAN THIS ONE?
WHUH.
BUT I WANTED-
I MEAN!
ARE YOU SURE IT'S-
POINT!
SECRET ENTRANCE
DUNGEON BELOW!
...
WELL.
THERE MUST BE A HIDDEN SWITCH TO OPEN IT SOMEWHERE-
HONK.
IS THIS DOING ANYTHING?
NO.
HONK.

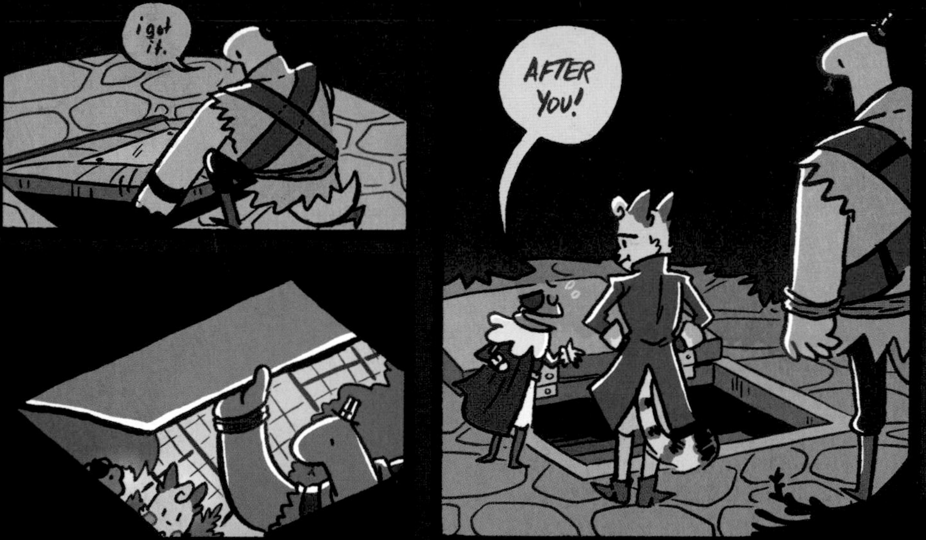
i got it.
AFTER YOU!

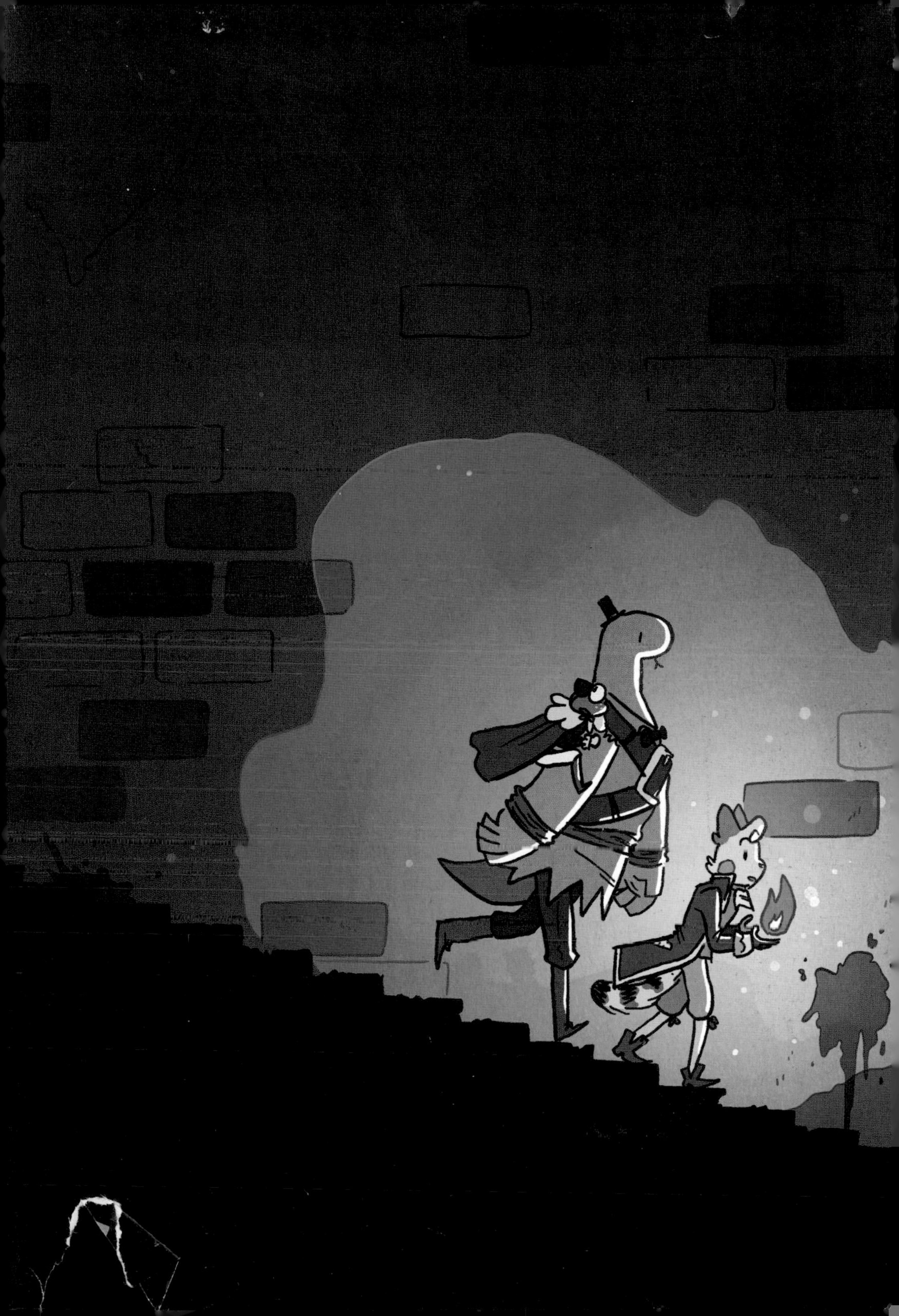

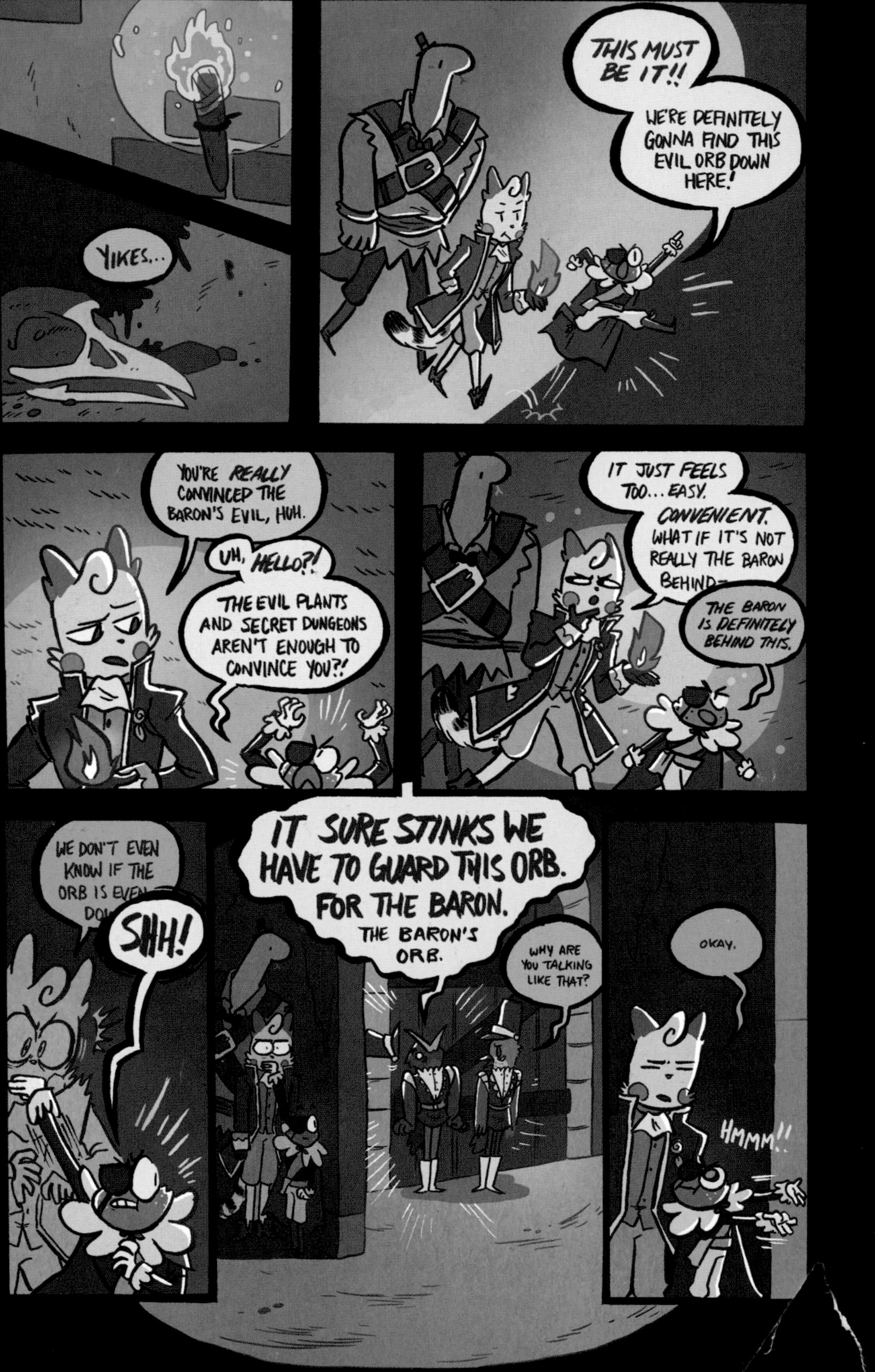
YIKES...
THIS MUST BE IT!!
WE'RE DEFINITELY GONNA FIND THIS EVIL ORB DOWN HERE!
YOU'RE REALLY CONVINCED THE BARON'S EVIL, HUH.
UH, HELLO?!
THE EVIL PLANTS AND SECRET DUNGEONS AREN'T ENOUGH TO CONVINCE YOU?!
IT JUST FEELS TOO... EASY.
CONVENIENT.
WHAT IF IT'S NOT REALLY THE BARON BEHIND–
THE BARON IS DEFINITELY BEHIND THIS.
WE DON'T EVEN KNOW IF THE ORB IS EVEN DO–
SHH!
IT SURE STINKS WE HAVE TO GUARD THIS ORB. FOR THE BARON.
THE BARON'S ORB.
WHY ARE YOU TALKING LIKE THAT?
OKAY.
HMMM!!

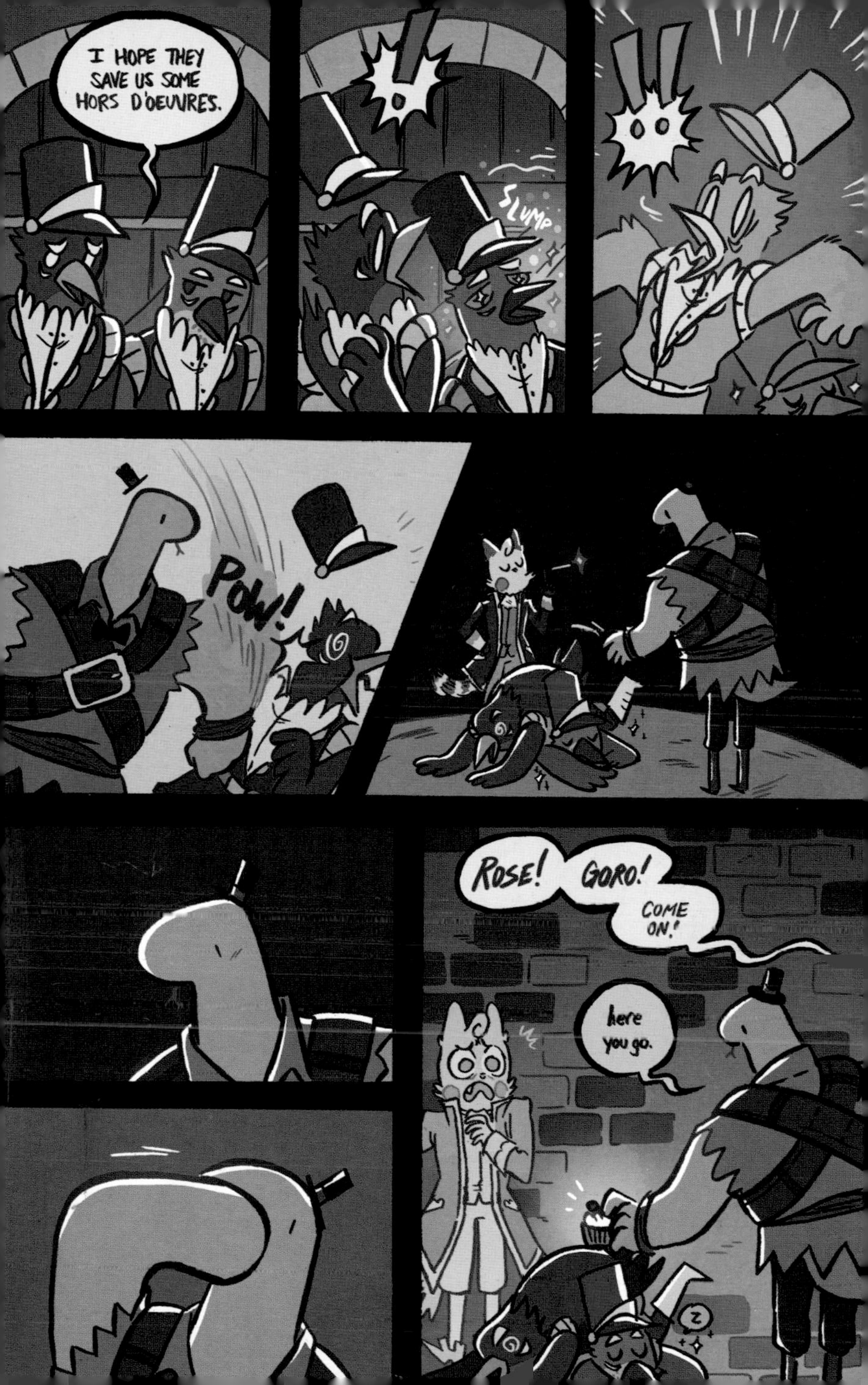
I HOPE THEY SAVE US SOME HORS D'OEUVRES.
SLUMP
POW!
ROSE!
GORO!
COME ON!
here you go.

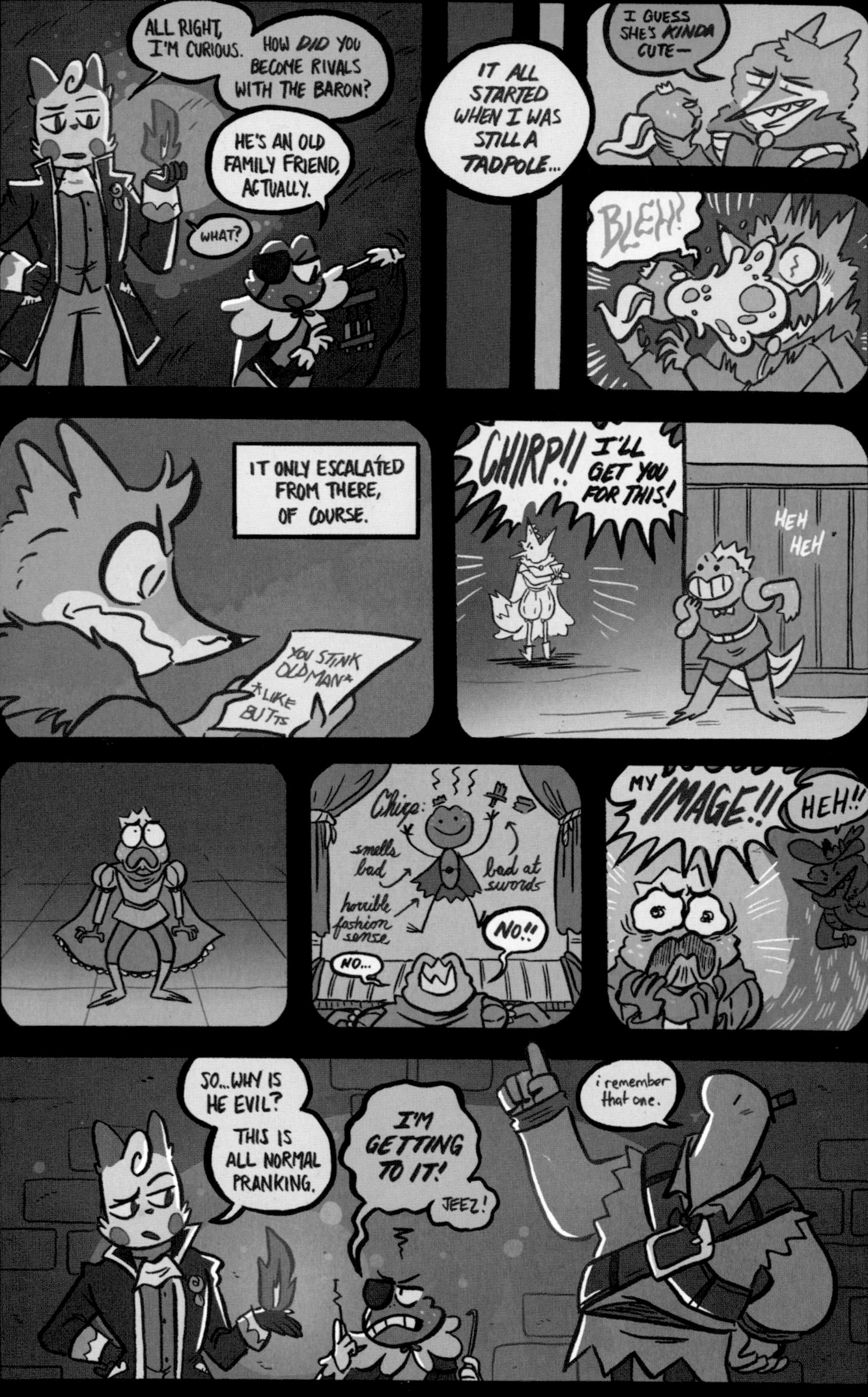

ALL RIGHT, I'M CURIOUS.
HOW DID YOU BECOME RIVALS WITH THE BARON?
HE'S AN OLD FAMILY FRIEND, ACTUALLY.
WHAT?
IT ALL STARTED WHEN I WAS STILL A TADPOLE...
I GUESS SHE'S KINDA CUTE—
BLEH!?
IT ONLY ESCALATED FROM THERE, OF COURSE.
YOU STINK OLD MAN* *LIKE BUTTS
CHIRP!!
I'LL GET YOU FOR THIS!
HEH HEH
Chirp:
smells bad
horrible fashion sense
bad at swords
NO...
NO!!
MY IMAGE!!
HEH!!
SO...WHY IS HE EVIL?
THIS IS ALL NORMAL PRANKING.
I'M GETTING TO IT!
JEEZ!
i remember that one.

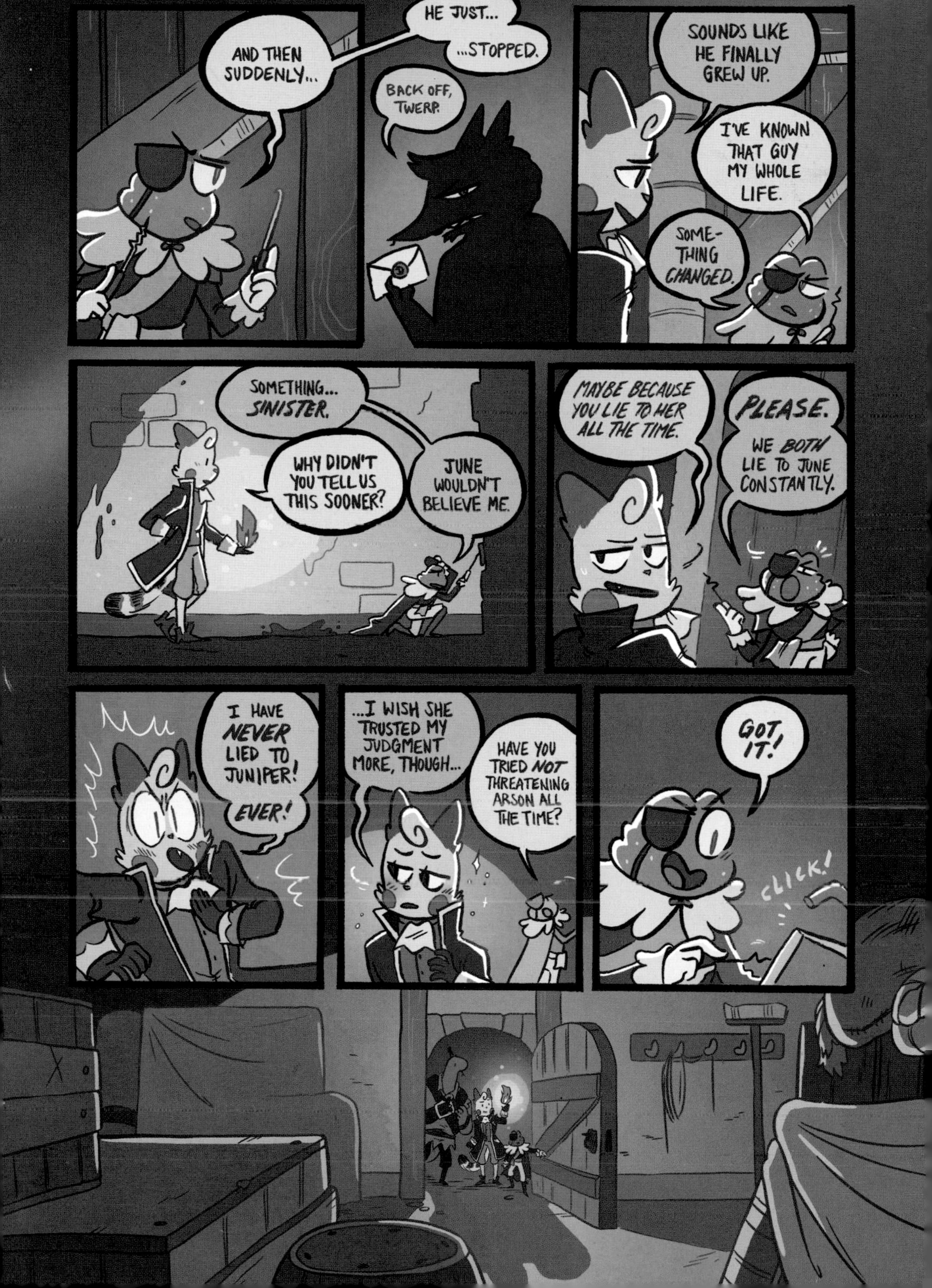
AND THEN SUDDENLY...
HE JUST...
...STOPPED.
BACK OFF, TWERP.
SOUNDS LIKE HE FINALLY GREW UP.
I'VE KNOWN THAT GUY MY WHOLE LIFE.
SOME-THING CHANGED.
SOMETHING... SINISTER.
WHY DIDN'T YOU TELL US THIS SOONER?
JUNE WOULDN'T BELIEVE ME.
MAYBE BECAUSE YOU LIE TO HER ALL THE TIME.
PLEASE.
WE BOTH LIE TO JUNE CONSTANTLY.
I HAVE NEVER LIED TO JUNIPER!
EVER!
...I WISH SHE TRUSTED MY JUDGMENT MORE, THOUGH...
HAVE YOU TRIED NOT THREATENING ARSON ALL THE TIME?
GOT IT!
CLICK!

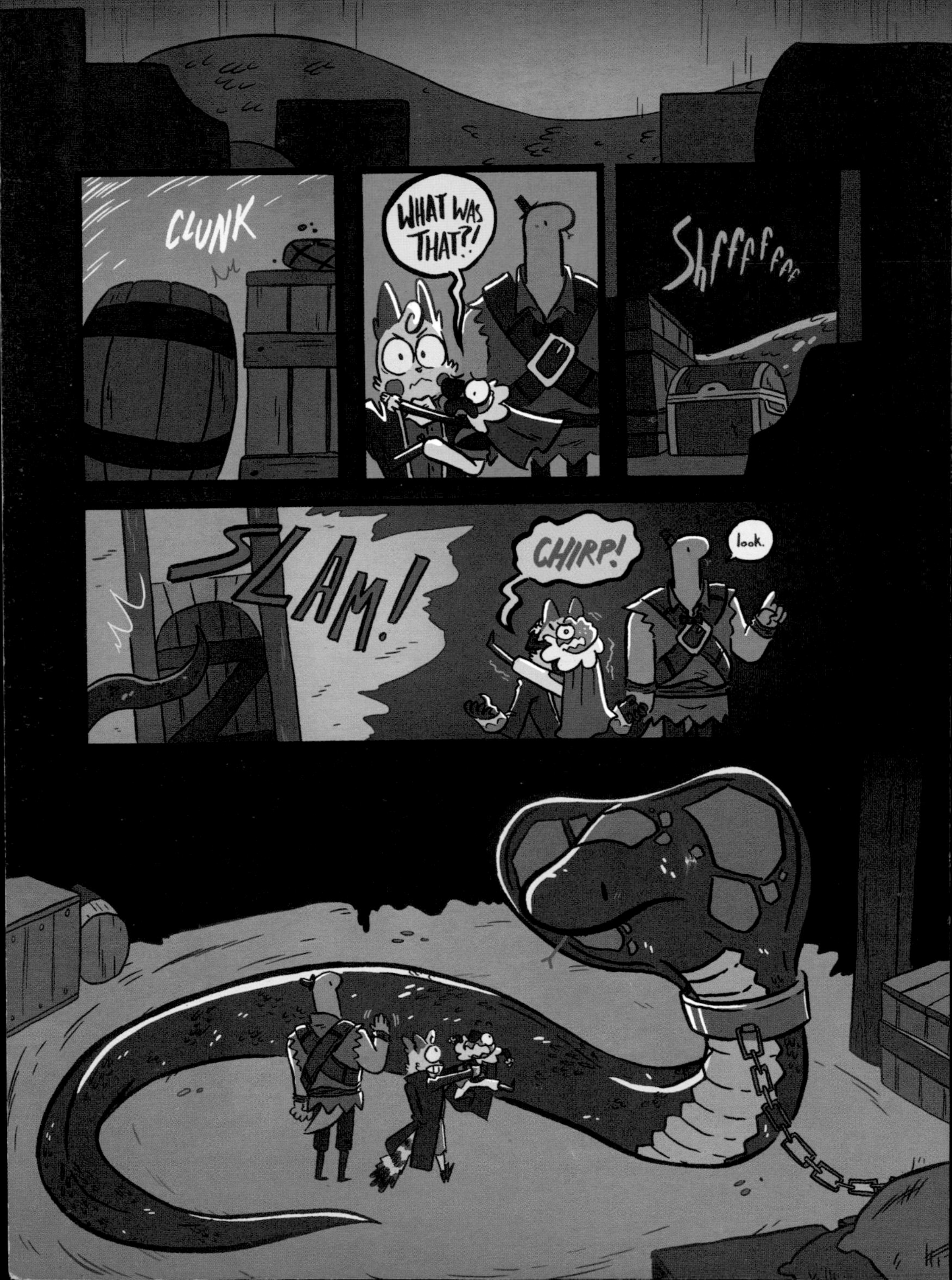
CLUNK
WHAT WAS THAT?!
Shffffff
SLAM!
CHIRP!
look.

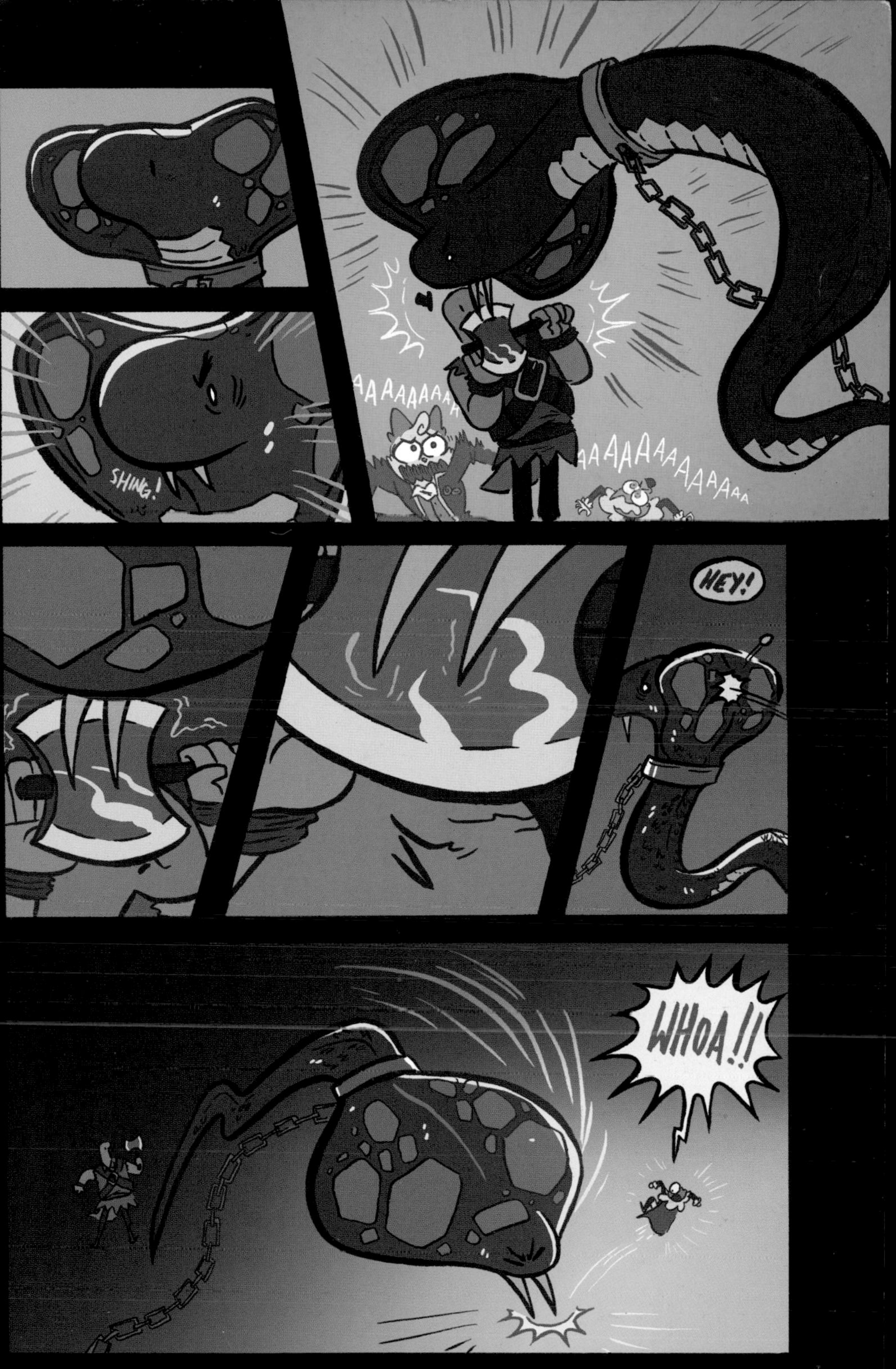
SHING!
AAAAAAAAA
AAAAAAAAAAAAAA
HEY!
WHOA!!

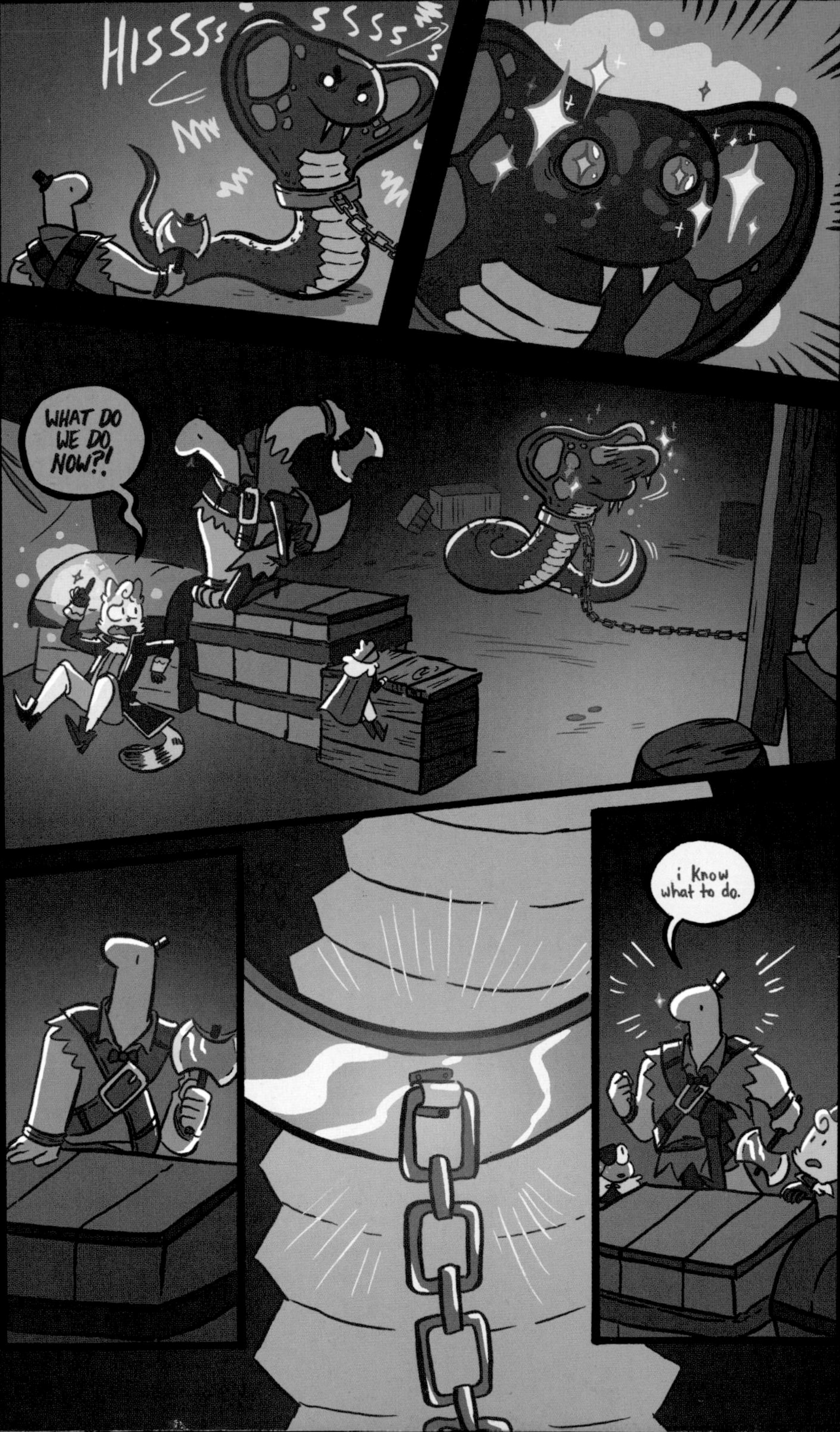
HISSSs SSSSs
WHAT DO WE DO NOW?!
i Know what to do.

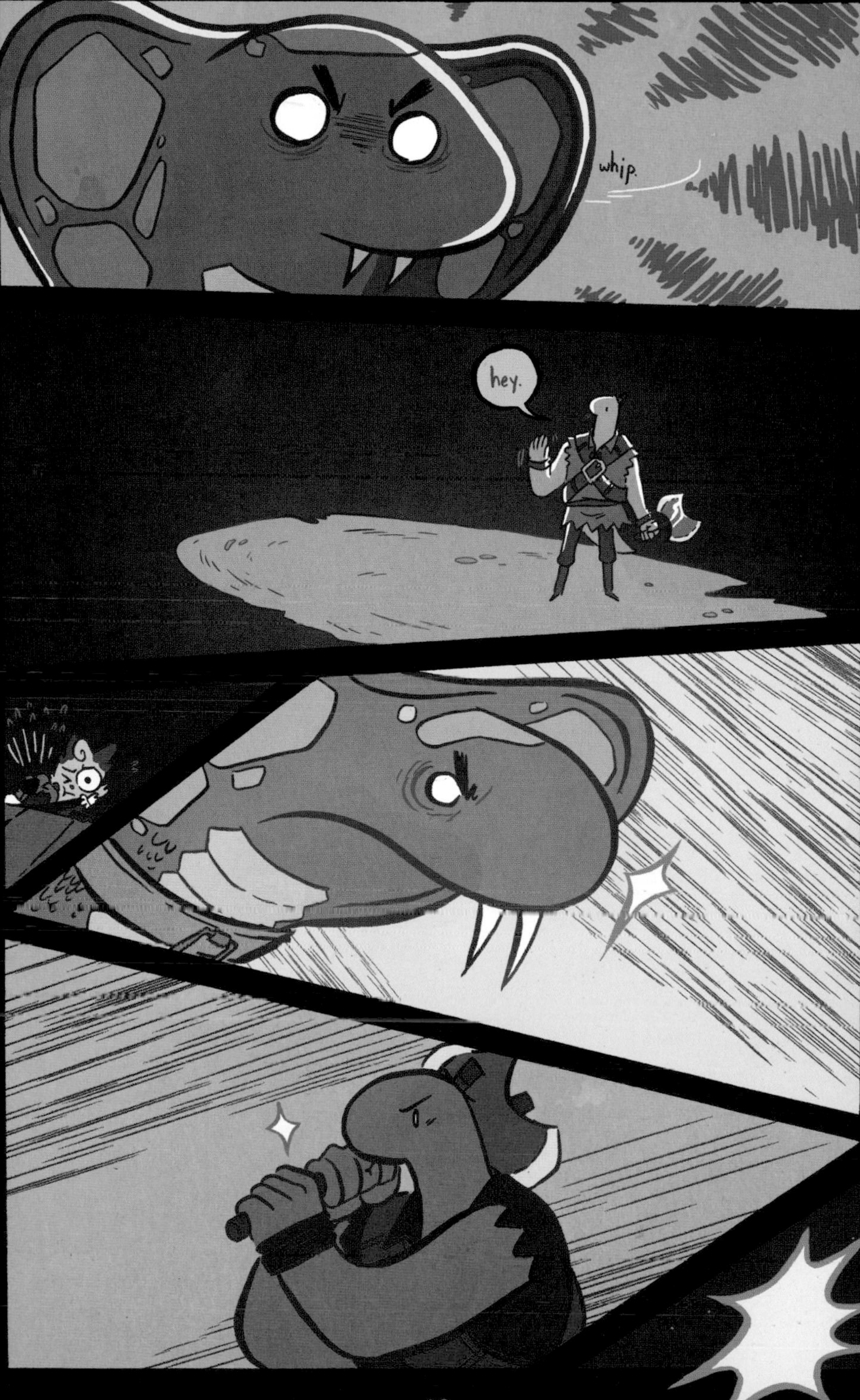
whip.
hey.

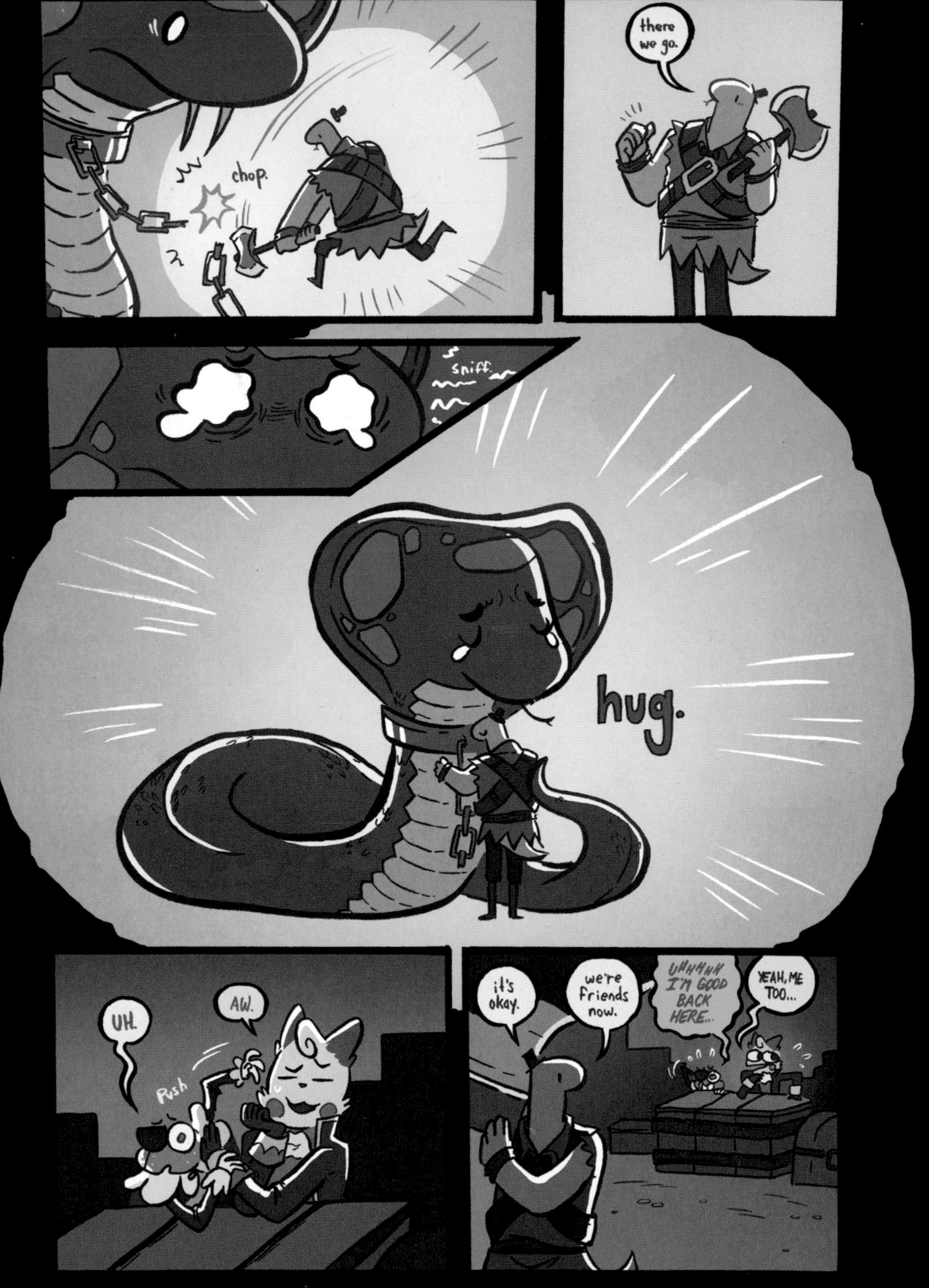
chop.
there we go.
sniff.
hug.
UH.
AW.
push
it's okay.
we're friends now.
UHHHNH I'M GOOD BACK HERE...
YEAH, ME TOO...

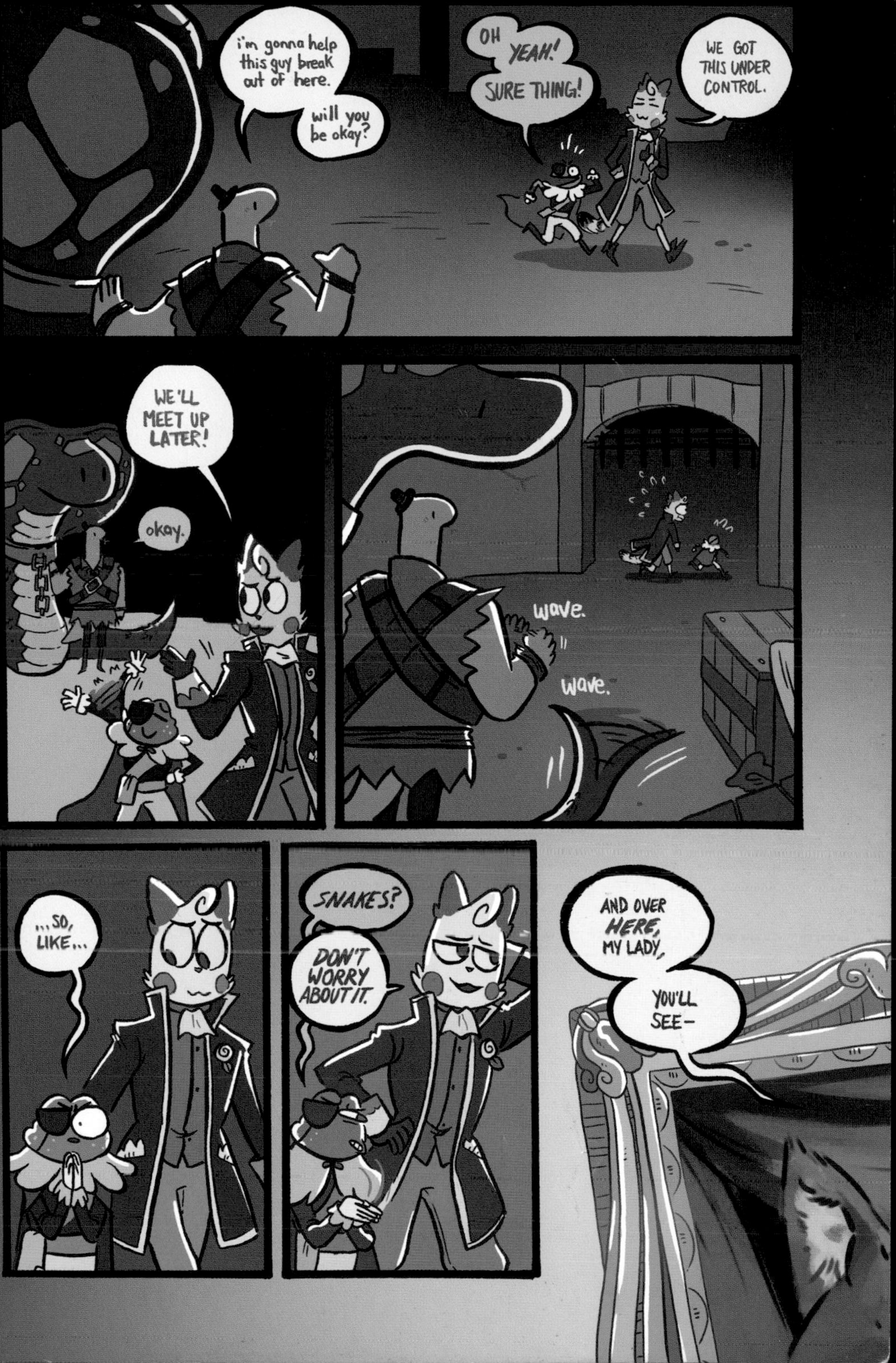
i'm gonna help this guy break out of here.
will you be okay?
OH YEAH! SURE THING!
WE GOT THIS UNDER CONTROL.
WE'LL MEET UP LATER!
okay.
wave.
wave.
...SO, LIKE...
SNAKES?
DON'T WORRY ABOUT IT.
AND OVER HERE, MY LADY,
YOU'LL SEE-

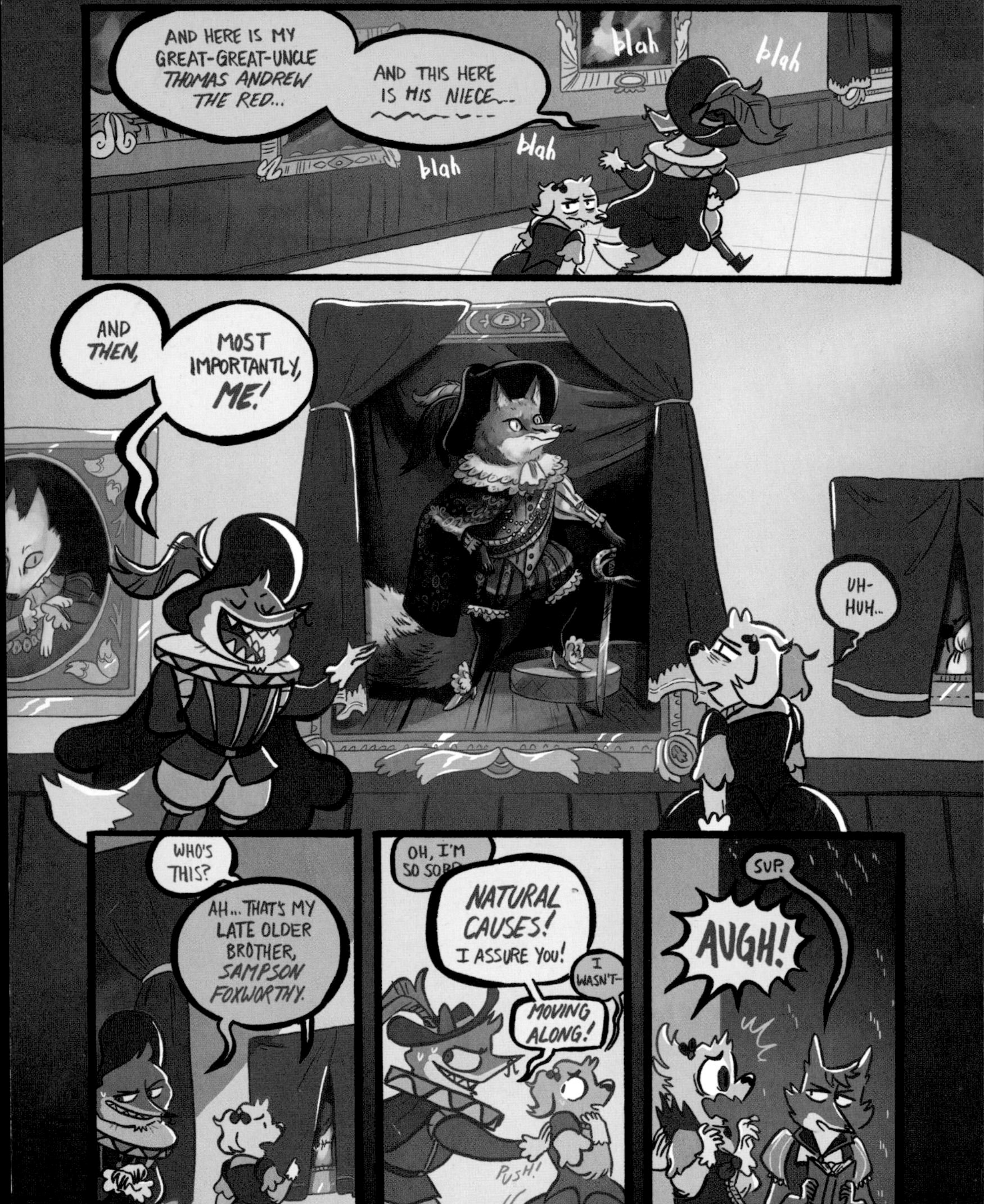
AND HERE IS MY GREAT-GREAT-UNCLE THOMAS ANDREW THE RED...
AND THIS HERE IS HIS NIECE...
blah
blah
blah
blah
AND THEN,
MOST IMPORTANTLY, ME!
UH-HUH...
WHO'S THIS?
AH... THAT'S MY LATE OLDER BROTHER, SAMPSON FOXWORTHY.
OH, I'M SO SORR
NATURAL CAUSES! I ASSURE YOU!
I WASN'T-
MOVING ALONG!
PUSH!
SUP.
AUGH!

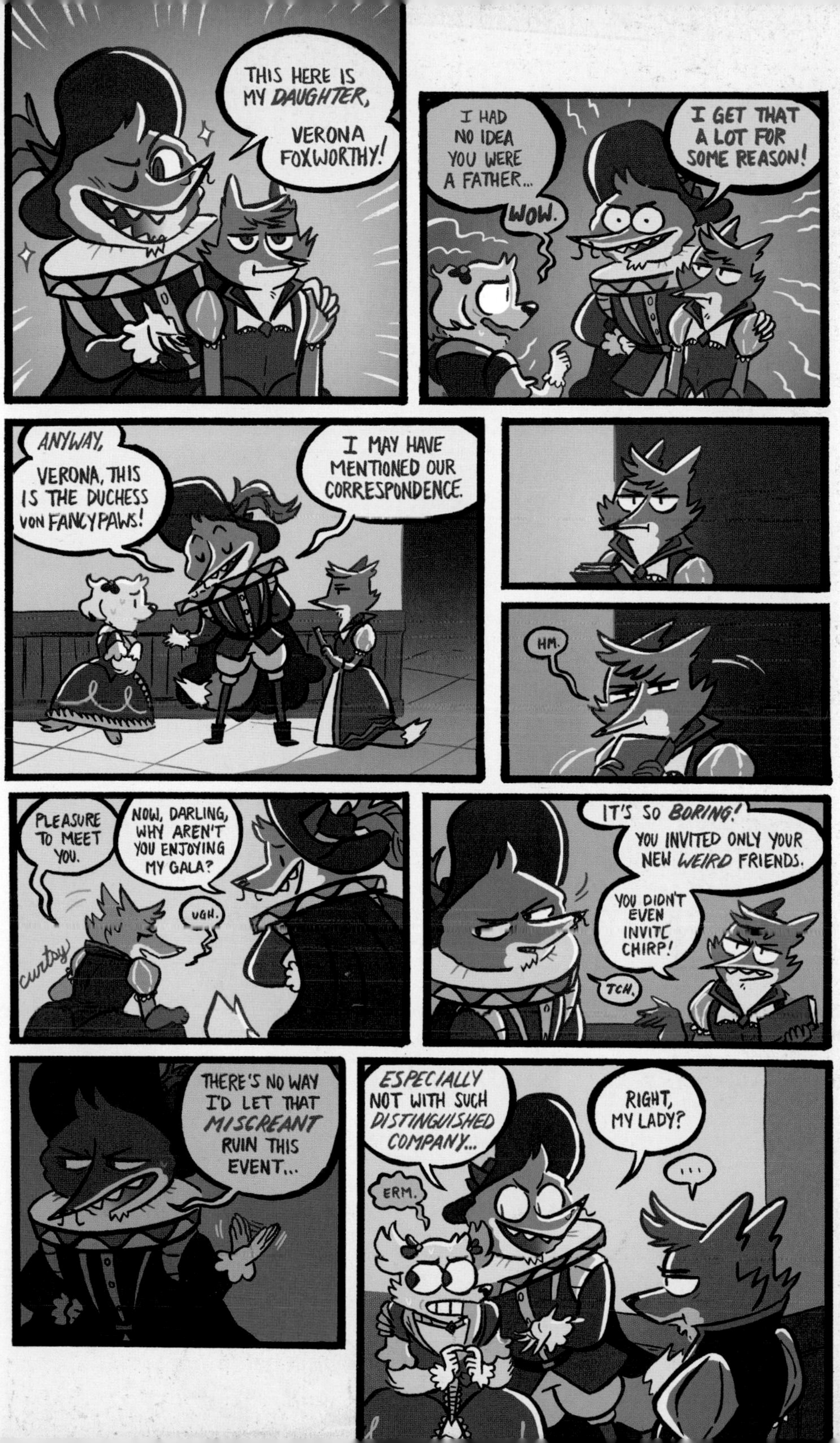
THIS HERE IS MY DAUGHTER, VERONA FOXWORTHY!
I HAD NO IDEA YOU WERE A FATHER...
WOW.
I GET THAT A LOT FOR SOME REASON!
ANYWAY, VERONA, THIS IS THE DUCHESS VON FANCYPAWS!
I MAY HAVE MENTIONED OUR CORRESPONDENCE.
HM.
PLEASURE TO MEET YOU.
curtsy
NOW, DARLING, WHY AREN'T YOU ENJOYING MY GALA?
UGH.
IT'S SO BORING!
YOU INVITED ONLY YOUR NEW WEIRD FRIENDS.
YOU DIDN'T EVEN INVITE CHIRP!
TCH.
THERE'S NO WAY I'D LET THAT MISCREANT RUIN THIS EVENT...
ESPECIALLY NOT WITH SUCH DISTINGUISHED COMPANY...
ERM.
RIGHT, MY LADY?
...

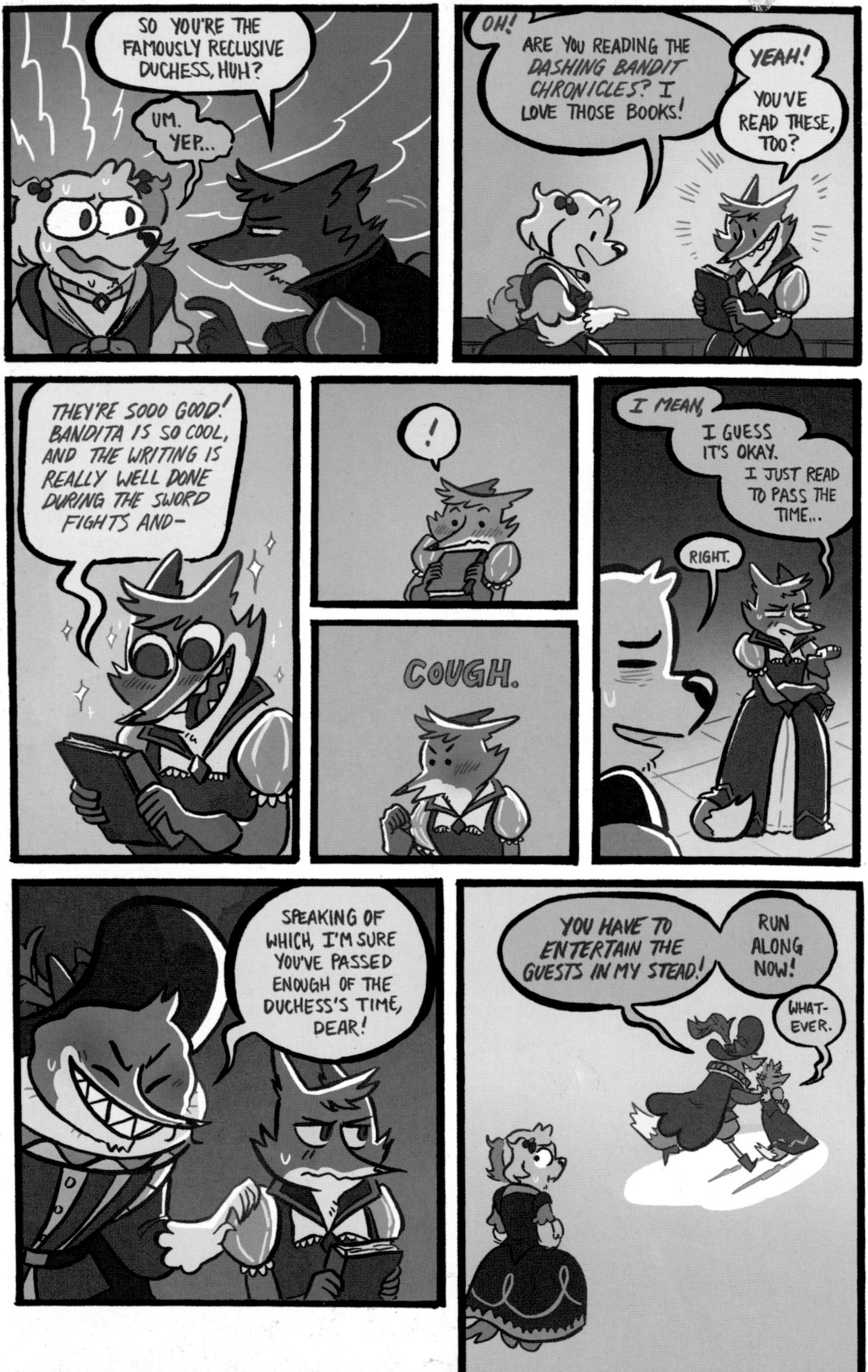
SO YOU'RE THE FAMOUSLY RECLUSIVE DUCHESS, HUH?
UM. YEP...
OH!
ARE YOU READING THE *DASHING BANDIT CHRONICLES*? I LOVE THOSE BOOKS!
YEAH!
YOU'VE READ THESE, TOO?
THEY'RE SOOO GOOD! BANDITA IS SO COOL, AND THE WRITING IS REALLY WELL DONE DURING THE SWORD FIGHTS AND-
!
COUGH.
I MEAN,
I GUESS IT'S OKAY.
I JUST READ TO PASS THE TIME...
RIGHT.
SPEAKING OF WHICH, I'M SURE YOU'VE PASSED ENOUGH OF THE DUCHESS'S TIME, DEAR!
YOU HAVE TO ENTERTAIN THE GUESTS IN MY STEAD!
RUN ALONG NOW!
WHAT-EVER.

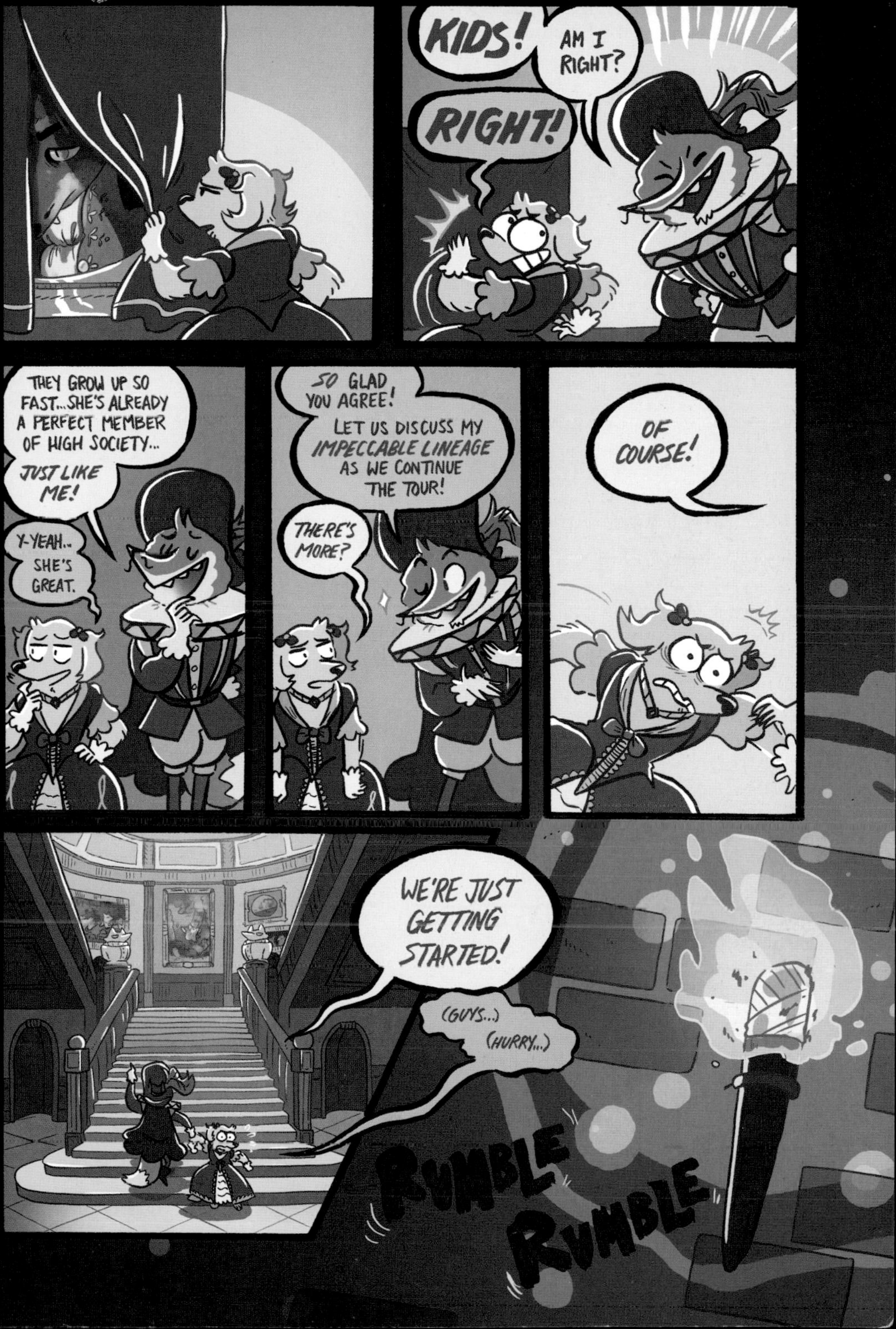
KIDS!
AM I RIGHT?
RIGHT!
THEY GROW UP SO FAST...SHE'S ALREADY A PERFECT MEMBER OF HIGH SOCIETY...
JUST LIKE ME!
Y-YEAH... SHE'S GREAT.
SO GLAD YOU AGREE!
LET US DISCUSS MY IMPECCABLE LINEAGE AS WE CONTINUE THE TOUR!
THERE'S MORE?
OF COURSE!
WE'RE JUST GETTING STARTED!
(GUYS...)
(HURRY...)
RUMBLE
RUMBLE

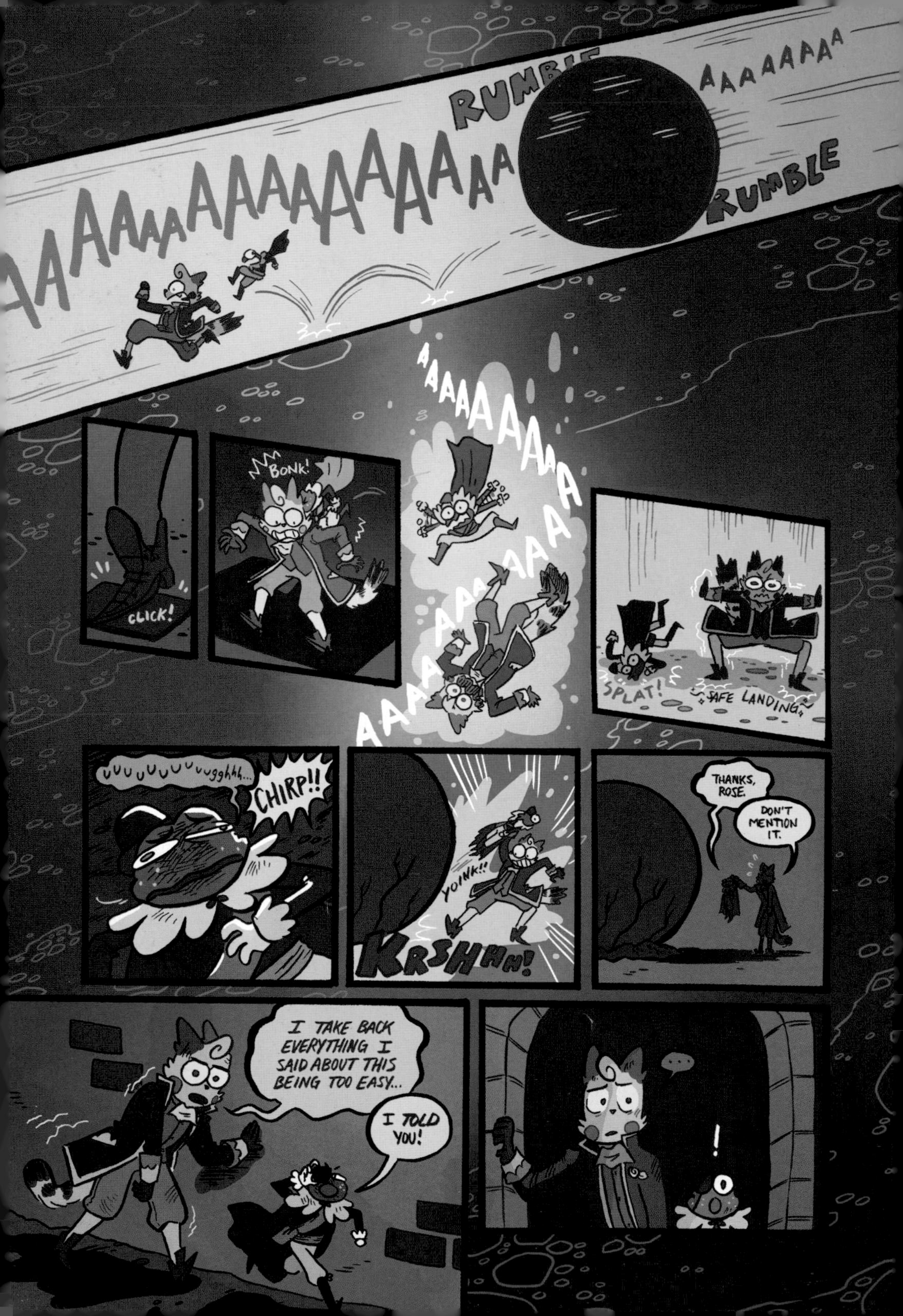

AAAAAAAAAAAAAAAAAAA
RUMBLE
AAAAAAA
RUMBLE
CLICK!
BONK!
AAAAAAAAAAAAAAAA
AAAAAAAAAAAAAA
SPLAT!
SAFE LANDING
UUUUUUUUuugghhh...
CHIRP!!
YOINK!!
KRSHHH!
THANKS, ROSE.
DON'T MENTION IT.
I TAKE BACK EVERYTHING I SAID ABOUT THIS BEING TOO EASY...
I TOLD YOU!
...
!

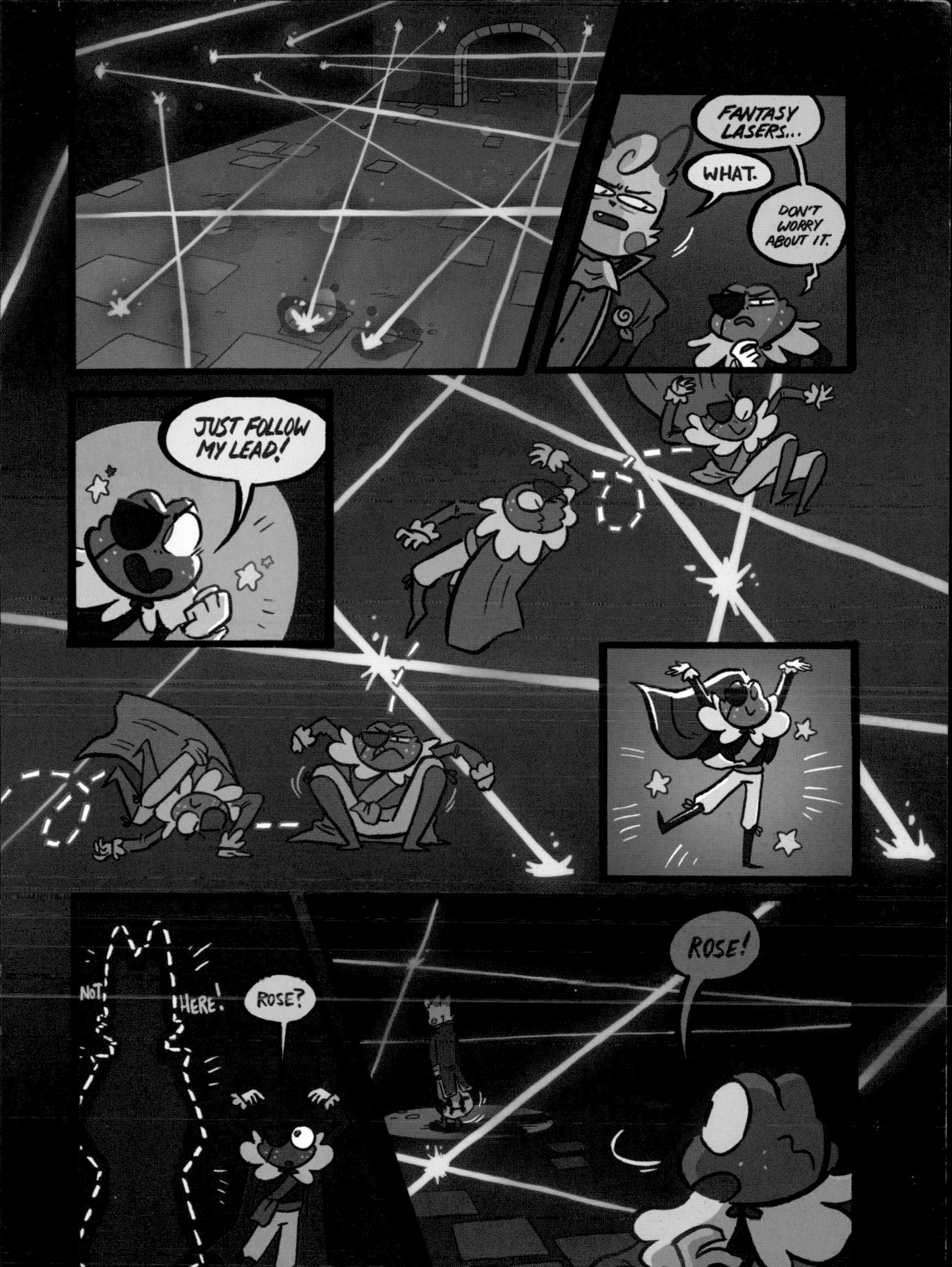
FANTASY LASERS...
WHAT.
DON'T WORRY ABOUT IT.
JUST FOLLOW MY LEAD!
NOT
HERE!
ROSE?
ROSE!

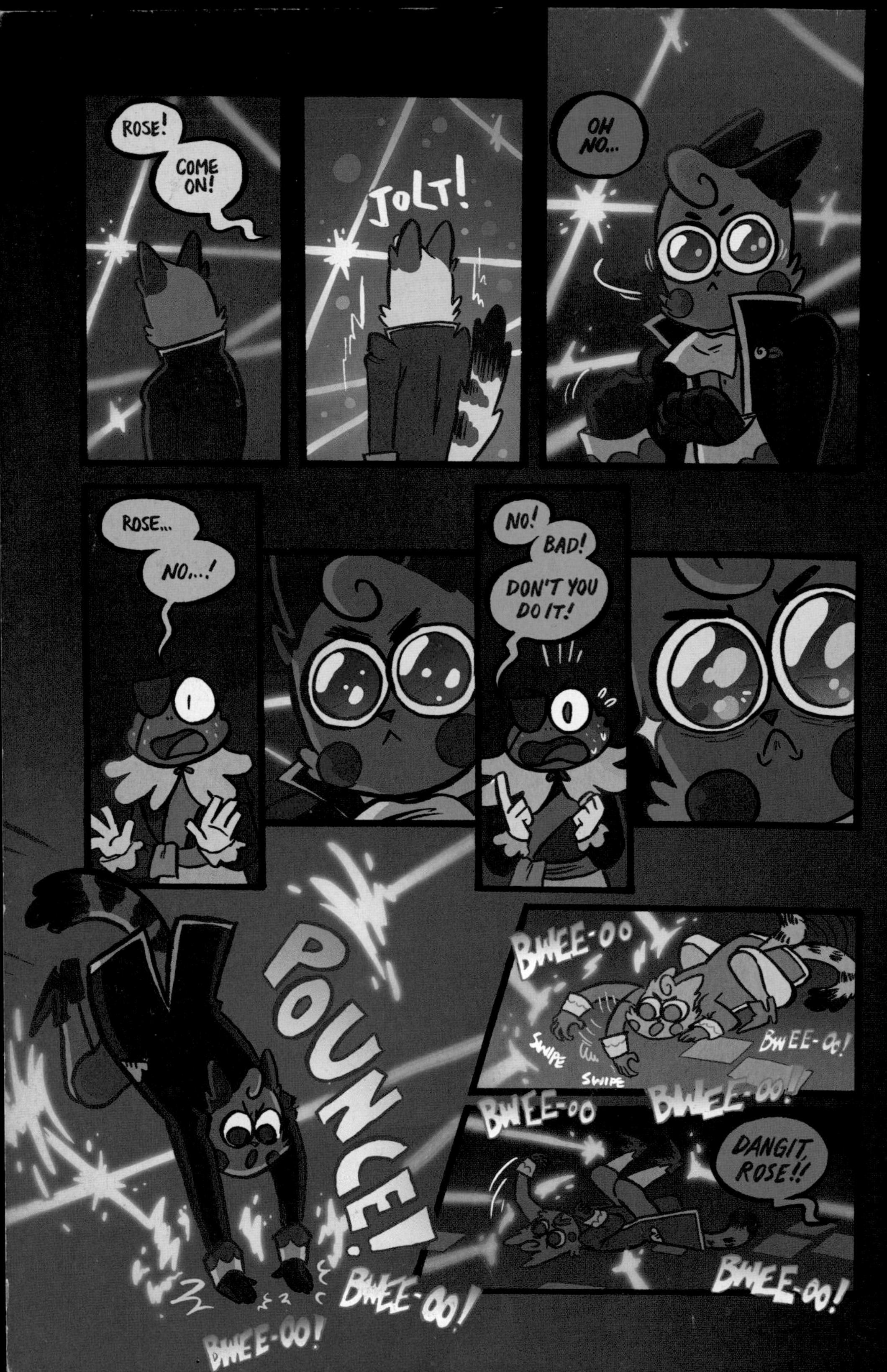
ROSE!
COME ON!
JOLT!
OH NO...
ROSE...
NO...!
NO!
BAD!
DON'T YOU DO IT!
POUNCE!
BWEE-OO!
BWEE-OO!
BWEE-OO
SWIPE
SWIPE
BWEE-OO!
BWEE-OO!!
BWEE-OO
DANGIT, ROSE!!
BWEE-OO!

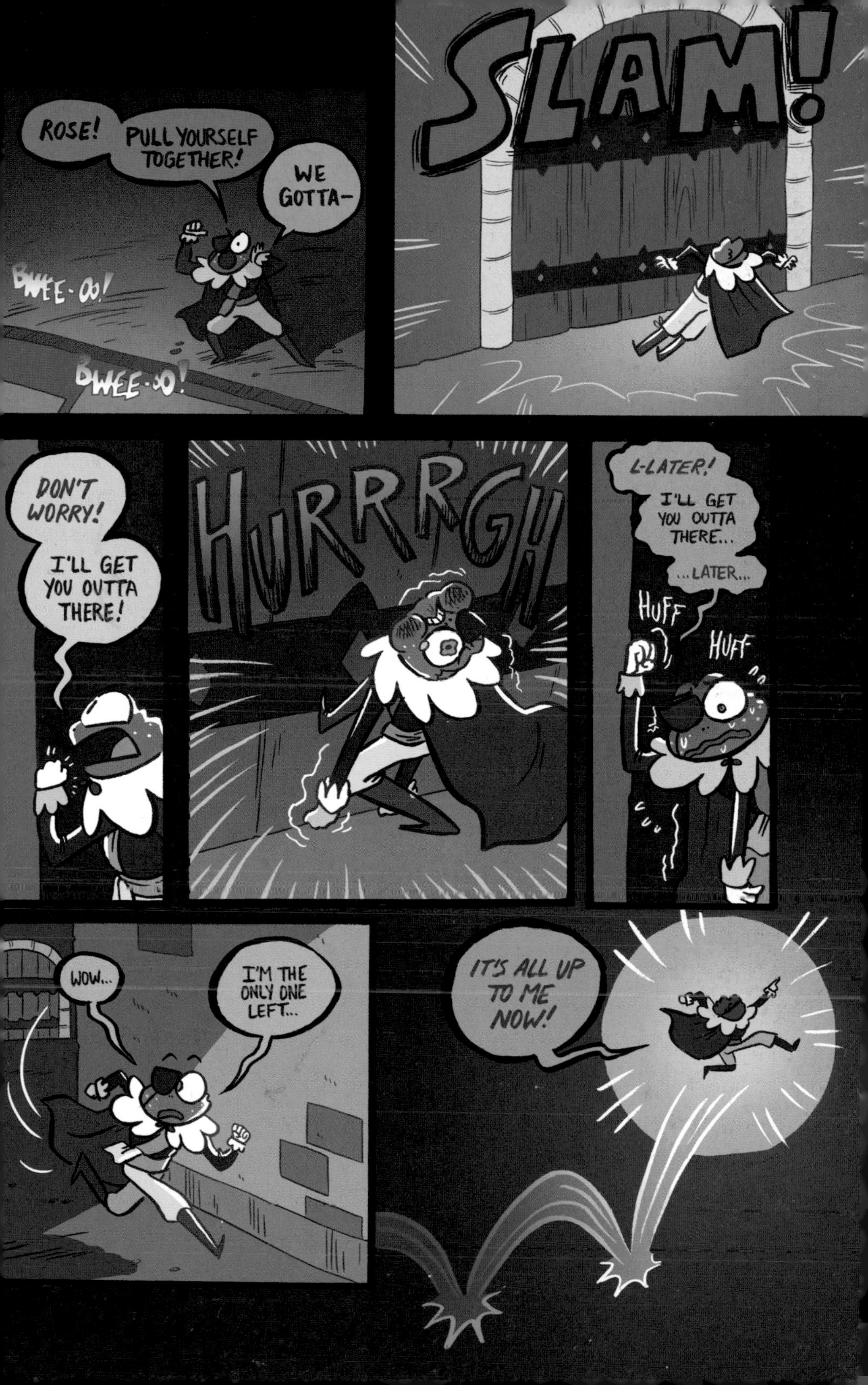
ROSE!
PULL YOURSELF TOGETHER!
WE GOTTA-
BWEE-OO!
BWEE-OO!
SLAM!
DON'T WORRY!
I'LL GET YOU OUTTA THERE!
HURRRGH
L-LATER!
I'LL GET YOU OUTTA THERE...
...LATER...
HUFF
HUFF
WOW...
I'M THE ONLY ONE LEFT...
IT'S ALL UP TO ME NOW!

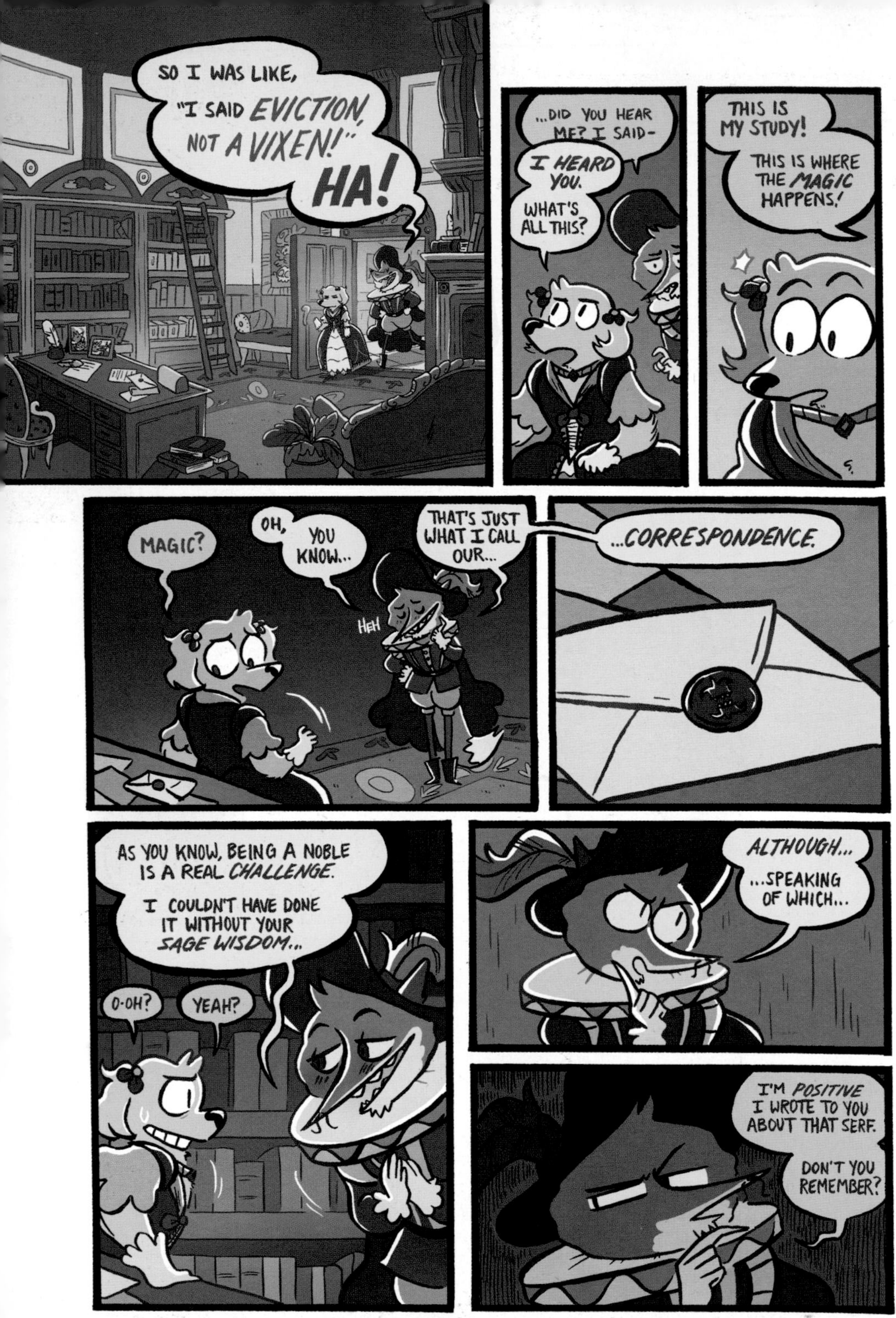

SO I WAS LIKE, "I SAID EVICTION, NOT A VIXEN!" HA!
...DID YOU HEAR ME? I SAID-
I HEARD YOU.
WHAT'S ALL THIS?
THIS IS MY STUDY!
THIS IS WHERE THE MAGIC HAPPENS!
MAGIC?
OH, YOU KNOW...
HEH
THAT'S JUST WHAT I CALL OUR...
...CORRESPONDENCE.
AS YOU KNOW, BEING A NOBLE IS A REAL CHALLENGE.
I COULDN'T HAVE DONE IT WITHOUT YOUR SAGE WISDOM...
O-OH?
YEAH?
ALTHOUGH...
...SPEAKING OF WHICH...
I'M POSITIVE I WROTE TO YOU ABOUT THAT SERF.
DON'T YOU REMEMBER?

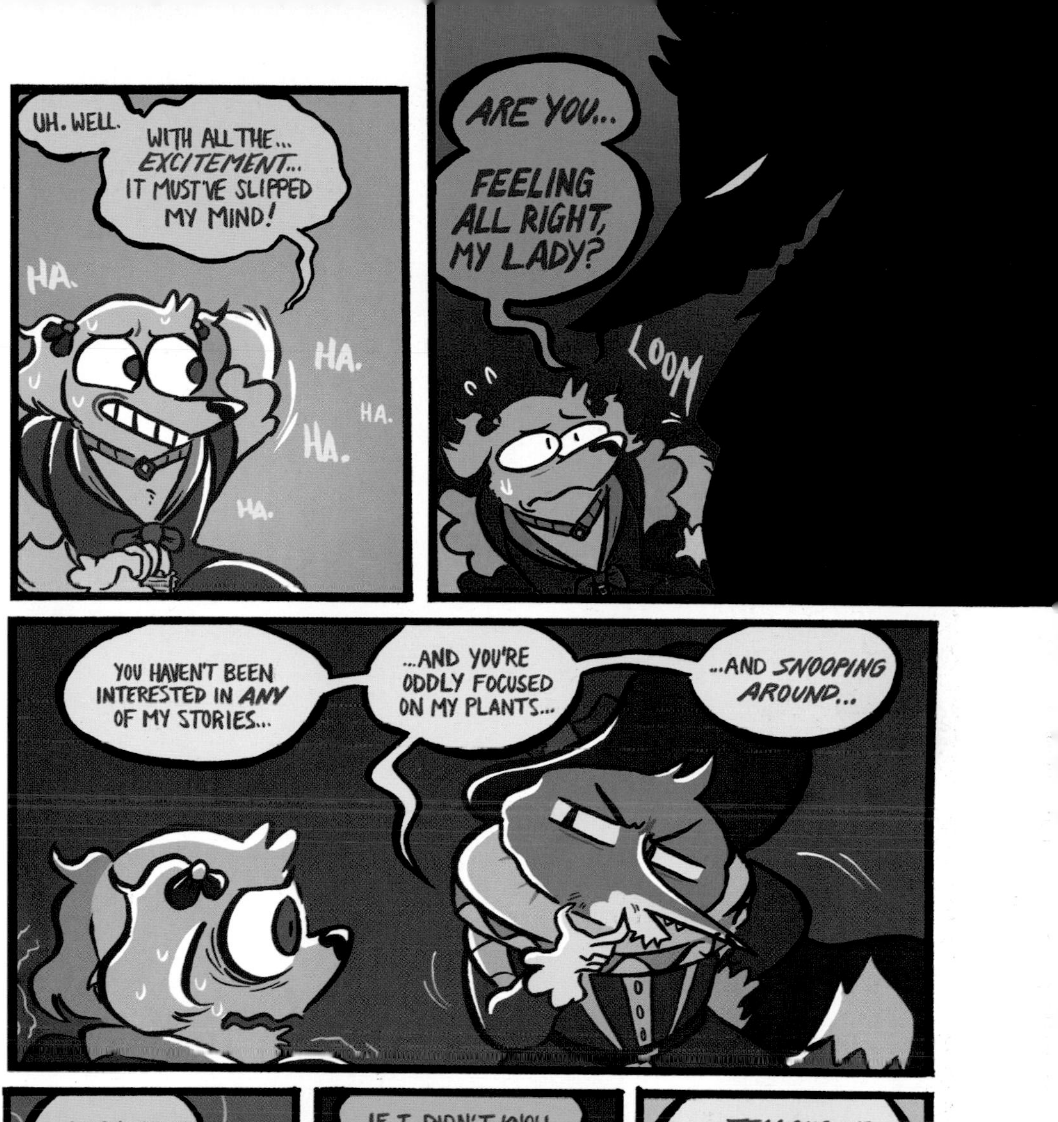
UH. WELL.
WITH ALL THE... EXCITEMENT... IT MUST'VE SLIPPED MY MIND!
HA.
HA.
HA.
HA.
HA.
ARE YOU...
FEELING ALL RIGHT, MY LADY?
LOOM
YOU HAVEN'T BEEN INTERESTED IN ANY OF MY STORIES...
...AND YOU'RE ODDLY FOCUSED ON MY PLANTS...
...AND SNOOPING AROUND...
...VERY UNLIKE YOURSELF.
IF I DIDN'T KNOW ANY BETTER, I'D SAY YOU'RE...
...JEALOUS OF HOW WELL I'M GETTING ALONG WITH JEREMY!
?!?!

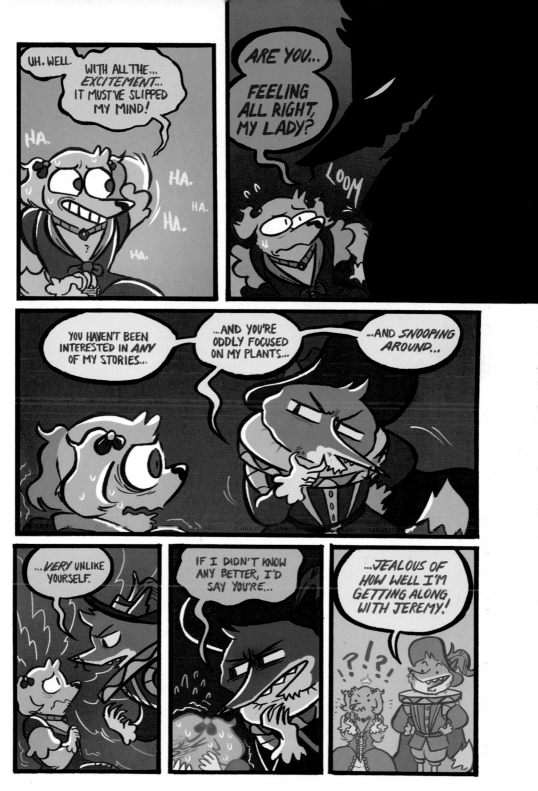

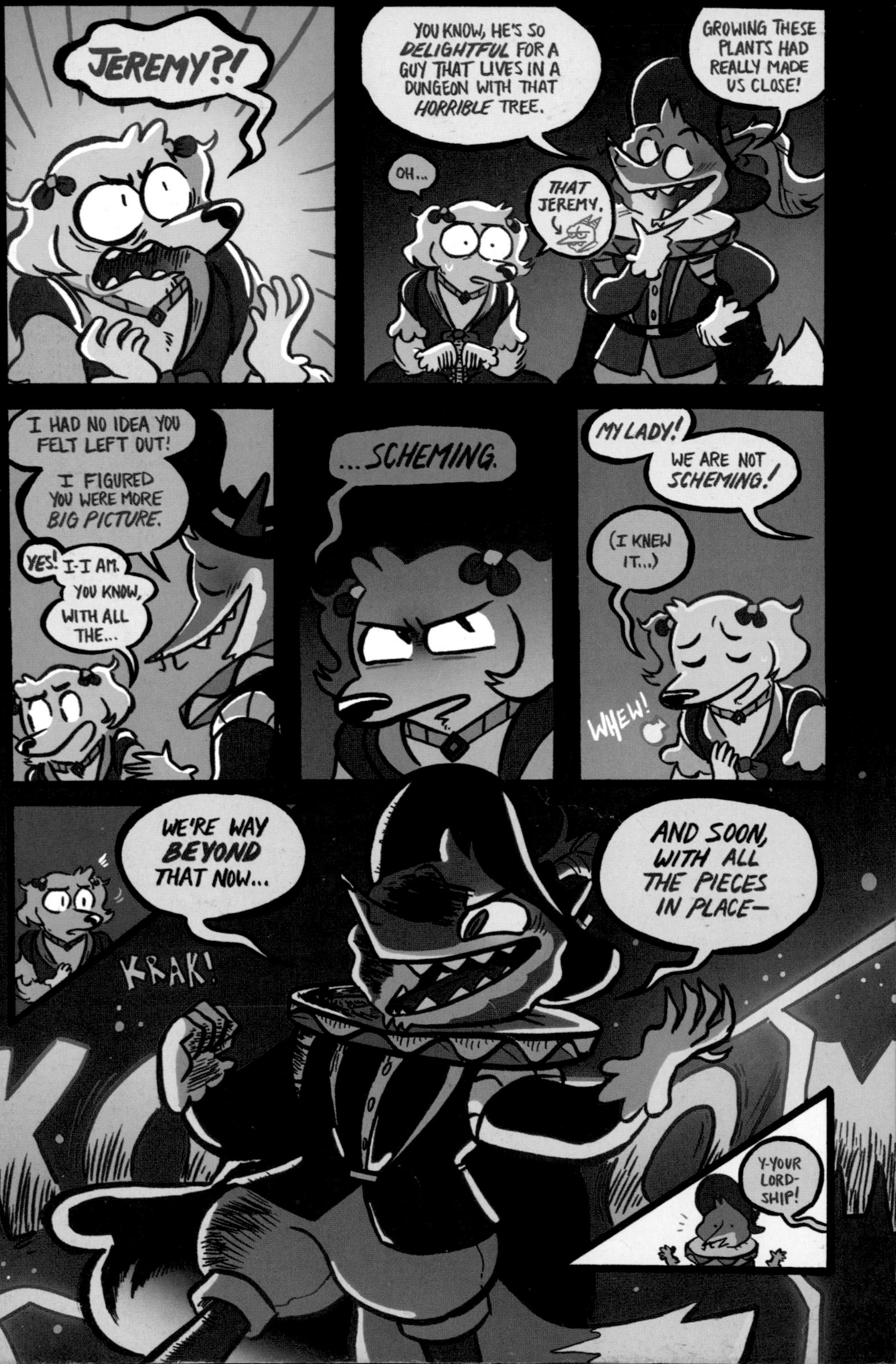

JEREMY?!
YOU KNOW, HE'S SO DELIGHTFUL FOR A GUY THAT LIVES IN A DUNGEON WITH THAT HORRIBLE TREE.
GROWING THESE PLANTS HAD REALLY MADE US CLOSE!
OH...
THAT JEREMY.
I HAD NO IDEA YOU FELT LEFT OUT!
I FIGURED YOU WERE MORE BIG PICTURE.
YES! I-I AM. YOU KNOW, WITH ALL THE...
...SCHEMING.
MY LADY!
WE ARE NOT SCHEMING!
(I KNEW IT...)
WHEW!
WE'RE WAY BEYOND THAT NOW...
KRAK!
AND SOON, WITH ALL THE PIECES IN PLACE—
Y-YOUR LORD-SHIP!

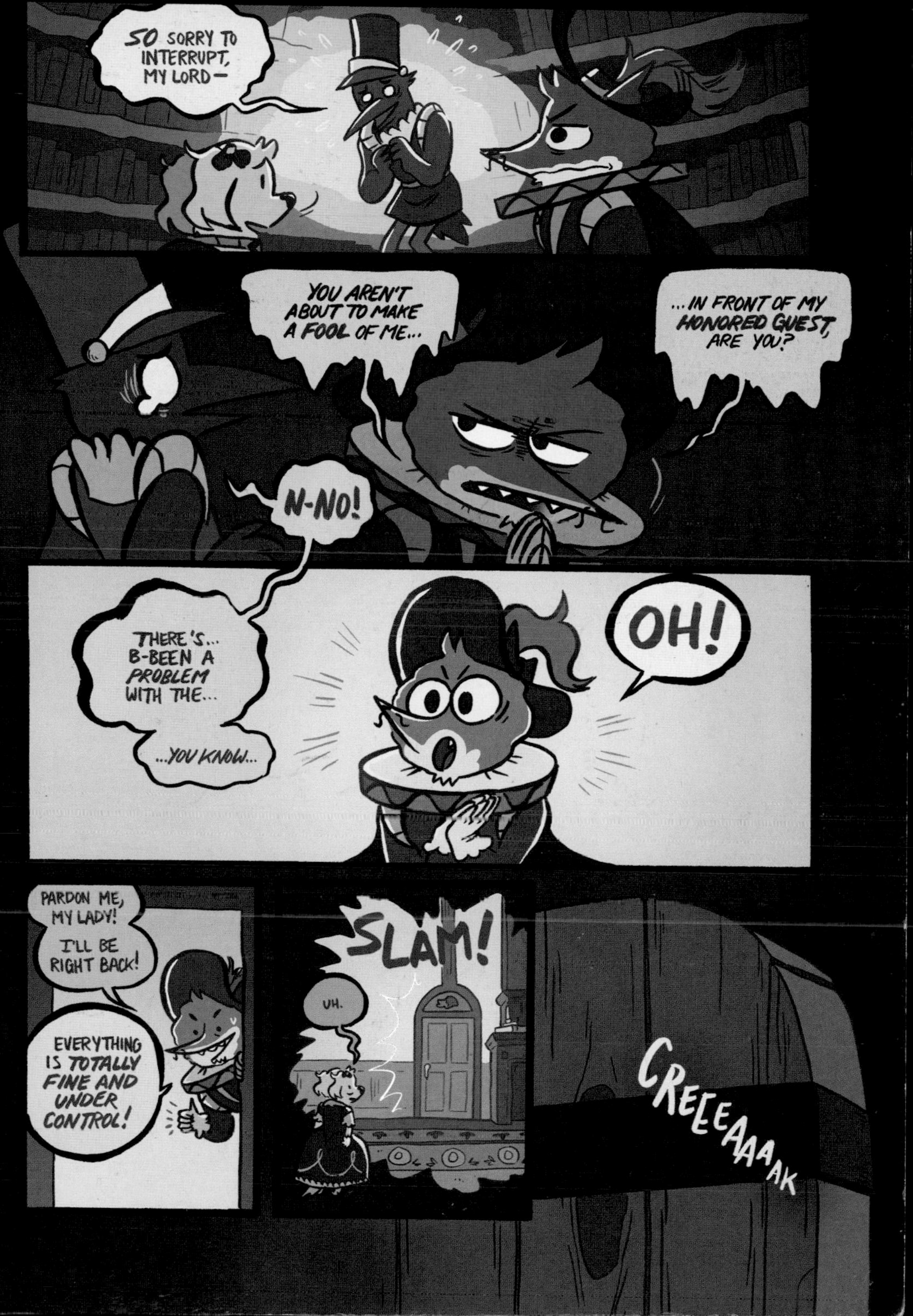
SO SORRY TO INTERRUPT, MY LORD—
YOU AREN'T ABOUT TO MAKE A FOOL OF ME...
...IN FRONT OF MY HONORED GUEST, ARE YOU?
N-NO!
THERE'S... B-BEEN A PROBLEM WITH THE...
...YOU KNOW...
OH!
PARDON ME, MY LADY!
I'LL BE RIGHT BACK!
EVERYTHING IS TOTALLY FINE AND UNDER CONTROL!
SLAM!
UH.
CREEEAAAAK

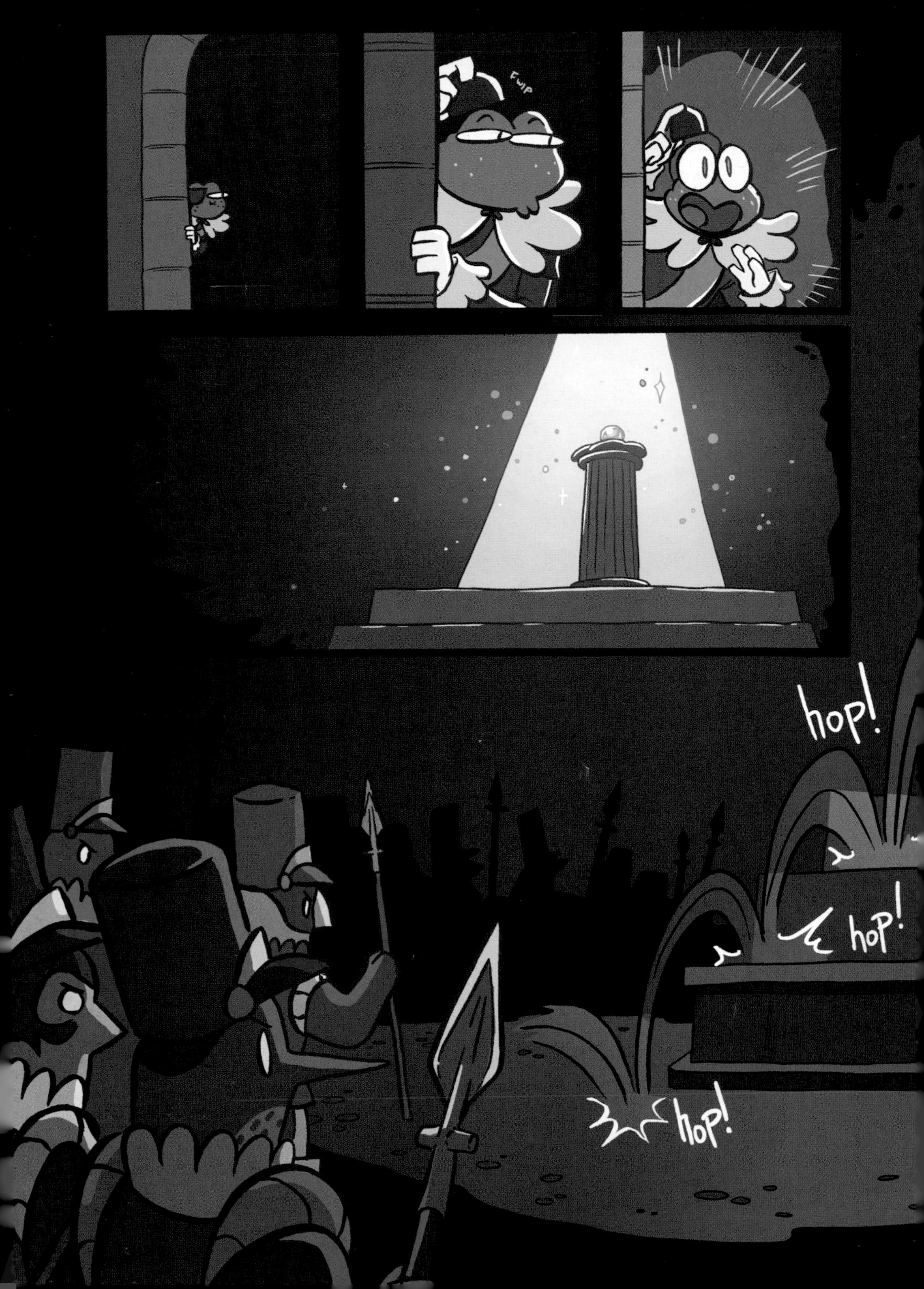
FWIP
hop!
hop!
hop!

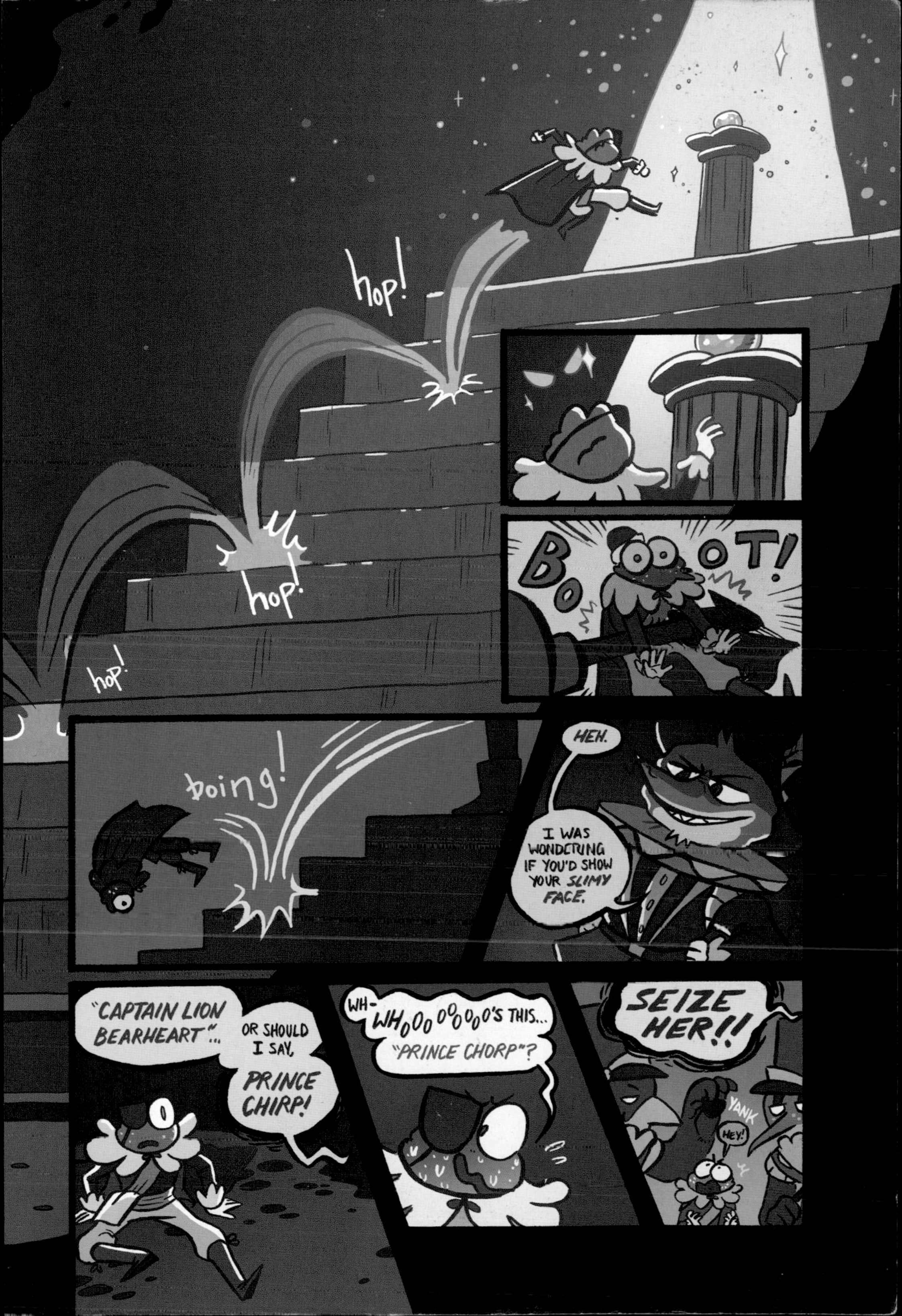
hop!
hop!
hop!
BOOOT!
boing!
HEH.
I WAS WONDERING IF YOU'D SHOW YOUR SLIMY FACE.
"CAPTAIN LION BEARHEART"...
OR SHOULD I SAY, PRINCE CHIRP!
WH- WHOOOOOOOO'S THIS... "PRINCE CHORP"?
SEIZE HER!!
YANK
HEY!

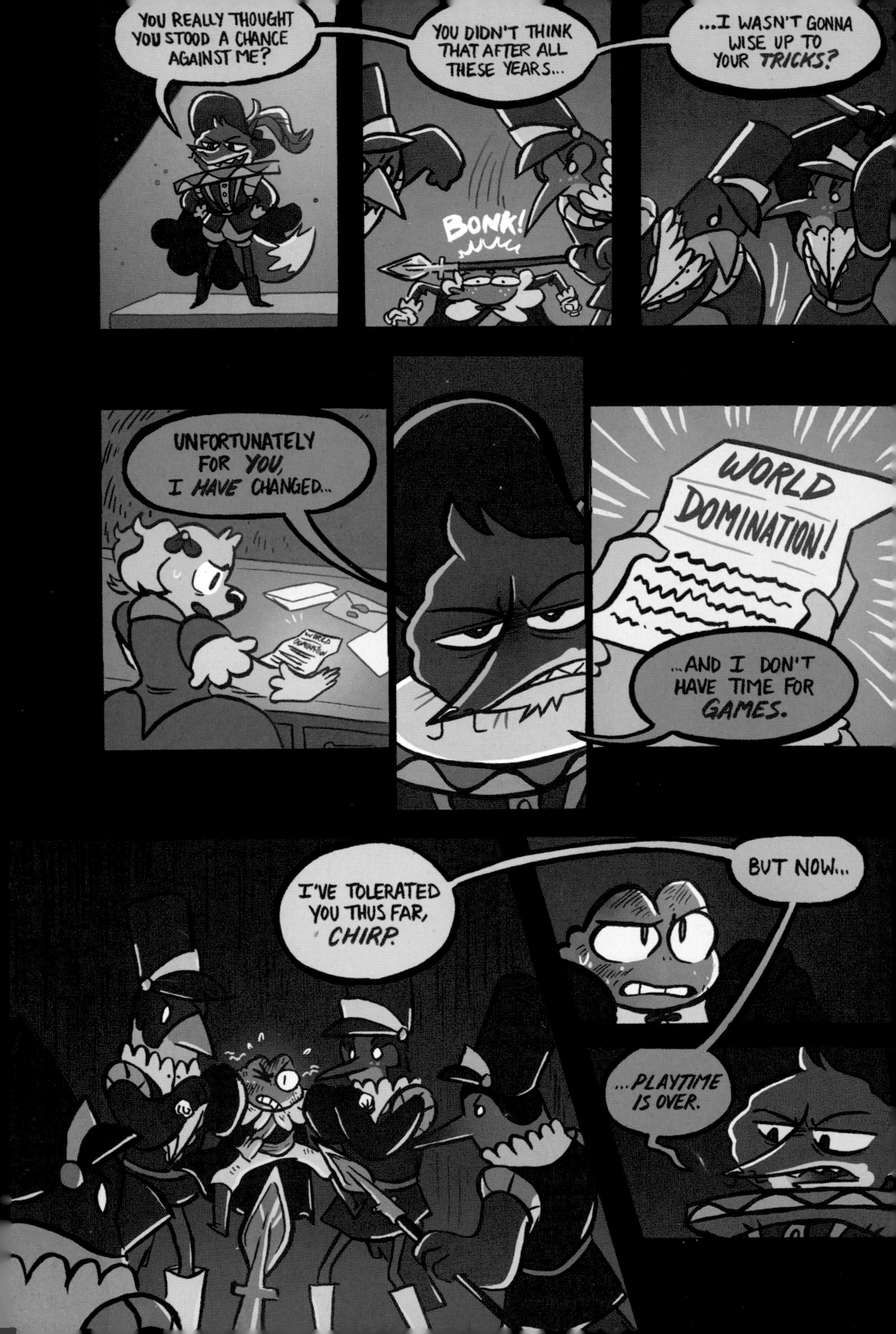
YOU REALLY THOUGHT YOU STOOD A CHANCE AGAINST ME?
YOU DIDN'T THINK THAT AFTER ALL THESE YEARS...
...I WASN'T GONNA WISE UP TO YOUR TRICKS?
BONK!
UNFORTUNATELY FOR YOU, I HAVE CHANGED...
WORLD DOMINATION!
...AND I DON'T HAVE TIME FOR GAMES.
I'VE TOLERATED YOU THUS FAR, CHIRP.
BUT NOW...
...PLAYTIME IS OVER.

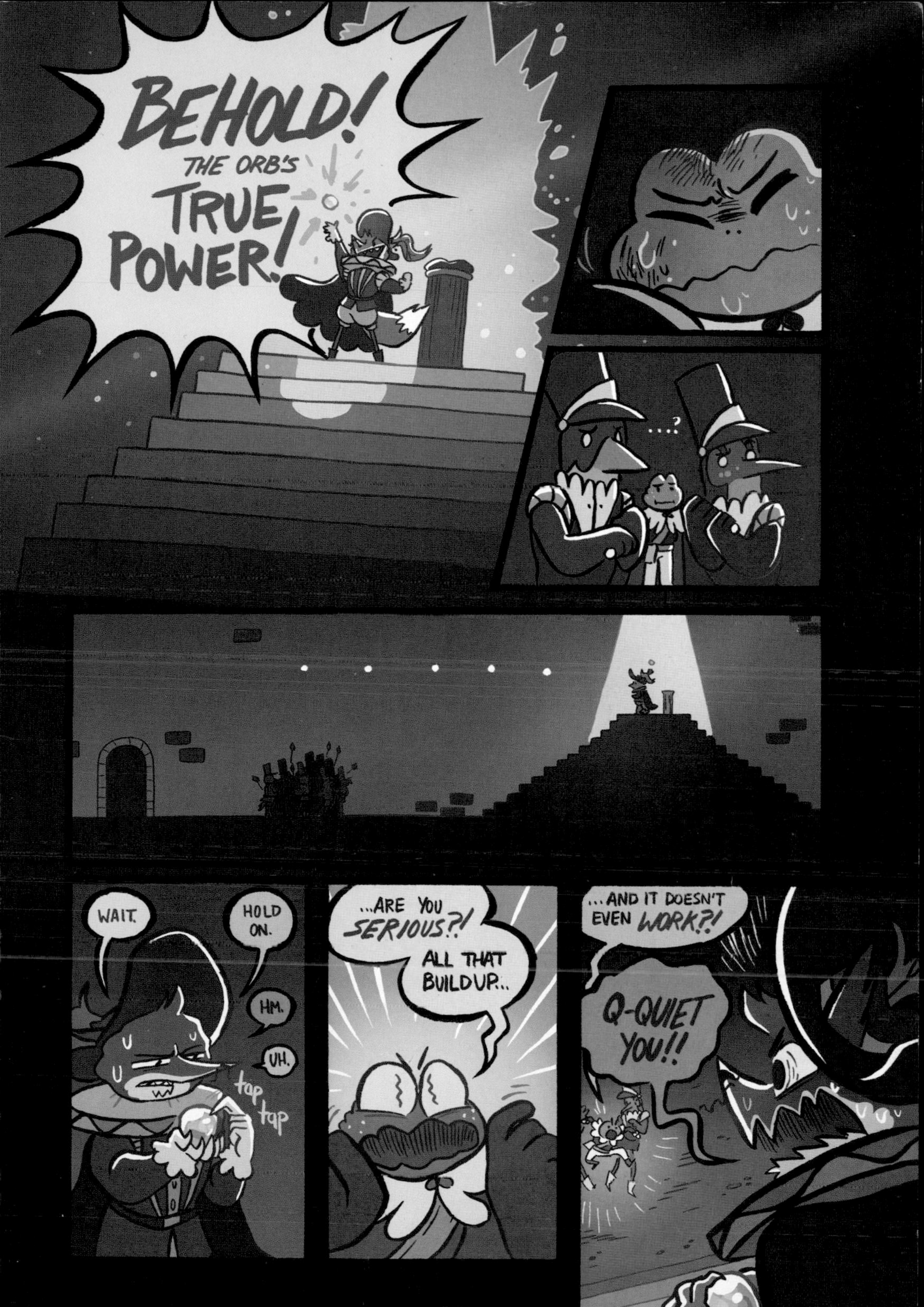
BEHOLD! THE ORB'S TRUE POWER!
...?
WAIT.
HOLD ON.
HM.
UH.
tap tap
...ARE YOU SERIOUS?!
ALL THAT BUILDUP...
...AND IT DOESN'T EVEN WORK?!
Q-QUIET YOU!!

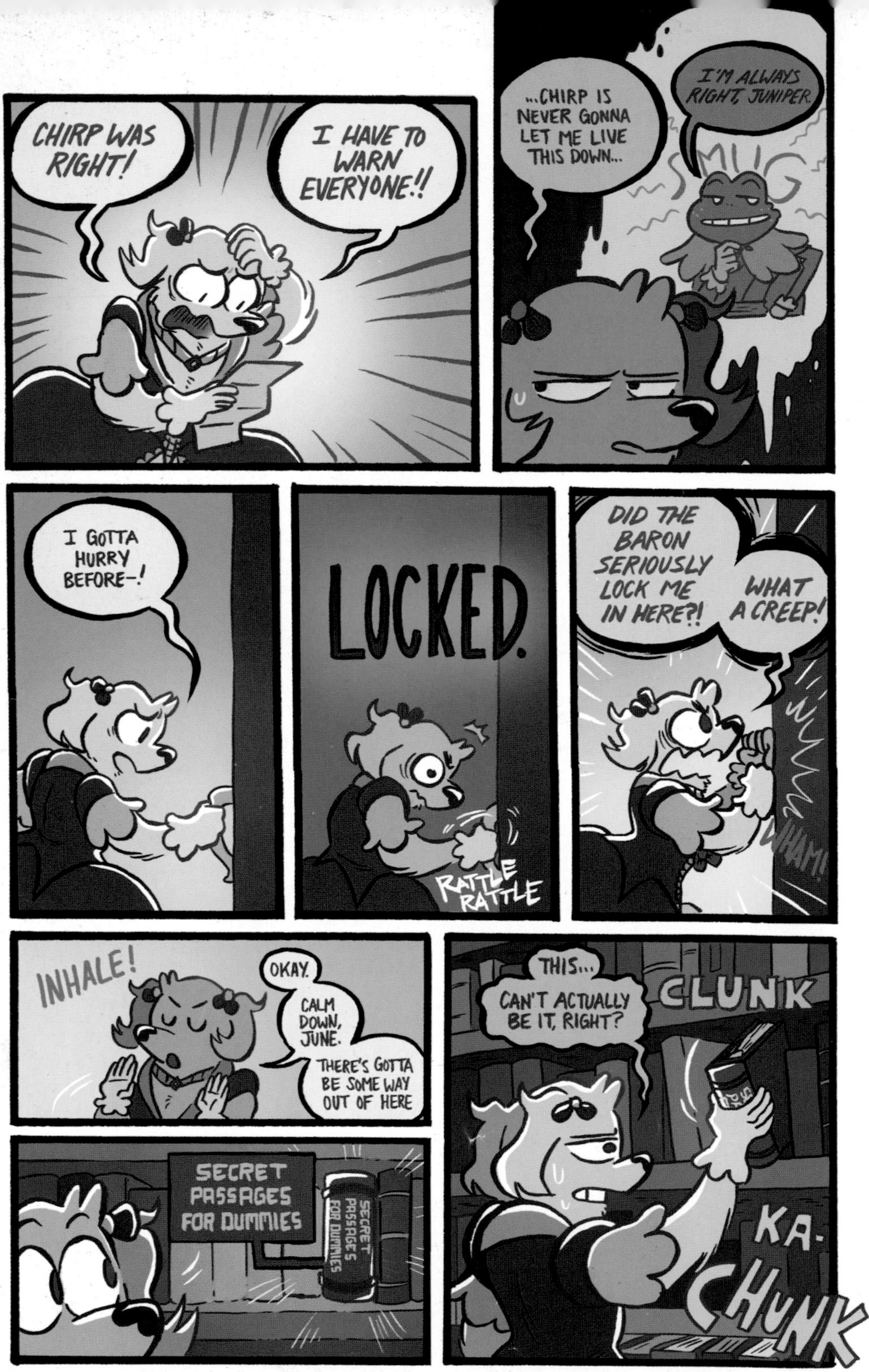
CHIRP WAS RIGHT!
I HAVE TO WARN EVERYONE!!
...CHIRP IS NEVER GONNA LET ME LIVE THIS DOWN...
I'M ALWAYS RIGHT, JUNIPER.
SMUG
I GOTTA HURRY BEFORE-!
LOCKED.
RATTLE RATTLE
DID THE BARON SERIOUSLY LOCK ME IN HERE?!
WHAT A CREEP!
WHAM!
INHALE!
OKAY.
CALM DOWN, JUNE.
THERE'S GOTTA BE SOME WAY OUT OF HERE
SECRET PASSAGES FOR DUMMIES
SECRET PASSAGES FOR DUMMIES
THIS...
CAN'T ACTUALLY BE IT, RIGHT?
CLUNK
KA-CHUNK

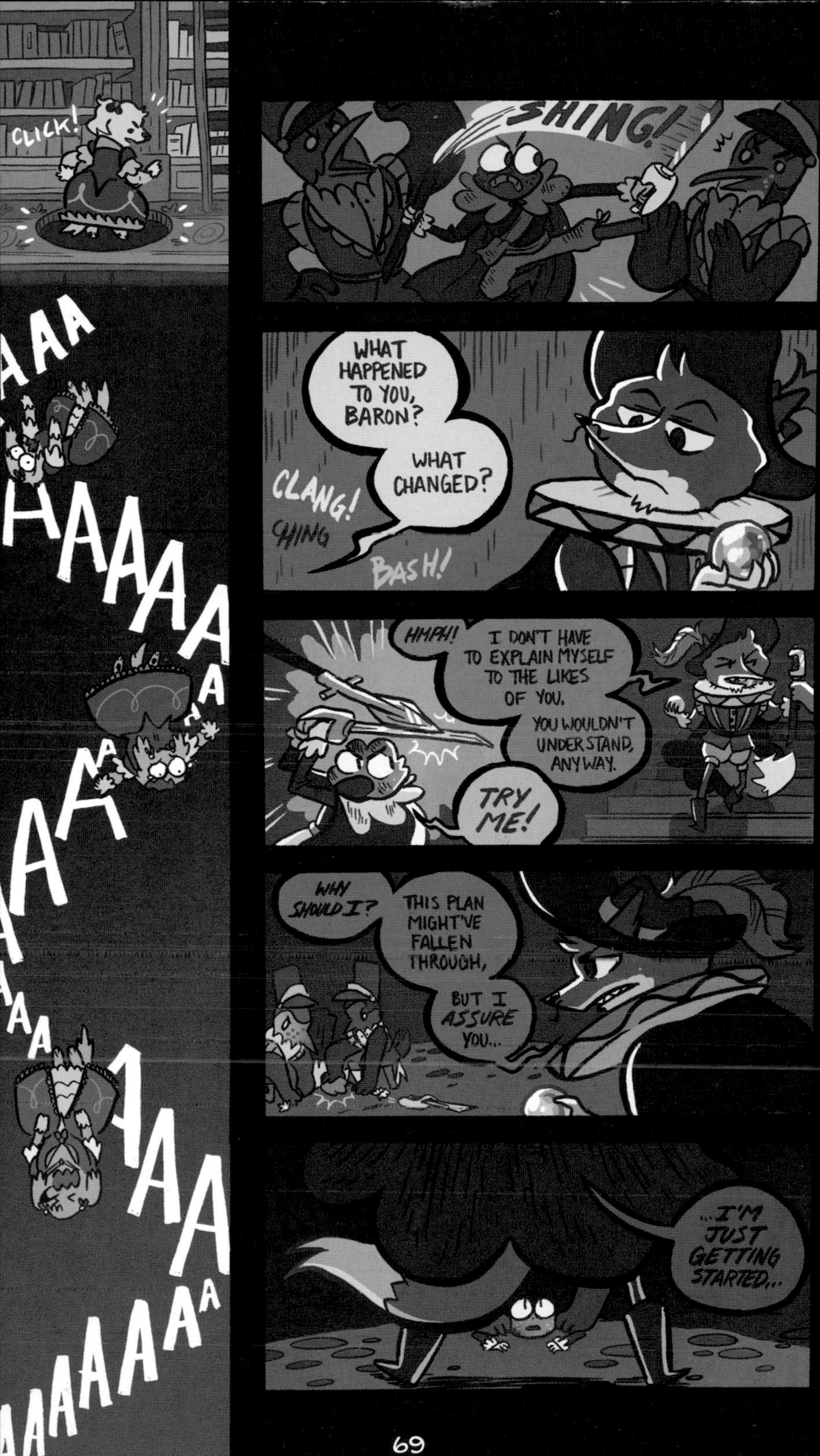
CLICK!
AAAAAAAAAAAAAAAAAAAAAAAAAAAAAAAAA
SHING!
WHAT HAPPENED TO YOU, BARON?
WHAT CHANGED?
CLANG!
CHING
BASH!
HMPH!
I DON'T HAVE TO EXPLAIN MYSELF TO THE LIKES OF YOU.
YOU WOULDN'T UNDERSTAND, ANYWAY.
TRY ME!
WHY SHOULD I?
THIS PLAN MIGHT'VE FALLEN THROUGH,
BUT I ASSURE YOU...
...I'M JUST GETTING STARTED...

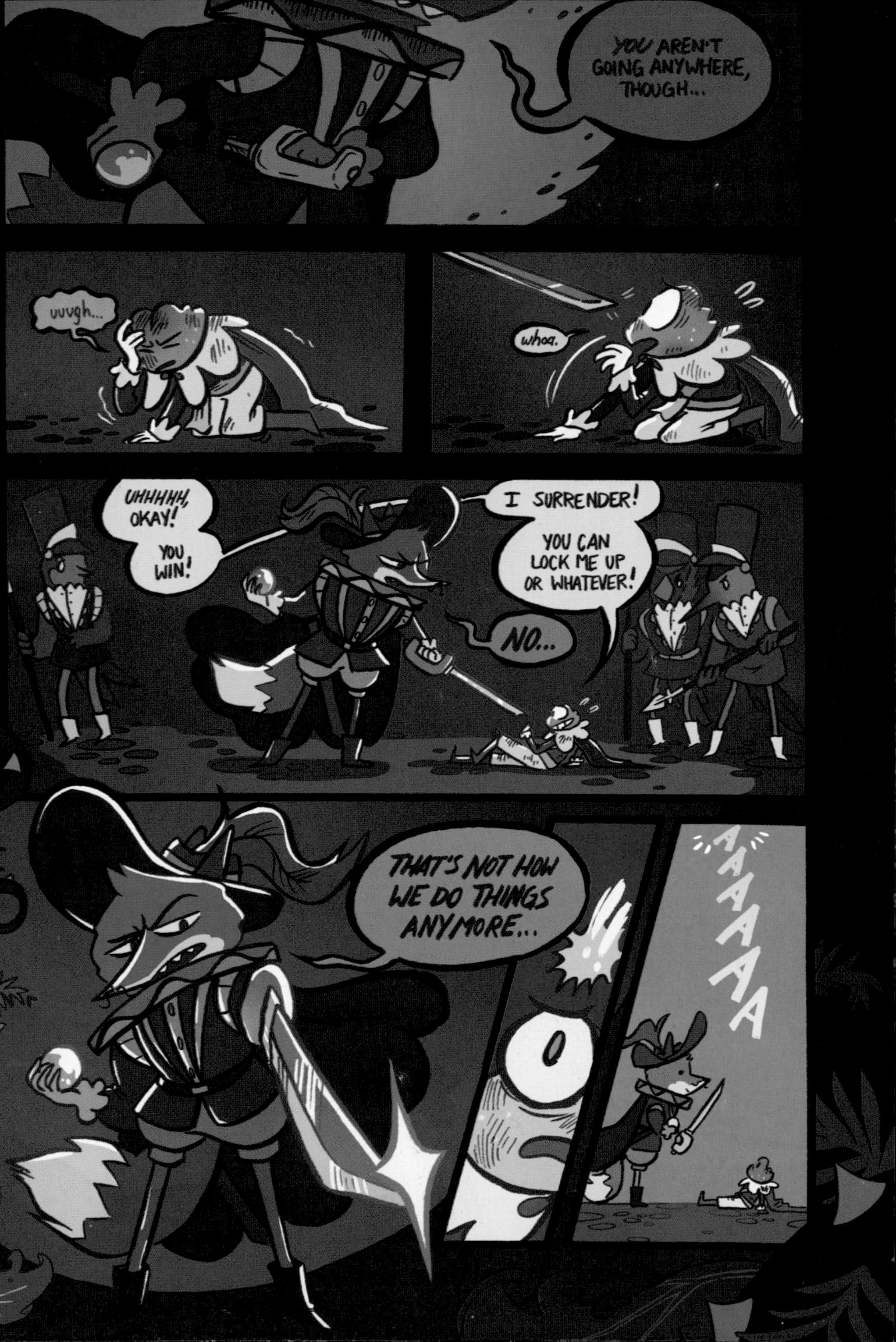
YOU AREN'T GOING ANYWHERE, THOUGH...
uuugh...
whoa.
UHHHHH, OKAY!
YOU WIN!
I SURRENDER!
YOU CAN LOCK ME UP OR WHATEVER!
NO...
THAT'S NOT HOW WE DO THINGS ANYMORE...
AAAAAAA

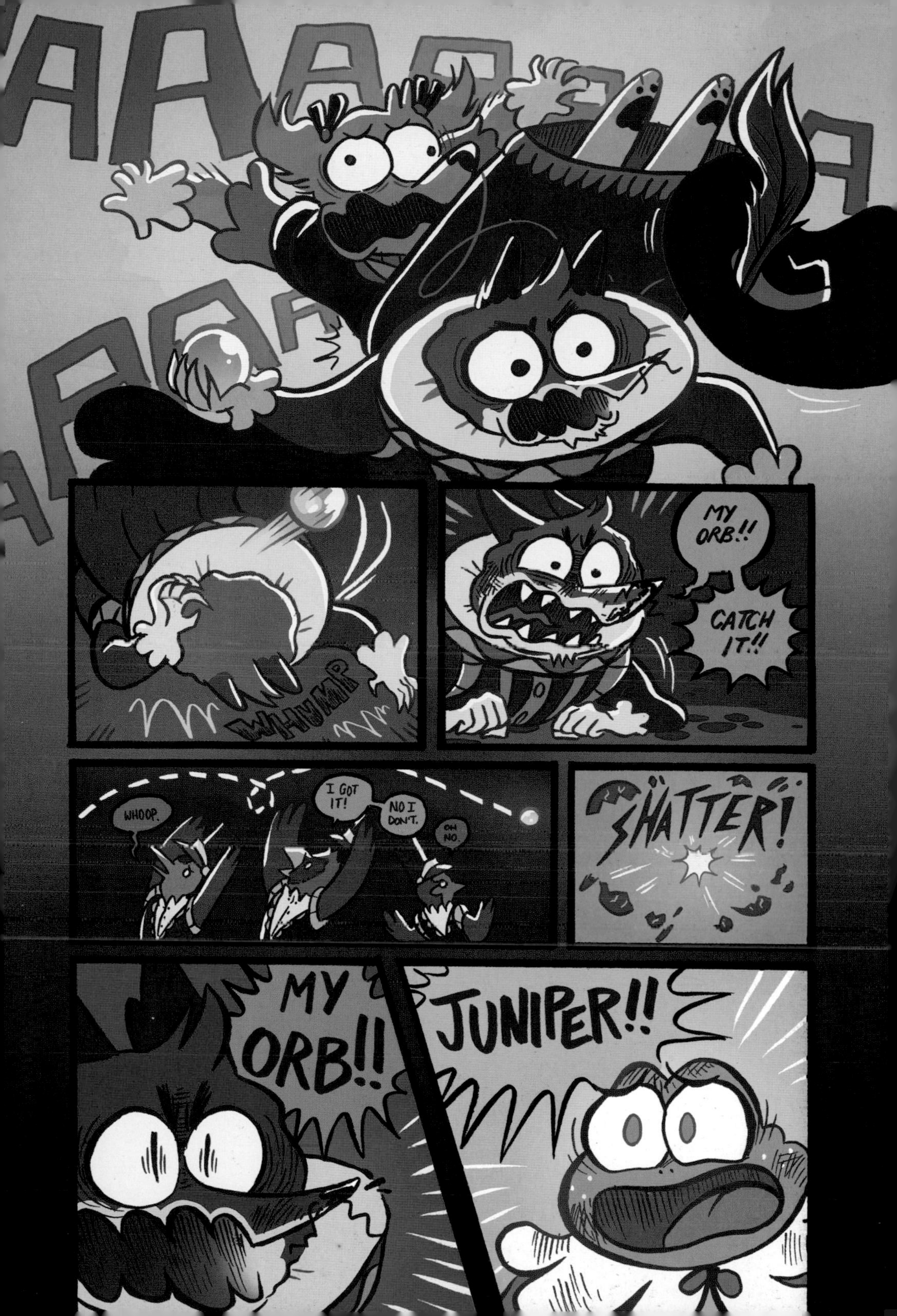
AAAAAAAAA
WHUMP
MY ORB!!
CATCH IT!!
WHOOP.
I GOT IT!
NO I DON'T.
OH NO.
SHATTER!
MY ORB!!
JUNIPER!!

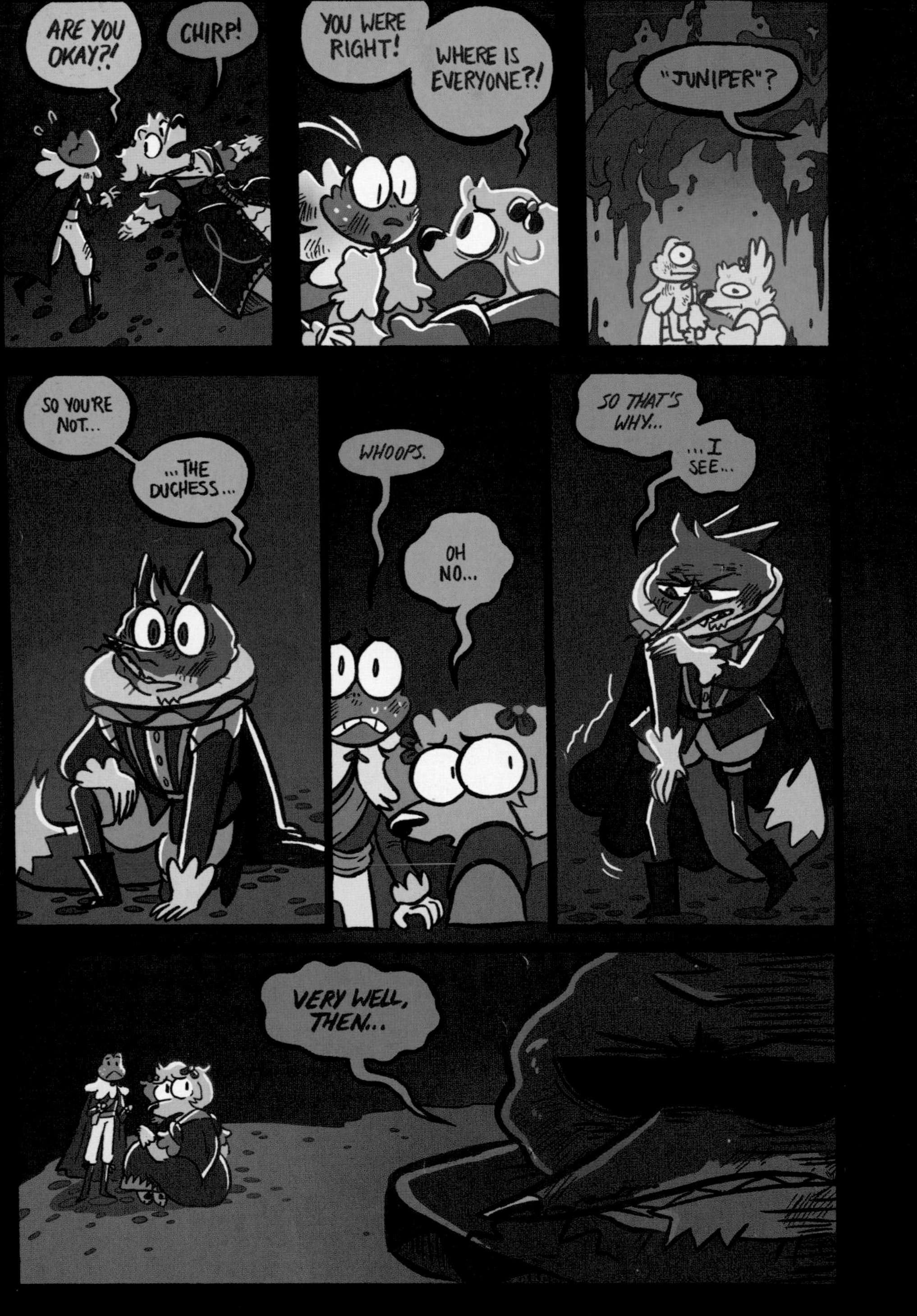
ARE YOU OKAY?!
CHIRP!
YOU WERE RIGHT!
WHERE IS EVERYONE?!
"JUNIPER"?
SO YOU'RE NOT...
...THE DUCHESS...
WHOOPS.
OH NO...
SO THAT'S WHY...
...I SEE...
VERY WELL, THEN...

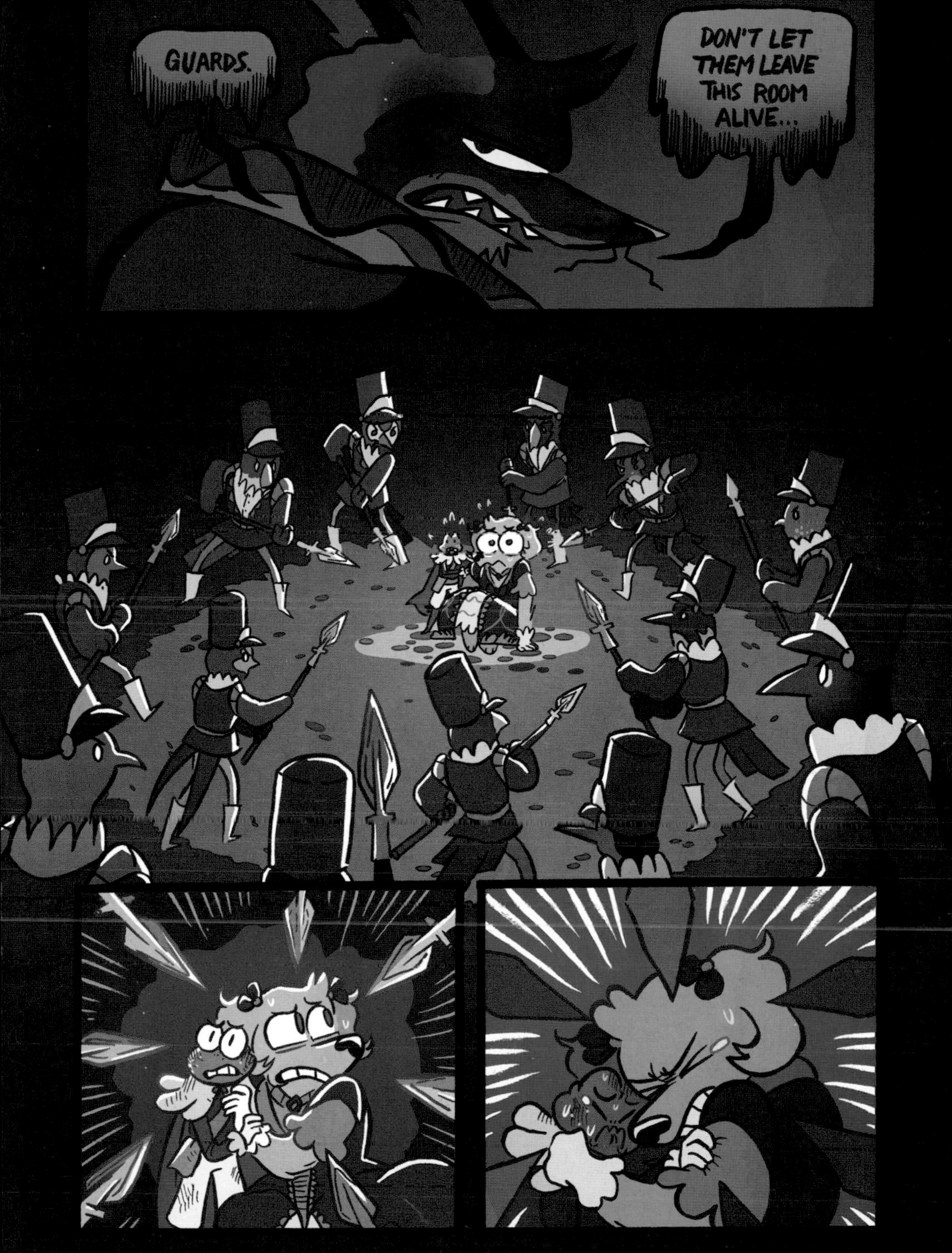
GUARDS.
DON'T LET THEM LEAVE THIS ROOM ALIVE...

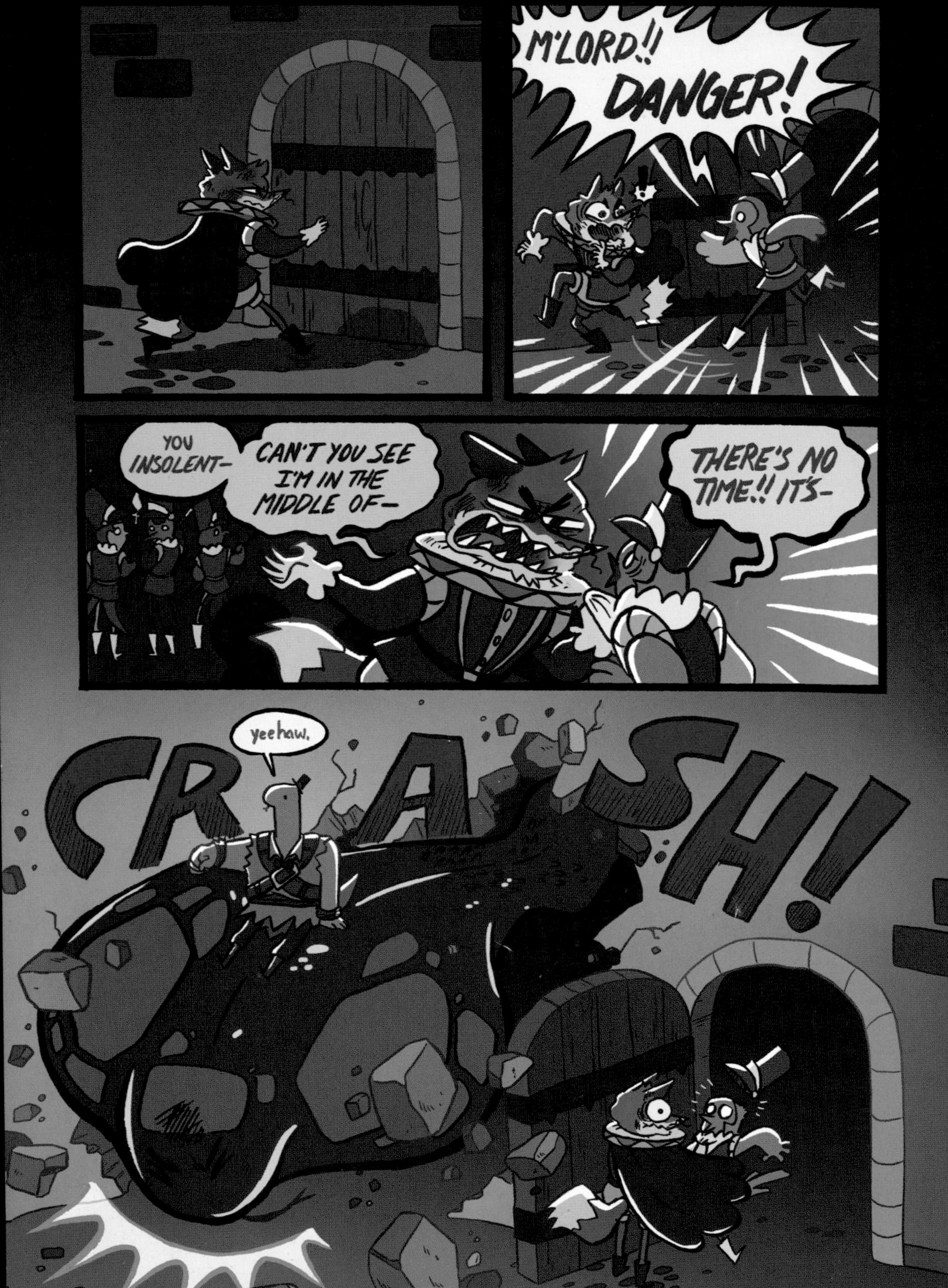
M'LORD!!
DANGER!
YOU INSOLENT-
CAN'T YOU SEE I'M IN THE MIDDLE OF-
THERE'S NO TIME!! IT'S-
yeehaw.
CRASH!

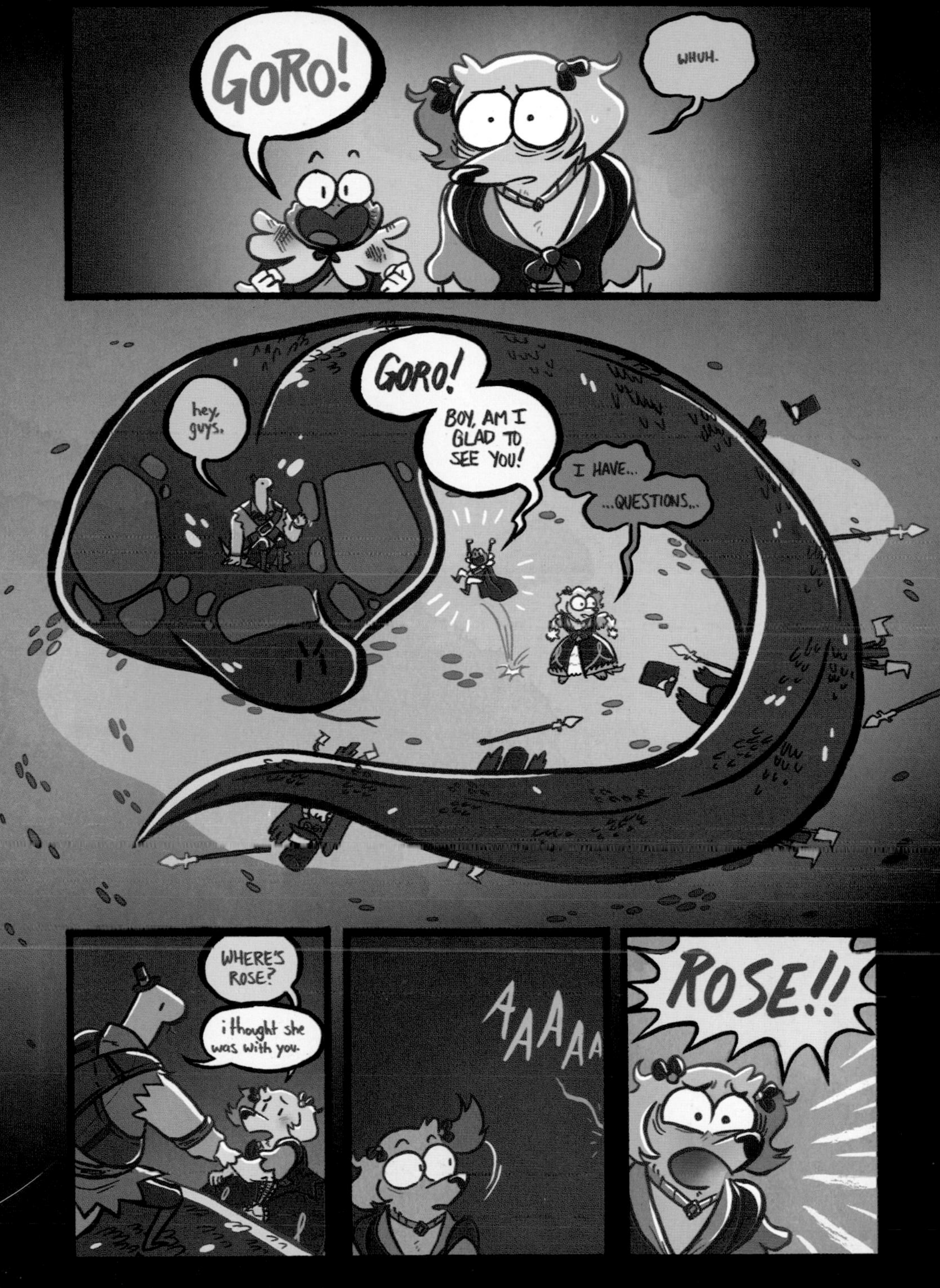
GORO!
WHUH.
hey, guys.
GORO!
BOY, AM I GLAD TO SEE YOU!
I HAVE...
...QUESTIONS...
WHERE'S ROSE?
i thought she was with you.
AAAAA
ROSE!!

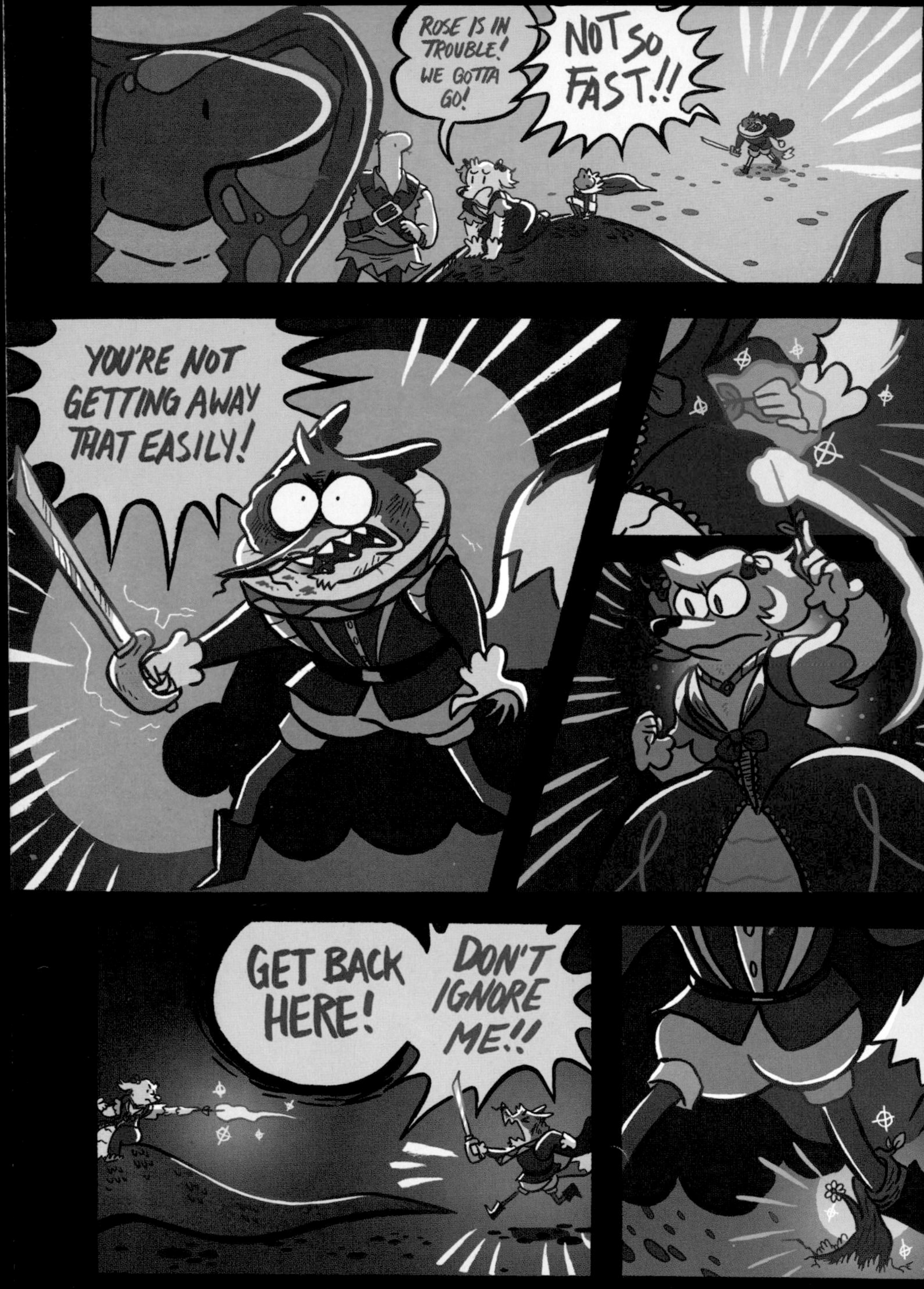
ROSE IS IN TROUBLE! WE GOTTA GO!
NOT SO FAST!!
YOU'RE NOT GETTING AWAY THAT EASILY!
GET BACK HERE!
DON'T IGNORE ME!!

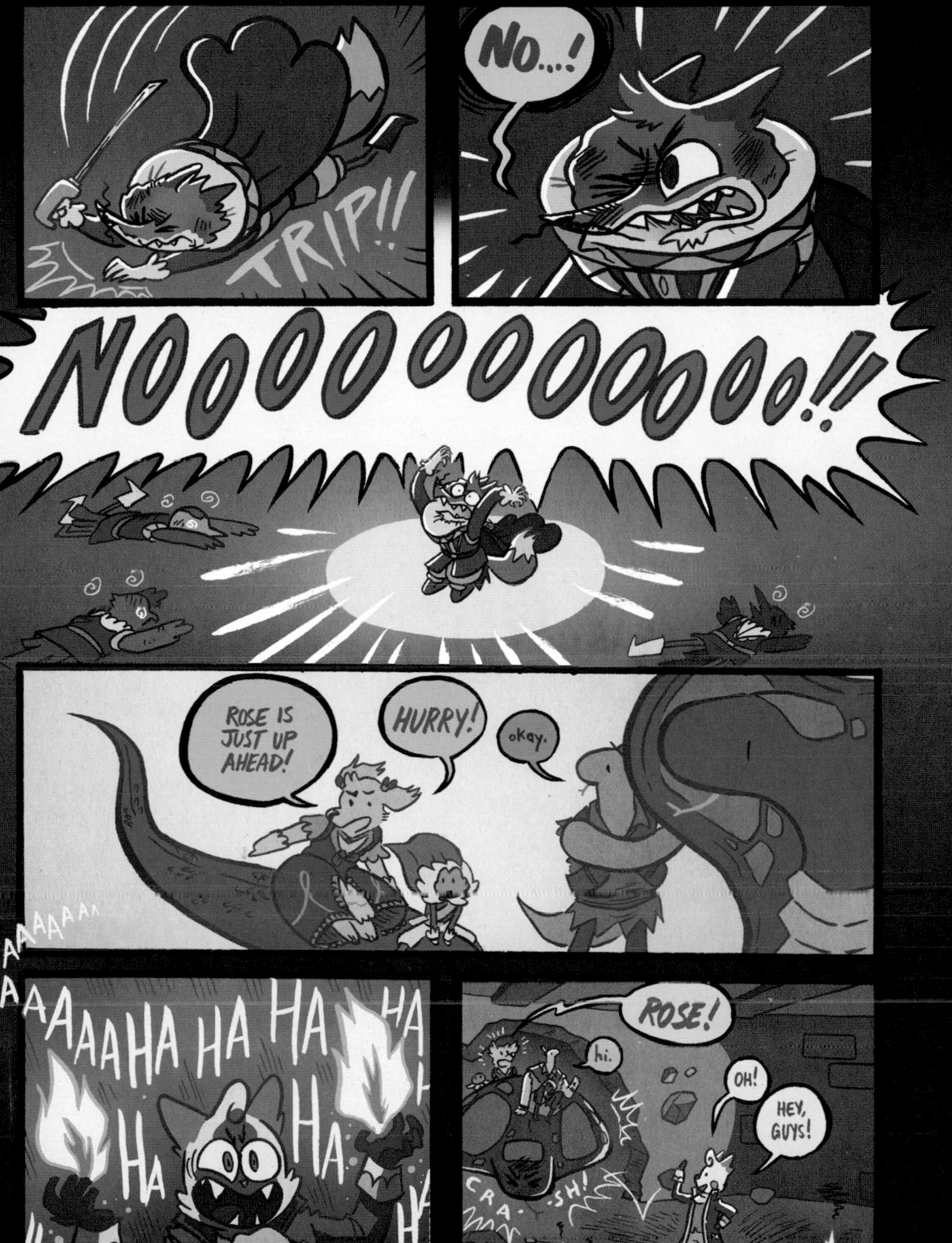
TRIP!!
NO...!
NOOOOOOOOOOOoo!!
ROSE IS JUST UP AHEAD!
HURRY!
okay.
AAAAAAA
AAAAAHA HA HA HA
HA HA HA HA HA HA HA HA HA
ROSE!
hi.
OH!
HEY, GUYS!
CRA- -SH!

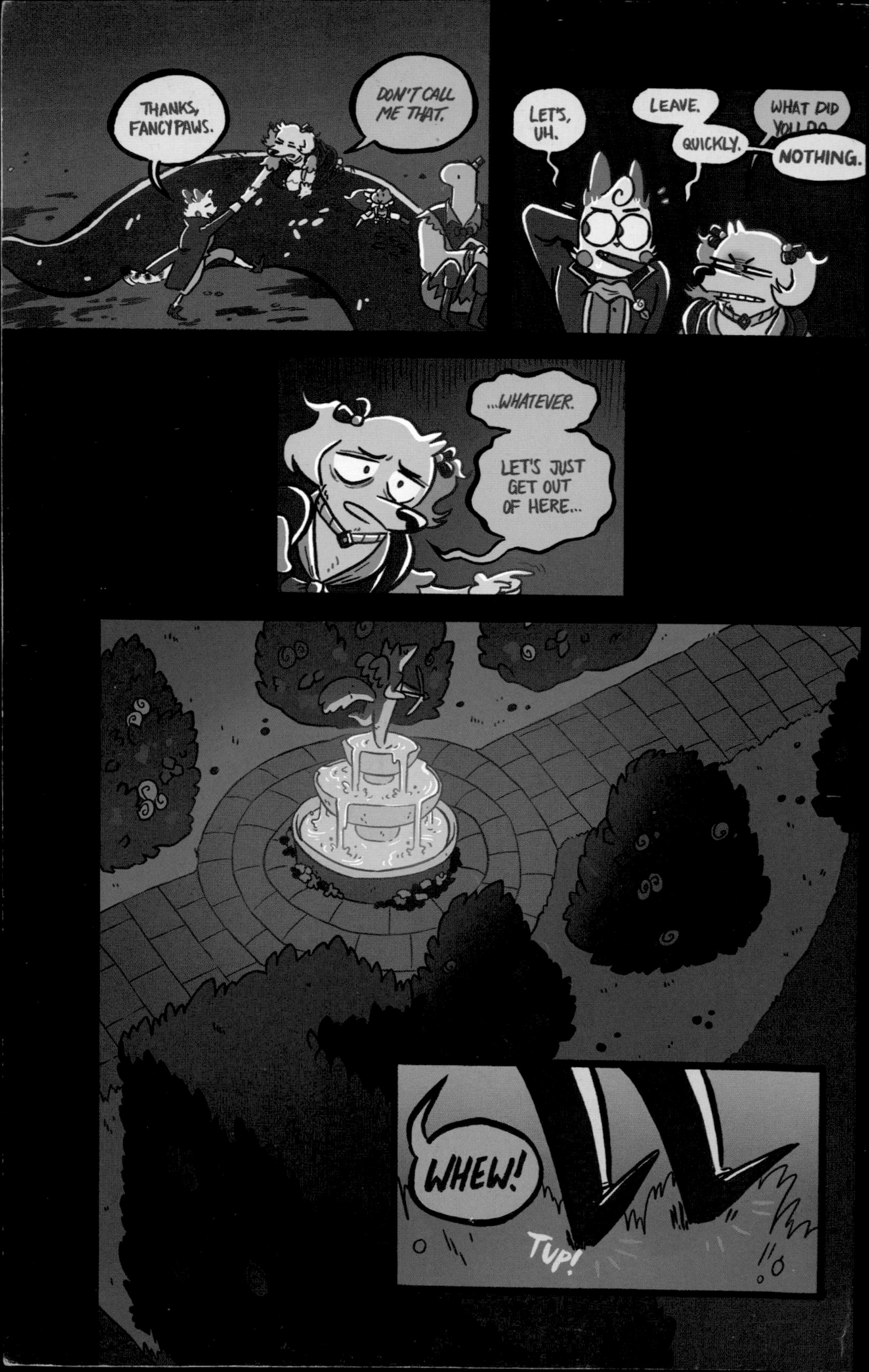

THANKS, FANCYPAWS.
DON'T CALL ME THAT.
LET'S, UH.
LEAVE.
QUICKLY.
WHAT DID YOU DO
NOTHING.
...WHATEVER.
LET'S JUST GET OUT OF HERE...
WHEW!
TUP!

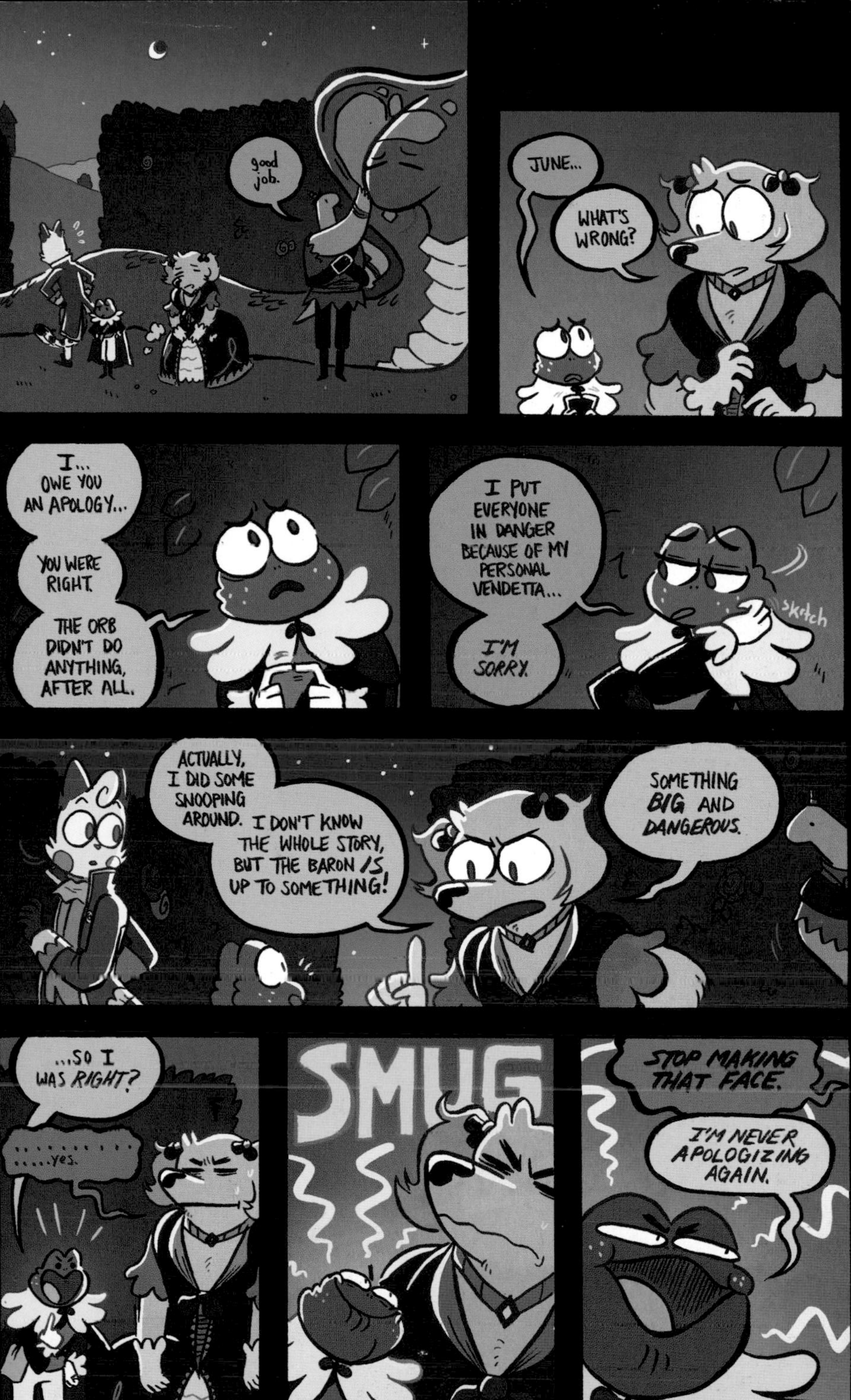

good job.
JUNE...
WHAT'S WRONG?
I... OWE YOU AN APOLOGY...
YOU WERE RIGHT.
THE ORB DIDN'T DO ANYTHING, AFTER ALL.
I PUT EVERYONE IN DANGER BECAUSE OF MY PERSONAL VENDETTA...
I'M SORRY.
sktch
ACTUALLY, I DID SOME SNOOPING AROUND. I DON'T KNOW THE WHOLE STORY, BUT THE BARON IS UP TO SOMETHING!
SOMETHING BIG AND DANGEROUS.
...SO I WAS RIGHT?
...............yes.
SMUG
STOP MAKING THAT FACE.
I'M NEVER APOLOGIZING AGAIN.

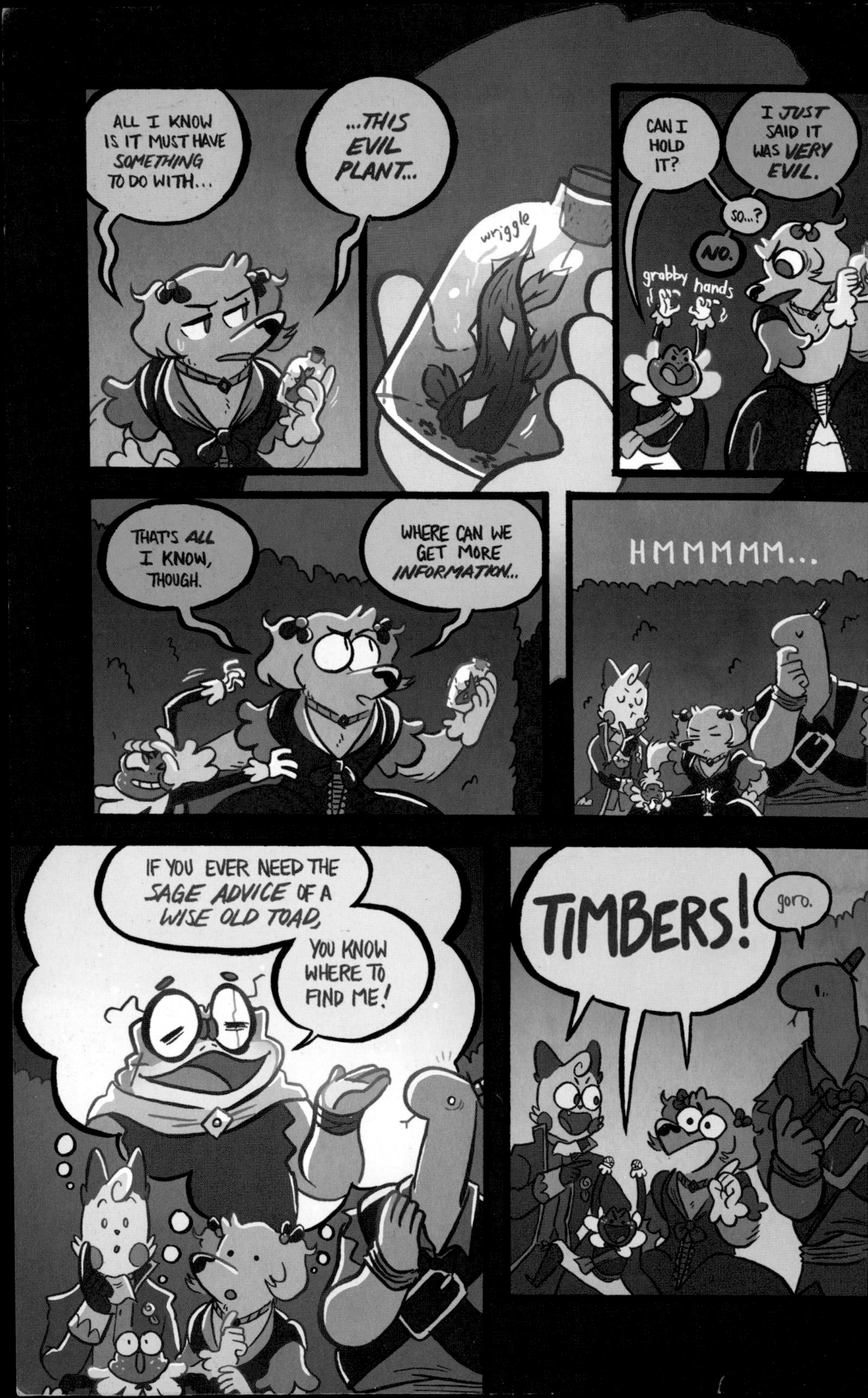
ALL I KNOW IS IT MUST HAVE SOMETHING TO DO WITH...
...THIS EVIL PLANT...
wriggle
CAN I HOLD IT?
I JUST SAID IT WAS VERY EVIL.
SO...?
NO.
grabby hands
THAT'S ALL I KNOW, THOUGH.
WHERE CAN WE GET MORE INFORMATION...
HMMMMM...
IF YOU EVER NEED THE SAGE ADVICE OF A WISE OLD TOAD,
YOU KNOW WHERE TO FIND ME!
TIMBERS!
goro.

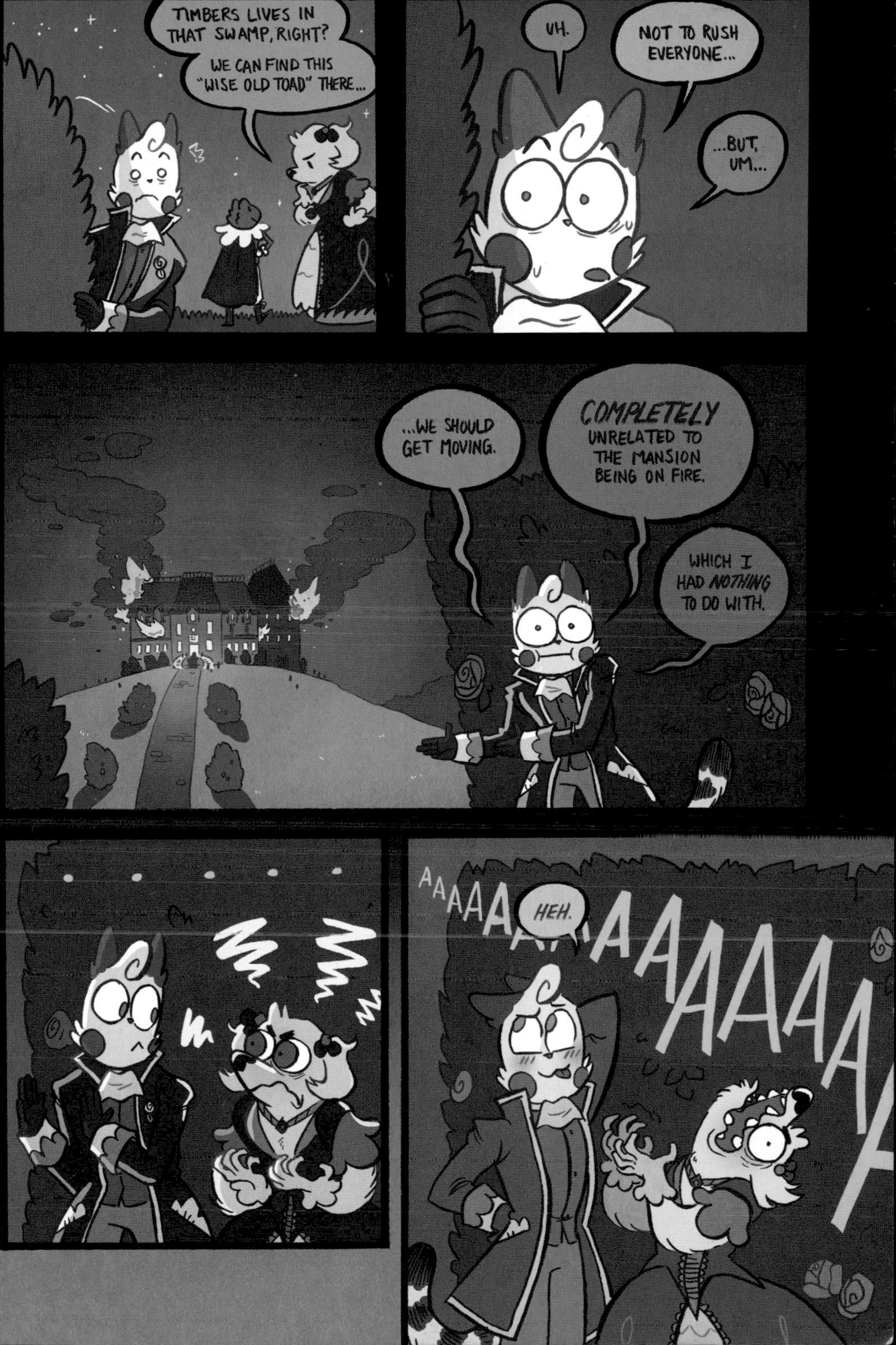
TIMBERS LIVES IN THAT SWAMP, RIGHT?
WE CAN FIND THIS "WISE OLD TOAD" THERE...
UH.
NOT TO RUSH EVERYONE...
...BUT, UM...
...WE SHOULD GET MOVING.
COMPLETELY UNRELATED TO THE MANSION BEING ON FIRE.
WHICH I HAD NOTHING TO DO WITH.
AAAAAAAAAAAAAAAAAAA
HEH.

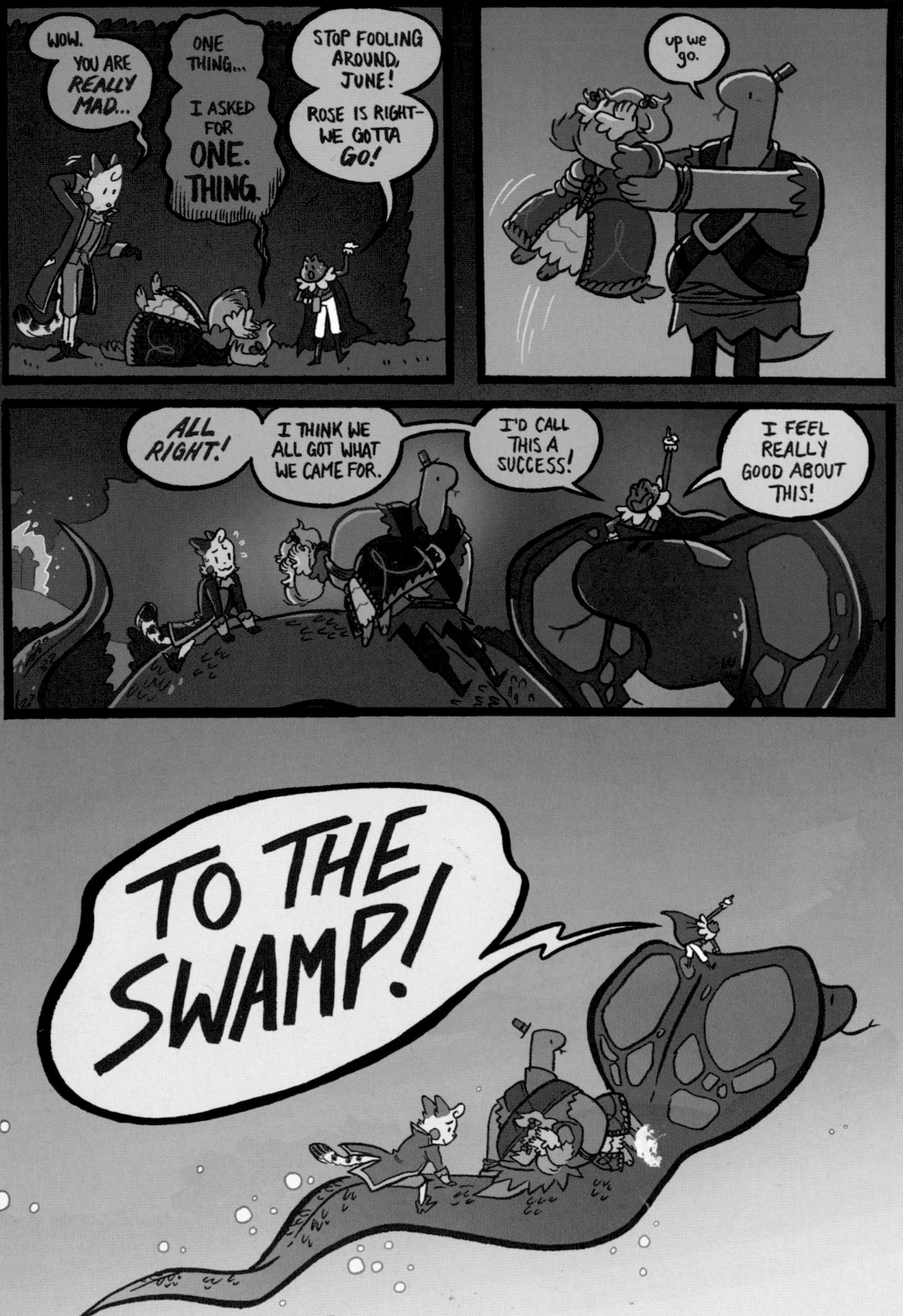
WOW. YOU ARE REALLY MAD...
ONE THING... I ASKED FOR ONE. THING.
STOP FOOLING AROUND, JUNE!
ROSE IS RIGHT- WE GOTTA GO!
up we go.
ALL RIGHT!
I THINK WE ALL GOT WHAT WE CAME FOR.
I'D CALL THIS A SUCCESS!
I FEEL REALLY GOOD ABOUT THIS!
TO THE SWAMP!

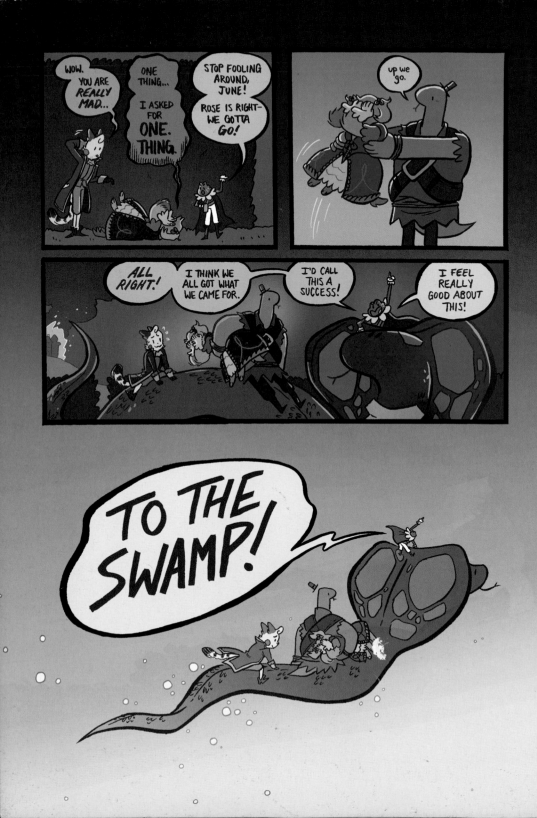

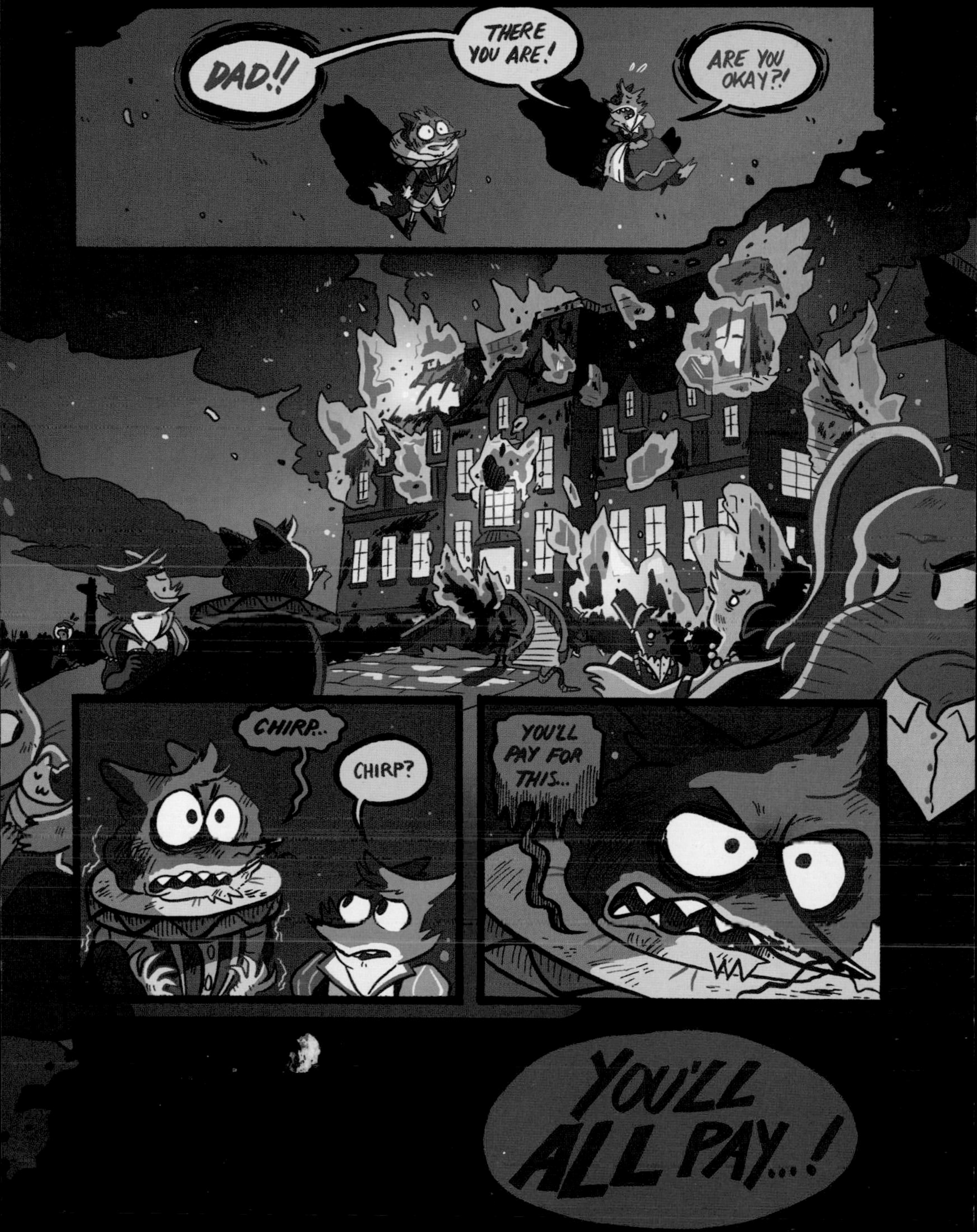
DAD!!
THERE YOU ARE!
ARE YOU OKAY?!
CHIRP...
CHIRP?
YOU'LL PAY FOR THIS...
YOU'LL ALL PAY...!

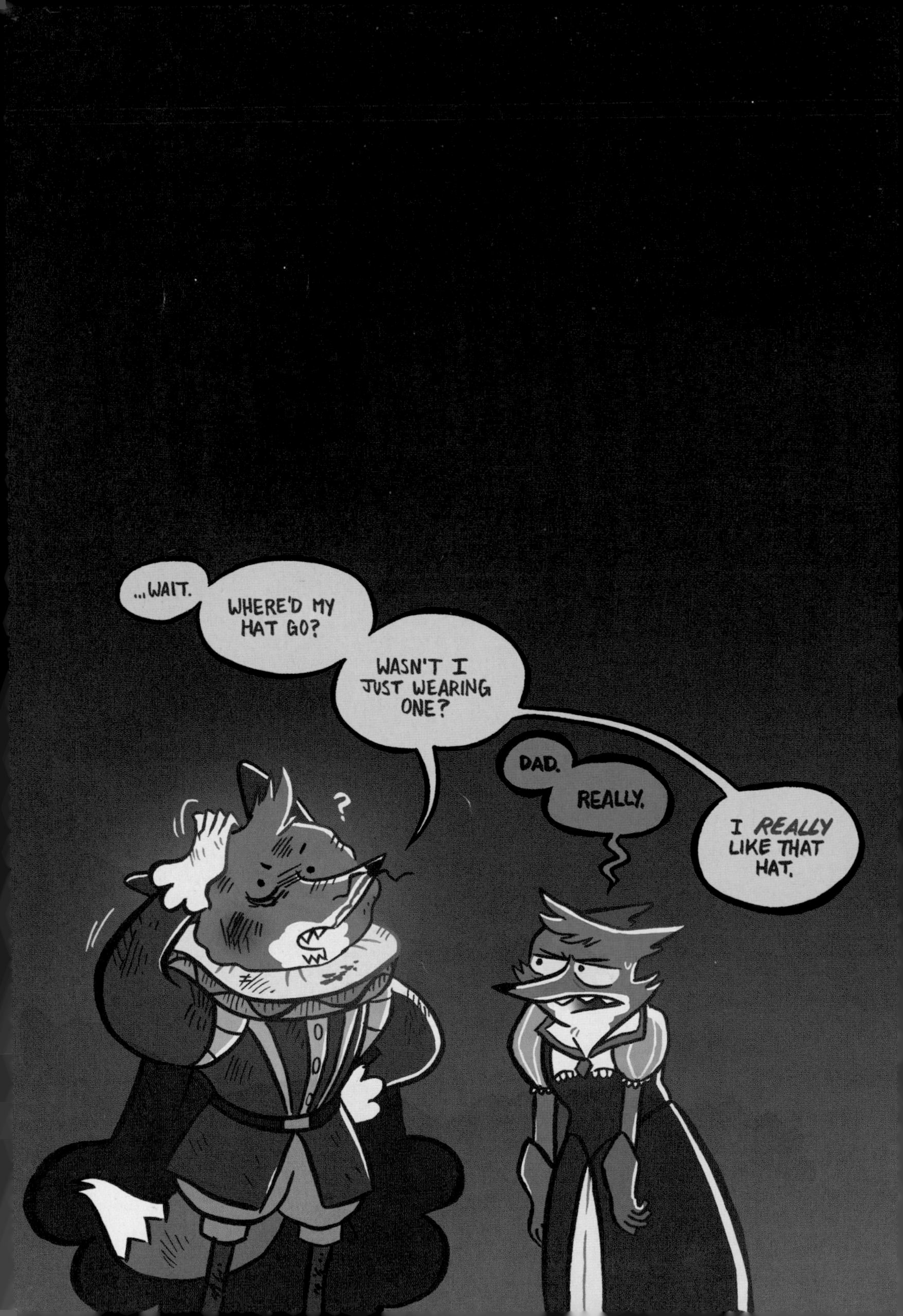
...WAIT.
WHERE'D MY HAT GO?
WASN'T I JUST WEARING ONE?
DAD.
REALLY.
I *REALLY* LIKE THAT HAT.

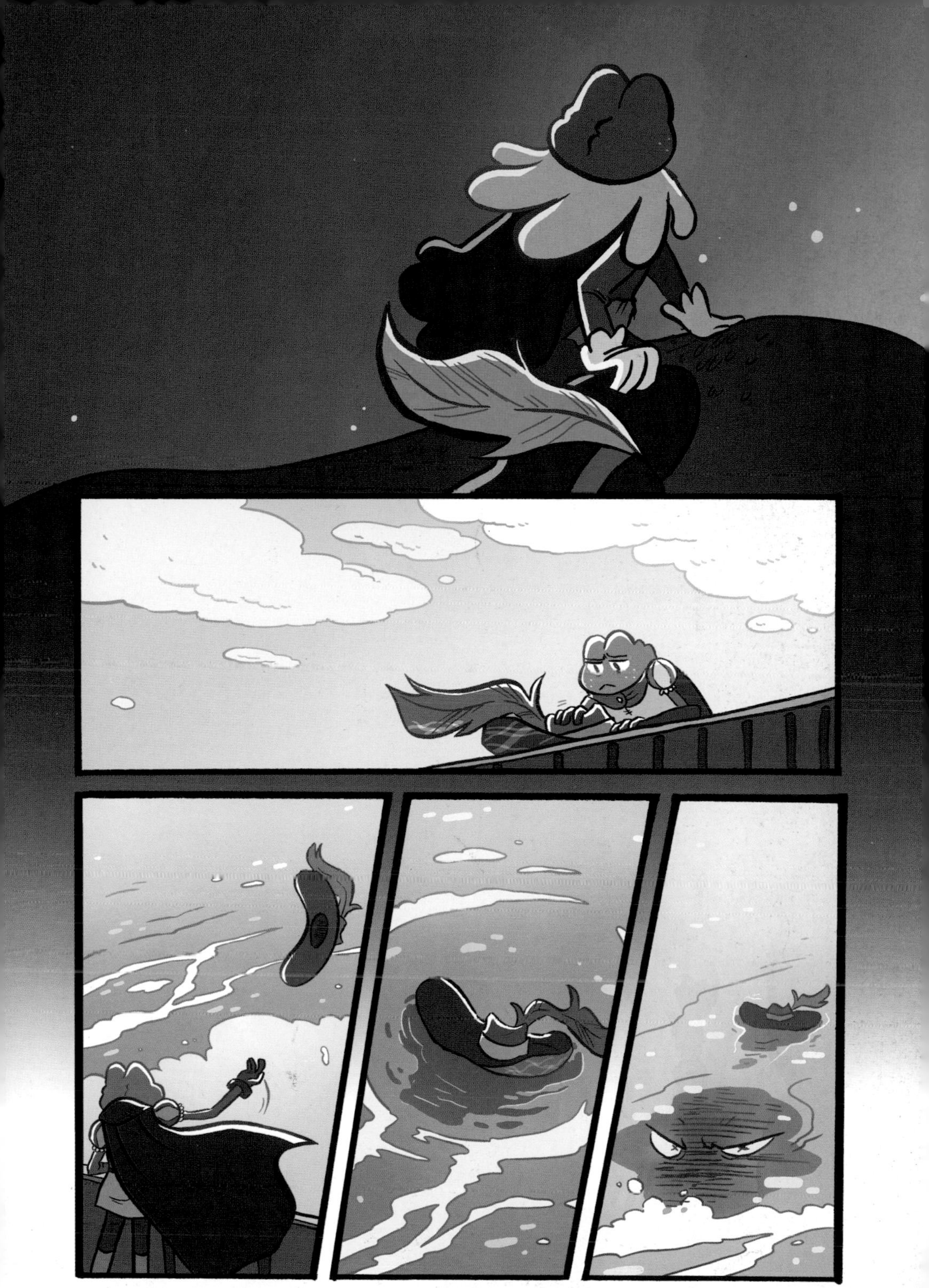

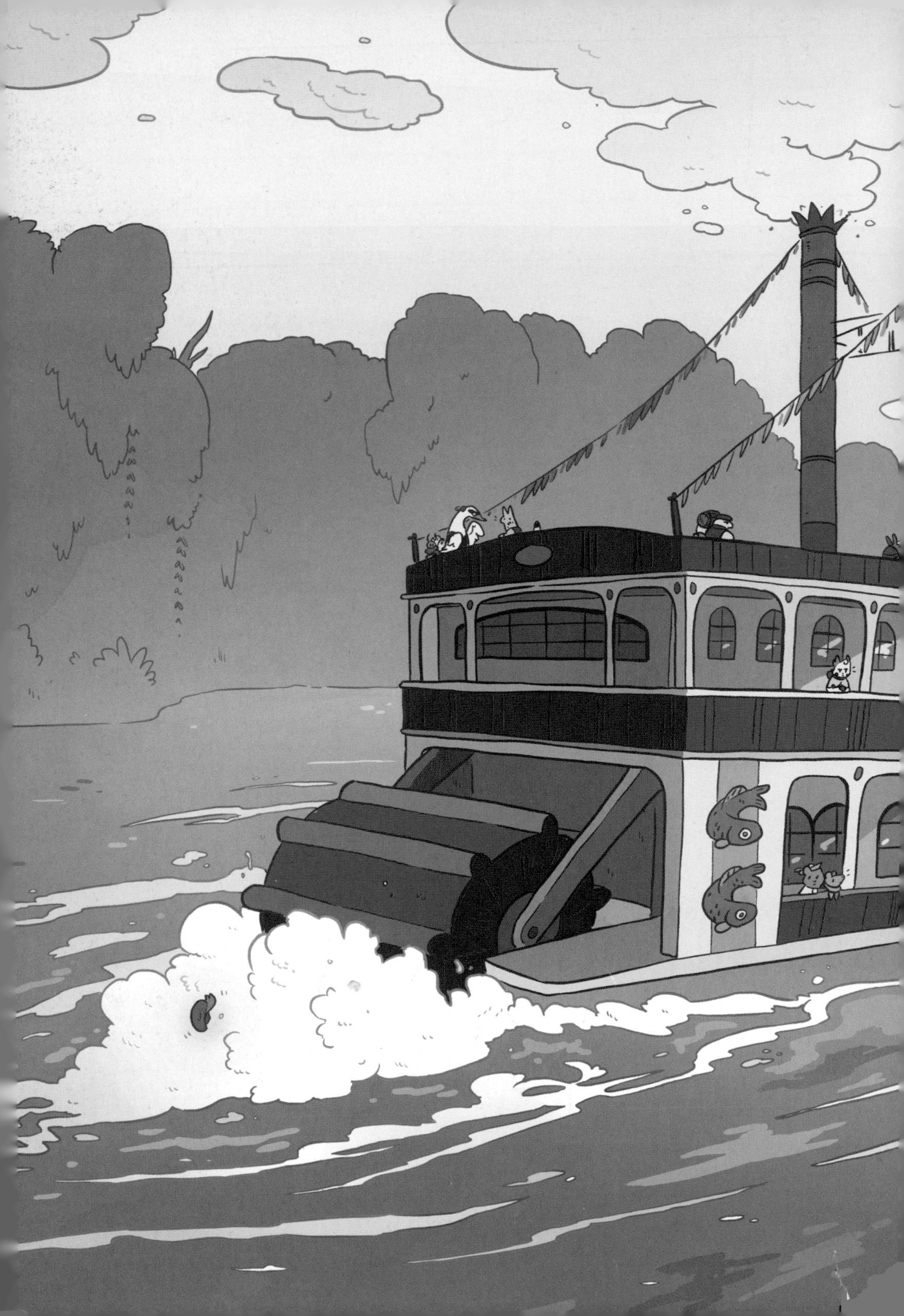

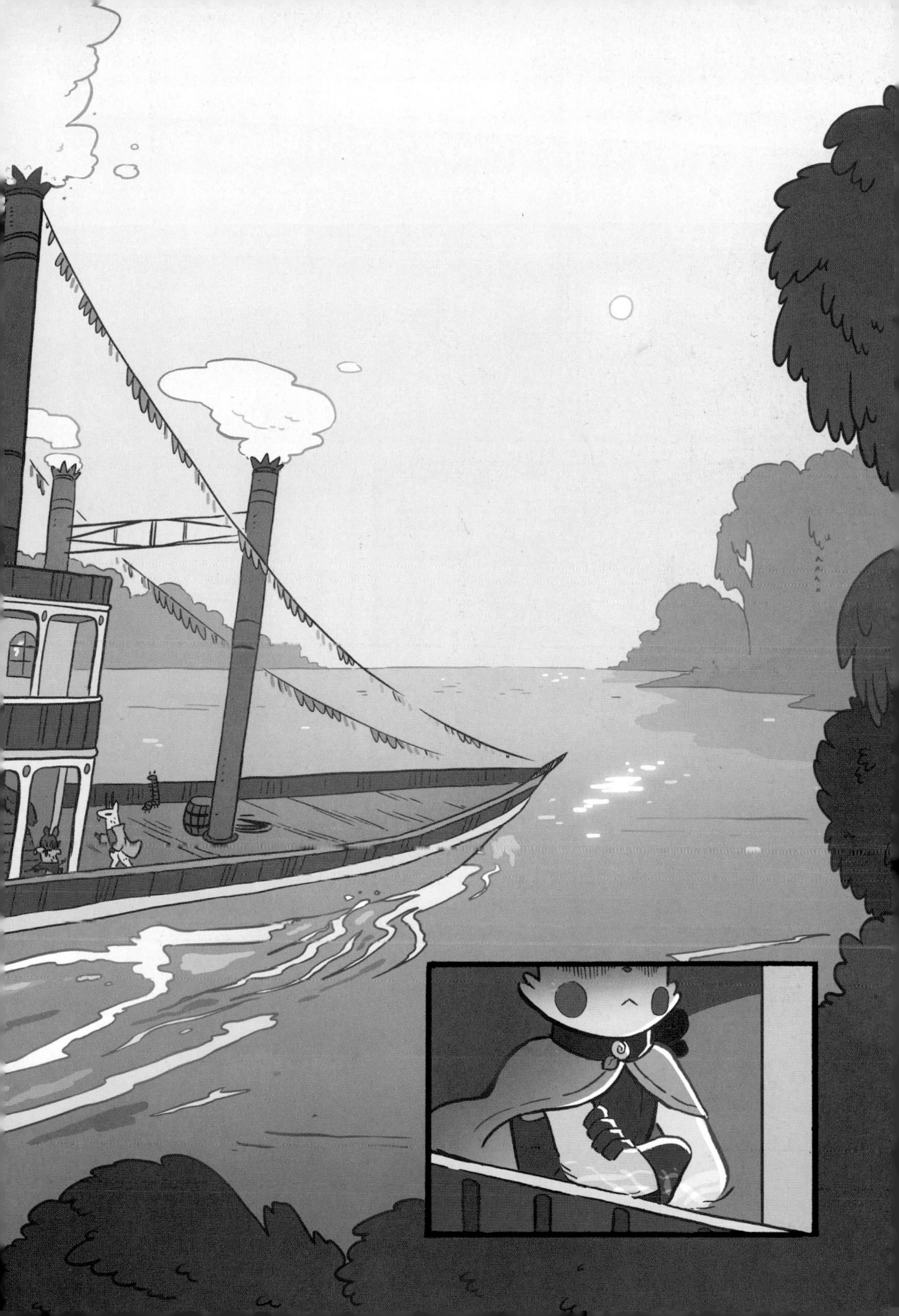

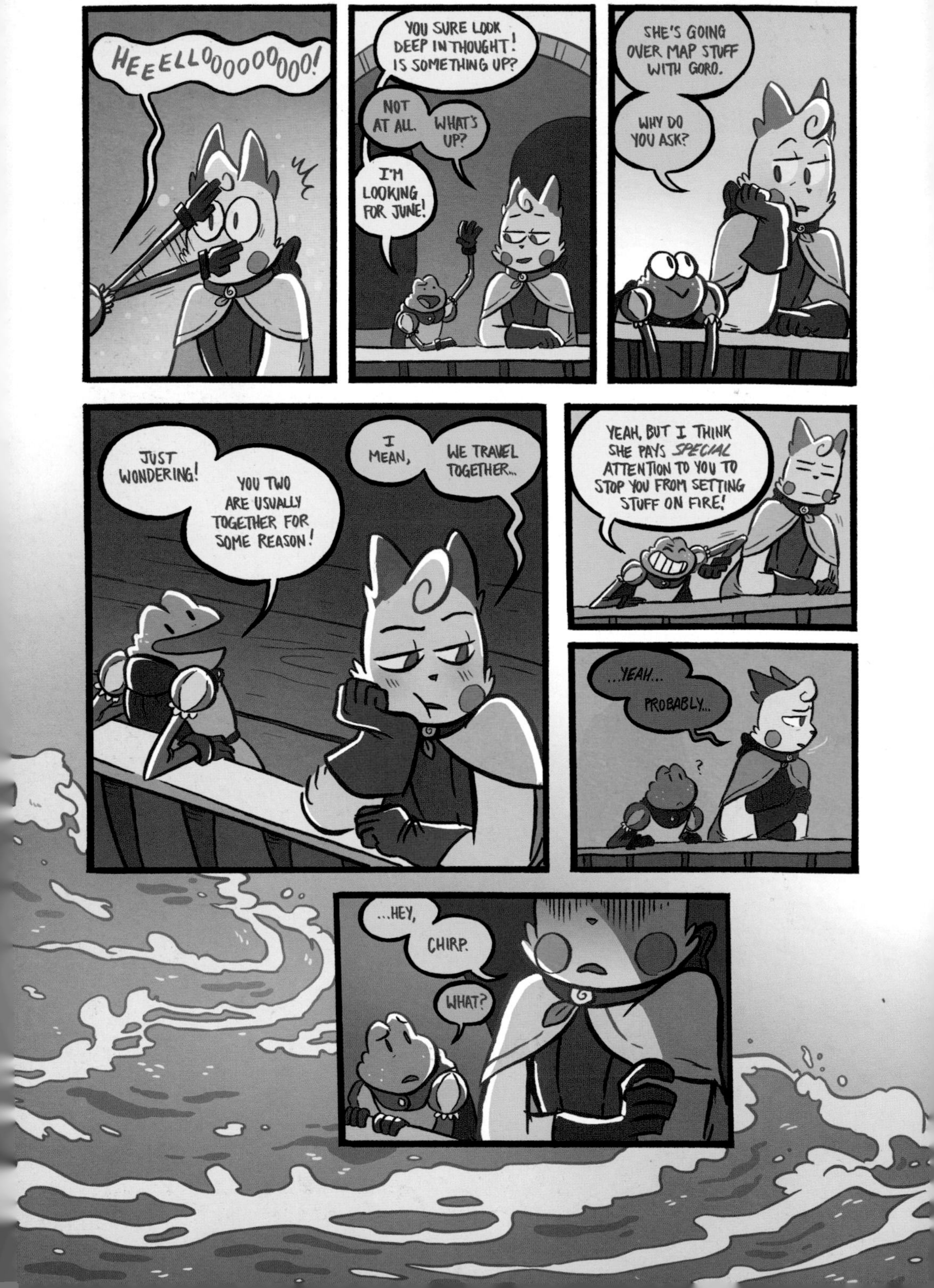
HEEELLOOOOOOOOO!
YOU SURE LOOK DEEP IN THOUGHT! IS SOMETHING UP?
NOT AT ALL.
WHAT'S UP?
I'M LOOKING FOR JUNE!
SHE'S GOING OVER MAP STUFF WITH GORO.
WHY DO YOU ASK?
JUST WONDERING!
YOU TWO ARE USUALLY TOGETHER FOR SOME REASON!
I MEAN,
WE TRAVEL TOGETHER...
YEAH, BUT I THINK SHE PAYS SPECIAL ATTENTION TO YOU TO STOP YOU FROM SETTING STUFF ON FIRE!
...YEAH...
PROBABLY...
?
...HEY,
CHIRP.
WHAT?

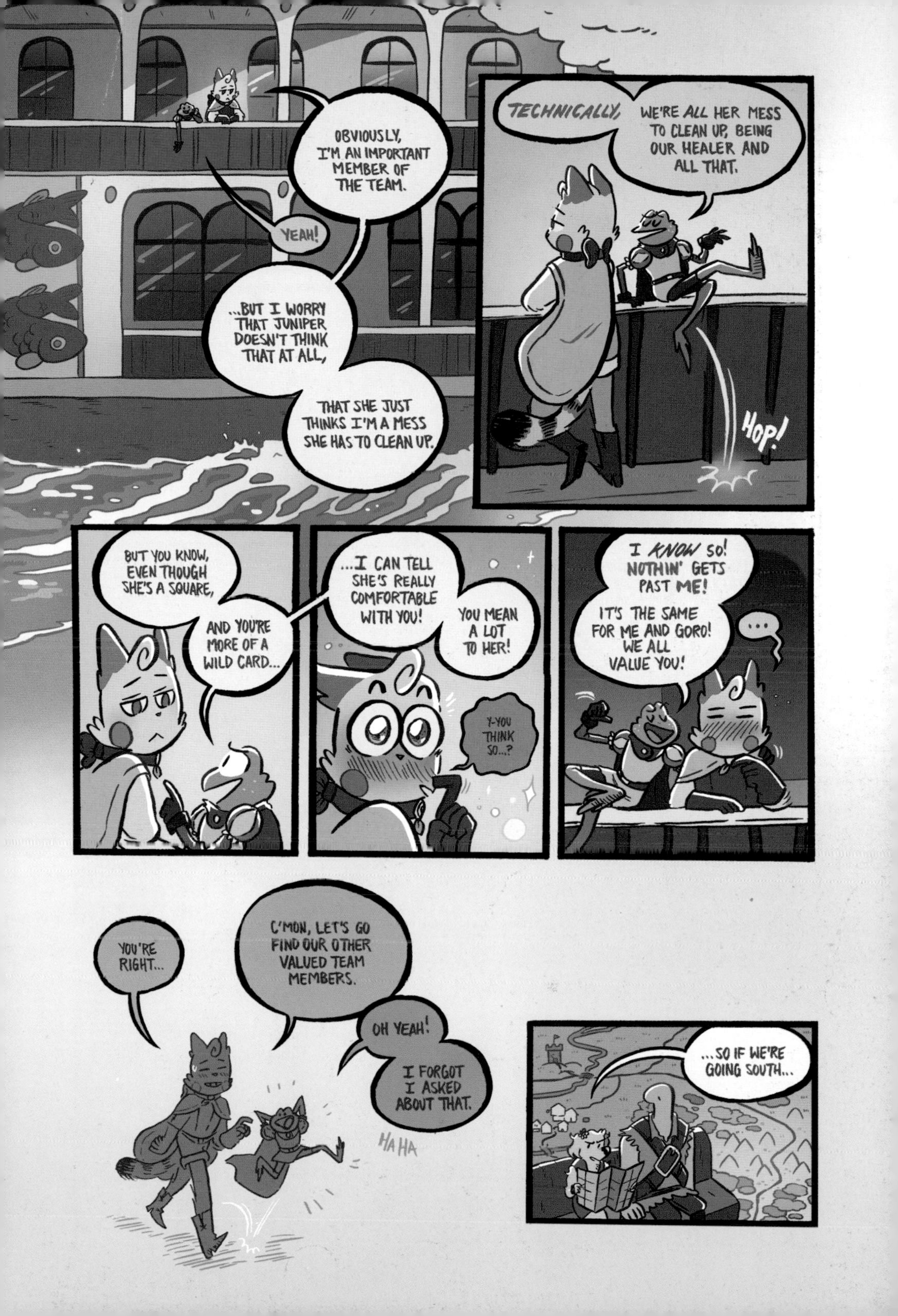

OBVIOUSLY, I'M AN IMPORTANT MEMBER OF THE TEAM.
YEAH!
...BUT I WORRY THAT JUNIPER DOESN'T THINK THAT AT ALL,
THAT SHE JUST THINKS I'M A MESS SHE HAS TO CLEAN UP.
TECHNICALLY,
WE'RE ALL HER MESS TO CLEAN UP, BEING OUR HEALER AND ALL THAT.
HOP!
BUT YOU KNOW, EVEN THOUGH SHE'S A SQUARE,
AND YOU'RE MORE OF A WILD CARD...
...I CAN TELL SHE'S REALLY COMFORTABLE WITH YOU!
YOU MEAN A LOT TO HER!
Y-YOU THINK SO...?
I KNOW SO! NOTHIN' GETS PAST ME!
IT'S THE SAME FOR ME AND GORO! WE ALL VALUE YOU!
...
YOU'RE RIGHT...
C'MON, LET'S GO FIND OUR OTHER VALUED TEAM MEMBERS.
OH YEAH!
I FORGOT I ASKED ABOUT THAT.
HA HA
...SO IF WE'RE GOING SOUTH...

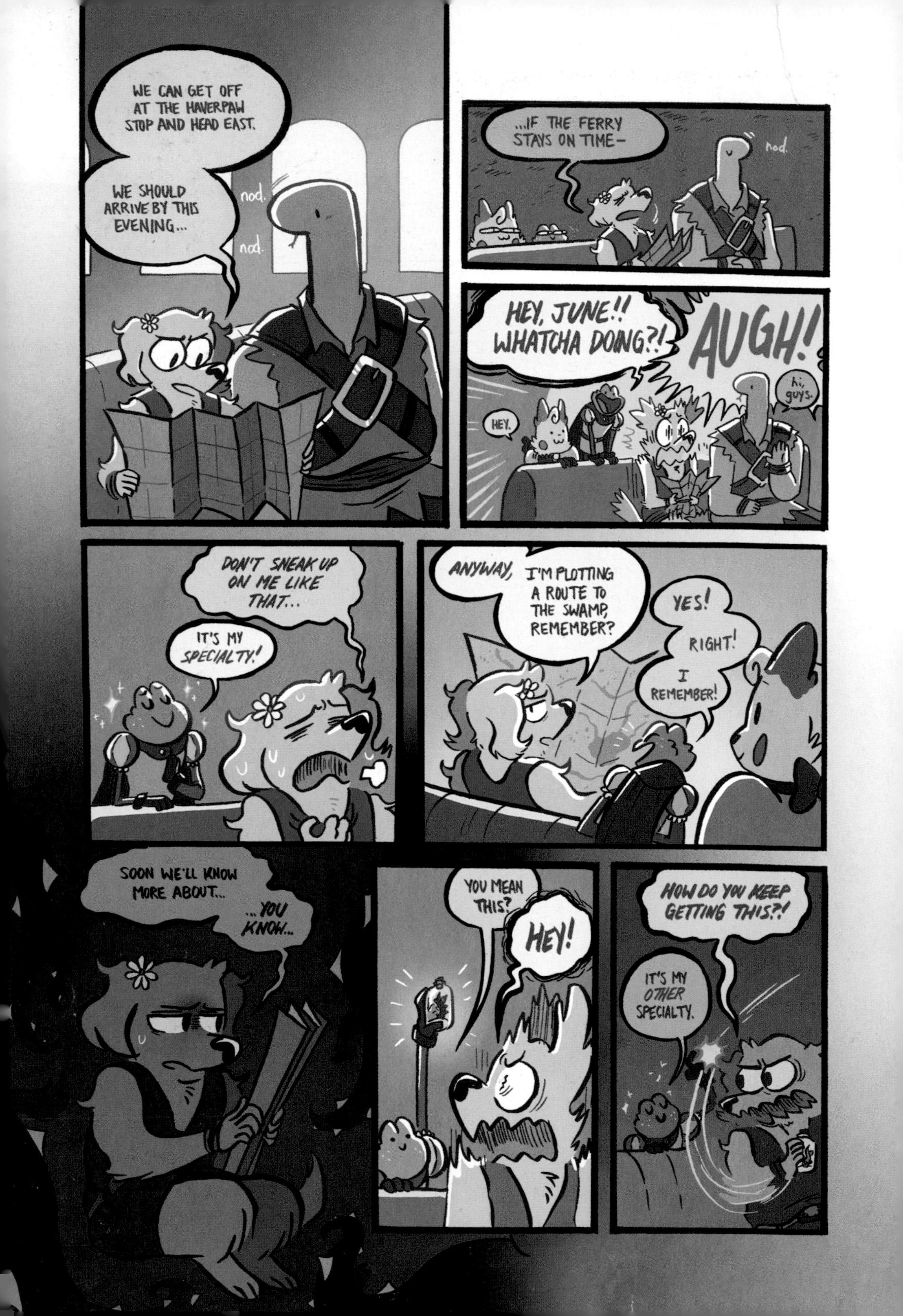
WE CAN GET OFF AT THE HAVERPAW STOP AND HEAD EAST.
WE SHOULD ARRIVE BY THIS EVENING...
nod.
nod.
...IF THE FERRY STAYS ON TIME—
nod.
HEY, JUNE!! WHATCHA DOING?!
AUGH!
hi, guys.
HEY.
DON'T SNEAK UP ON ME LIKE THAT...
IT'S MY SPECIALTY!
ANYWAY,
I'M PLOTTING A ROUTE TO THE SWAMP, REMEMBER?
YES!
RIGHT!
I REMEMBER!
SOON WE'LL KNOW MORE ABOUT...
...YOU KNOW...
YOU MEAN THIS?
HEY!
HOW DO YOU KEEP GETTING THIS?!
IT'S MY OTHER SPECIALTY.

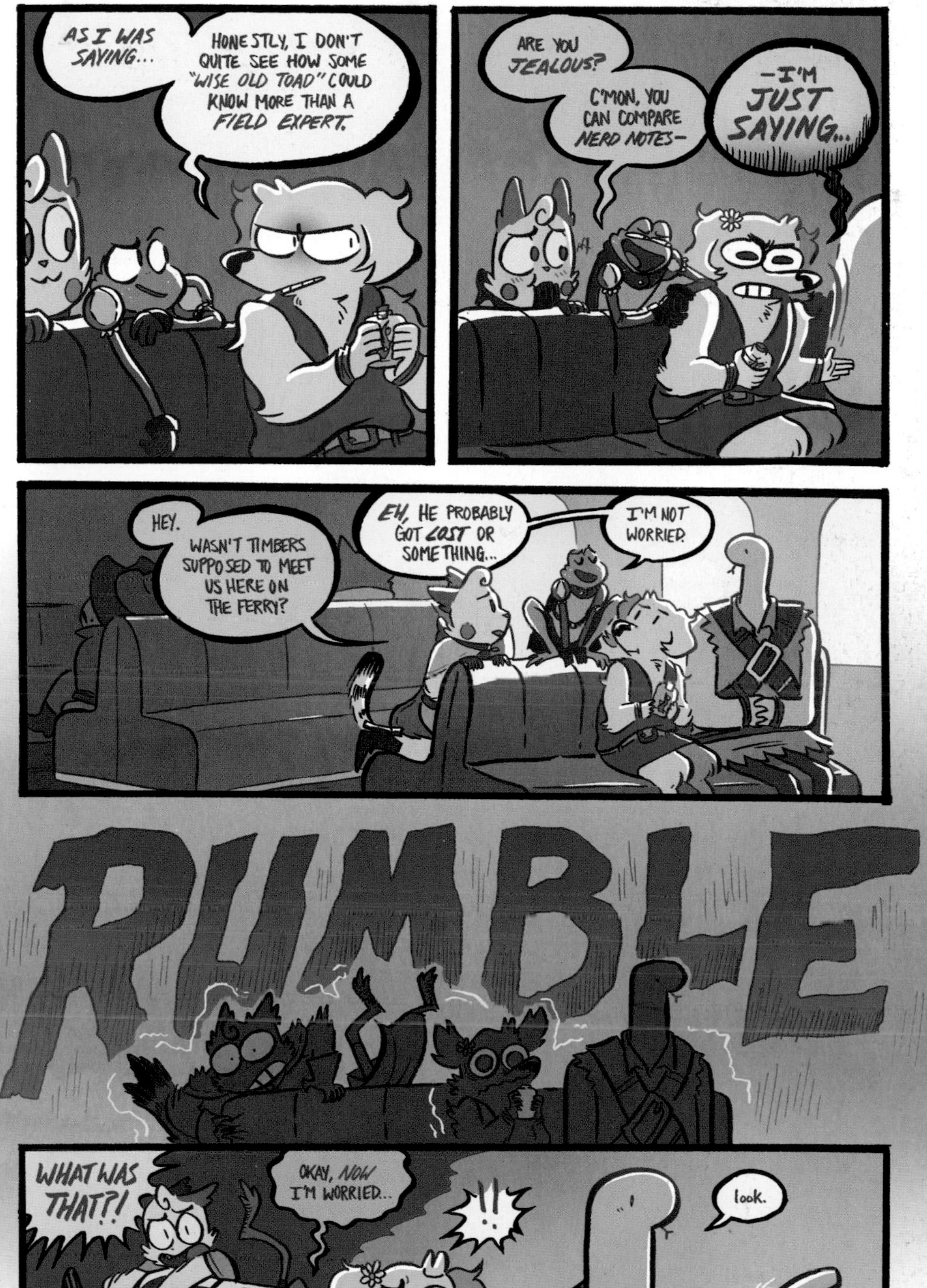
AS I WAS SAYING...
HONESTLY, I DON'T QUITE SEE HOW SOME "WISE OLD TOAD" COULD KNOW MORE THAN A FIELD EXPERT.
ARE YOU JEALOUS?
C'MON, YOU CAN COMPARE NERD NOTES—
—I'M JUST SAYING...
HEY.
WASN'T TIMBERS SUPPOSED TO MEET US HERE ON THE FERRY?
EH, HE PROBABLY GOT LOST OR SOMETHING...
I'M NOT WORRIED.
RUMBLE
WHAT WAS THAT?!
OKAY, NOW I'M WORRIED...
!!
look.

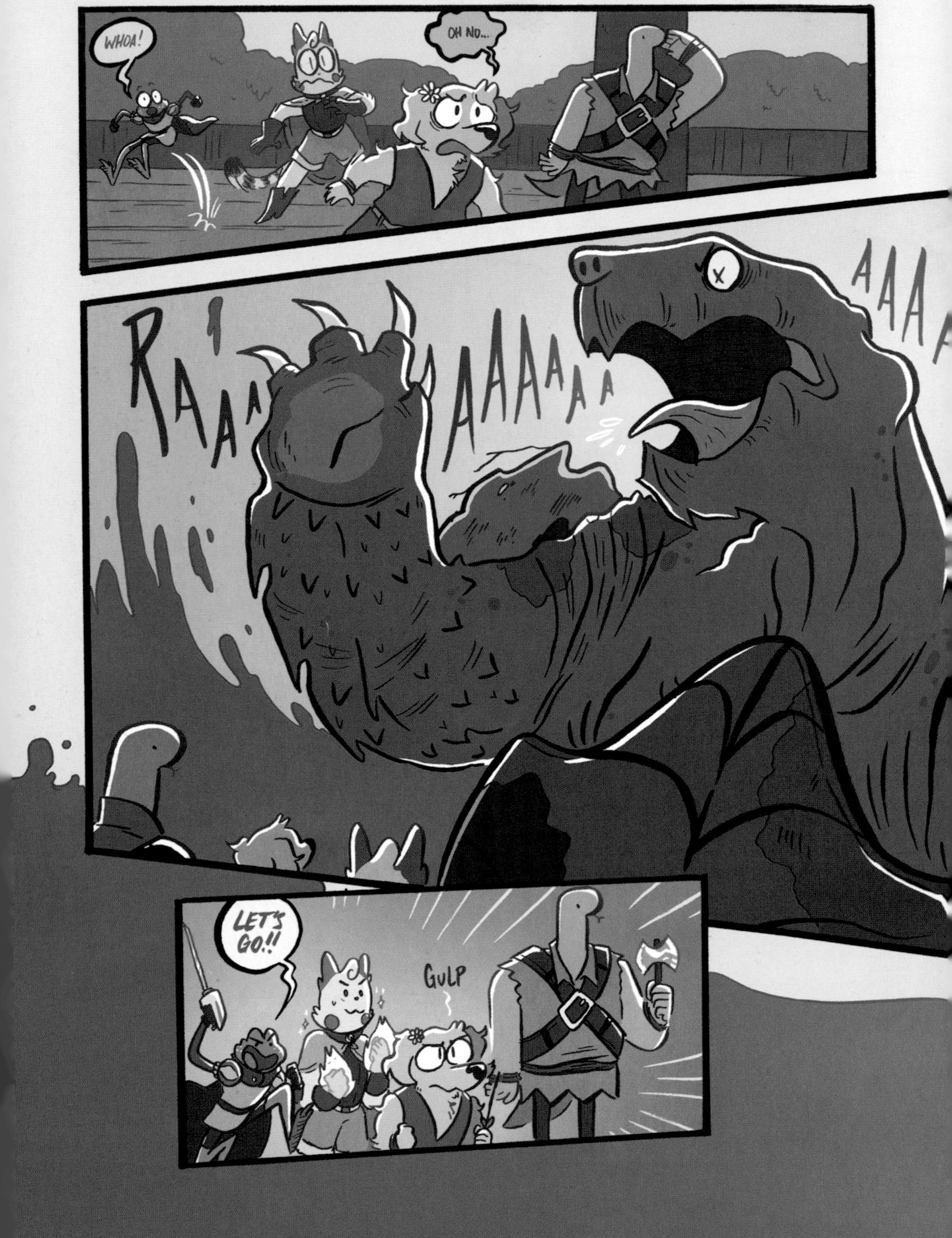
WHOA!
OH NO...
RAAAA AAAAAAAA AAAA
LET'S GO!!
GULP

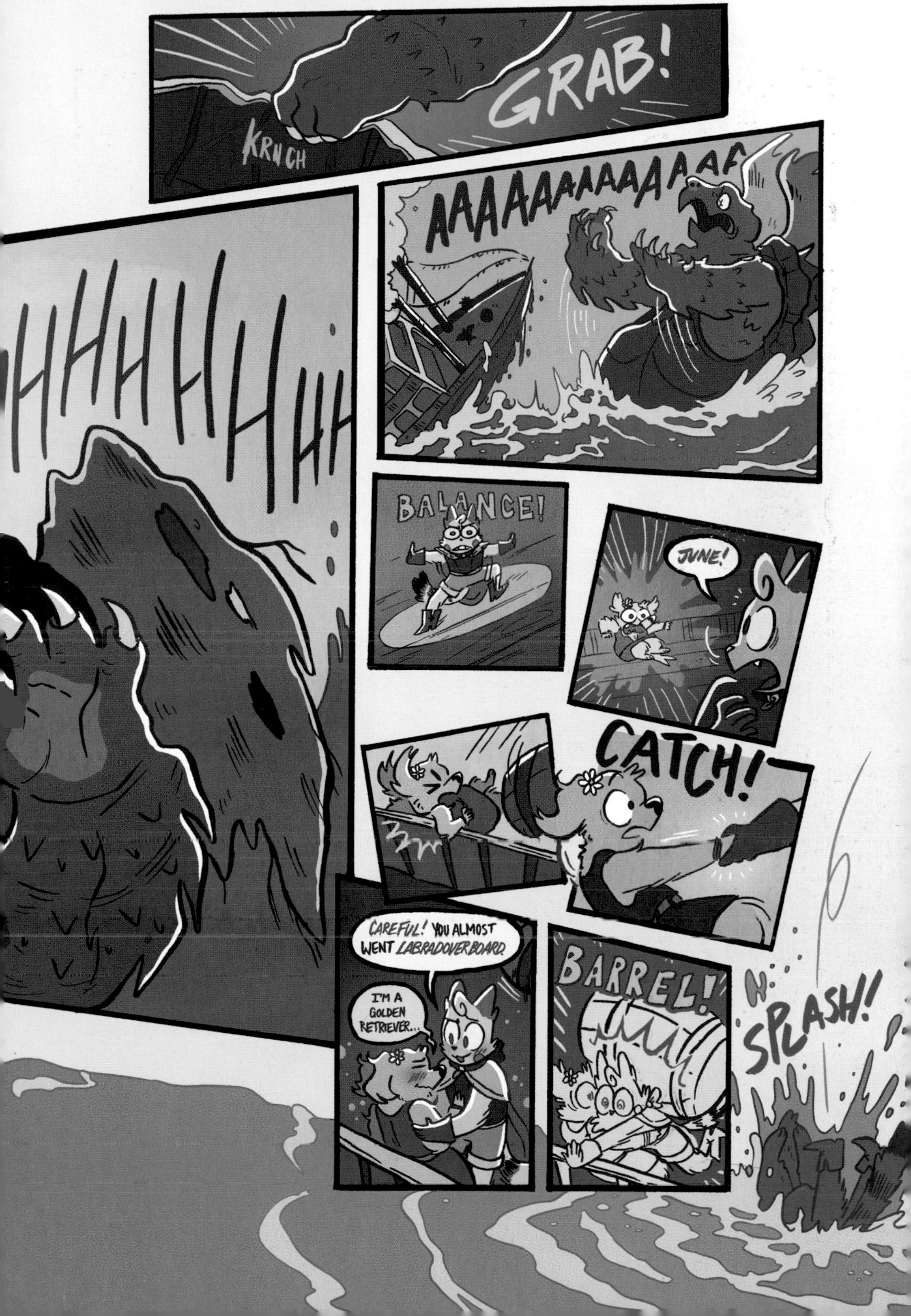
GRAB!
KRNCH
AAAAAAAAAAAAF
HHHHHHHHHHHH
BALANCE!
JUNE!
CATCH!
CAREFUL! YOU ALMOST WENT LABRADOVERBOARD.
I'M A GOLDEN RETRIEVER...
BARREL!
SPLASH!

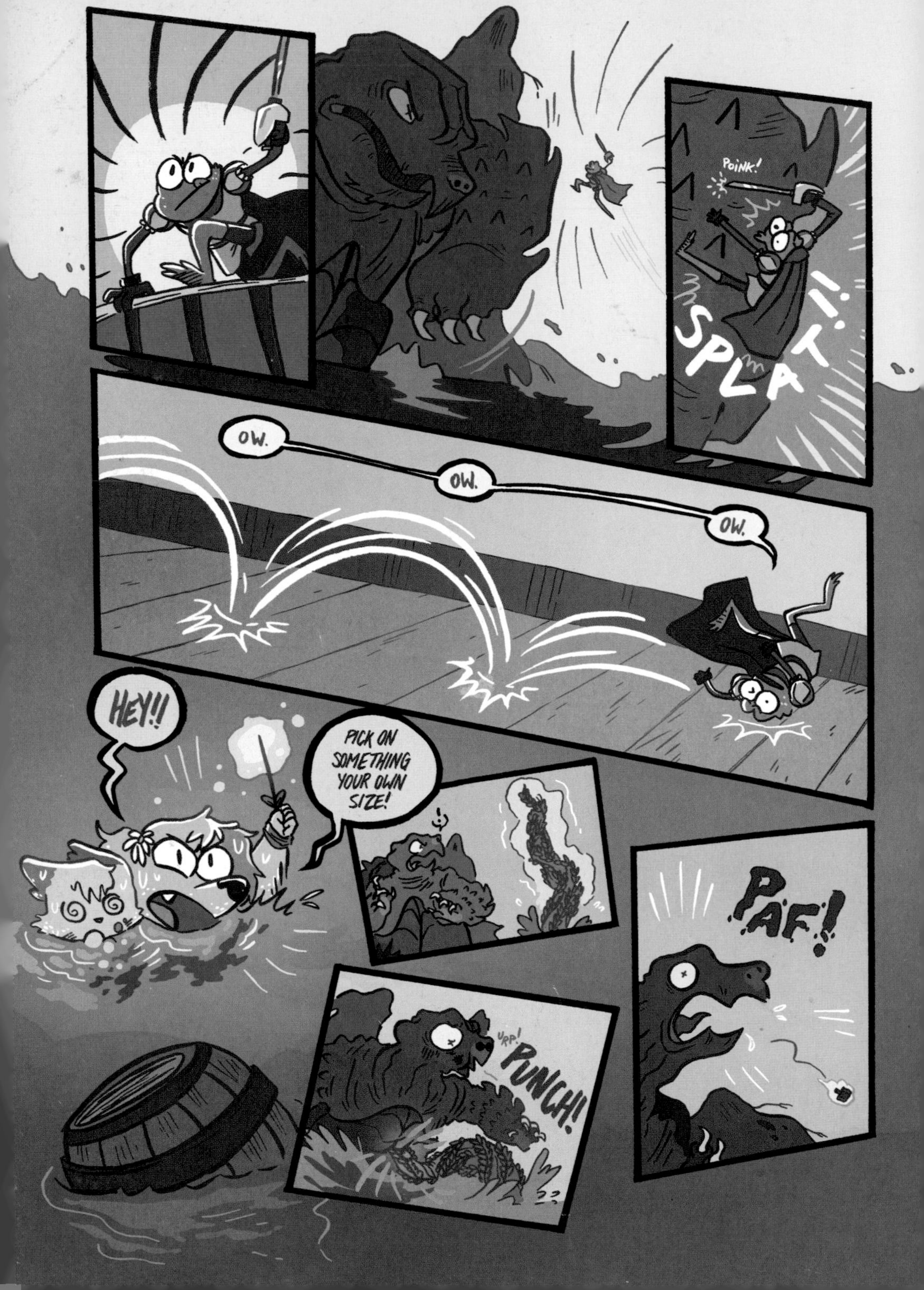
POINK!
SPLAT!!
OW.
OW.
OW.
HEY!!
PICK ON SOMETHING YOUR OWN SIZE!
PAF!
URP!
PUNCH!

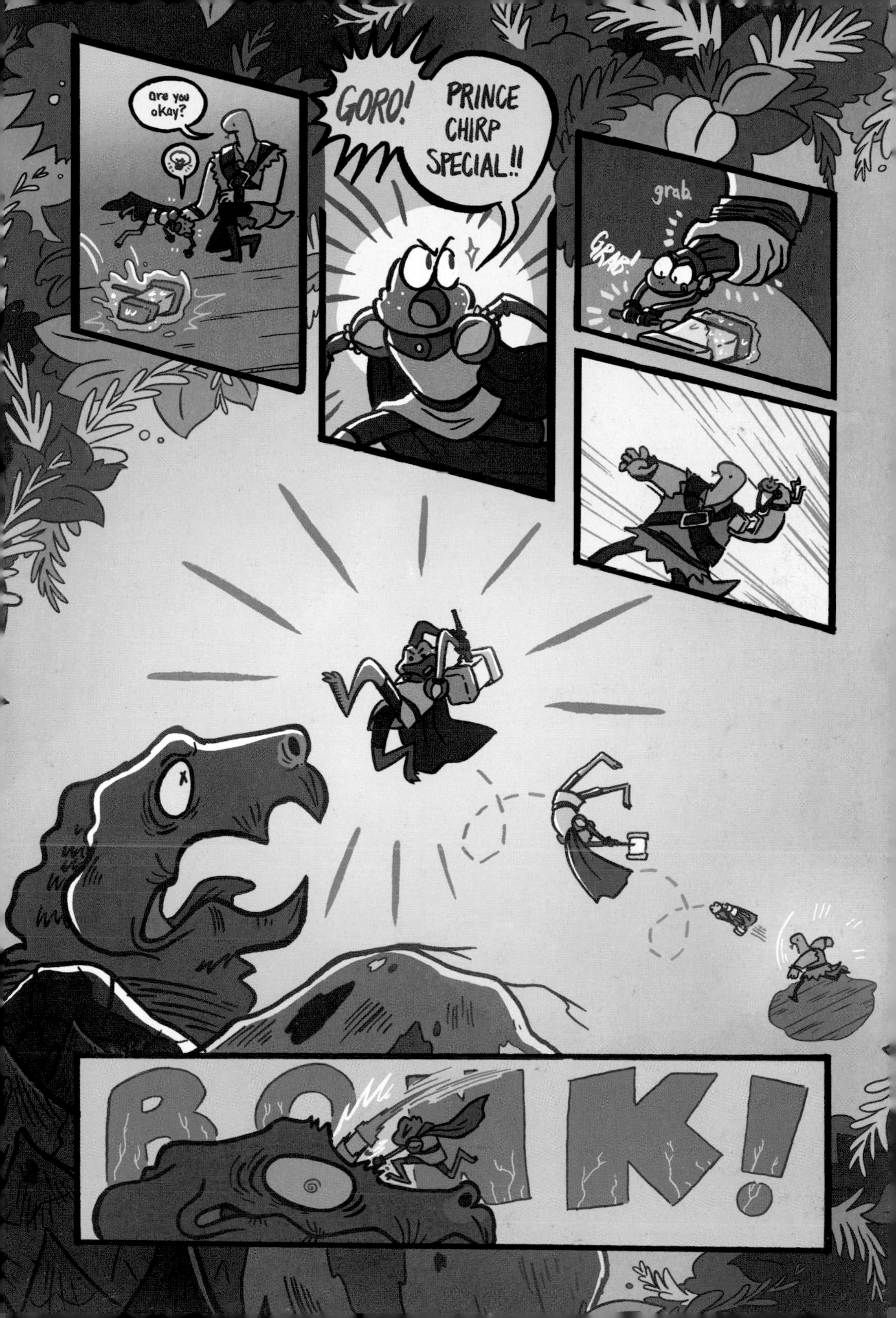
are you okay?
GORO!
PRINCE CHIRP SPECIAL!!
grab
GRAB!
BONK!

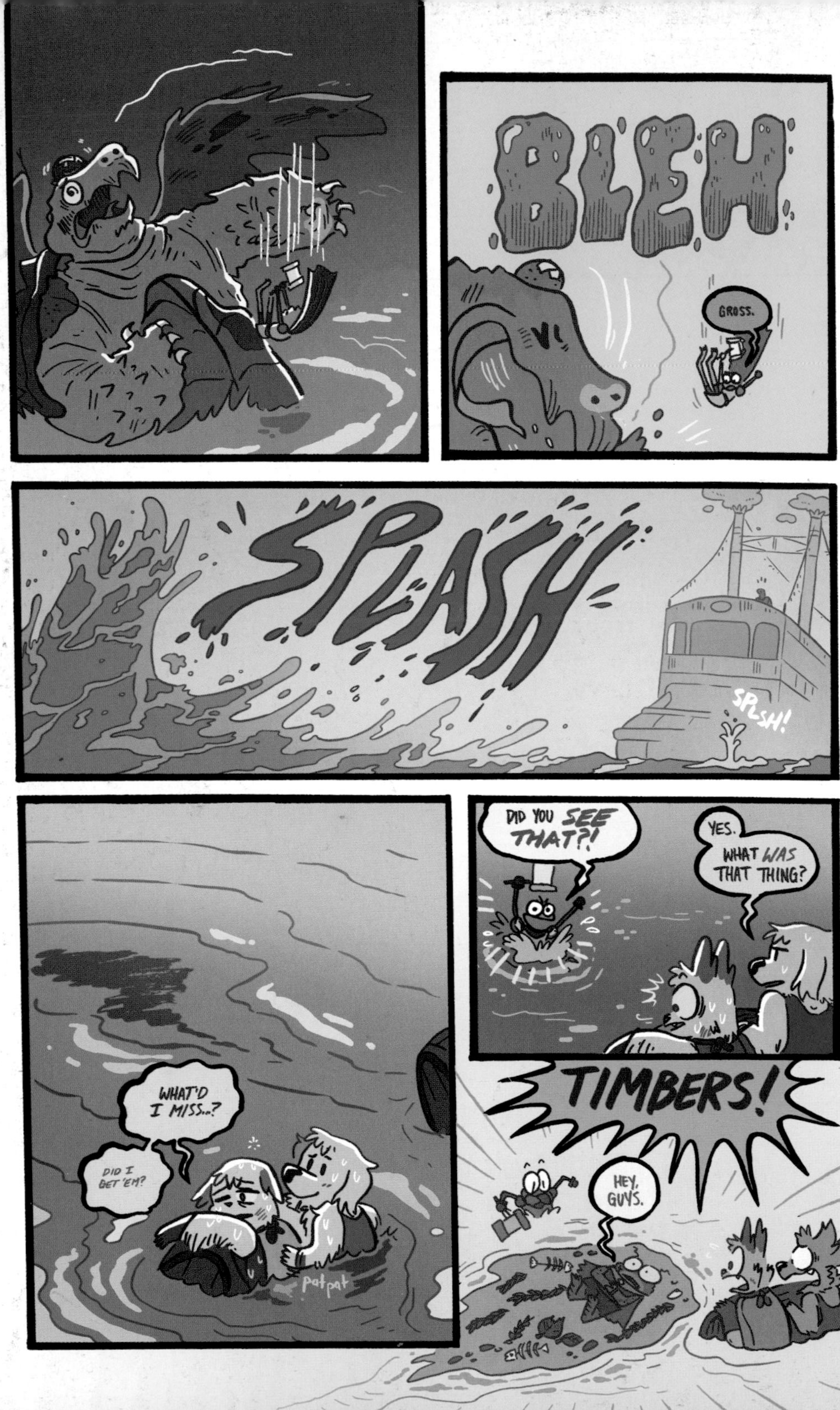
BLEH
GROSS.
SPLASH
SPLSH!
WHAT'D I MISS...?
DID I GET 'EM?
patpat
DID YOU SEE THAT?!
YES. WHAT WAS THAT THING?
TIMBERS!
HEY, GUYS.

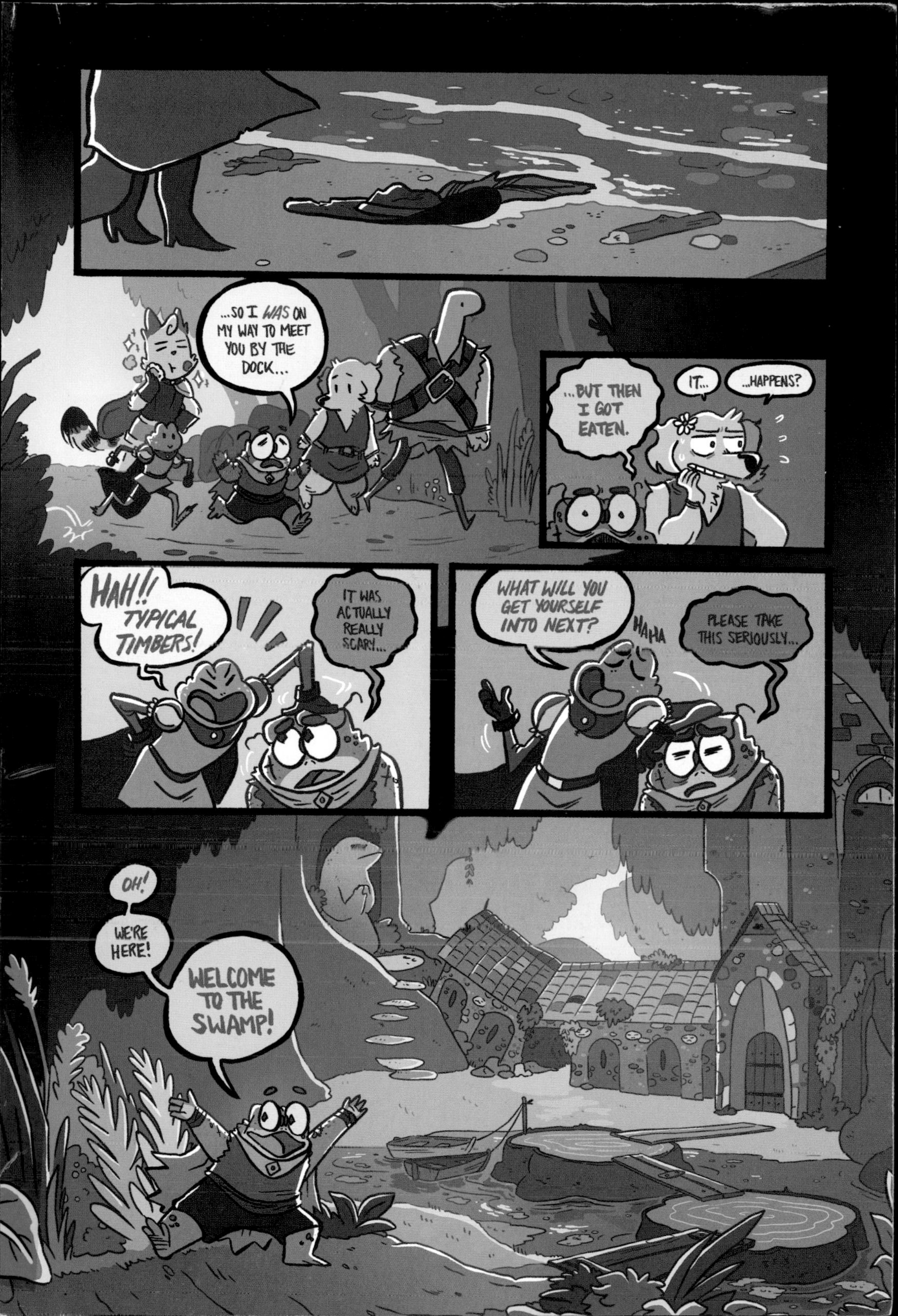
...SO I WAS ON MY WAY TO MEET YOU BY THE DOCK...
...BUT THEN I GOT EATEN.
IT...
...HAPPENS?
HAH!! TYPICAL TIMBERS!
IT WAS ACTUALLY REALLY SCARY...
WHAT WILL YOU GET YOURSELF INTO NEXT?
HAHA
PLEASE TAKE THIS SERIOUSLY...
OH!
WE'RE HERE!
WELCOME TO THE SWAMP!

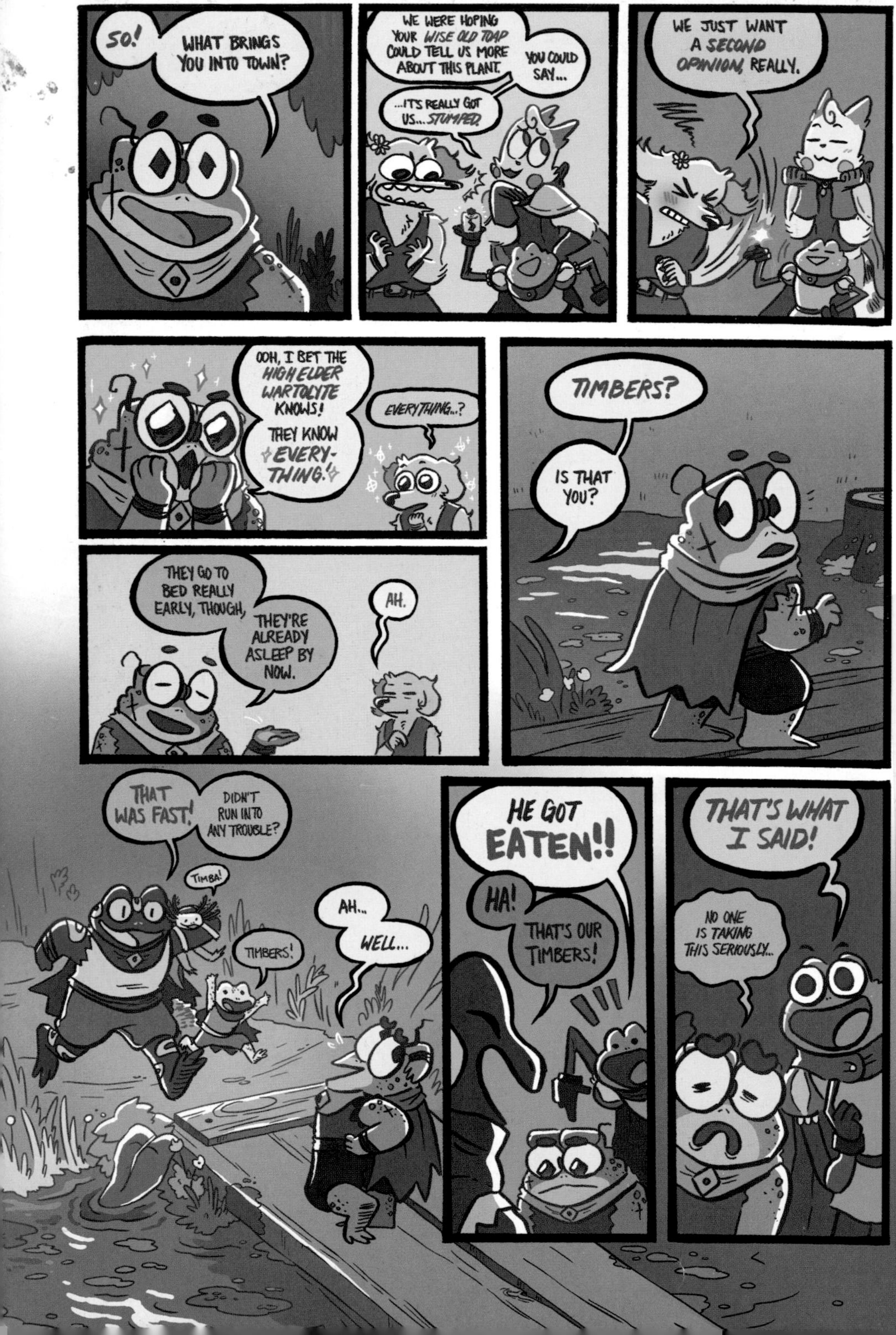

SO!
WHAT BRINGS YOU INTO TOWN?
WE WERE HOPING YOUR WISE OLD TOAD COULD TELL US MORE ABOUT THIS PLANT.
YOU COULD SAY...
...IT'S REALLY GOT US... STUMPED.
WE JUST WANT A SECOND OPINION, REALLY.
OOH, I BET THE HIGH ELDER WARTOLYTE KNOWS!
THEY KNOW EVERYTHING!
EVERYTHING..?
THEY GO TO BED REALLY EARLY, THOUGH.
THEY'RE ALREADY ASLEEP BY NOW.
AH.
TIMBERS?
IS THAT YOU?
THAT WAS FAST!
DIDN'T RUN INTO ANY TROUBLE?
TIMBA!
TIMBERS!
AH...
WELL...
HE GOT EATEN!!
HA!
THAT'S OUR TIMBERS!
THAT'S WHAT I SAID!
NO ONE IS TAKING THIS SERIOUSLY...

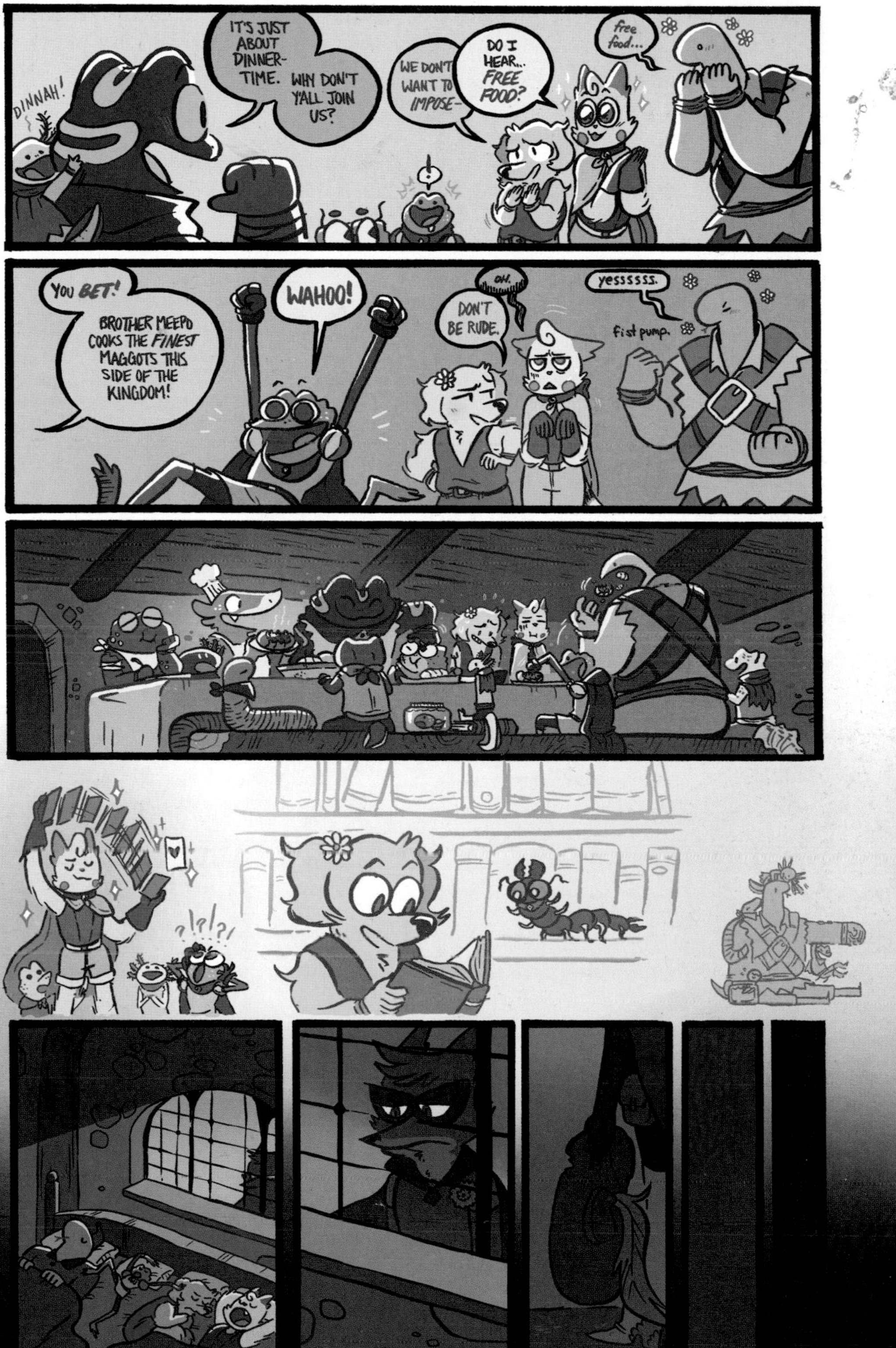
DINNAH!
IT'S JUST ABOUT DINNER-TIME. WHY DON'T Y'ALL JOIN US?
WE DON'T WANT TO IMPOSE-
DO I HEAR... FREE FOOD?
free food...
YOU BET!
BROTHER MEEPO COOKS THE FINEST MAGGOTS THIS SIDE OF THE KINGDOM!
WAHOO!
DON'T BE RUDE.
OH.
yessssss.
fist pump.

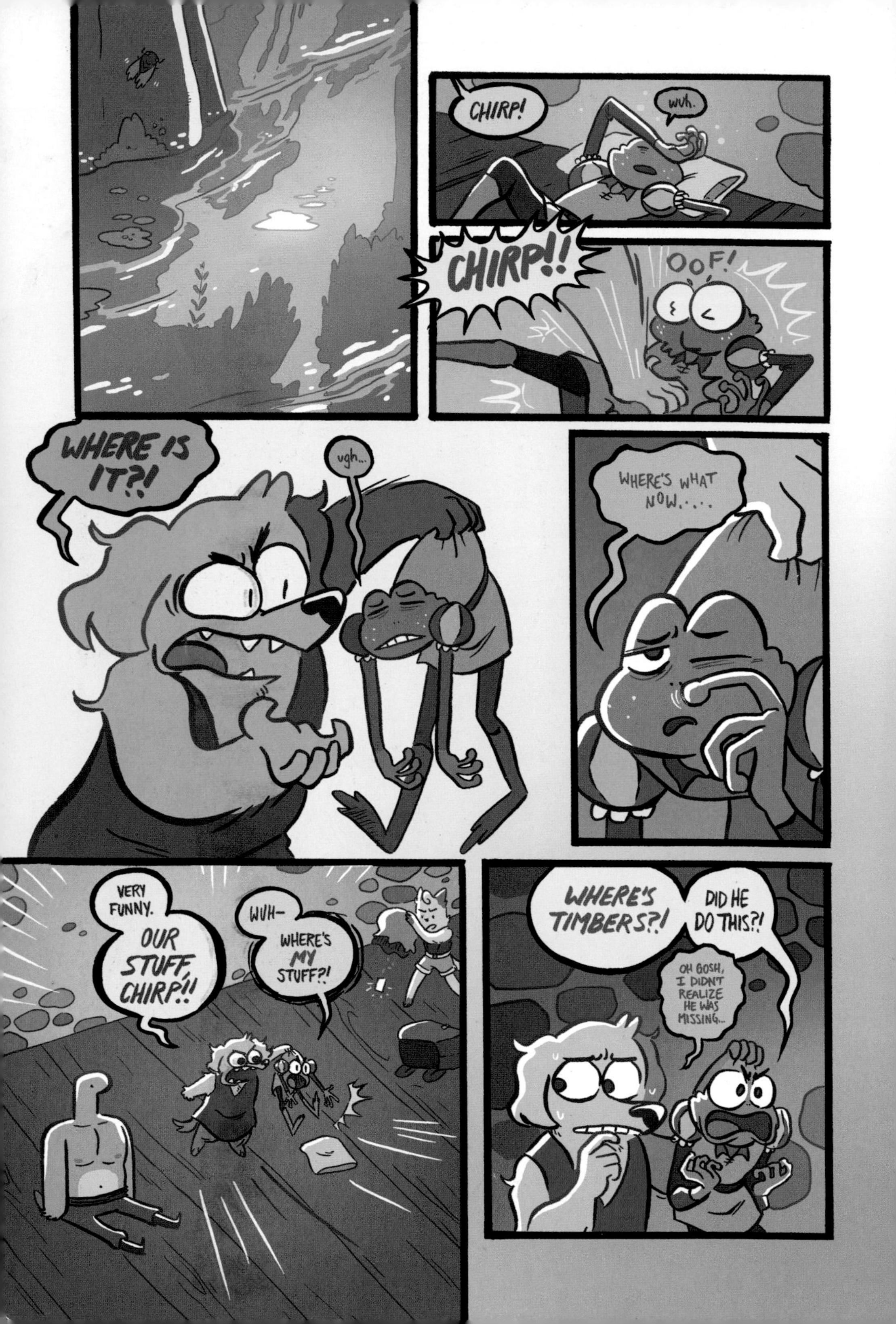
CHIRP!
wuh.
CHIRP!!
OOF!
WHERE IS IT?!
ugh...
WHERE'S WHAT NOW.....
VERY FUNNY.
OUR STUFF, CHIRP!!
WUH-
WHERE'S MY STUFF?!
WHERE'S TIMBERS?!
DID HE DO THIS?!
OH GOSH, I DIDN'T REALIZE HE WAS MISSING...

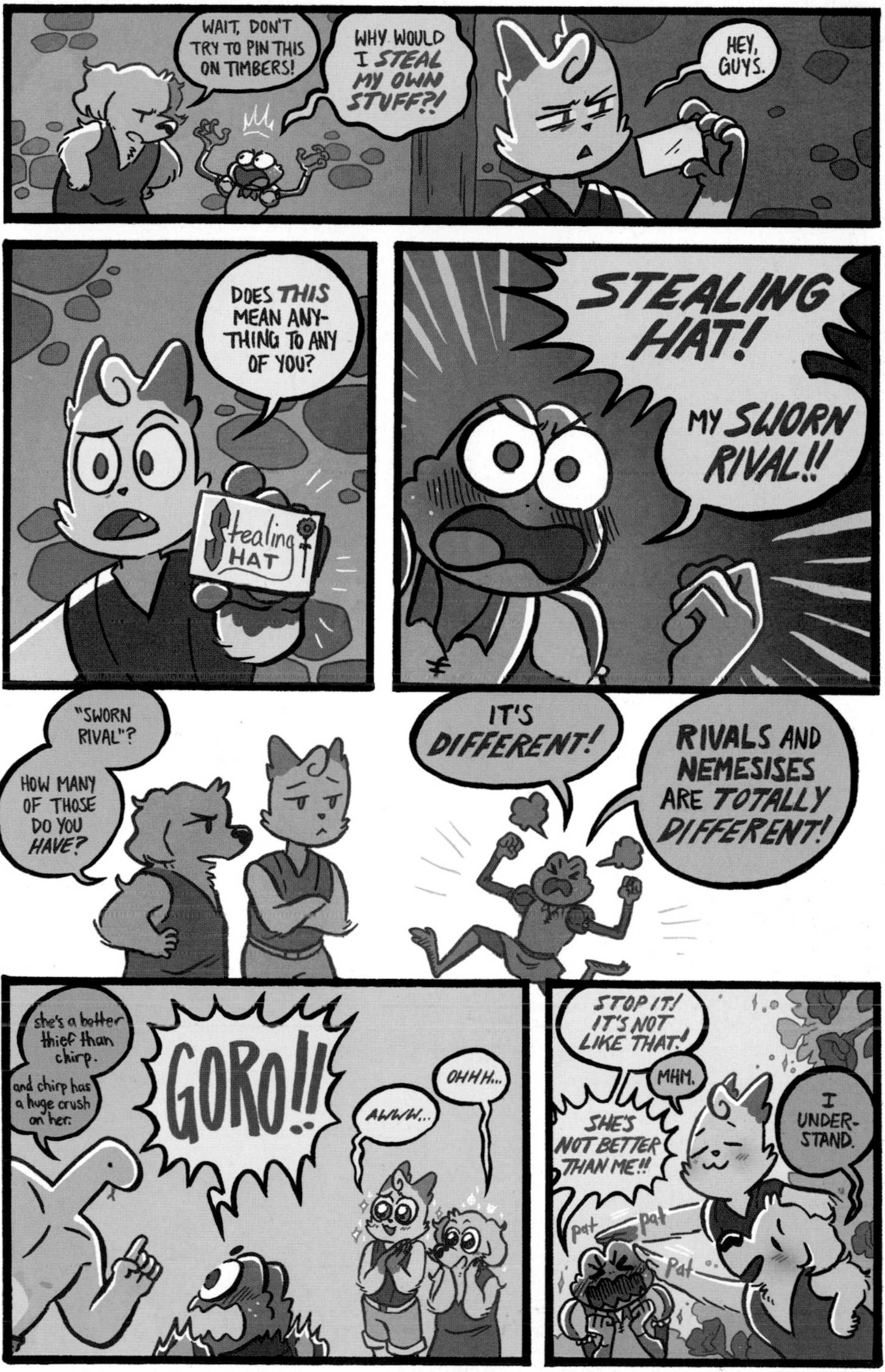
WAIT, DON'T TRY TO PIN THIS ON TIMBERS!
WHY WOULD I STEAL MY OWN STUFF?!
HEY, GUYS.
DOES THIS MEAN ANY-THING TO ANY OF YOU?
Stealing HAT
STEALING HAT!
MY SWORN RIVAL!!
"SWORN RIVAL"?
HOW MANY OF THOSE DO YOU HAVE?
IT'S DIFFERENT!
RIVALS AND NEMESISES ARE TOTALLY DIFFERENT!
she's a better thief than chirp.
and chirp has a huge crush on her.
GORO!!
AWWW...
OHHH...
STOP IT! IT'S NOT LIKE THAT!
MHM.
SHE'S NOT BETTER THAN ME!!
I UNDER-STAND.
pat
pat
pat

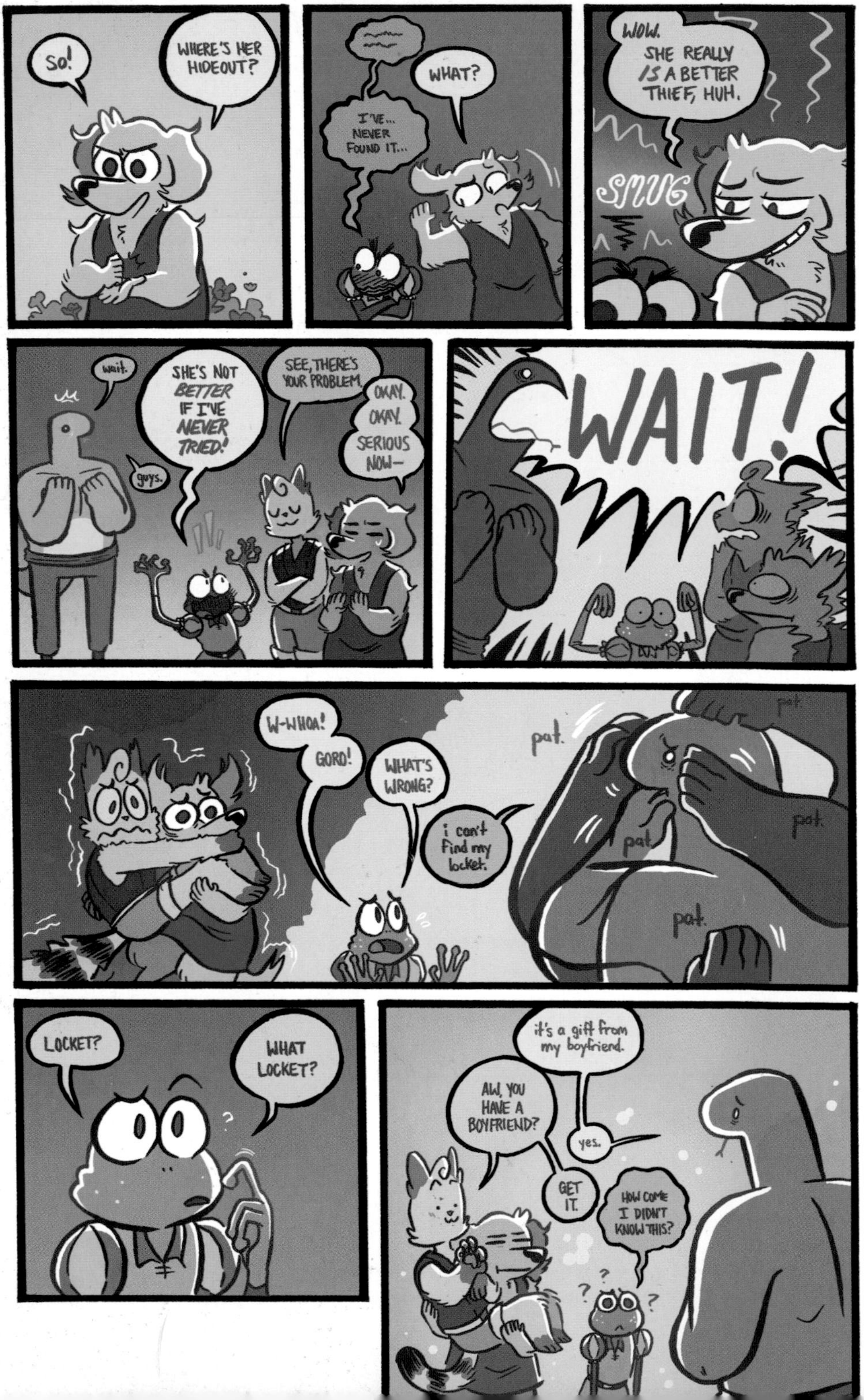

SO!
WHERE'S HER HIDEOUT?
I'VE... NEVER FOUND IT...
WHAT?
WOW. SHE REALLY IS A BETTER THIEF, HUH.
SMUG
wait.
SHE'S NOT BETTER IF I'VE NEVER TRIED!
guys.
SEE, THERE'S YOUR PROBLEM.
OKAY. OKAY. SERIOUS NOW—
WAIT!
W-WHOA!
GORD!
WHAT'S WRONG?
i can't find my locket.
pat.
pat.
pat.
pat.
pat.
LOCKET?
WHAT LOCKET?
it's a gift from my boyfriend.
AW, YOU HAVE A BOYFRIEND?
yes.
GET IT.
HOW COME I DIDN'T KNOW THIS?

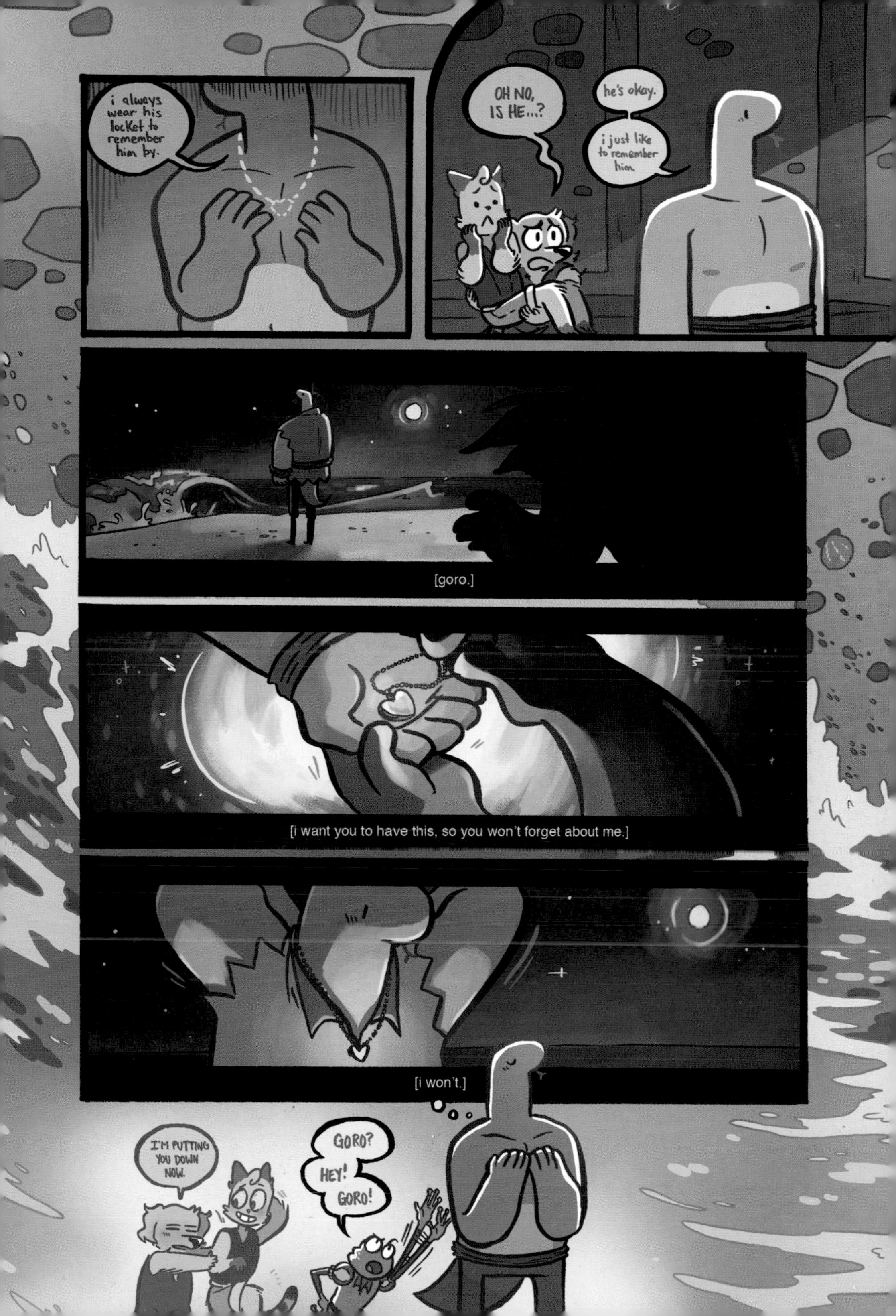
i always wear his locket to remember him by.
OH NO, IS HE...?
he's okay.
i just like to remember him.
[goro.]
[i want you to have this, so you won't forget about me.]
[i won't.]
I'M PUTTING YOU DOWN NOW.
GORO?
HEY!
GORO!

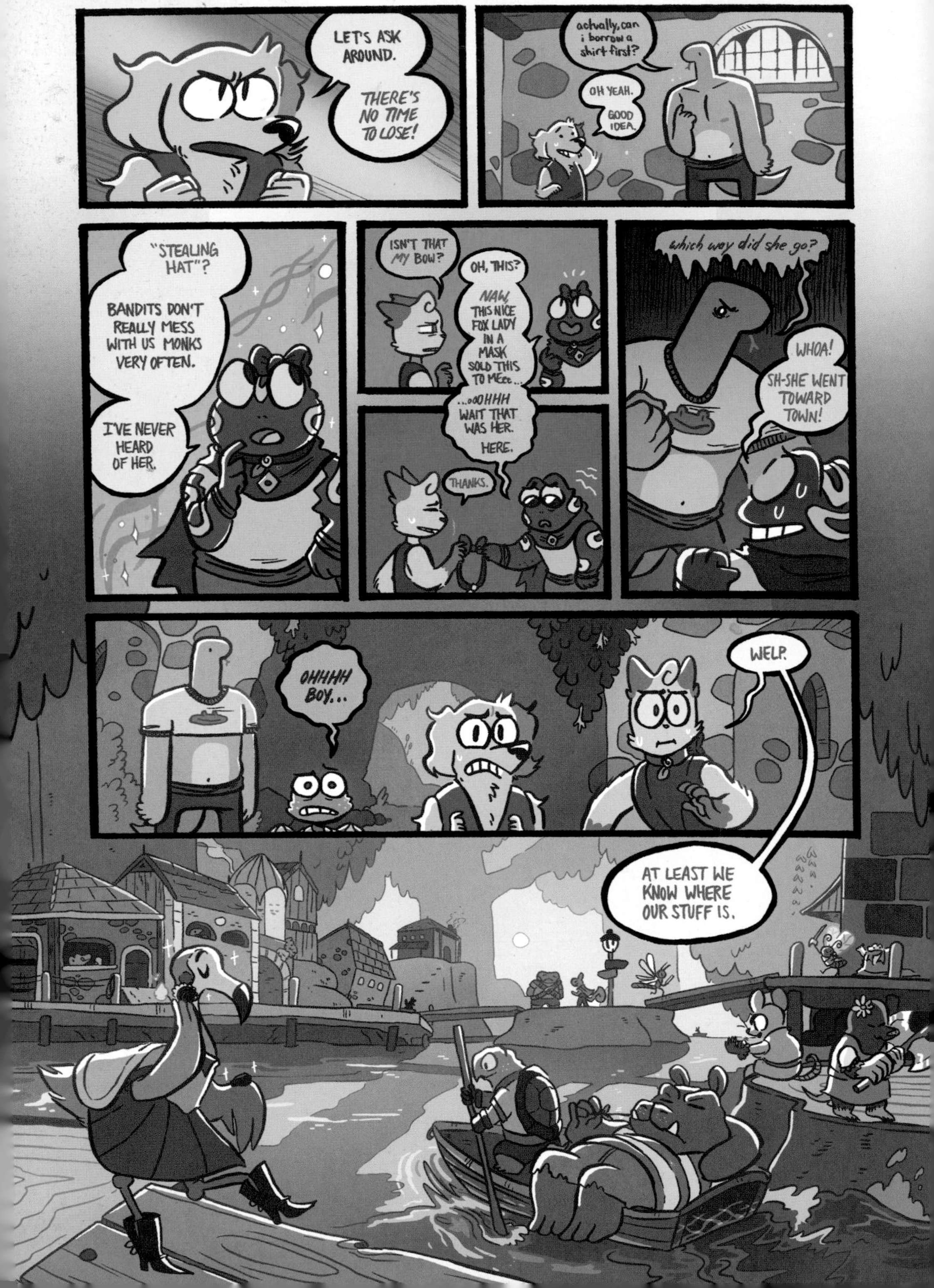
LET'S ASK AROUND.
THERE'S NO TIME TO LOSE!
actually, can i borrow a shirt first?
OH YEAH.
GOOD IDEA.
"STEALING HAT"?
BANDITS DON'T REALLY MESS WITH US MONKS VERY OFTEN.
I'VE NEVER HEARD OF HER.
ISN'T THAT MY BOW?
OH, THIS?
NAW, THIS NICE FOX LADY IN A MASK SOLD THIS TO ME...
...OOOHHH WAIT THAT WAS HER.
HERE.
THANKS.
which way did she go?
WHOA!
SH-SHE WENT TOWARD TOWN!
OHHHH BOY...
WELP.
AT LEAST WE KNOW WHERE OUR STUFF IS.

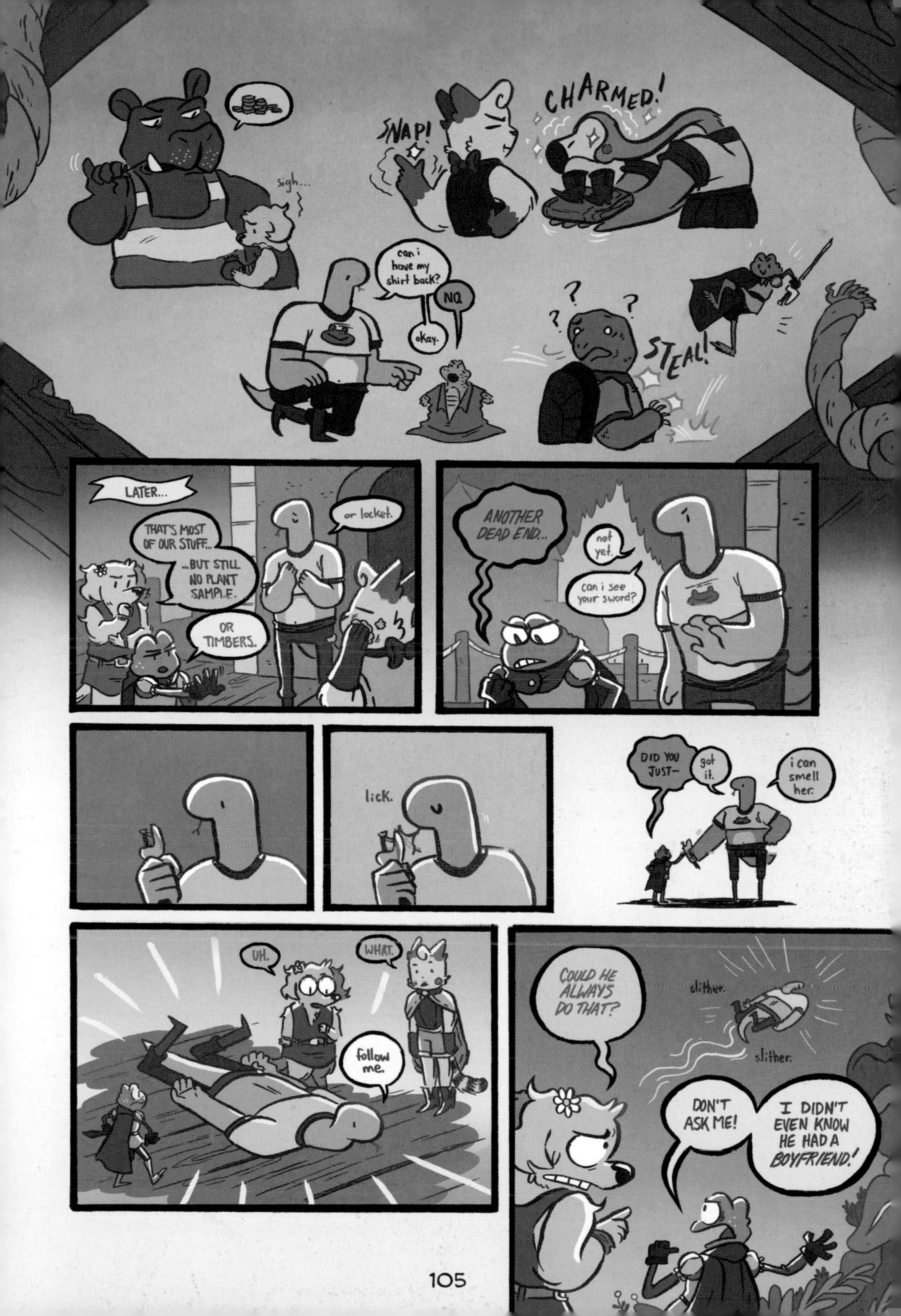

sigh...
SNAP!
CHARMED!
can i have my shirt back?
NO.
okay.
?
?
?
STEAL!
LATER...
THAT'S MOST OF OUR STUFF...
...BUT STILL NO PLANT SAMPLE.
or locket.
OR TIMBERS.
ANOTHER DEAD END...
not yet.
can i see your sword?
lick.
DID YOU JUST–
got it.
i can smell her.
UH.
WHAT.
follow me.
COULD HE ALWAYS DO THAT?
slither.
slither.
DON'T ASK ME!
I DIDN'T EVEN KNOW HE HAD A BOYFRIEND!

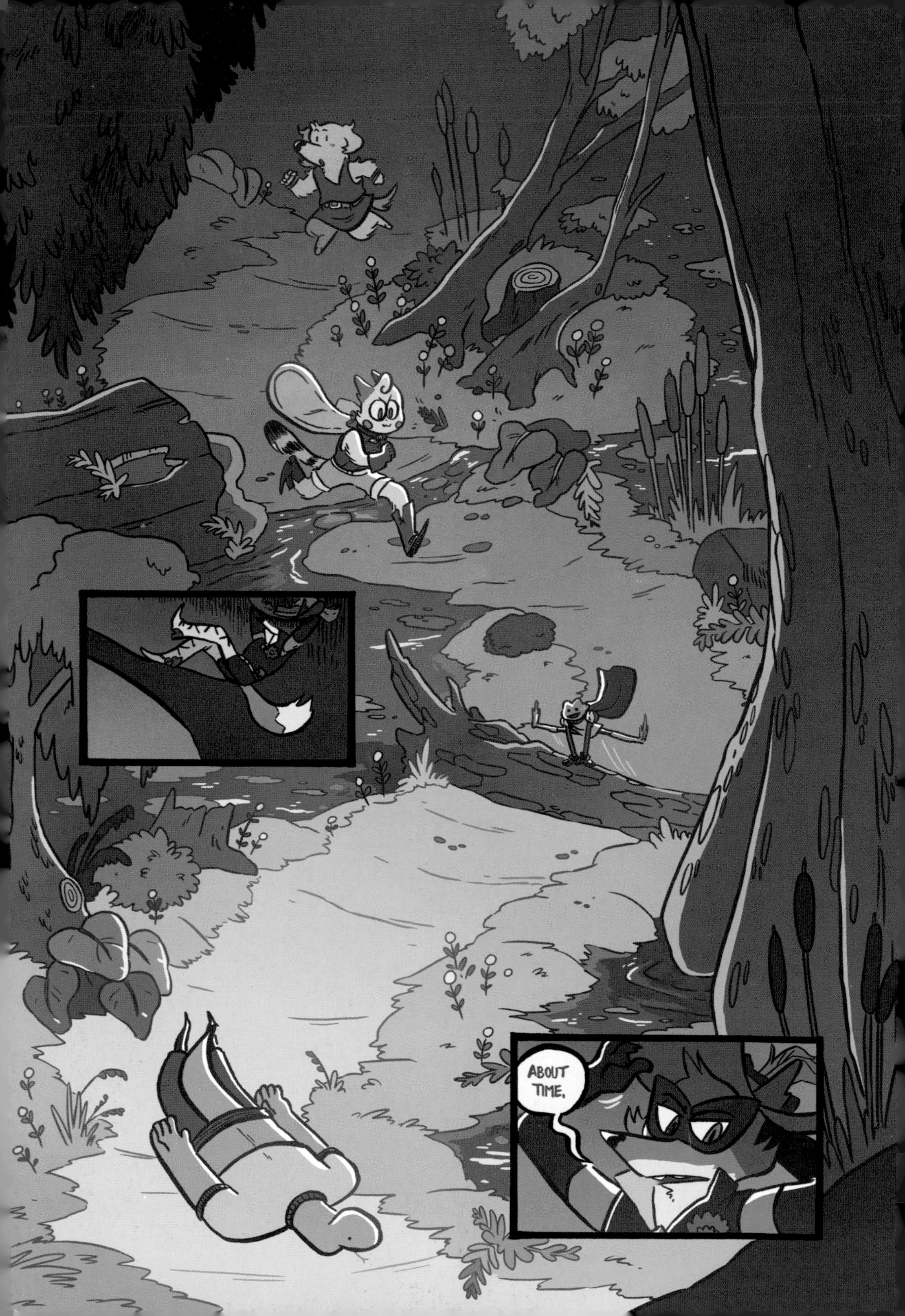
ABOUT TIME.

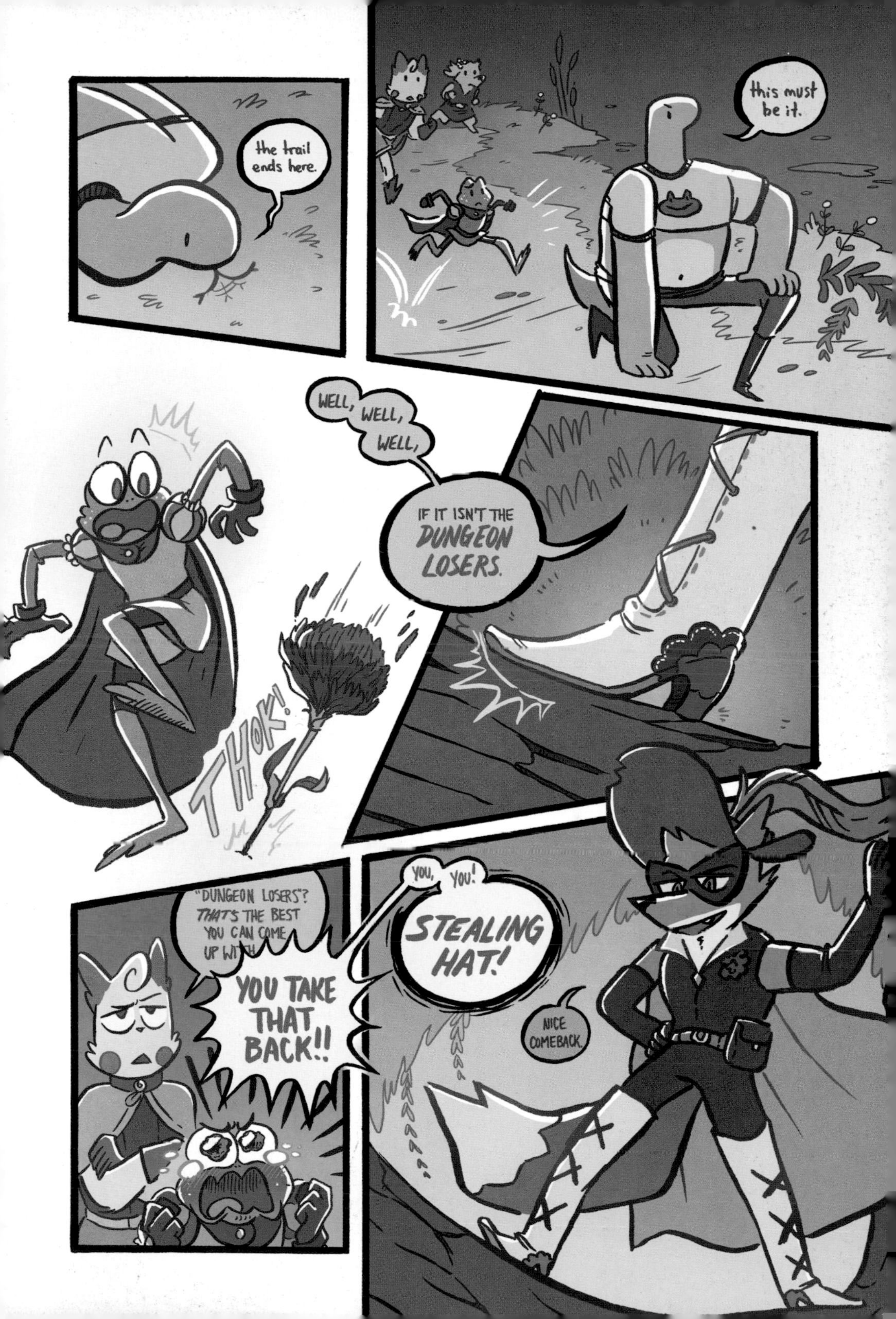
the trail ends here.
this must be it.
WELL, WELL, WELL,
IF IT ISN'T THE DUNGEON LOSERS.
THOK!
"DUNGEON LOSERS"? THAT'S THE BEST YOU CAN COME UP WITH
YOU TAKE THAT BACK!!
YOU, YOU!
STEALING HAT!
NICE COMEBACK.

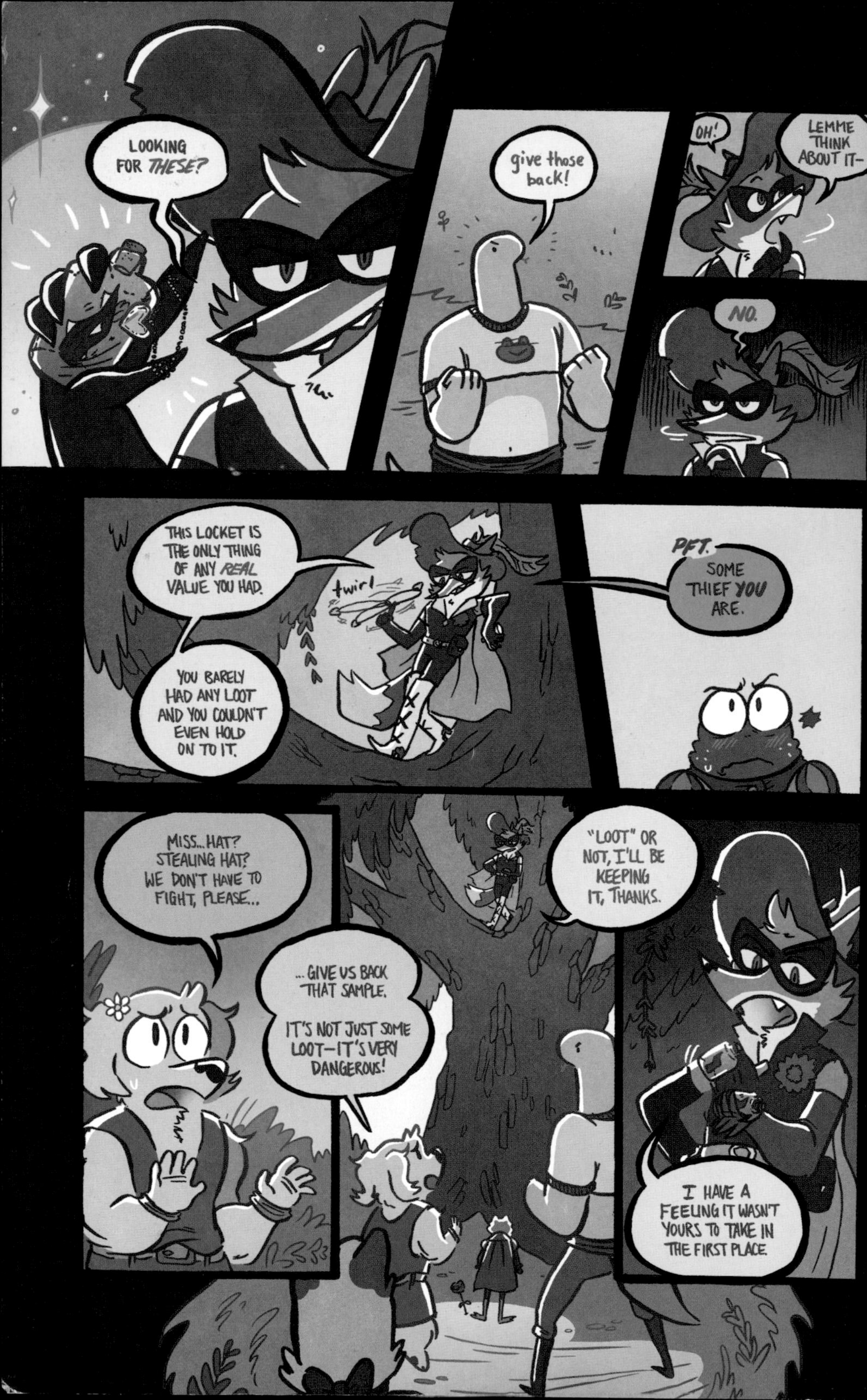

LOOKING FOR THESE?
give those back!
OH!
LEMME THINK ABOUT IT–
NO.
THIS LOCKET IS THE ONLY THING OF ANY REAL VALUE YOU HAD.
twirl
YOU BARELY HAD ANY LOOT AND YOU COULDN'T EVEN HOLD ON TO IT.
PFT.
SOME THIEF YOU ARE.
MISS...HAT? STEALING HAT? WE DON'T HAVE TO FIGHT, PLEASE...
...GIVE US BACK THAT SAMPLE.
IT'S NOT JUST SOME LOOT—IT'S VERY DANGEROUS!
"LOOT" OR NOT, I'LL BE KEEPING IT, THANKS.
I HAVE A FEELING IT WASN'T YOURS TO TAKE IN THE FIRST PLACE.

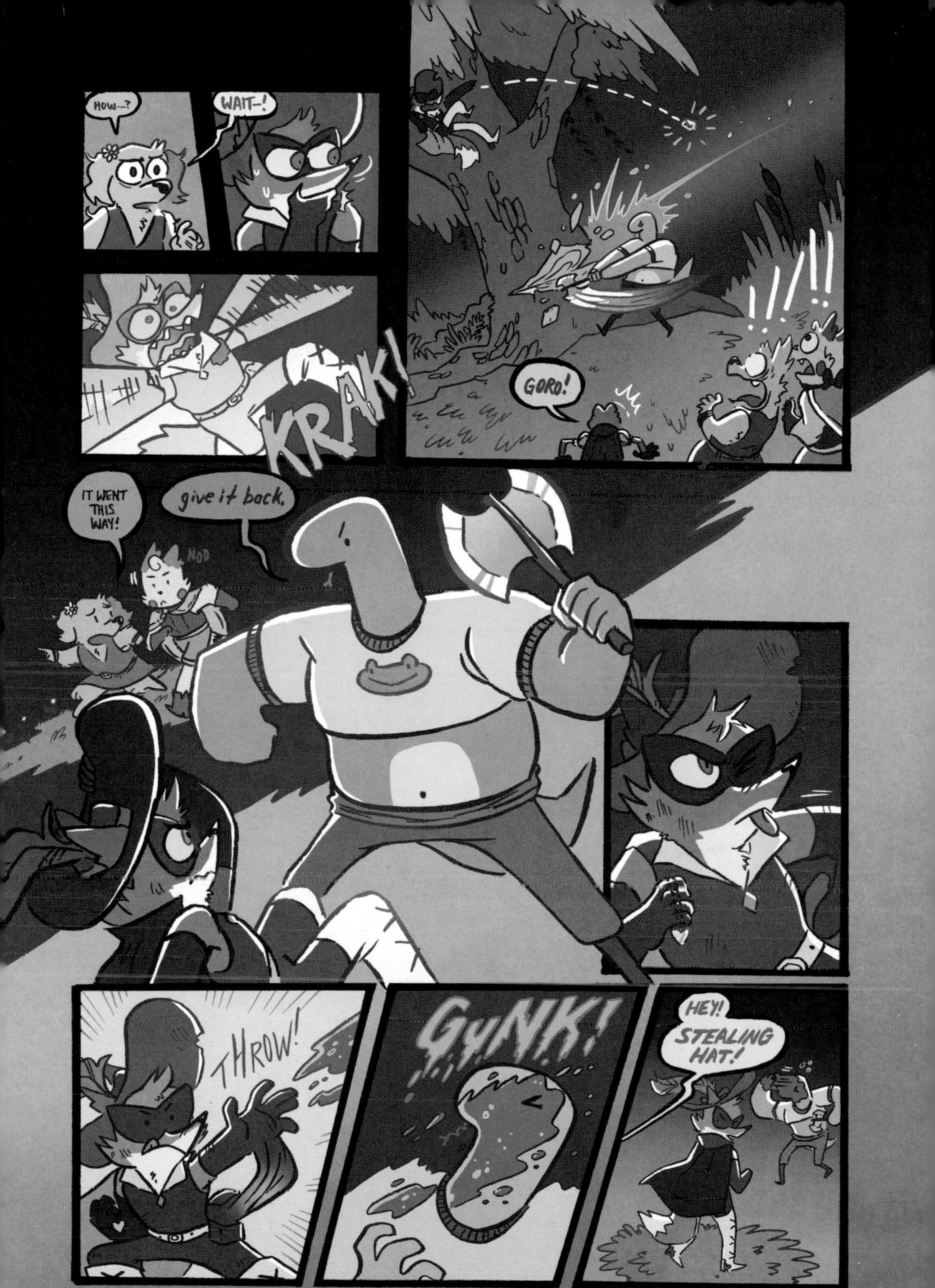

HOW...?
WAIT-!
KRAK!
GORO!
IT WENT THIS WAY!
give it back.
NOD
THROW!
GUNK!
HEY!
STEALING HAT!

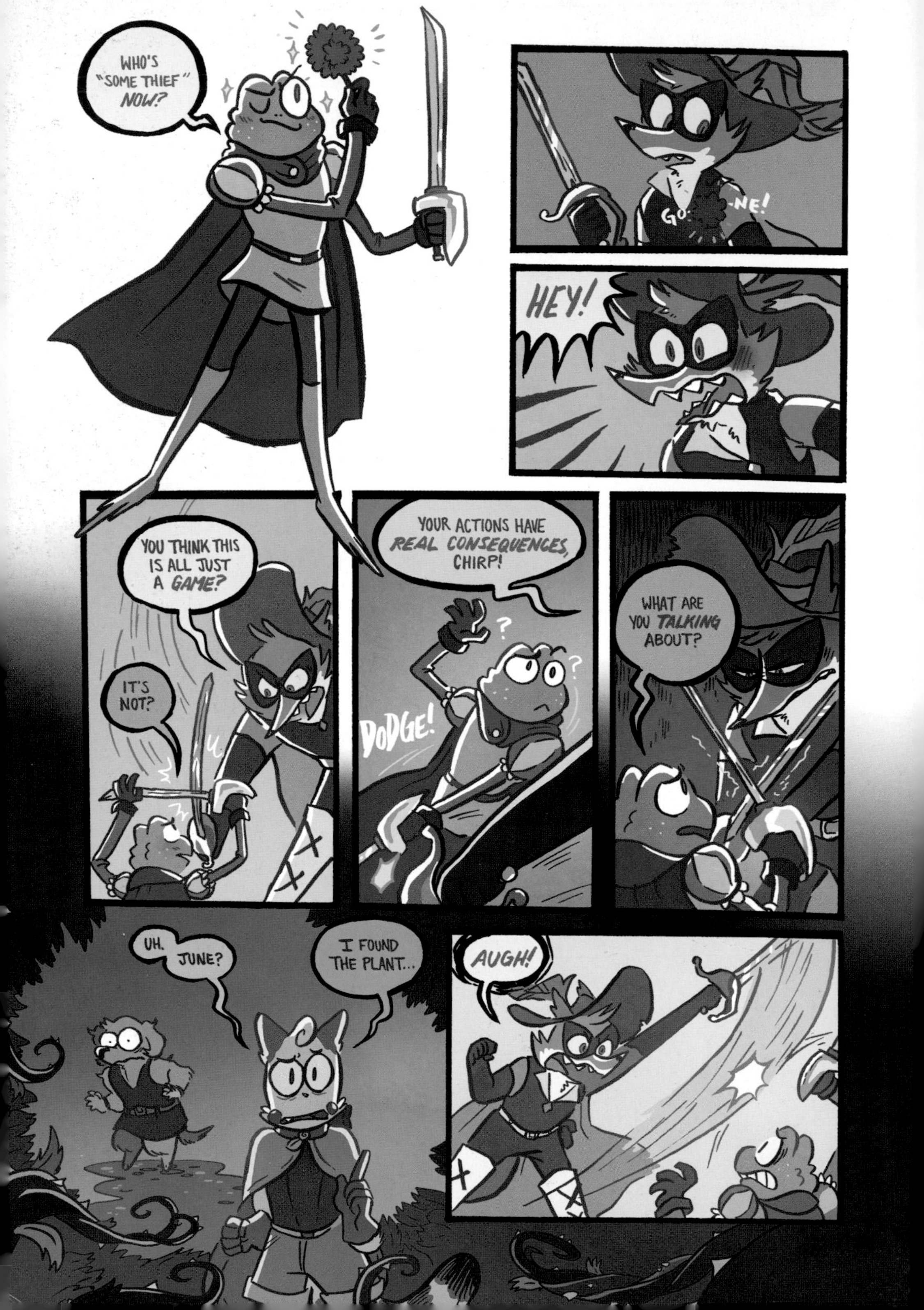

WHO'S "SOME THIEF" NOW?
GO- -NE!
HEY!
YOU THINK THIS IS ALL JUST A GAME?
IT'S NOT?
YOUR ACTIONS HAVE REAL CONSEQUENCES, CHIRP!
DODGE!
WHAT ARE YOU TALKING ABOUT?
UH. JUNE?
I FOUND THE PLANT...
AUGH!

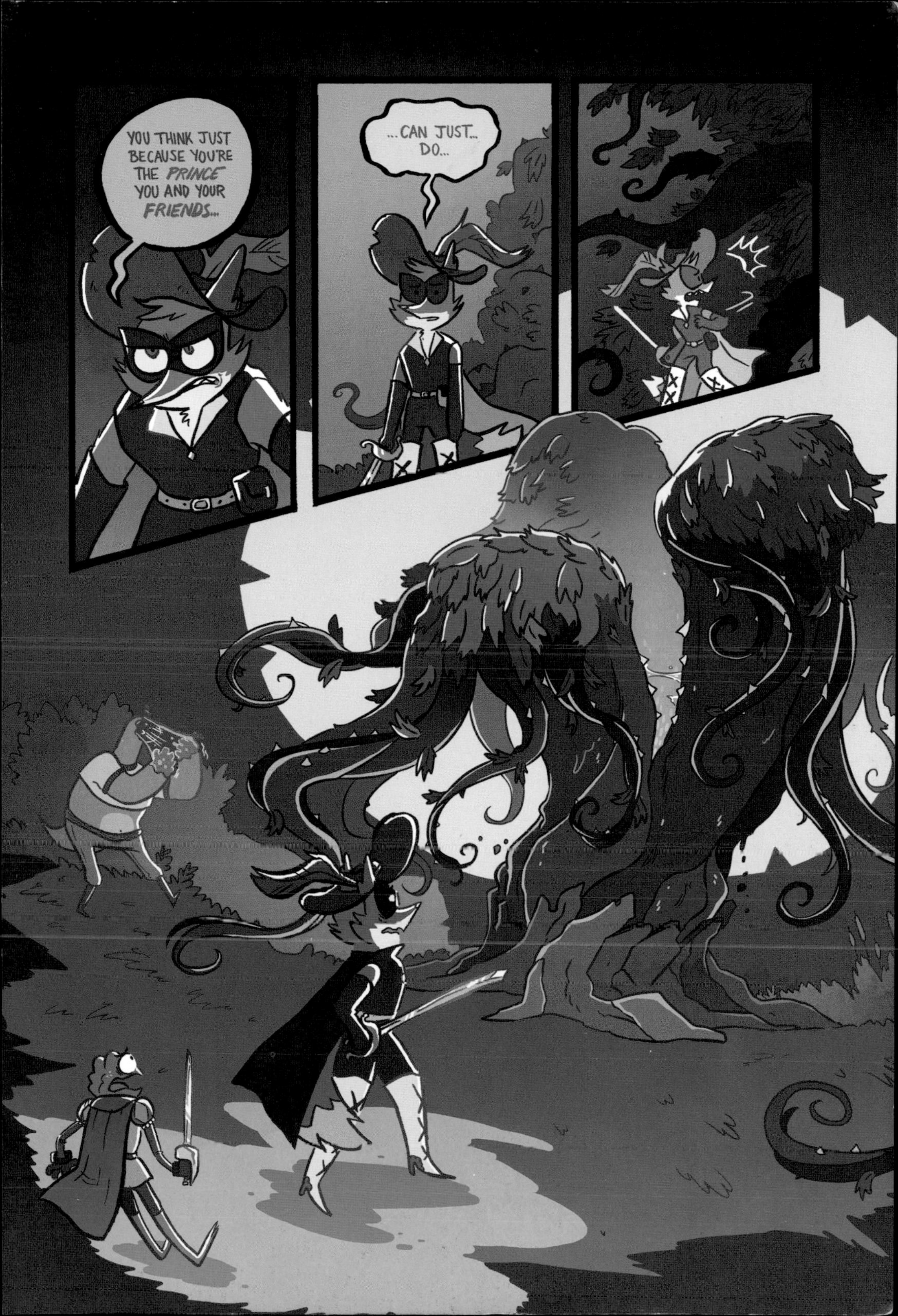
YOU THINK JUST BECAUSE YOU'RE THE *PRINCE* YOU AND YOUR *FRIENDS*...
...CAN JUST... DO...

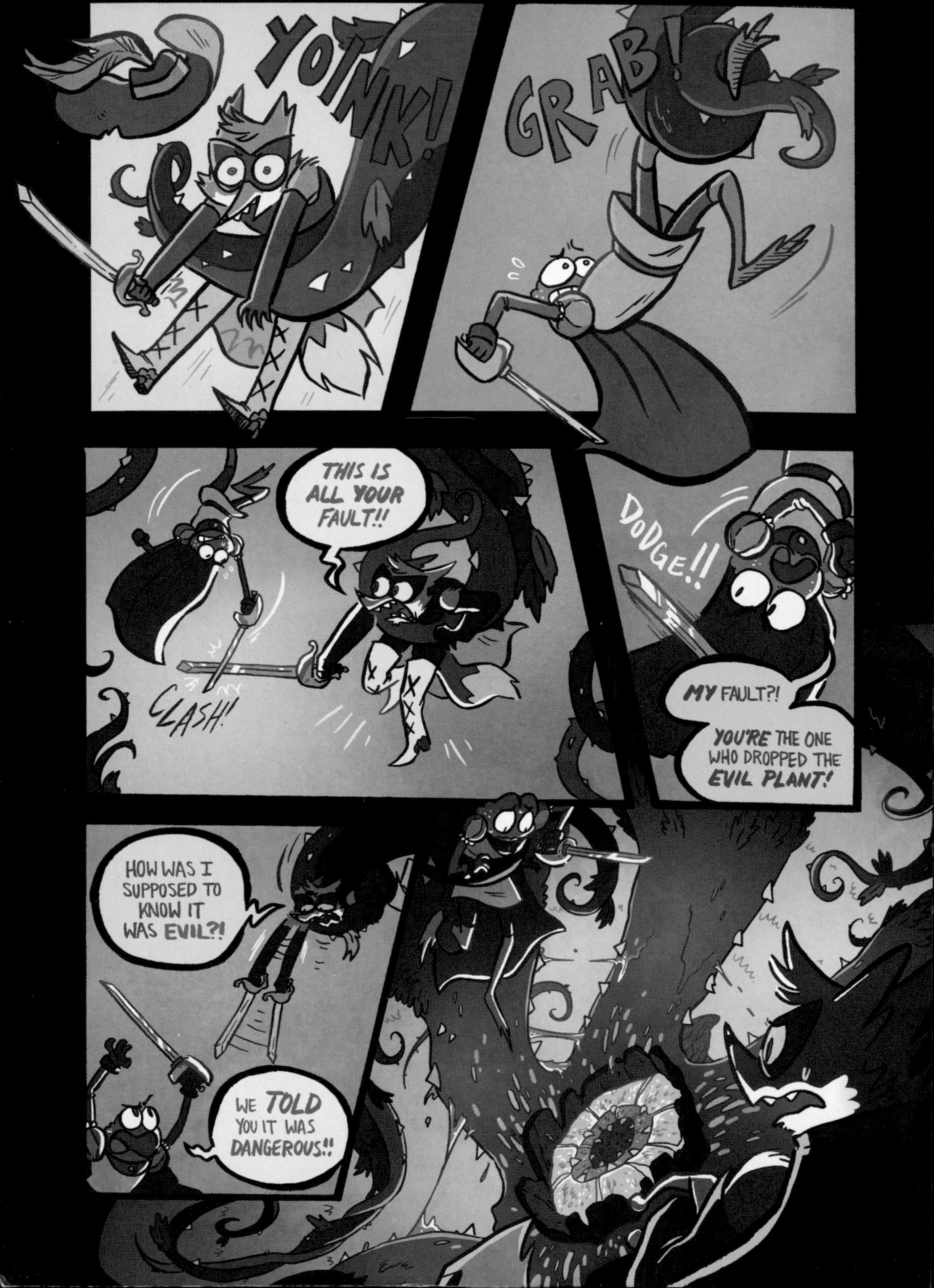
YOINK!
GRAB!
THIS IS ALL YOUR FAULT!!
CLASH!
DODGE!!
MY FAULT?!
YOU'RE THE ONE WHO DROPPED THE EVIL PLANT!
HOW WAS I SUPPOSED TO KNOW IT WAS EVIL?!
WE TOLD YOU IT WAS DANGEROUS!!

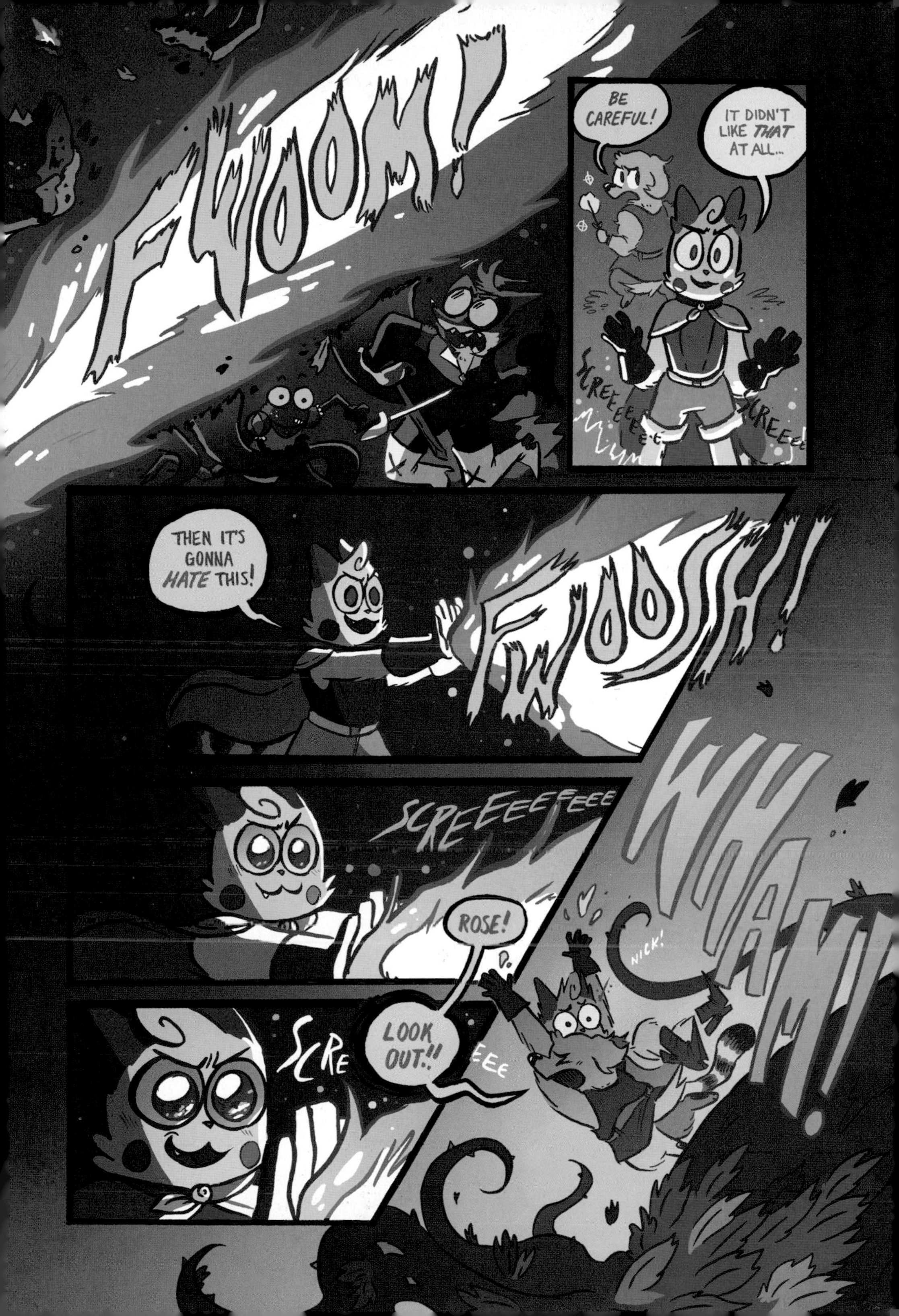
FWOOM!
BE CAREFUL!
IT DIDN'T LIKE THAT AT ALL...
SCREEEEEE
SCREEEEE
THEN IT'S GONNA HATE THIS!
FWOOSH!
SCREEEEEEEEE
WHAM!
ROSE!
NICK!
SCRE
LOOK OUT!!
EEE

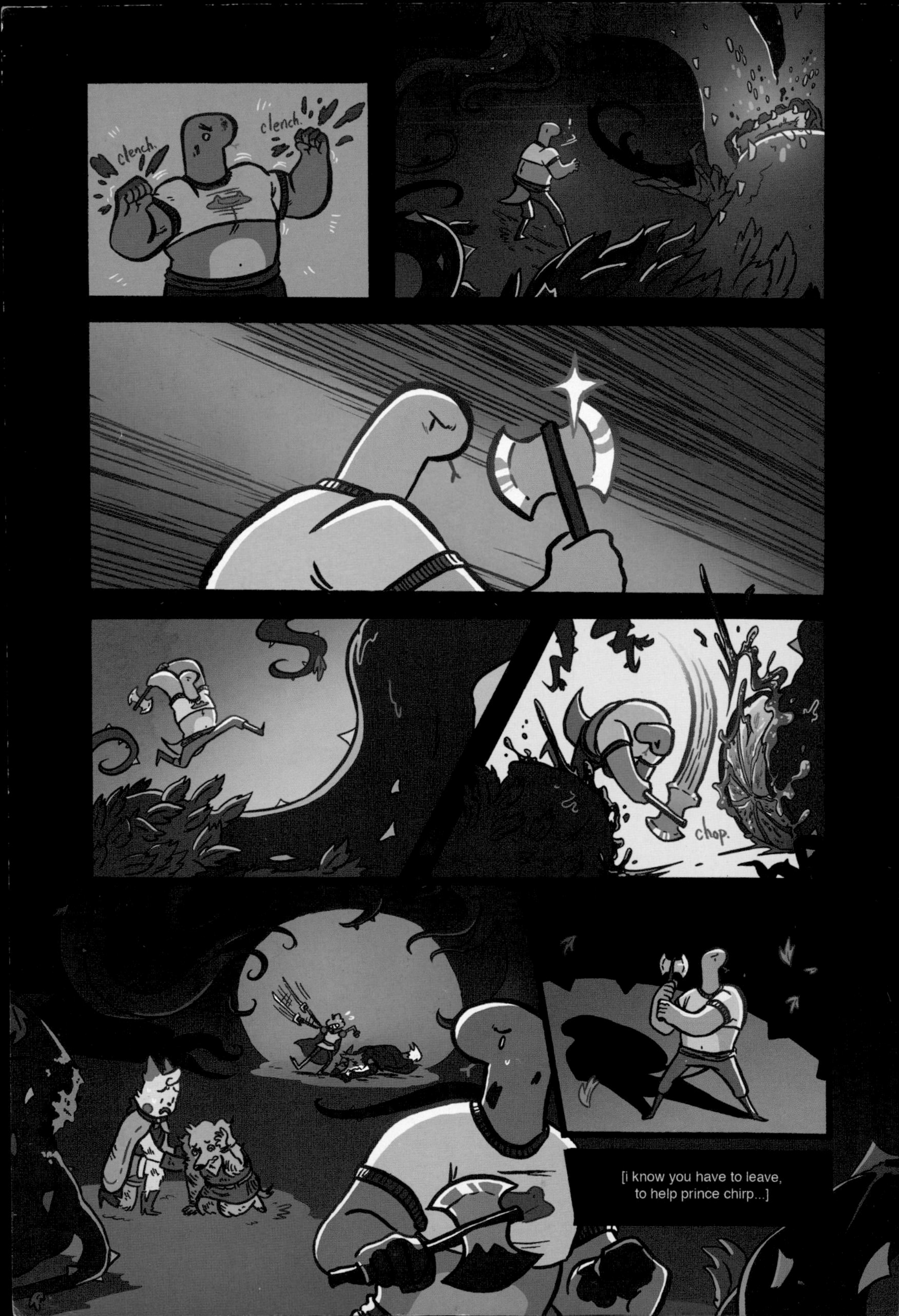
clench.
clench.
chop.
[i know you have to leave,
to help prince chirp...]

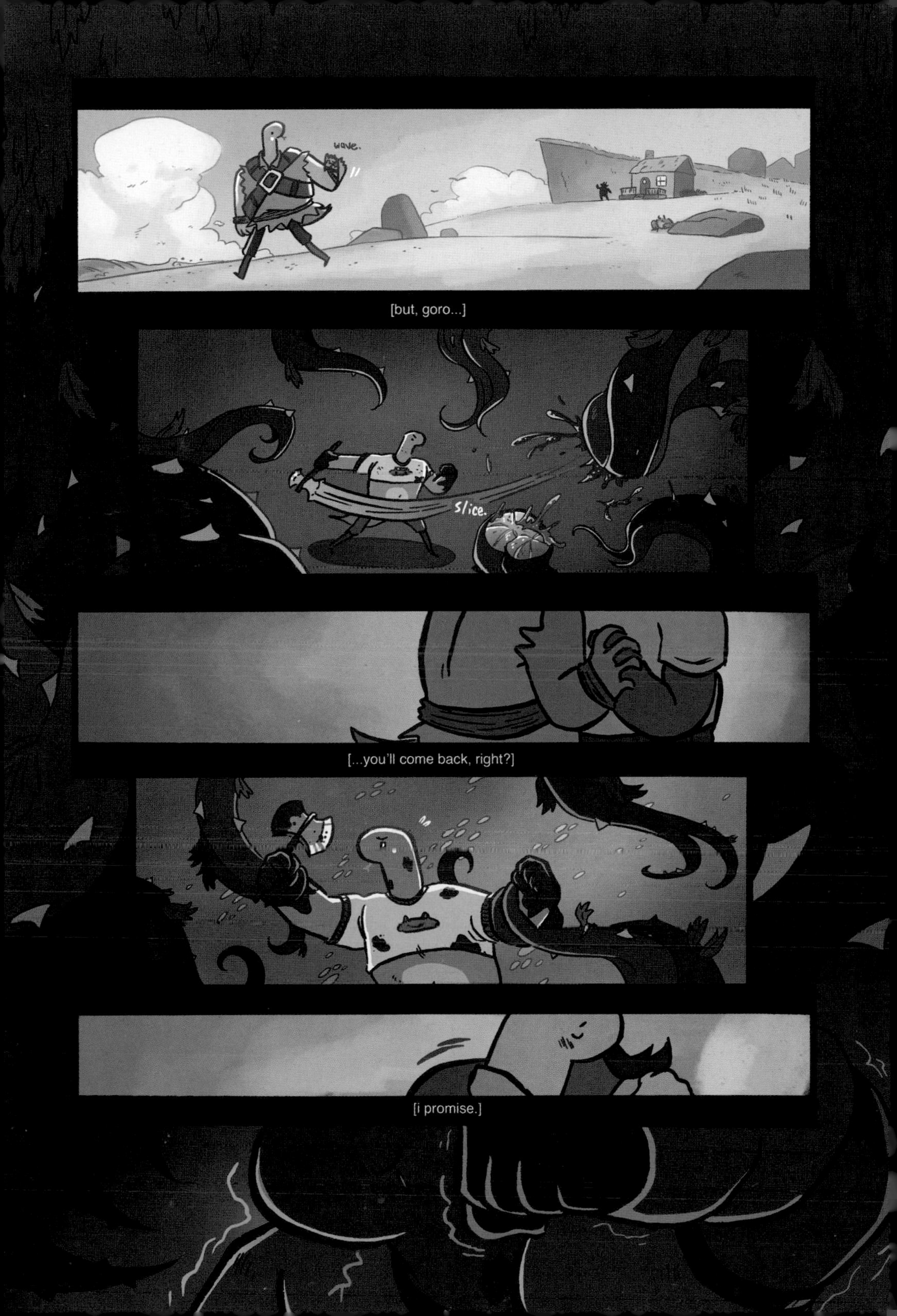
wave.
[but, goro...]
slice.
[...you'll come back, right?]
[i promise.]

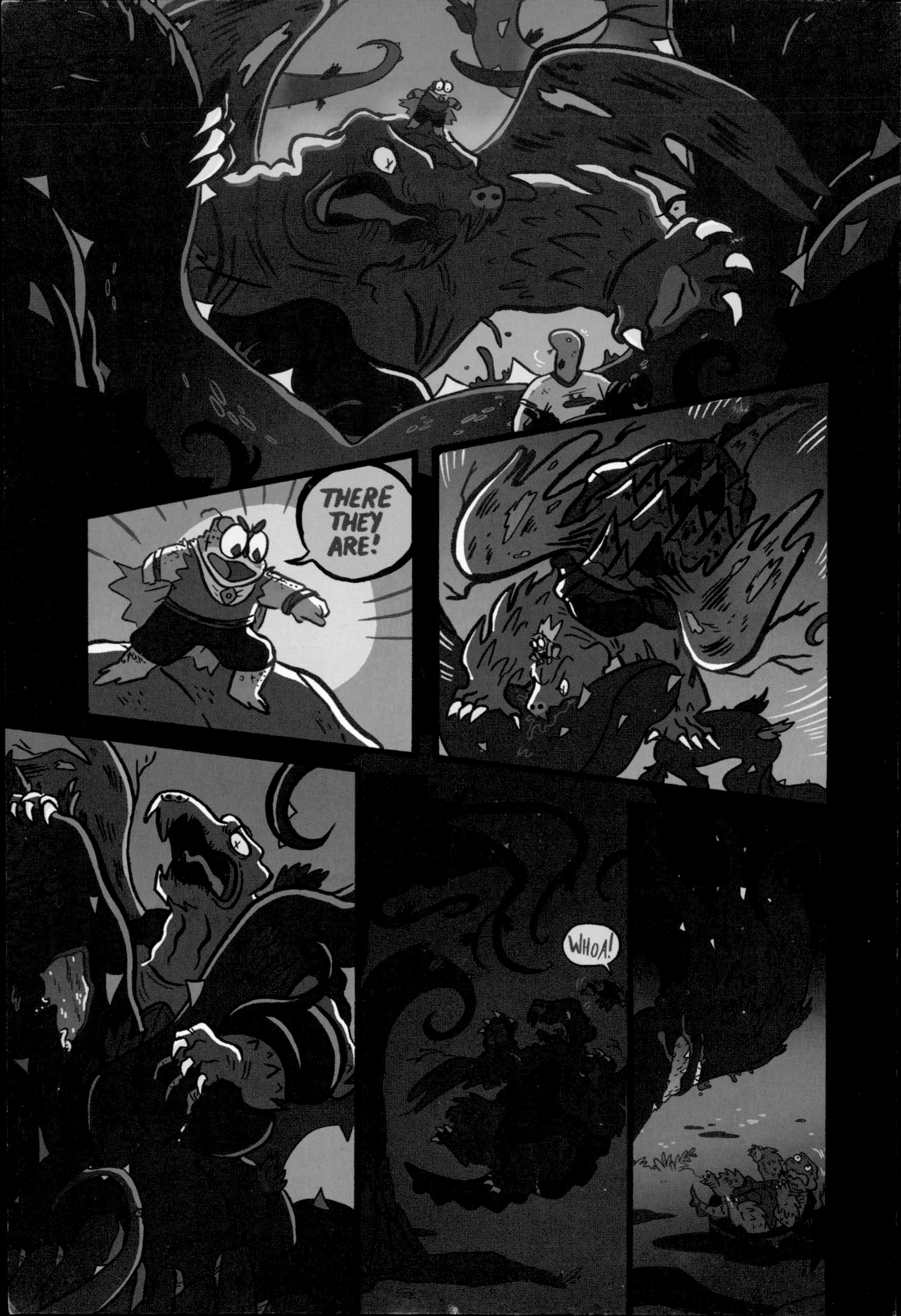
THERE THEY ARE!
WHOA!

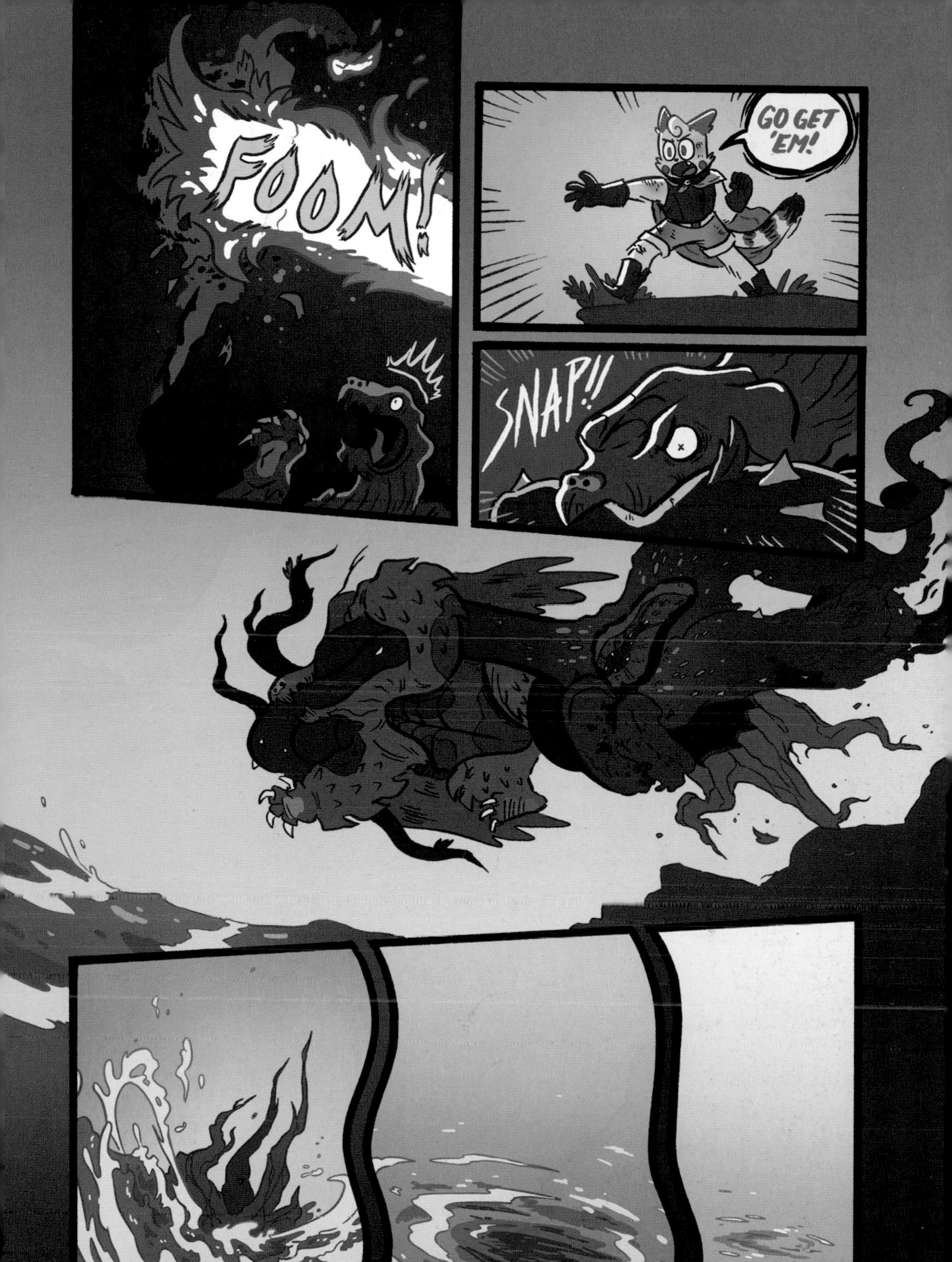
FOOM!
GO GET 'EM!
SNAP!!

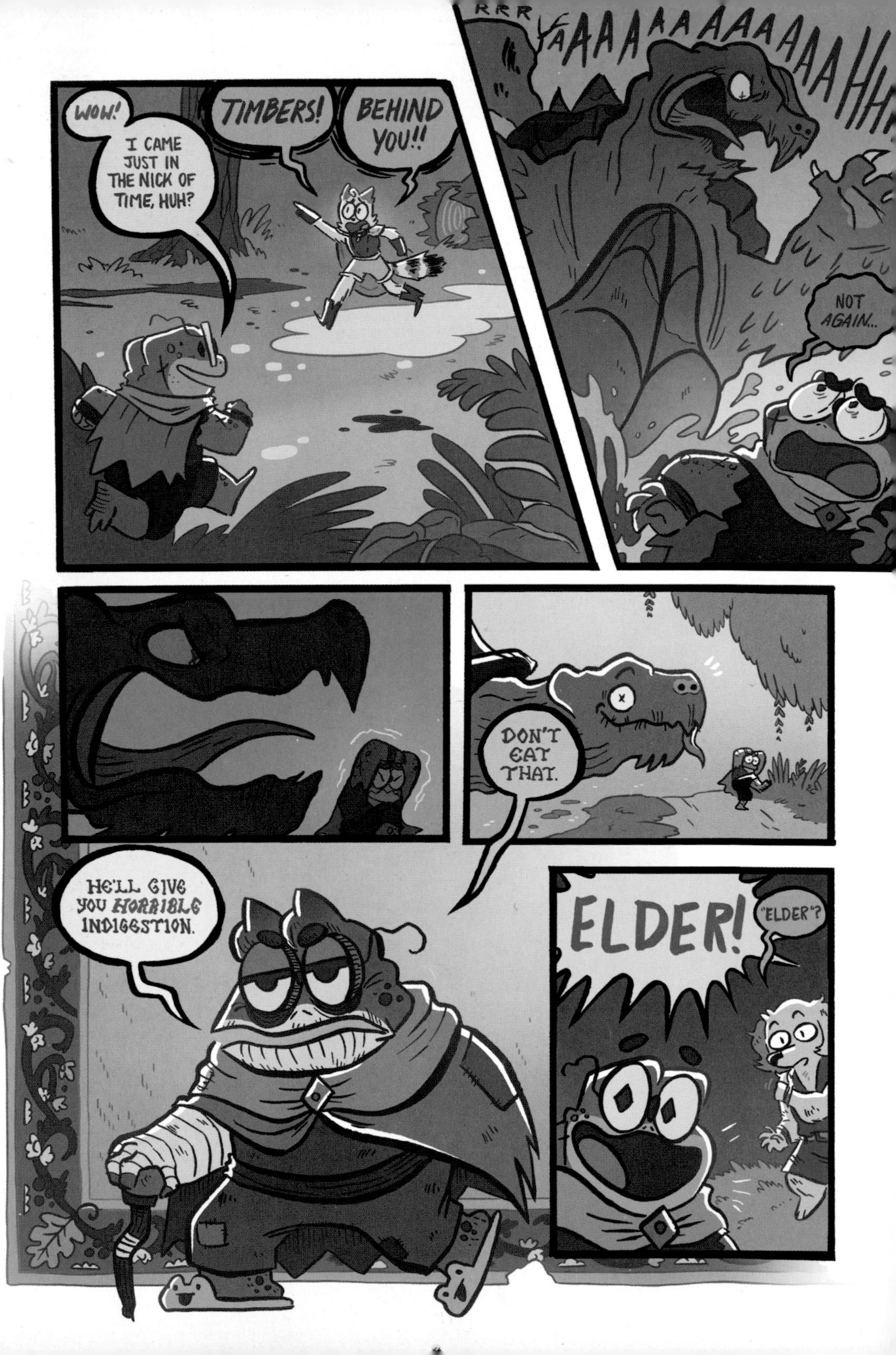

WOW!
I CAME JUST IN THE NICK OF TIME, HUH?
TIMBERS!
BEHIND YOU!!
RRRAAAAAAAAAAAHHH
NOT AGAIN...
DON'T EAT THAT.
HE'LL GIVE YOU HORRIBLE INDIGESTION.
ELDER!
"ELDER"?

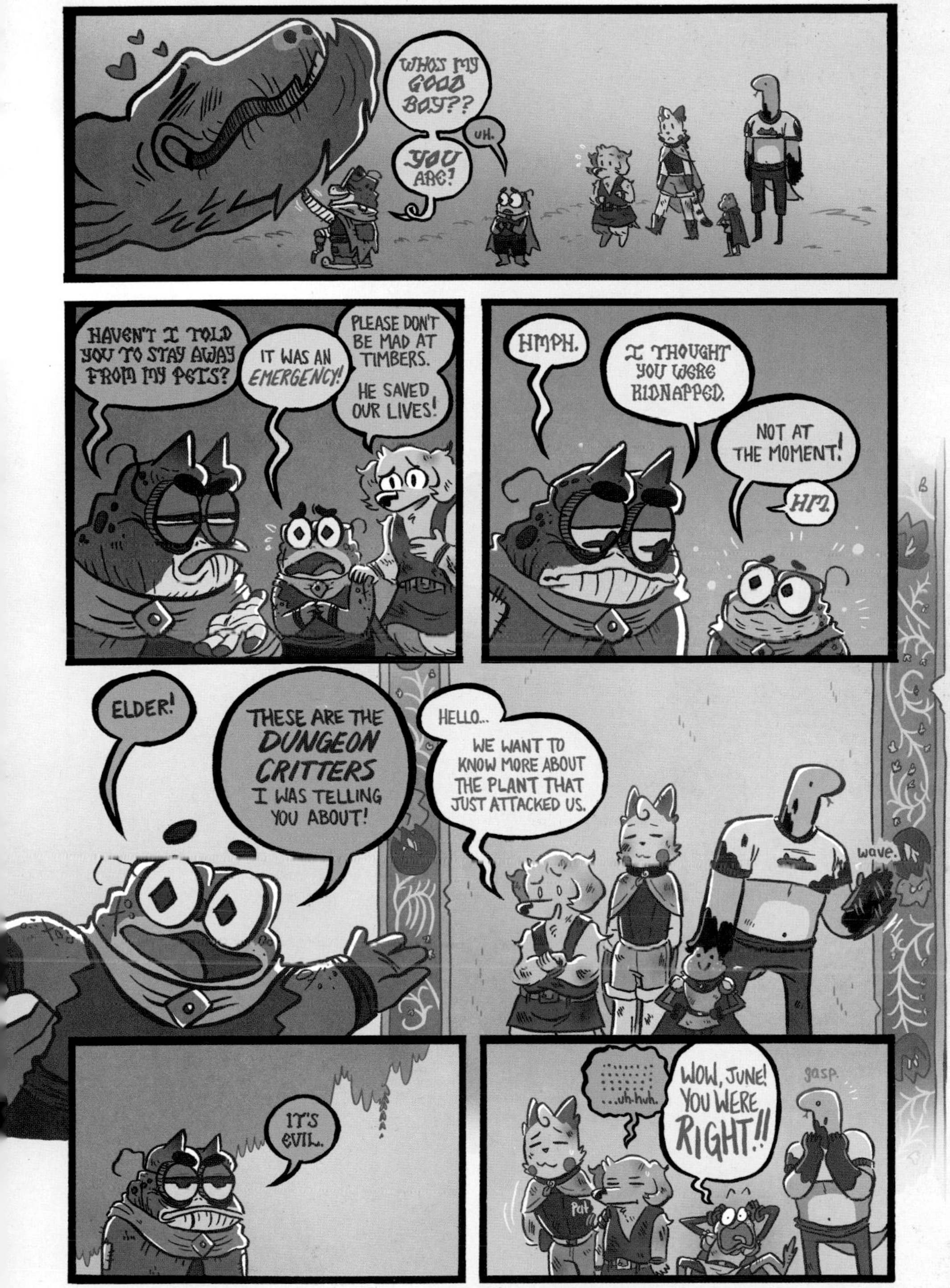
WHO'S MY GOOD BOY??
YOU ARE!
UH.
HAVEN'T I TOLD YOU TO STAY AWAY FROM MY PETS?
IT WAS AN EMERGENCY!
PLEASE DON'T BE MAD AT TIMBERS.
HE SAVED OUR LIVES!
HMPH.
I THOUGHT YOU WERE KIDNAPPED.
NOT AT THE MOMENT!
HI!
ELDER!
THESE ARE THE DUNGEON CRITTERS I WAS TELLING YOU ABOUT!
HELLO...
WE WANT TO KNOW MORE ABOUT THE PLANT THAT JUST ATTACKED US.
wave.
IT'S EVIL.
...uh-huh.
WOW, JUNE! YOU WERE RIGHT!!
gasp.
pat

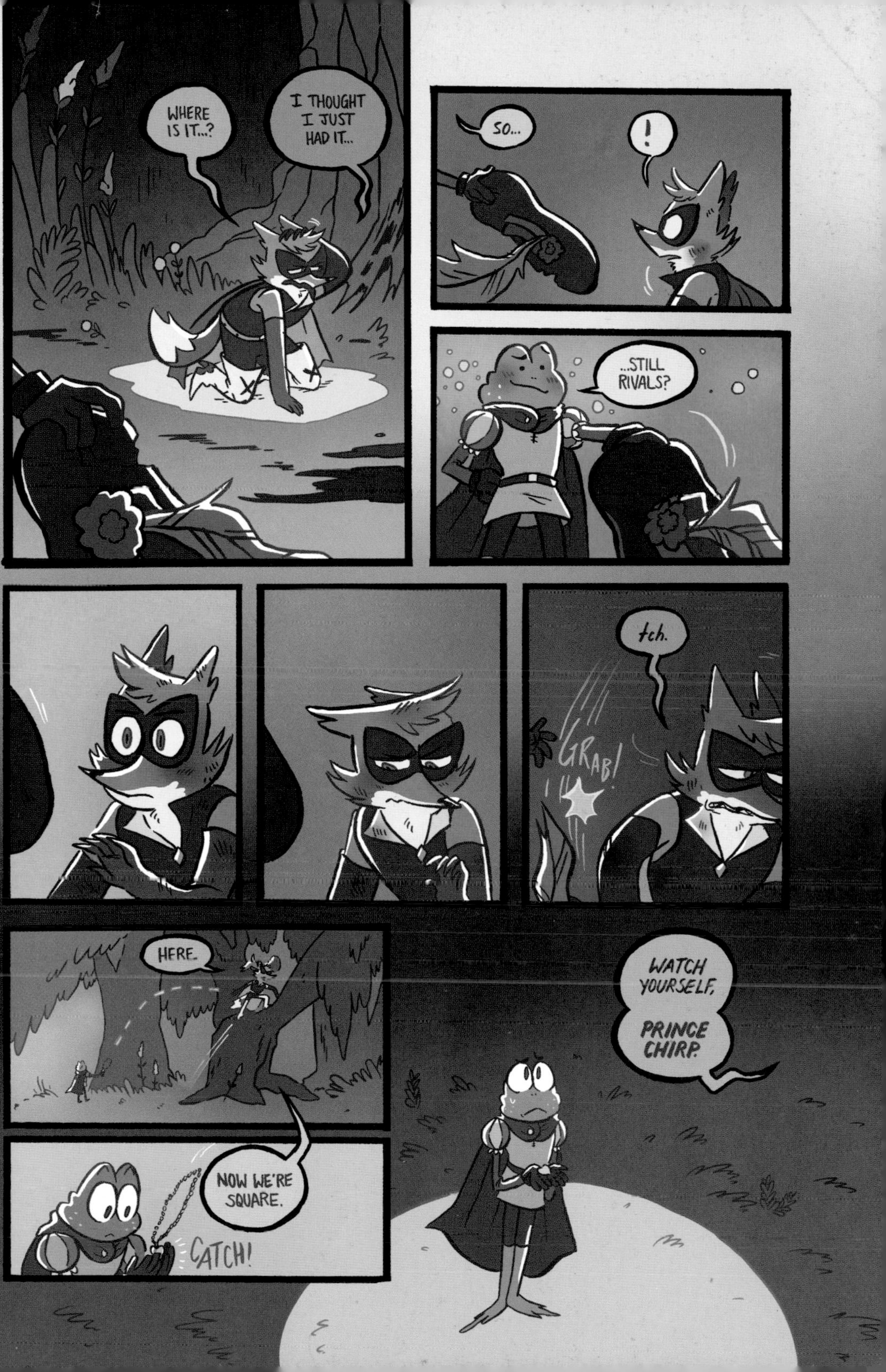
WHERE IS IT...?
I THOUGHT I JUST HAD IT...
SO...
!
...STILL RIVALS?
tch.
GRAB!
HERE.
NOW WE'RE SQUARE.
CATCH!
WATCH YOURSELF,
PRINCE CHIRP.

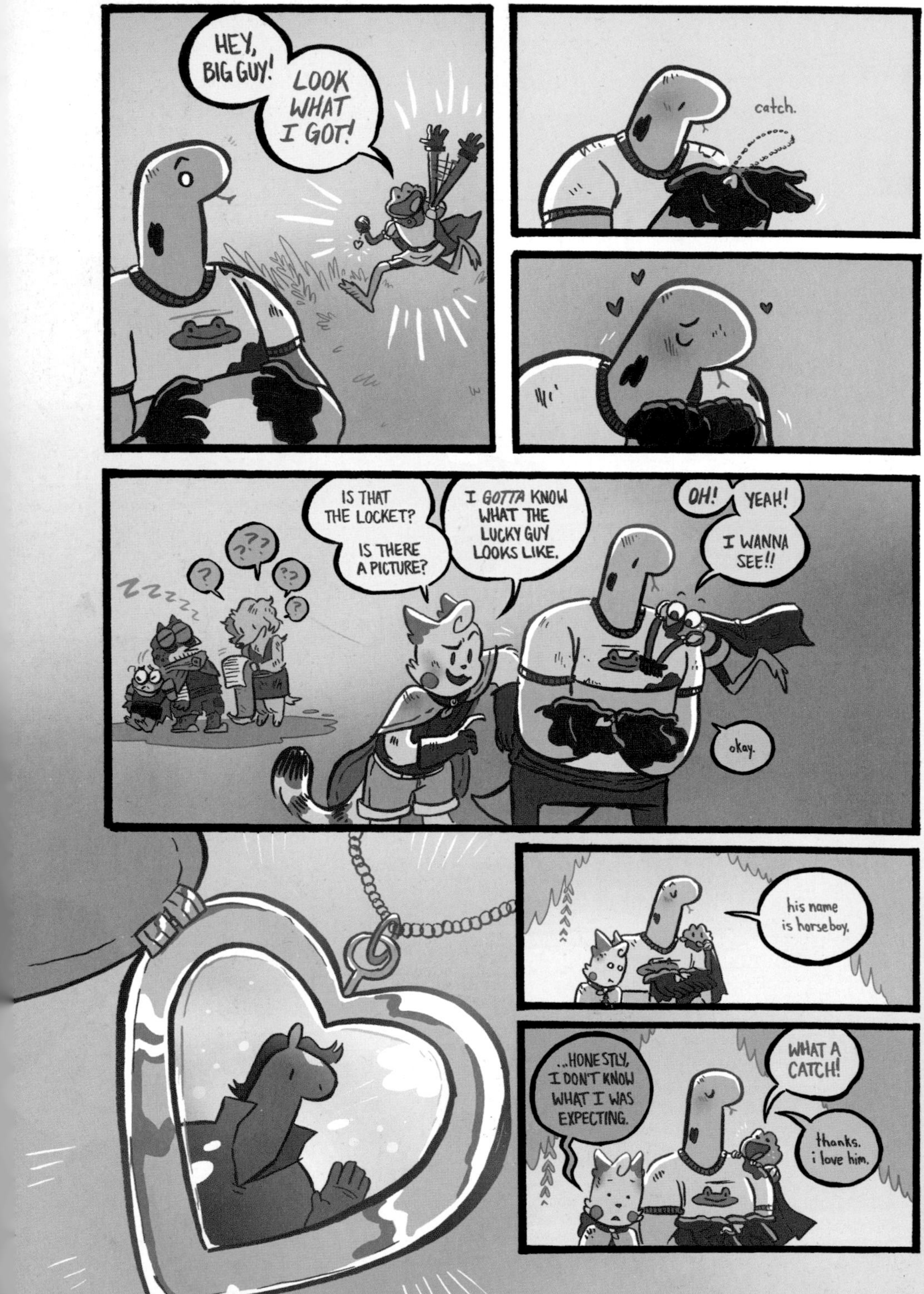
HEY, BIG GUY!
LOOK WHAT I GOT!
catch.
IS THAT THE LOCKET?
IS THERE A PICTURE?
I GOTTA KNOW WHAT THE LUCKY GUY LOOKS LIKE.
OH!
YEAH!
I WANNA SEE!!
okay.
his name is horseboy.
...HONESTLY, I DON'T KNOW WHAT I WAS EXPECTING.
WHAT A CATCH!
thanks. i love him.

123

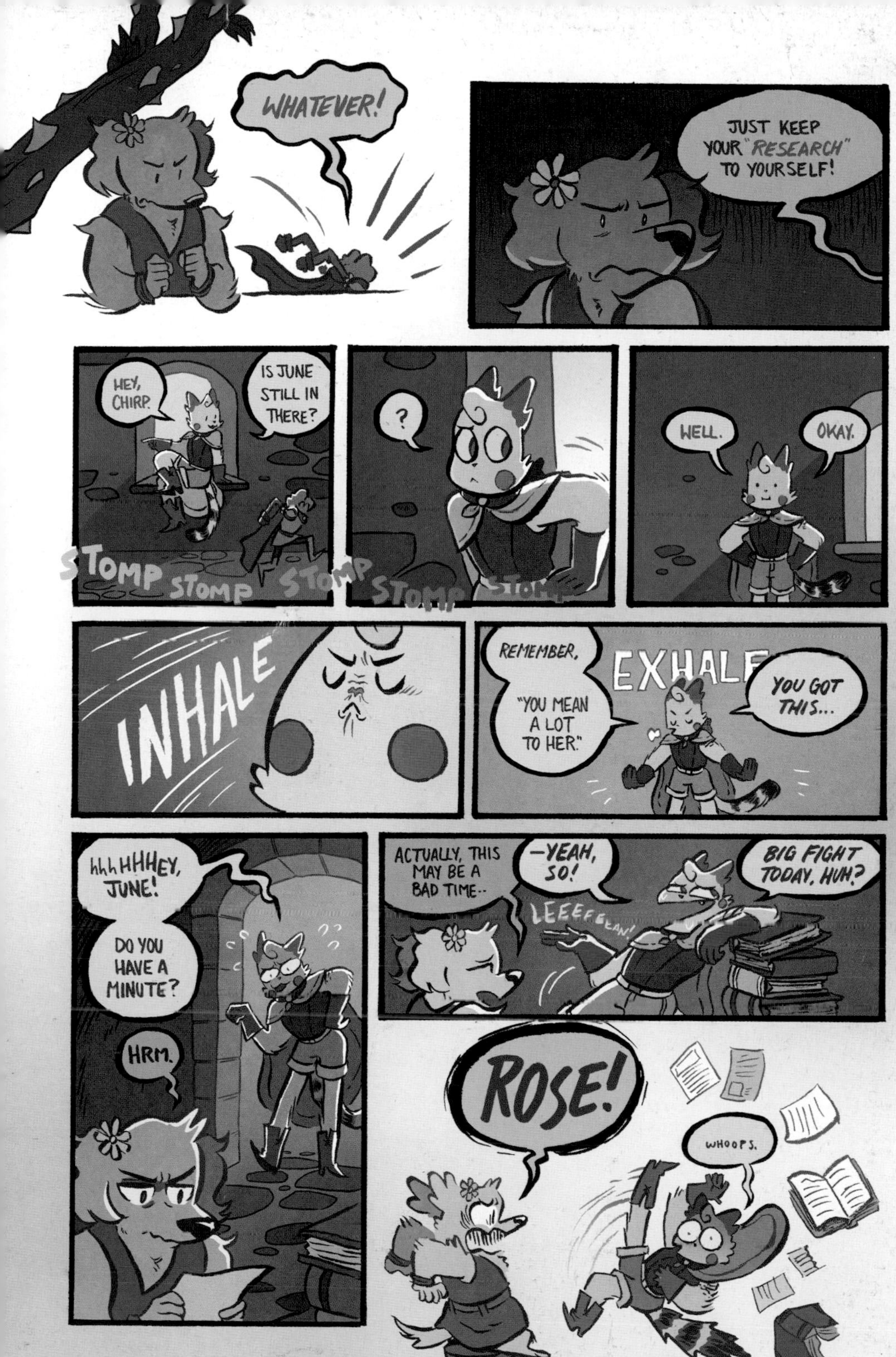
WHATEVER!
JUST KEEP YOUR "RESEARCH" TO YOURSELF!
HEY, CHIRP.
IS JUNE STILL IN THERE?
STOMP STOMP STOMP STOMP STOMP
?
WELL.
OKAY.
INHALE
REMEMBER,
"YOU MEAN A LOT TO HER."
EXHALE
YOU GOT THIS...
hhhHHHEY, JUNE!
DO YOU HAVE A MINUTE?
HRM.
ACTUALLY, THIS MAY BE A BAD TIME--
—YEAH, SO!
BIG FIGHT TODAY, HUH?
ROSE!
WHOOPS.

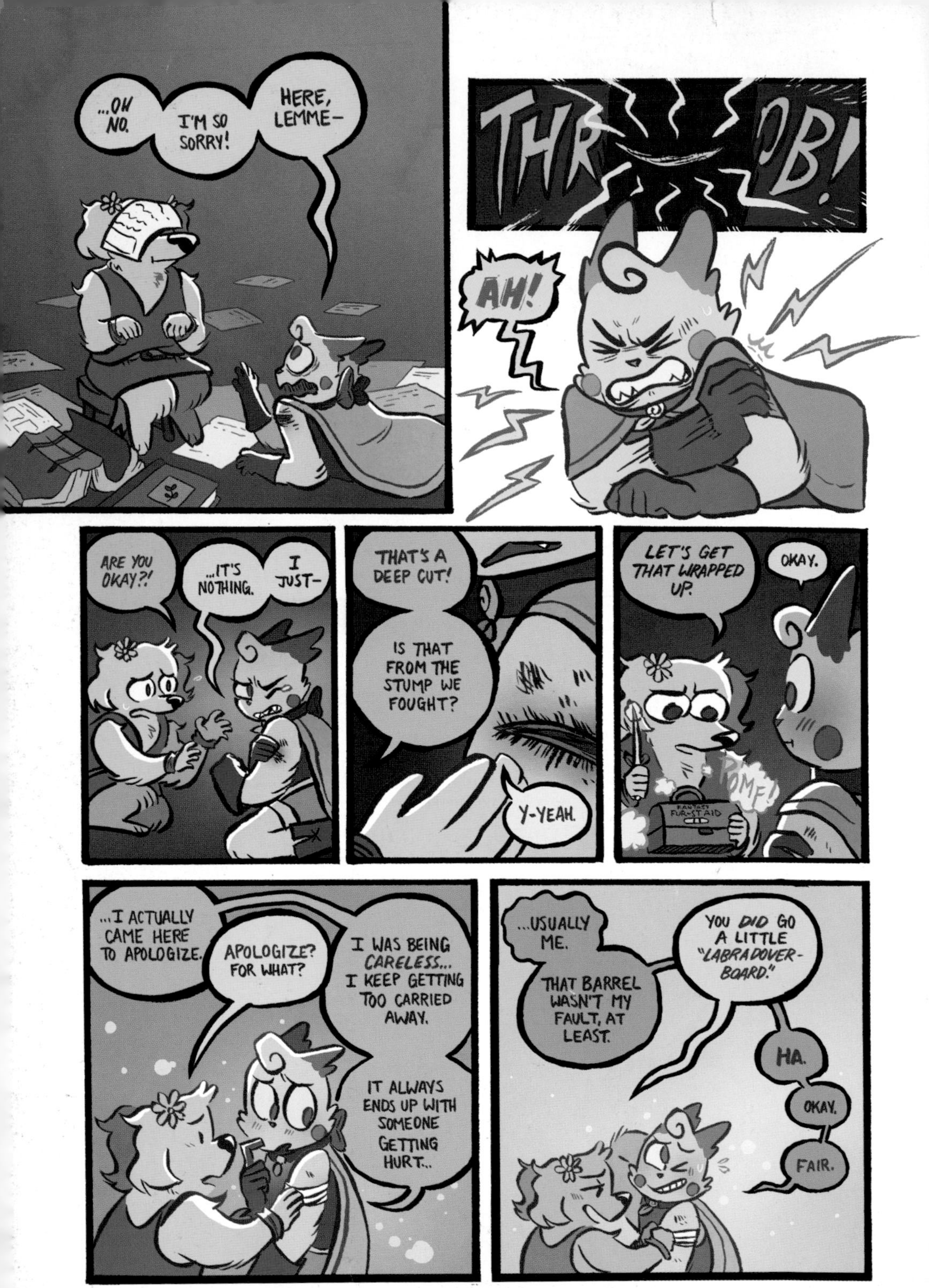
...OH NO.
I'M SO SORRY!
HERE, LEMME-
THROB!
AH!
ARE YOU OKAY?!
...IT'S NOTHING.
I JUST-
THAT'S A DEEP CUT!
IS THAT FROM THE STUMP WE FOUGHT?
Y-YEAH.
LET'S GET THAT WRAPPED UP.
OKAY.
POMF!
FANTASY FUR-ST AID
...I ACTUALLY CAME HERE TO APOLOGIZE.
APOLOGIZE? FOR WHAT?
I WAS BEING CARELESS... I KEEP GETTING TOO CARRIED AWAY.
IT ALWAYS ENDS UP WITH SOMEONE GETTING HURT...
...USUALLY ME.
THAT BARREL WASN'T MY FAULT, AT LEAST.
YOU DID GO A LITTLE "LABRADOVER-BOARD."
HA.
OKAY.
FAIR.

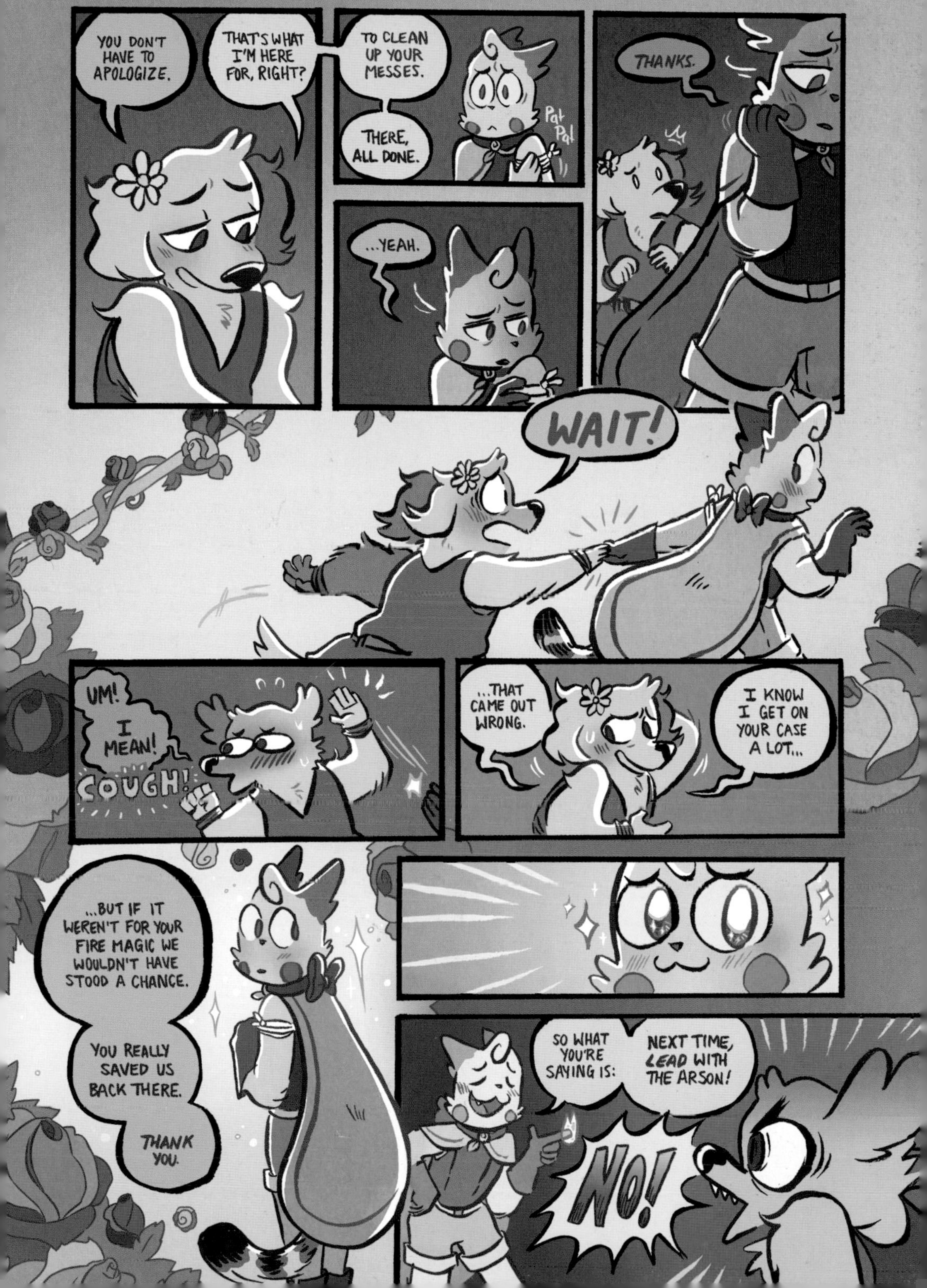
YOU DON'T HAVE TO APOLOGIZE.
THAT'S WHAT I'M HERE FOR, RIGHT?
TO CLEAN UP YOUR MESSES.
THERE, ALL DONE.
Pat Pat
...YEAH.
THANKS.
WAIT!
UM!
I MEAN!
COUGH!
...THAT CAME OUT WRONG.
I KNOW I GET ON YOUR CASE A LOT...
...BUT IF IT WEREN'T FOR YOUR FIRE MAGIC WE WOULDN'T HAVE STOOD A CHANCE.
YOU REALLY SAVED US BACK THERE.
THANK YOU.
SO WHAT YOU'RE SAYING IS:
NEXT TIME, LEAD WITH THE ARSON!
NO!

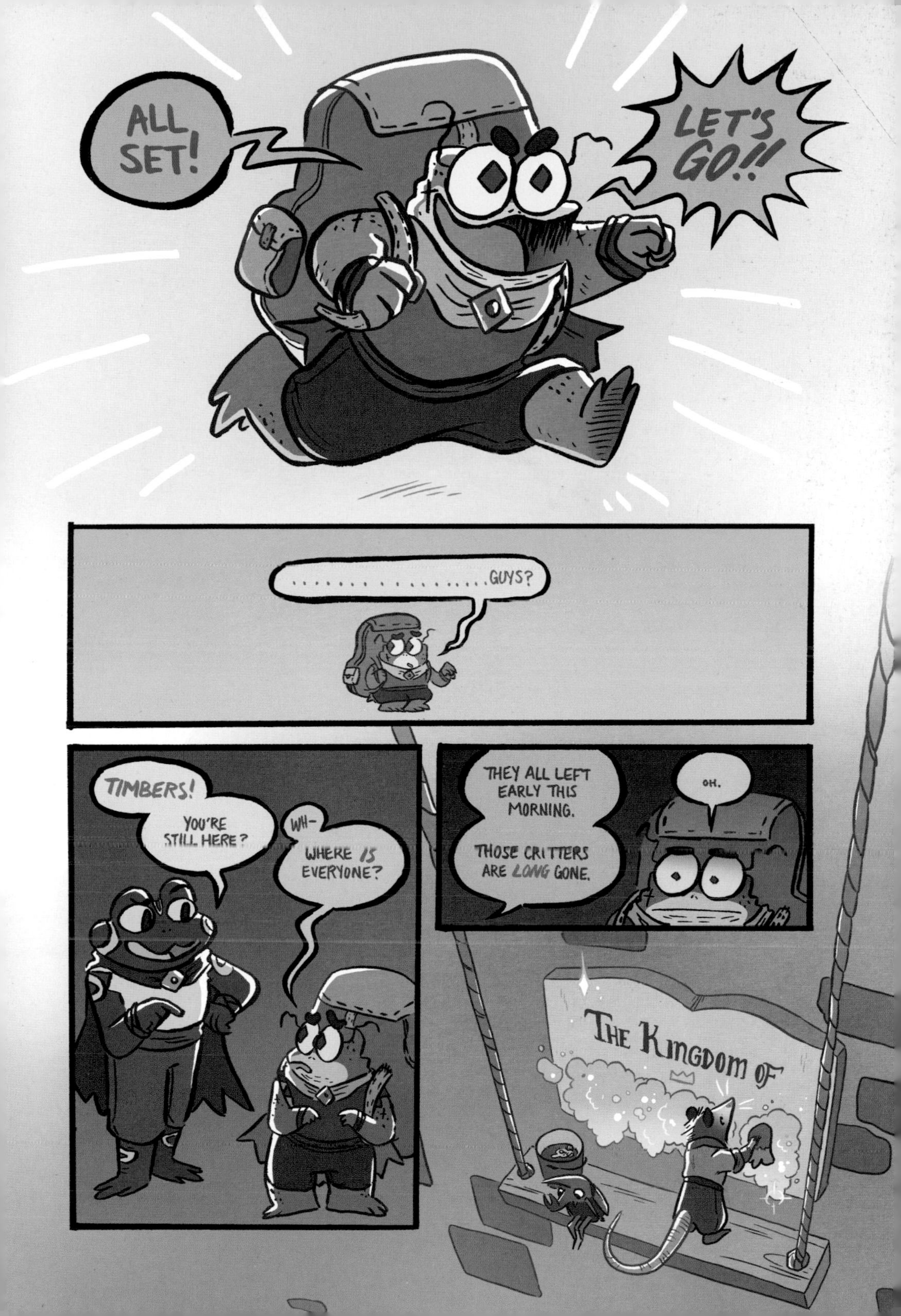
ALL SET!
LET'S GO!!
........................GUYS?
TIMBERS!
YOU'RE STILL HERE?
WH-
WHERE IS EVERYONE?
THEY ALL LEFT EARLY THIS MORNING.
THOSE CRITTERS ARE LONG GONE.
OH.
THE KINGDOM OF

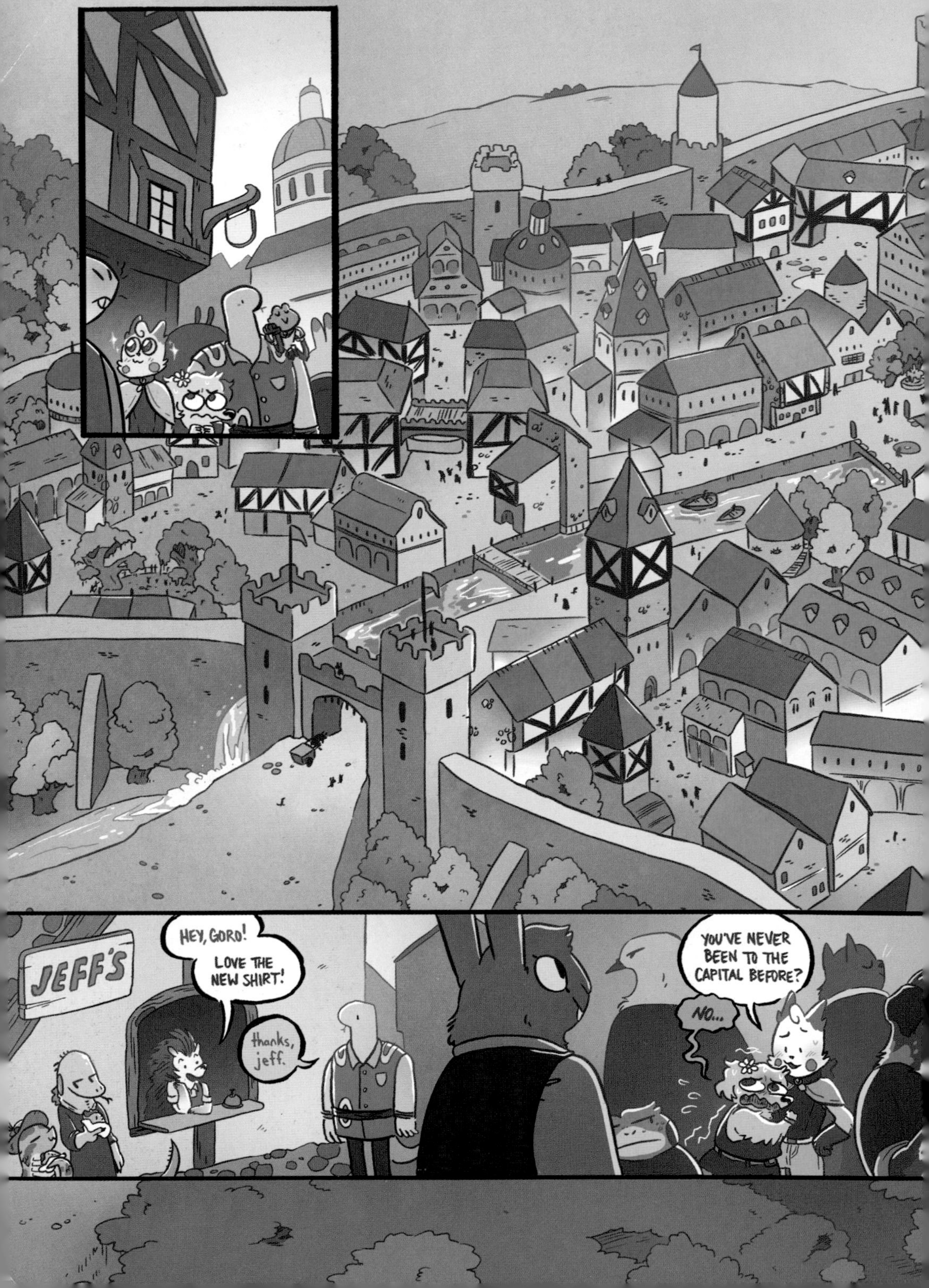
JEFF'S
HEY, GORO!
LOVE THE NEW SHIRT!
thanks, jeff.
YOU'VE NEVER BEEN TO THE CAPITAL BEFORE?
NO...

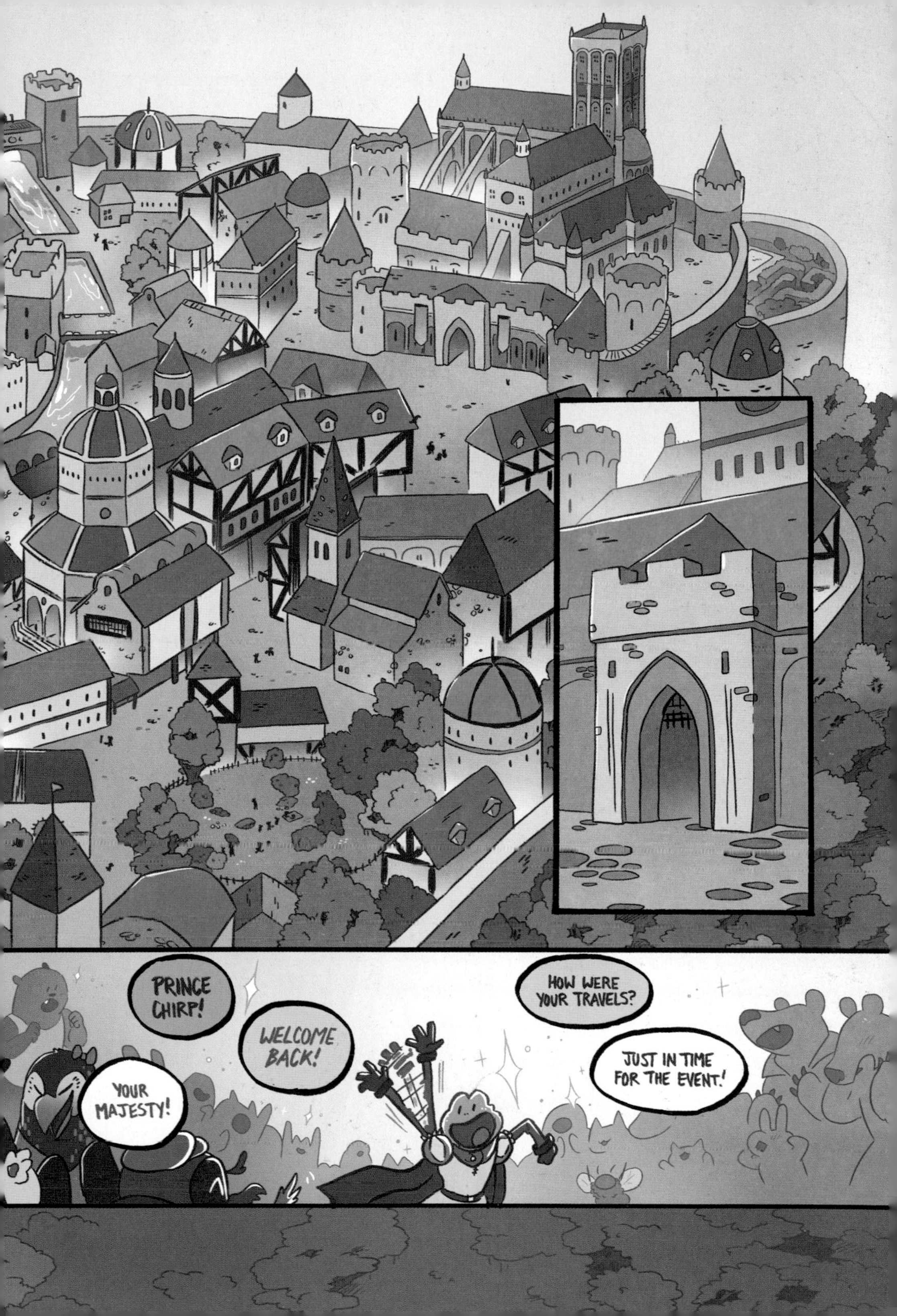
PRINCE CHIRP!
WELCOME BACK!
YOUR MAJESTY!
HOW WERE YOUR TRAVELS?
JUST IN TIME FOR THE EVENT!

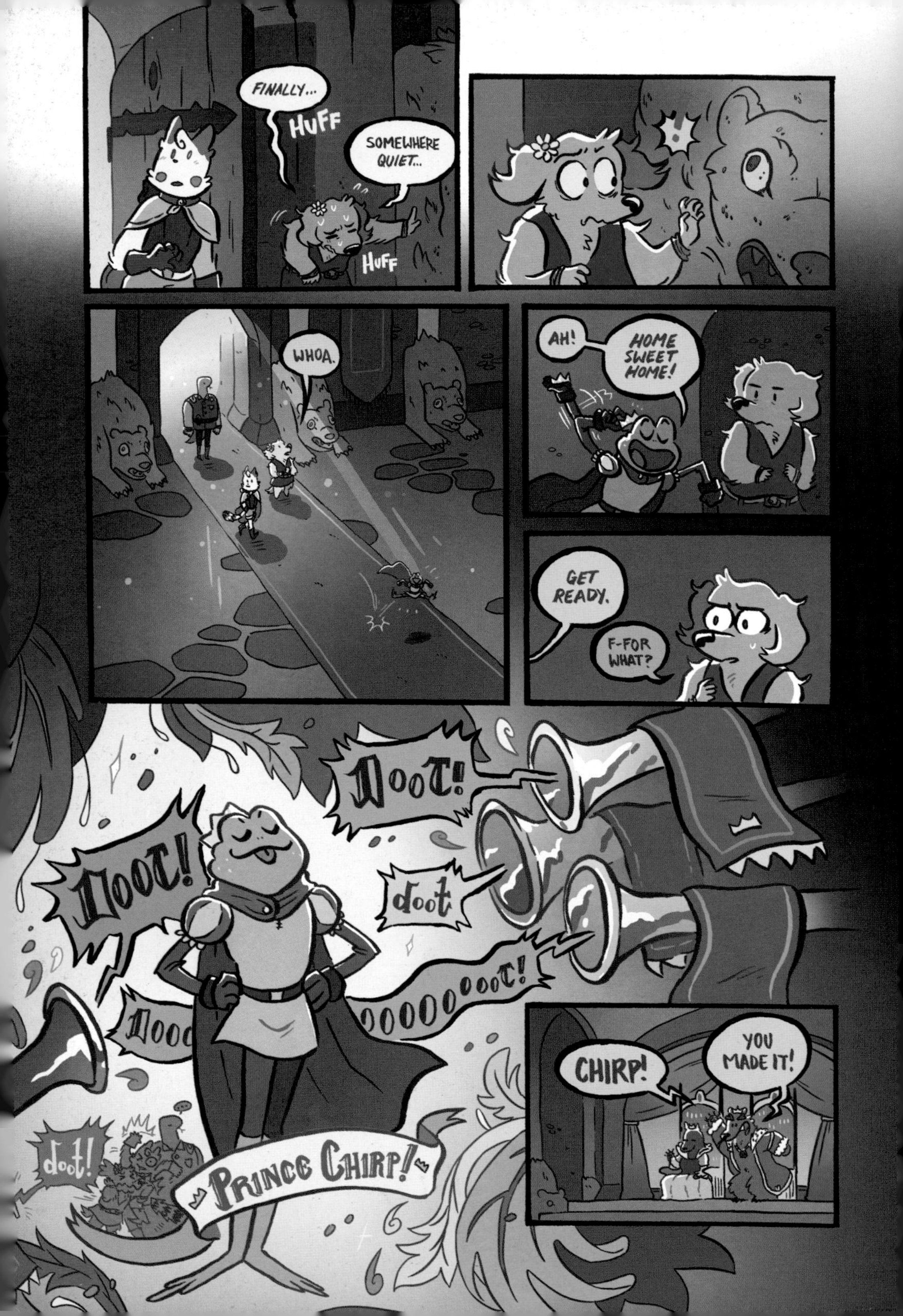

FINALLY...
HUFF
SOMEWHERE QUIET...
HUFF
!
WHOA.
AH!
HOME SWEET HOME!
GET READY.
F-FOR WHAT?
DOOT!
DOOT!
doot
DOOOOOOOOOOOOT!
doot!
PRINCE CHIRP!
CHIRP!
YOU MADE IT!

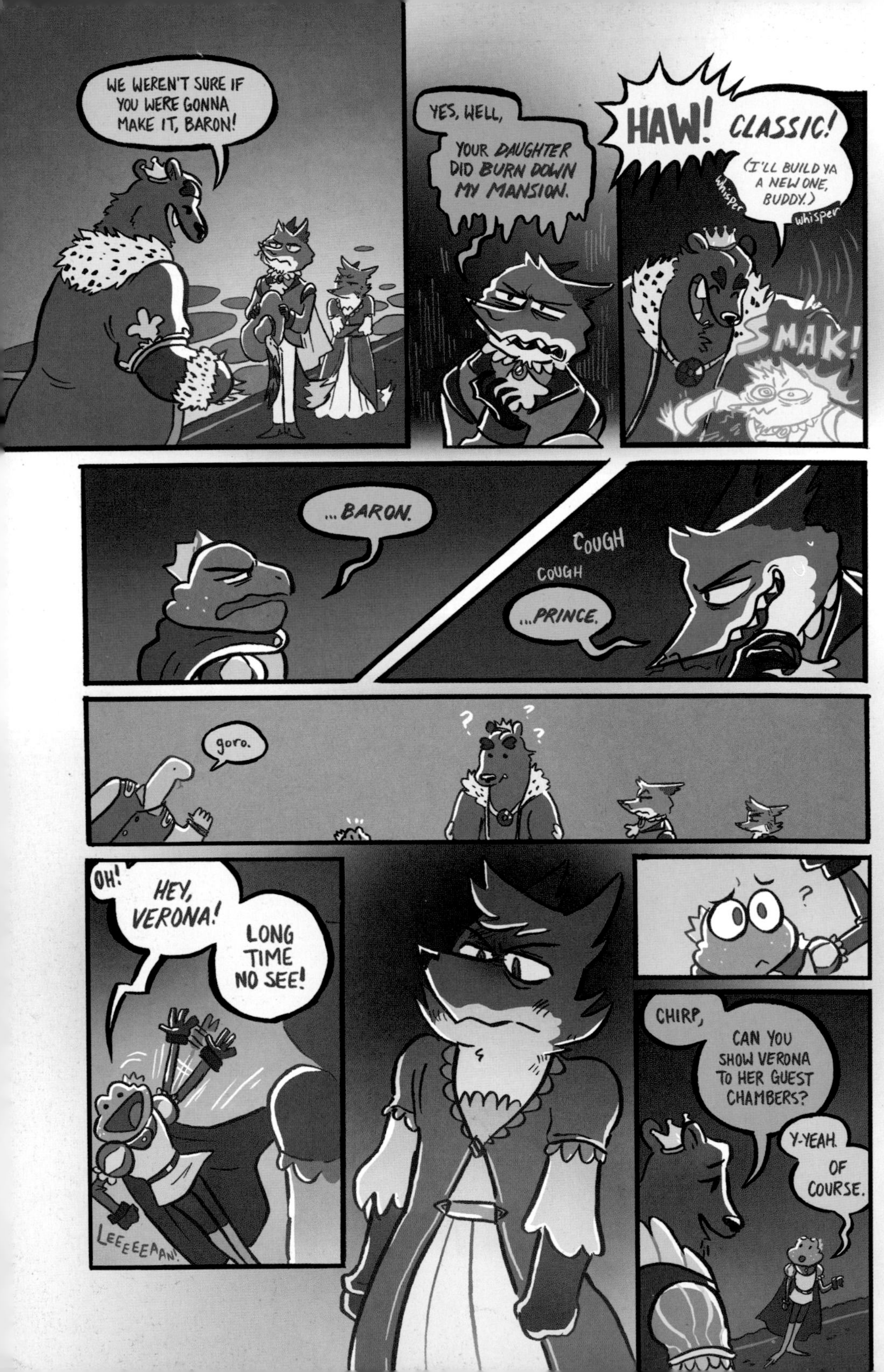
WE WEREN'T SURE IF YOU WERE GONNA MAKE IT, BARON!
YES, WELL,
YOUR DAUGHTER DID BURN DOWN MY MANSION.
HAW! CLASSIC!
(I'LL BUILD YA A NEW ONE, BUDDY.)
whisper
whisper
SMAK!
...BARON.
COUGH
COUGH
...PRINCE.
goro.
?
?
?
OH!
HEY, VERONA!
LONG TIME NO SEE!
LEEEEEAAN!
?
CHIRP,
CAN YOU SHOW VERONA TO HER GUEST CHAMBERS?
Y-YEAH.
OF COURSE.

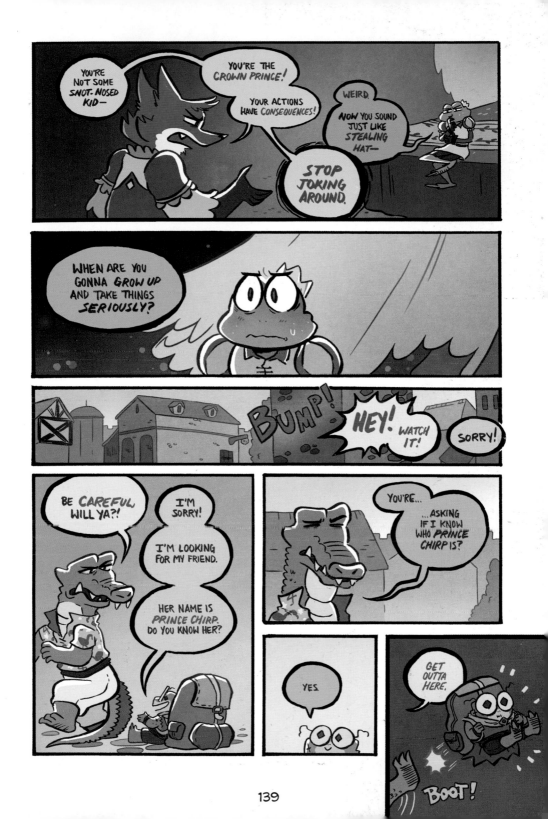

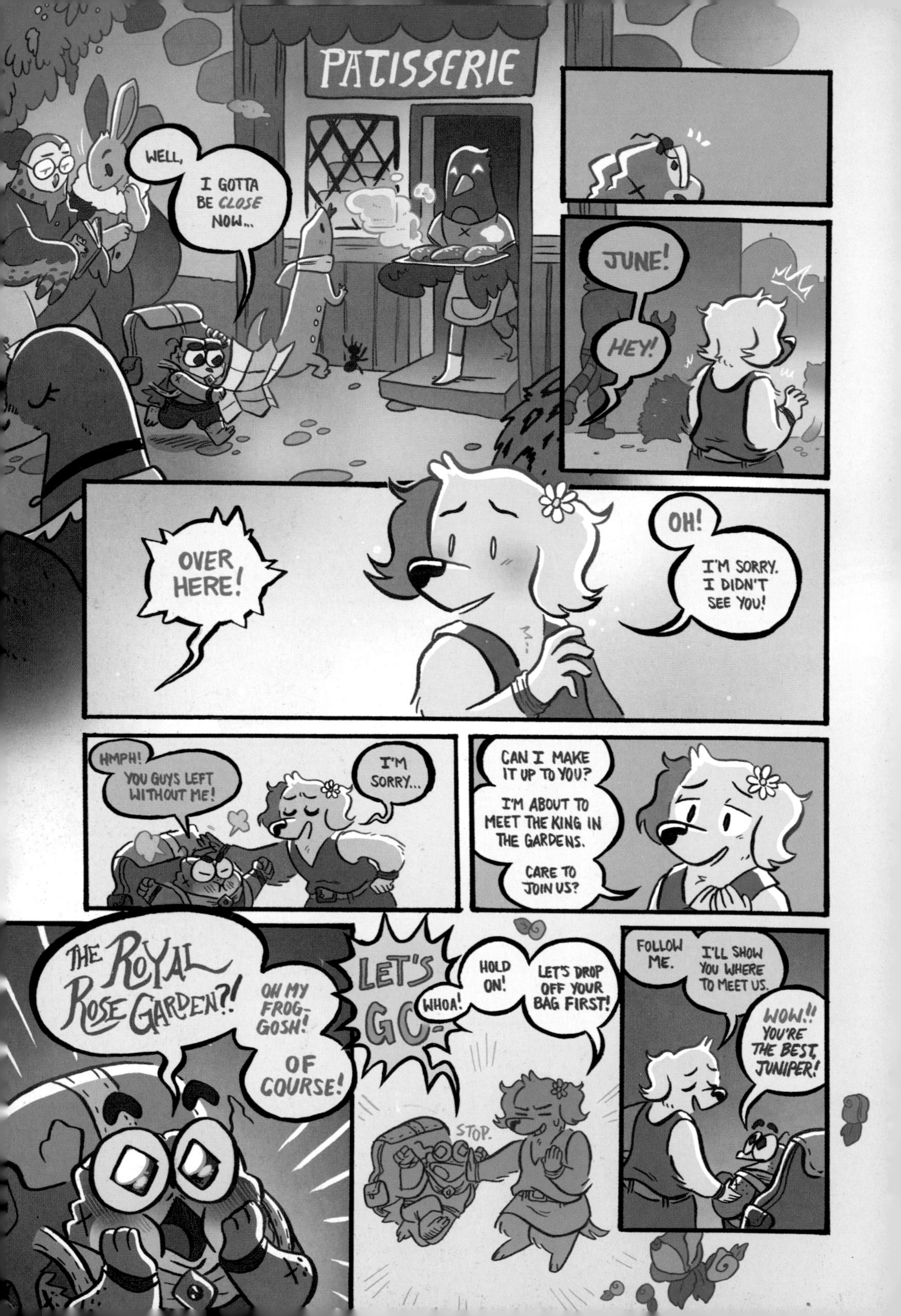
PATISSERIE
WELL,
I GOTTA BE CLOSE NOW...
JUNE!
HEY!
OVER HERE!
OH!
I'M SORRY. I DIDN'T SEE YOU!
HMPH! YOU GUYS LEFT WITHOUT ME!
I'M SORRY...
CAN I MAKE IT UP TO YOU?
I'M ABOUT TO MEET THE KING IN THE GARDENS.
CARE TO JOIN US?
THE ROYAL ROSE GARDEN?!
OH MY FROG-GOSH!
OF COURSE!
LET'S GO-
WHOA!
HOLD ON!
LET'S DROP OFF YOUR BAG FIRST!
STOP.
FOLLOW ME.
I'LL SHOW YOU WHERE TO MEET US.
WOW!! YOU'RE THE BEST, JUNIPER!

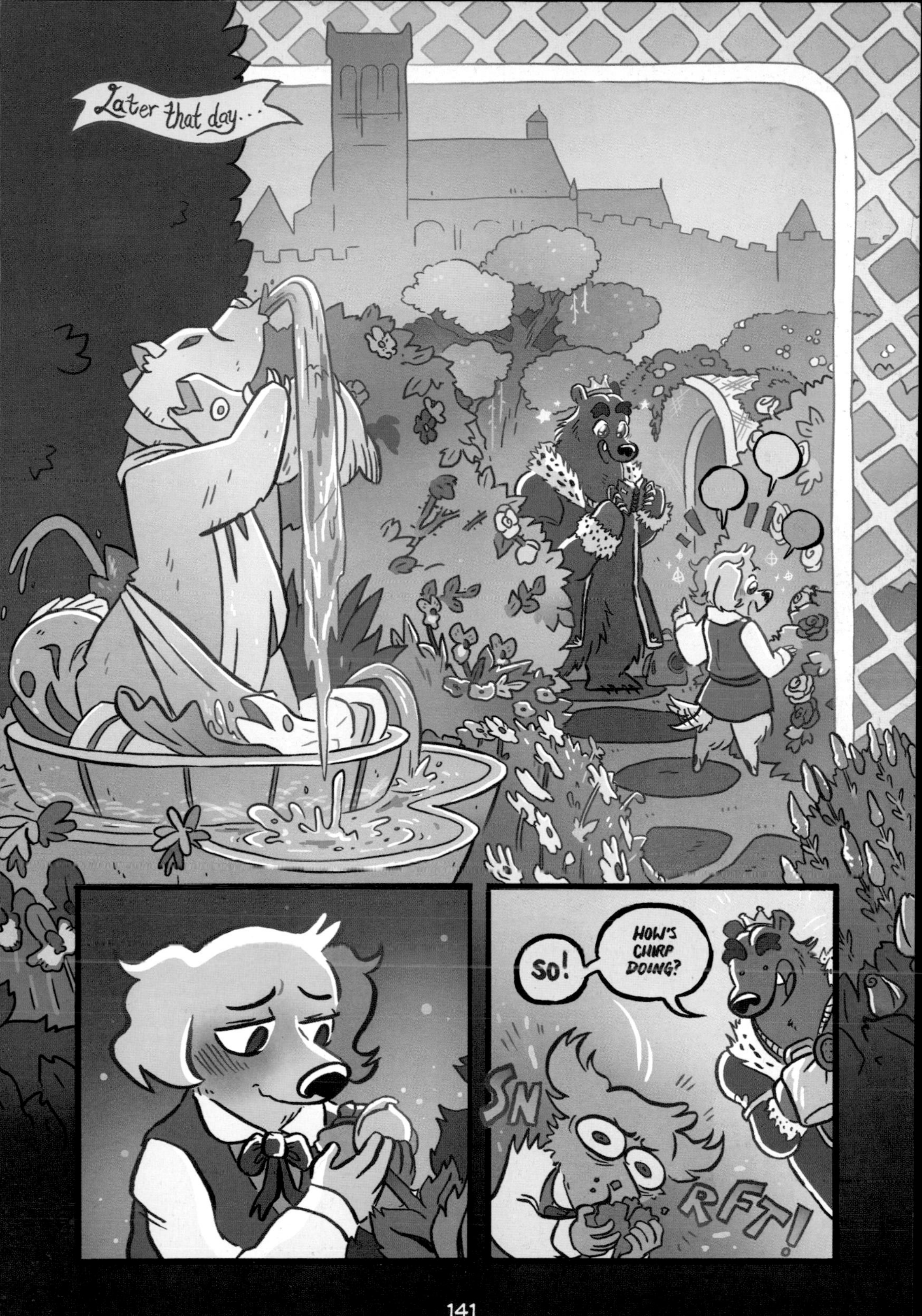
Later that day...
SO!
HOW'S CHIRP DOING?
SNORFT!

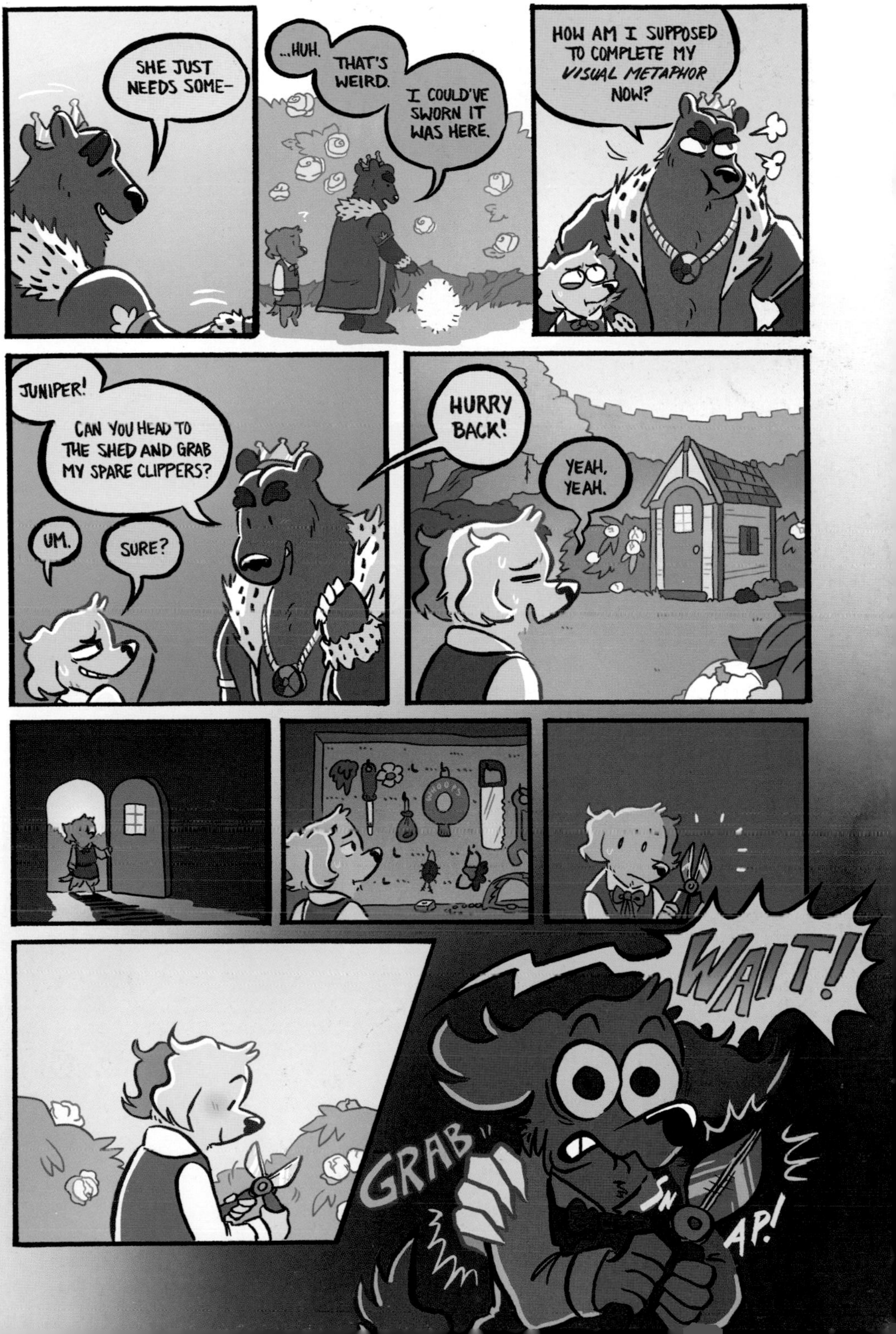

SHE JUST NEEDS SOME–
...HUH.
THAT'S WEIRD.
I COULD'VE SWORN IT WAS HERE.
HOW AM I SUPPOSED TO COMPLETE MY *VISUAL METAPHOR* NOW?
JUNIPER!
CAN YOU HEAD TO THE SHED AND GRAB MY SPARE CLIPPERS?
UM.
SURE?
HURRY BACK!
YEAH, YEAH.
WAIT!
GRAB
SNAP!

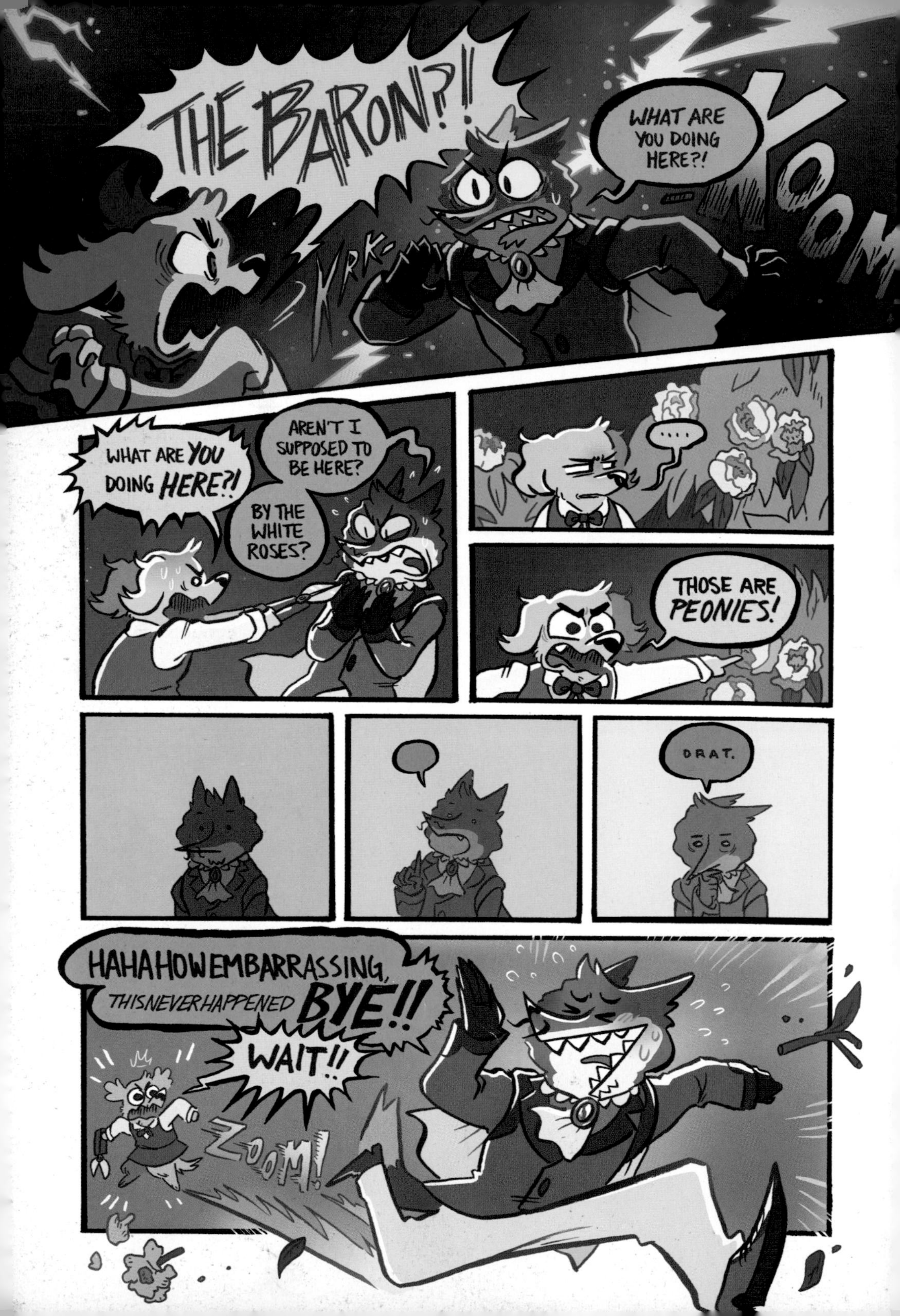
THE BARON?!!
WHAT ARE YOU DOING HERE?!
KRK-
WHAT ARE YOU DOING HERE?!
AREN'T I SUPPOSED TO BE HERE?
BY THE WHITE ROSES?
....
THOSE ARE PEONIES!
DRAT.
HAHAHOWEMBARRASSING, THISNEVERHAPPENED BYE!!
WAIT!!
ZOOM!

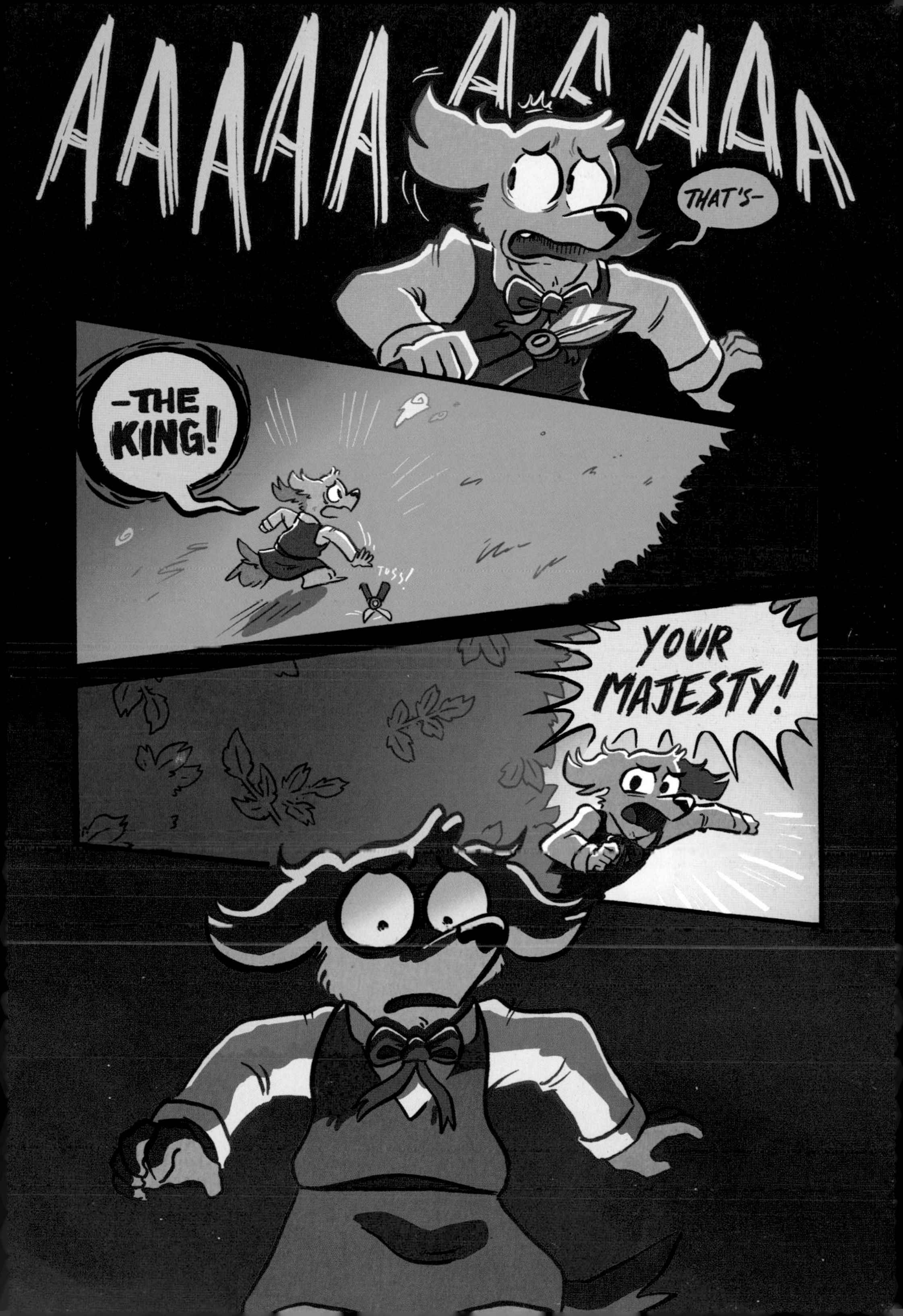
AAAAAAAAAAA
THAT'S–
–THE KING!
TOSS!
YOUR MAJESTY!

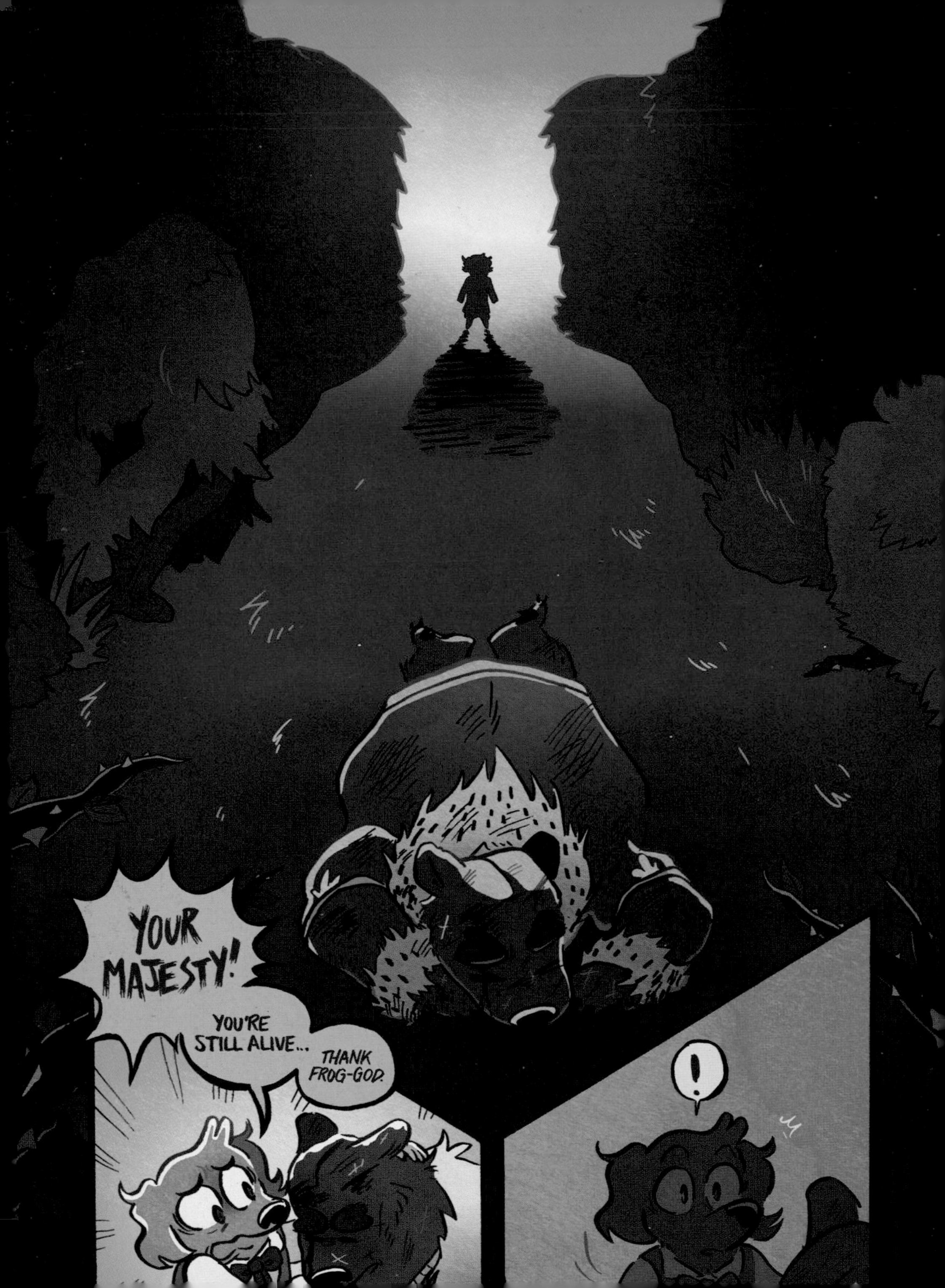
YOUR MAJESTY!
YOU'RE STILL ALIVE...
THANK FROG-GOD.
!

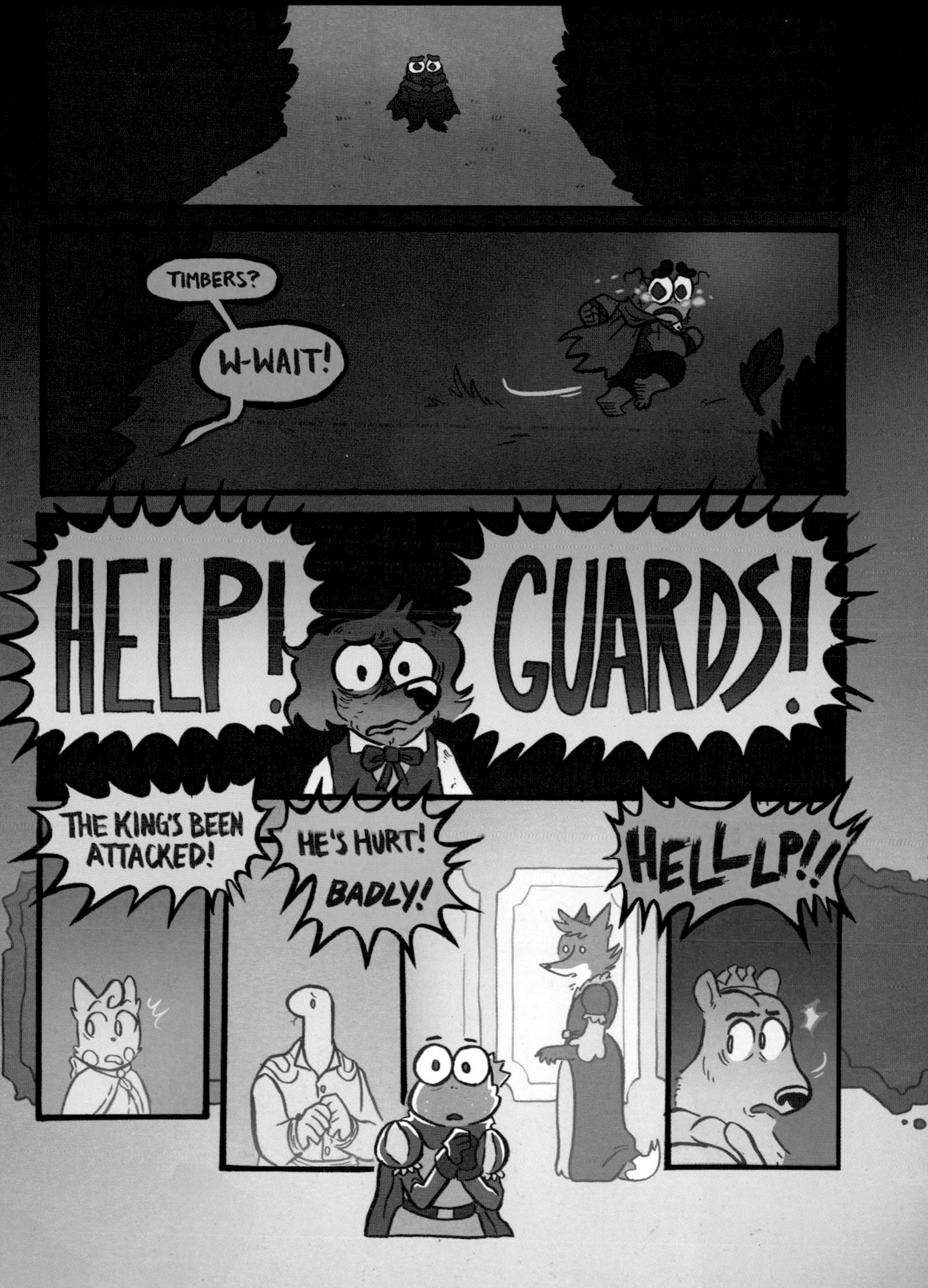
TIMBERS?
W-WAIT!
HELP! GUARDS!
THE KING'S BEEN ATTACKED!
HE'S HURT!
BADLY!
HELLLP!!

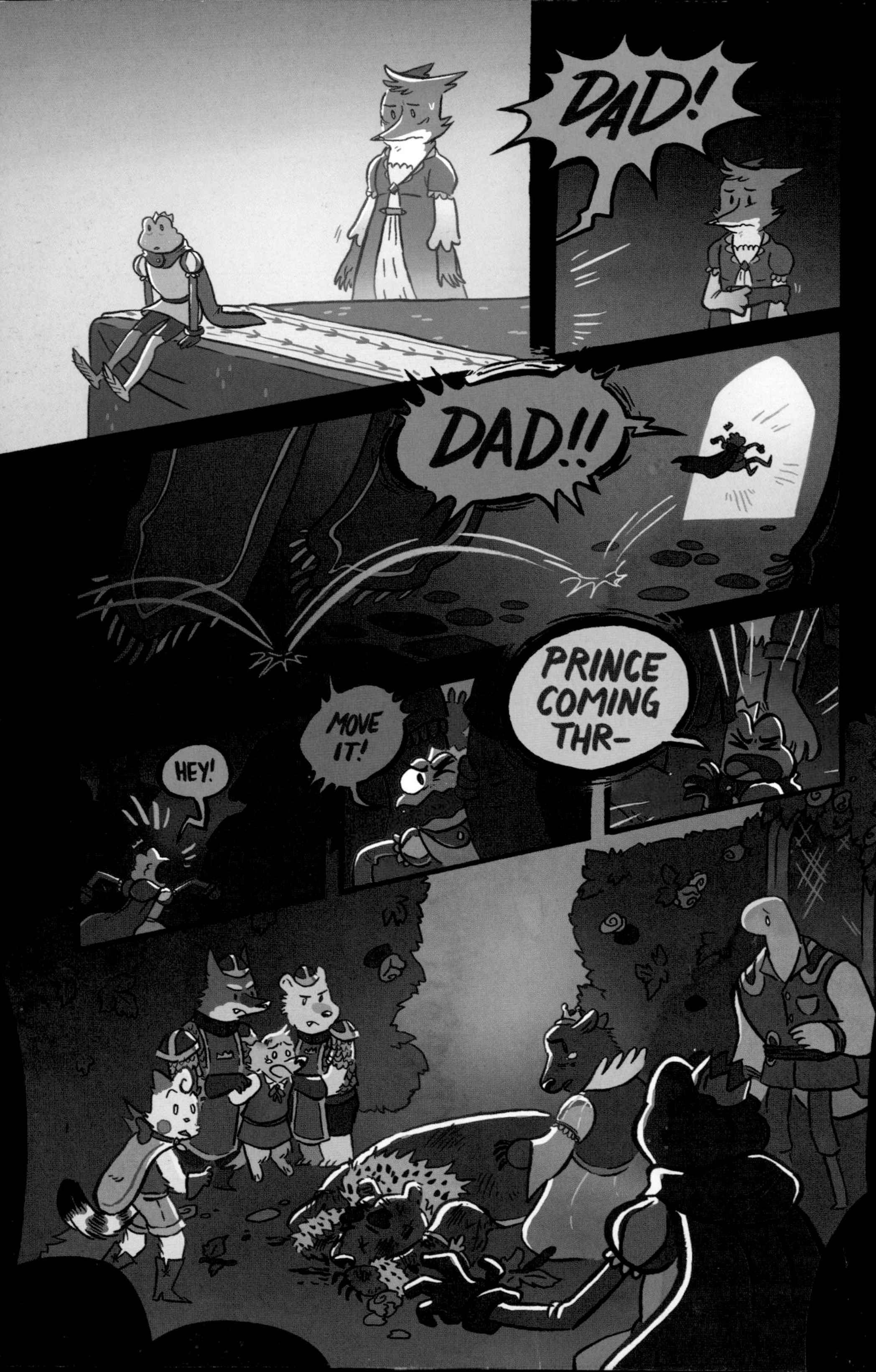
DAD!
DAD!!
HEY!
MOVE IT!
PRINCE COMING THR-

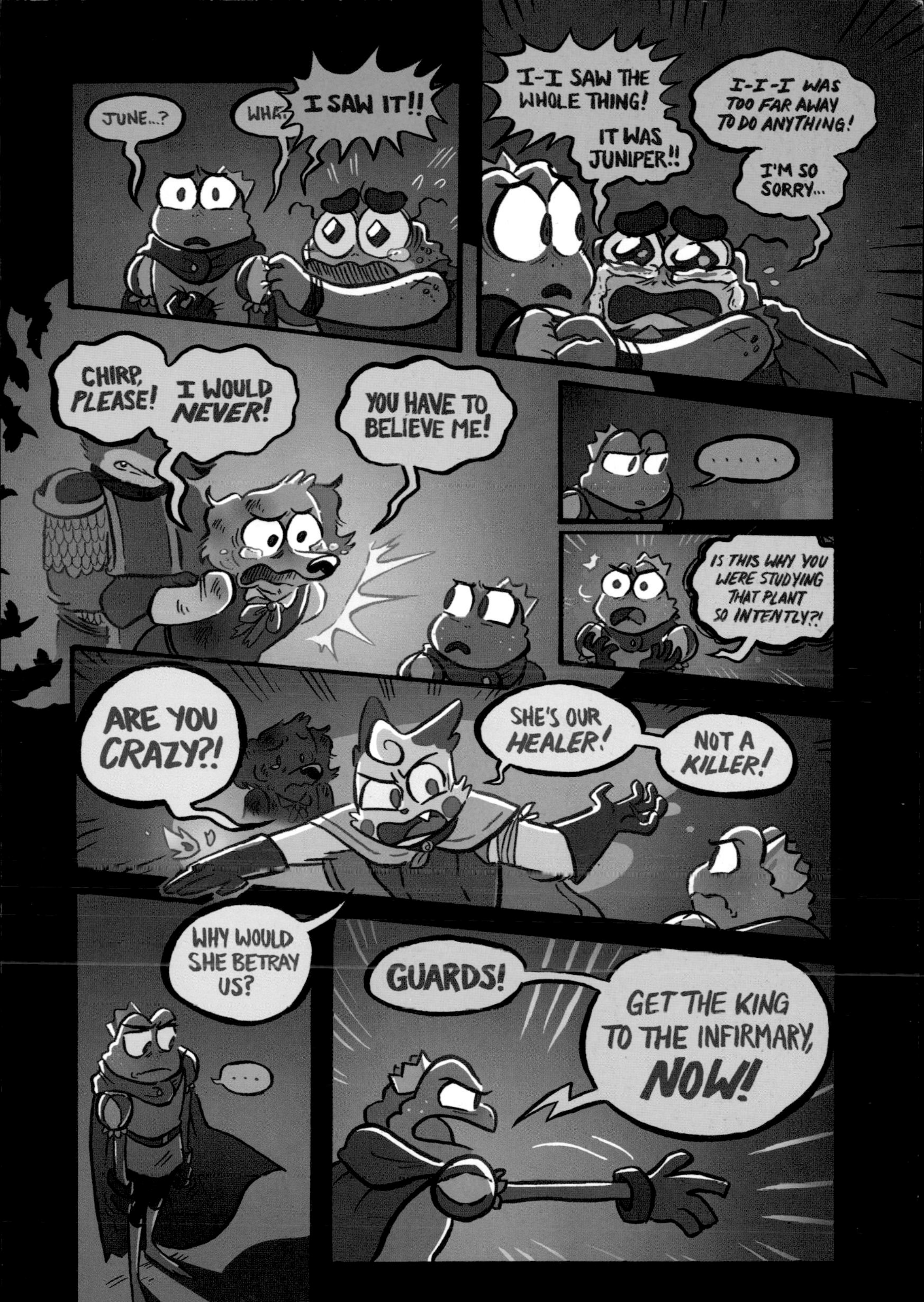
JUNE...?
WHA-
I SAW IT!!
I-I SAW THE WHOLE THING!
IT WAS JUNIPER!!
I-I-I WAS TOO FAR AWAY TO DO ANYTHING!
I'M SO SORRY...
CHIRP, PLEASE!
I WOULD NEVER!
YOU HAVE TO BELIEVE ME!
......
IS THIS WHY YOU WERE STUDYING THAT PLANT SO INTENTLY?!
ARE YOU CRAZY?!
SHE'S OUR HEALER!
NOT A KILLER!
WHY WOULD SHE BETRAY US?
...
GUARDS!
GET THE KING TO THE INFIRMARY, NOW!

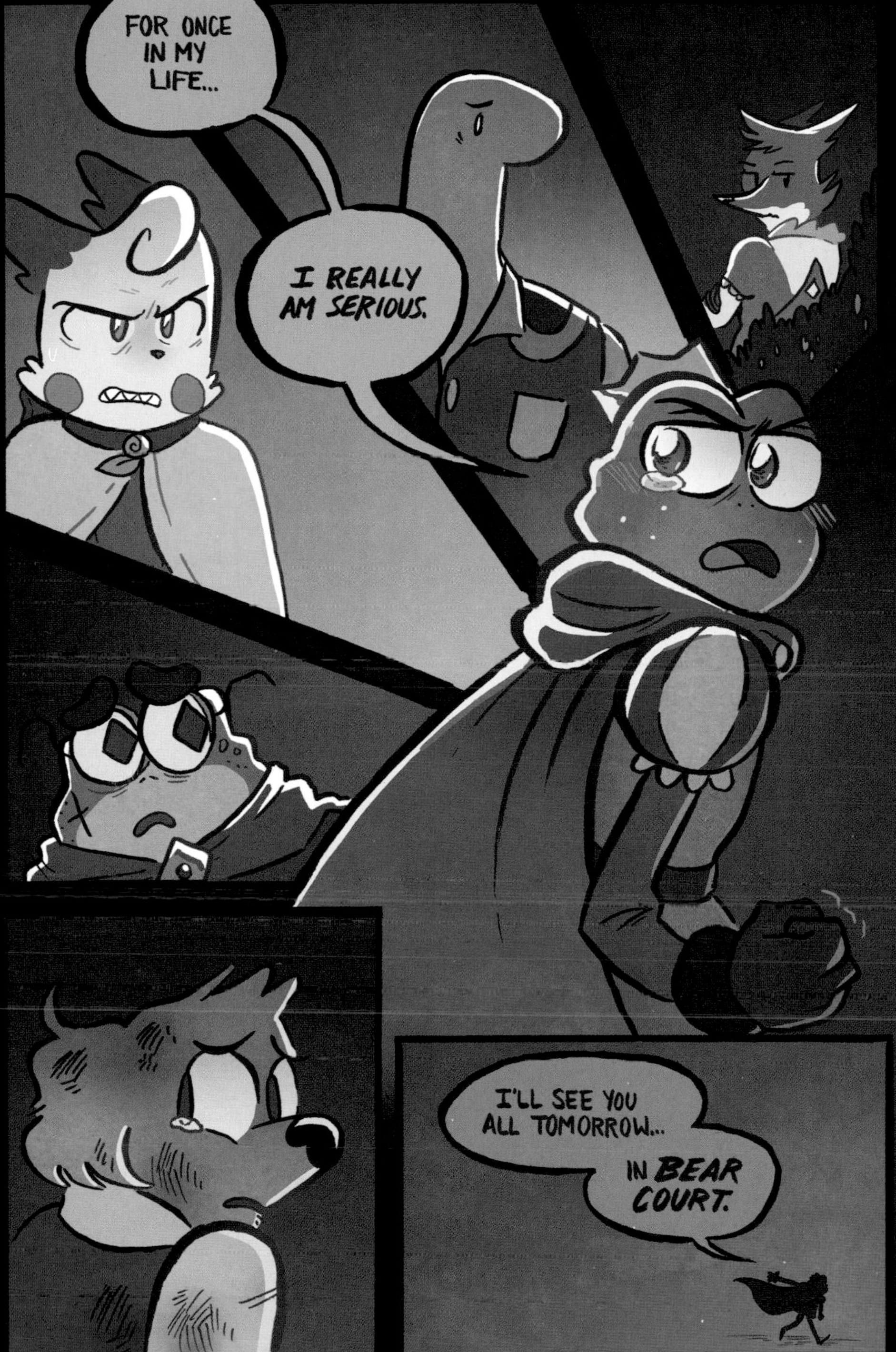
FOR ONCE IN MY LIFE...
I REALLY AM SERIOUS.
I'LL SEE YOU ALL TOMORROW...
IN BEAR COURT.

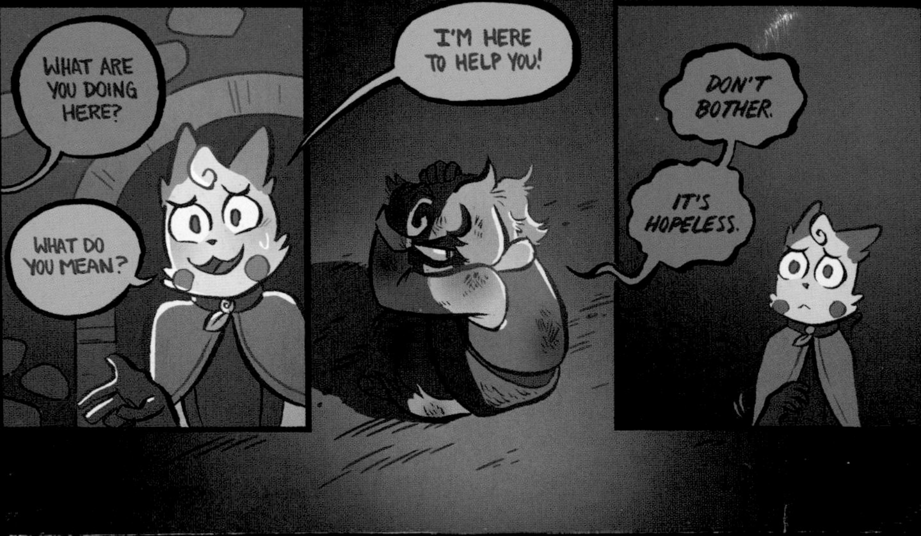
WHAT ARE YOU DOING HERE?
I'M HERE TO HELP YOU!
WHAT DO YOU MEAN?
DON'T BOTHER.
IT'S HOPELESS.

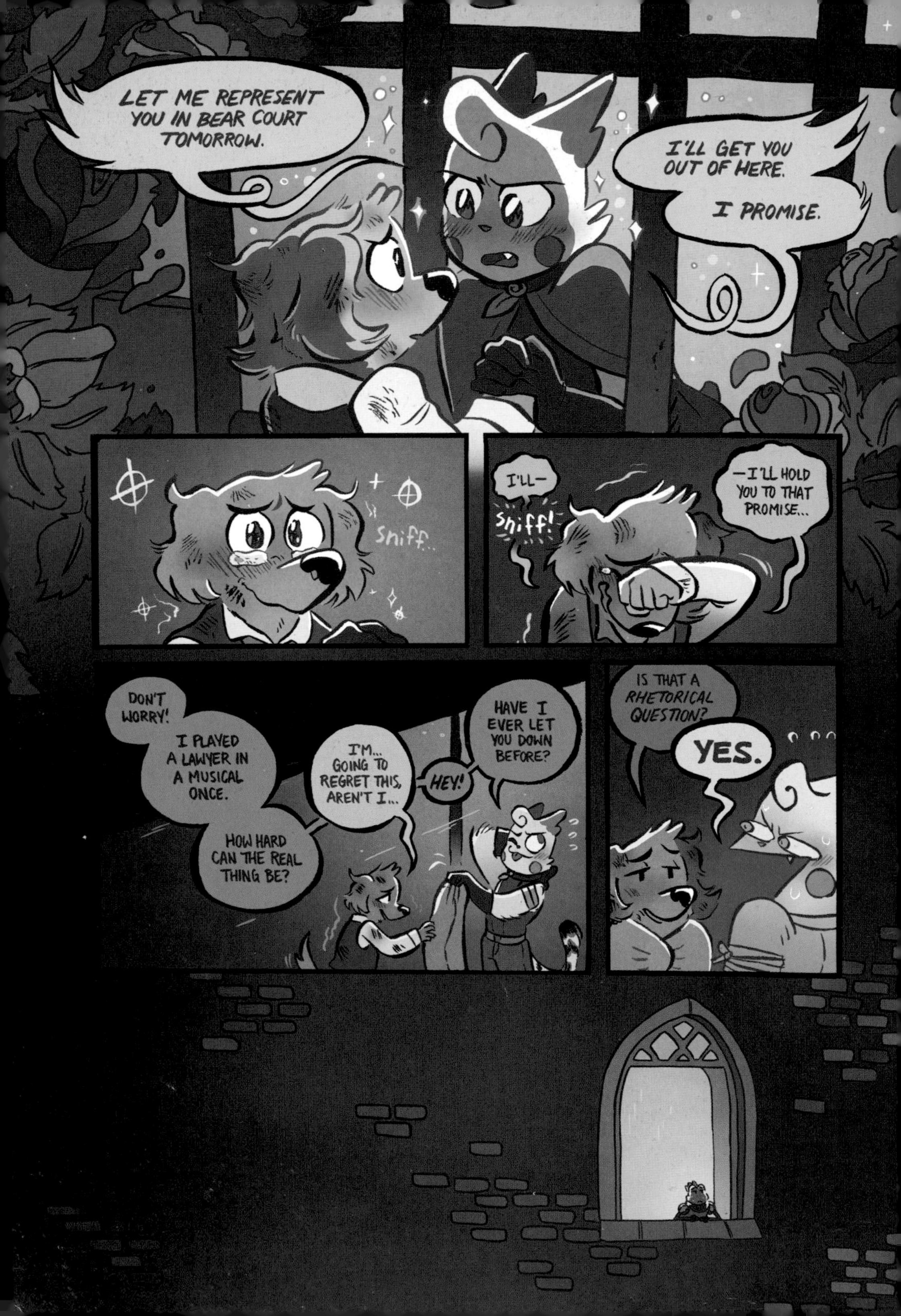
LET ME REPRESENT YOU IN BEAR COURT TOMORROW.
I'LL GET YOU OUT OF HERE.
I PROMISE.
sniff...
I'LL—
sniff!
—I'LL HOLD YOU TO THAT PROMISE...
DON'T WORRY!
I PLAYED A LAWYER IN A MUSICAL ONCE.
HOW HARD CAN THE REAL THING BE?
I'M... GOING TO REGRET THIS, AREN'T I...
HEY!
HAVE I EVER LET YOU DOWN BEFORE?
IS THAT A RHETORICAL QUESTION?
YES.

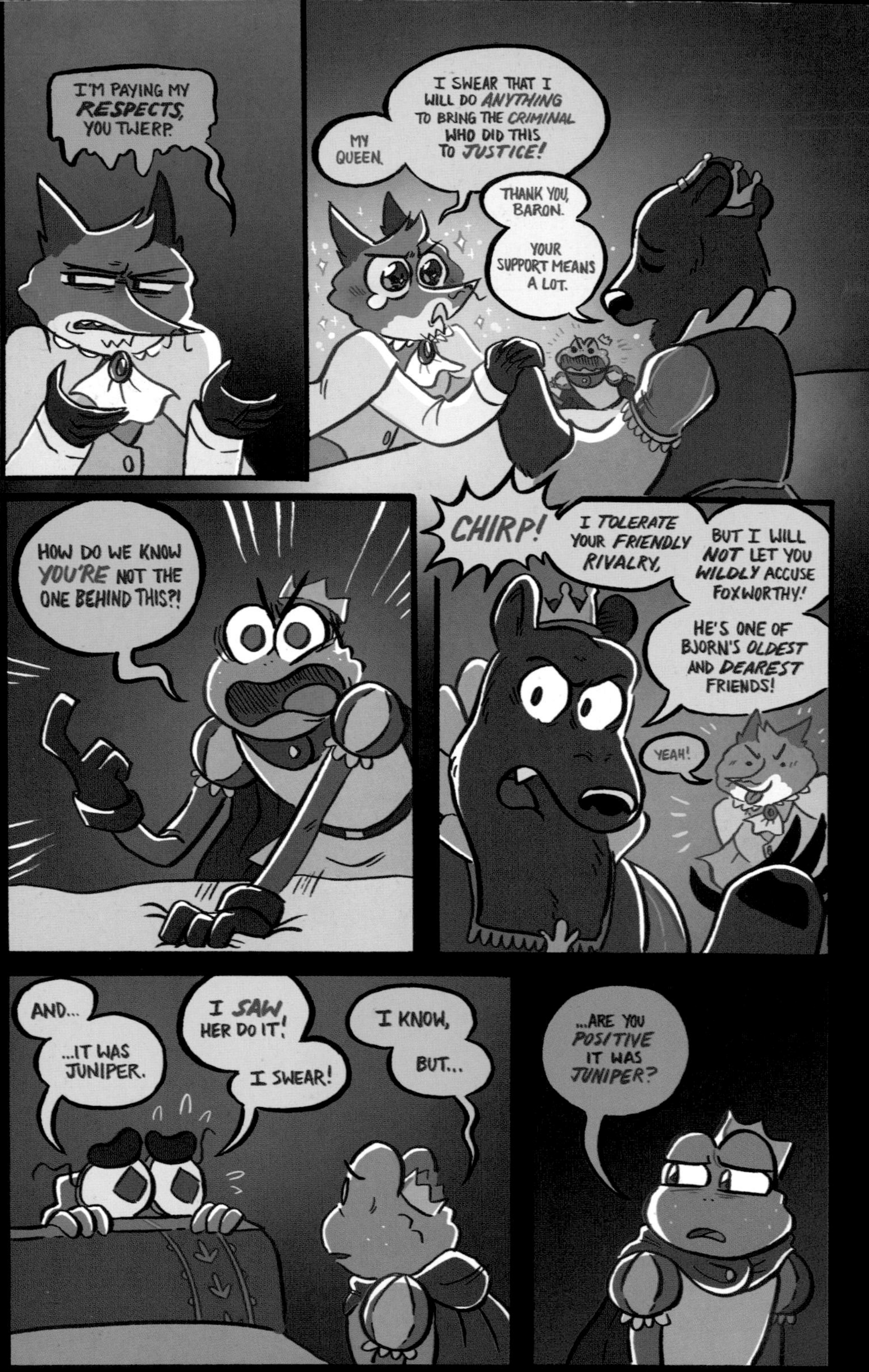
I'M PAYING MY RESPECTS, YOU TWERP.
MY QUEEN.
I SWEAR THAT I WILL DO ANYTHING TO BRING THE CRIMINAL WHO DID THIS TO JUSTICE!
THANK YOU, BARON.
YOUR SUPPORT MEANS A LOT.
HOW DO WE KNOW YOU'RE NOT THE ONE BEHIND THIS?!
CHIRP!
I TOLERATE YOUR FRIENDLY RIVALRY,
BUT I WILL NOT LET YOU WILDLY ACCUSE FOXWORTHY!
HE'S ONE OF BJORN'S OLDEST AND DEAREST FRIENDS!
YEAH!
AND...
...IT WAS JUNIPER.
I SAW HER DO IT!
I SWEAR!
I KNOW,
BUT...
...ARE YOU POSITIVE IT WAS JUNIPER?

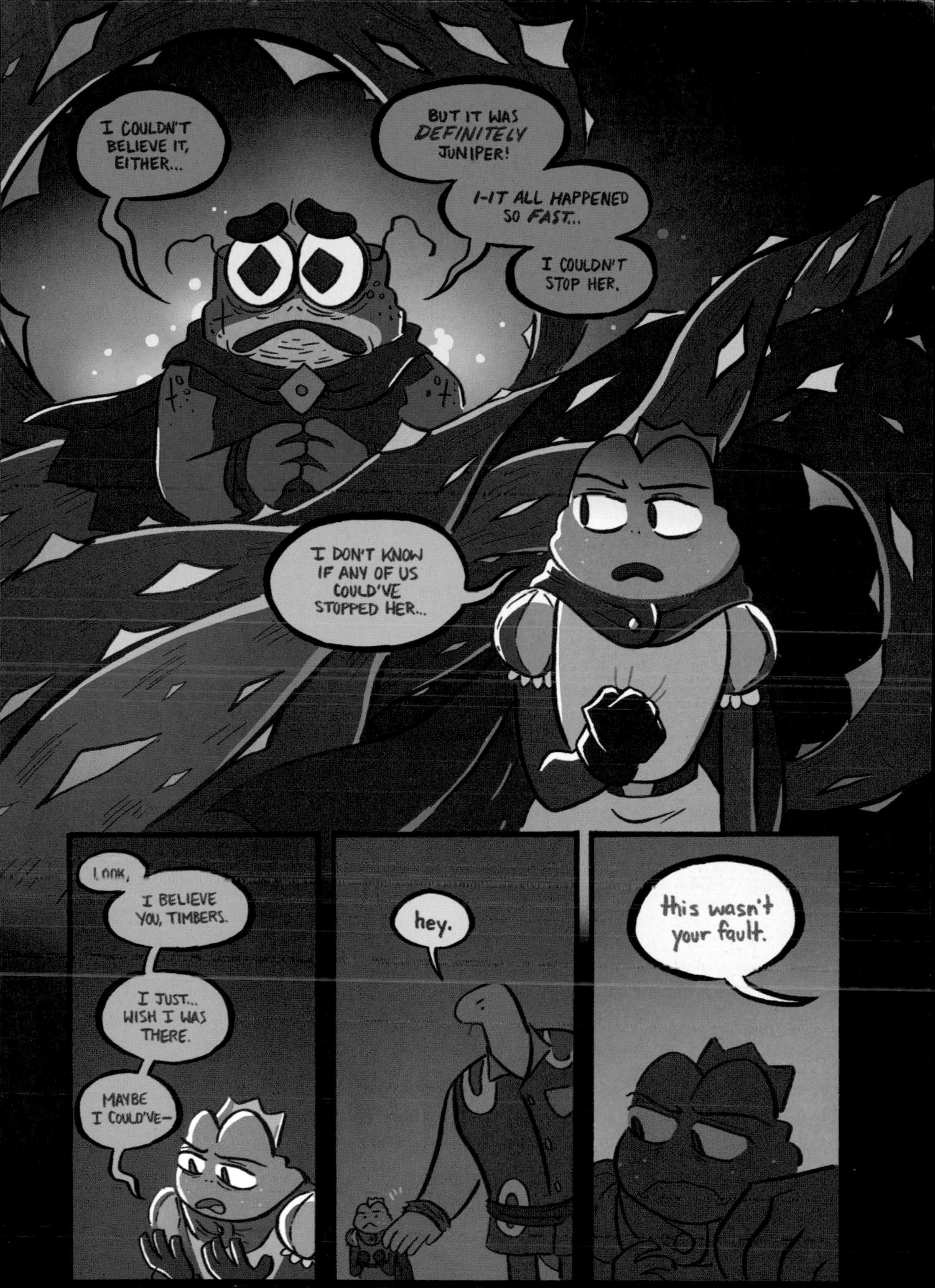

I COULDN'T BELIEVE IT, EITHER...
BUT IT WAS DEFINITELY JUNIPER!
I-IT ALL HAPPENED SO FAST...
I COULDN'T STOP HER.
I DON'T KNOW IF ANY OF US COULD'VE STOPPED HER...
LOOK,
I BELIEVE YOU, TIMBERS.
I JUST... WISH I WAS THERE.
MAYBE I COULD'VE—
hey.
this wasn't your fault.

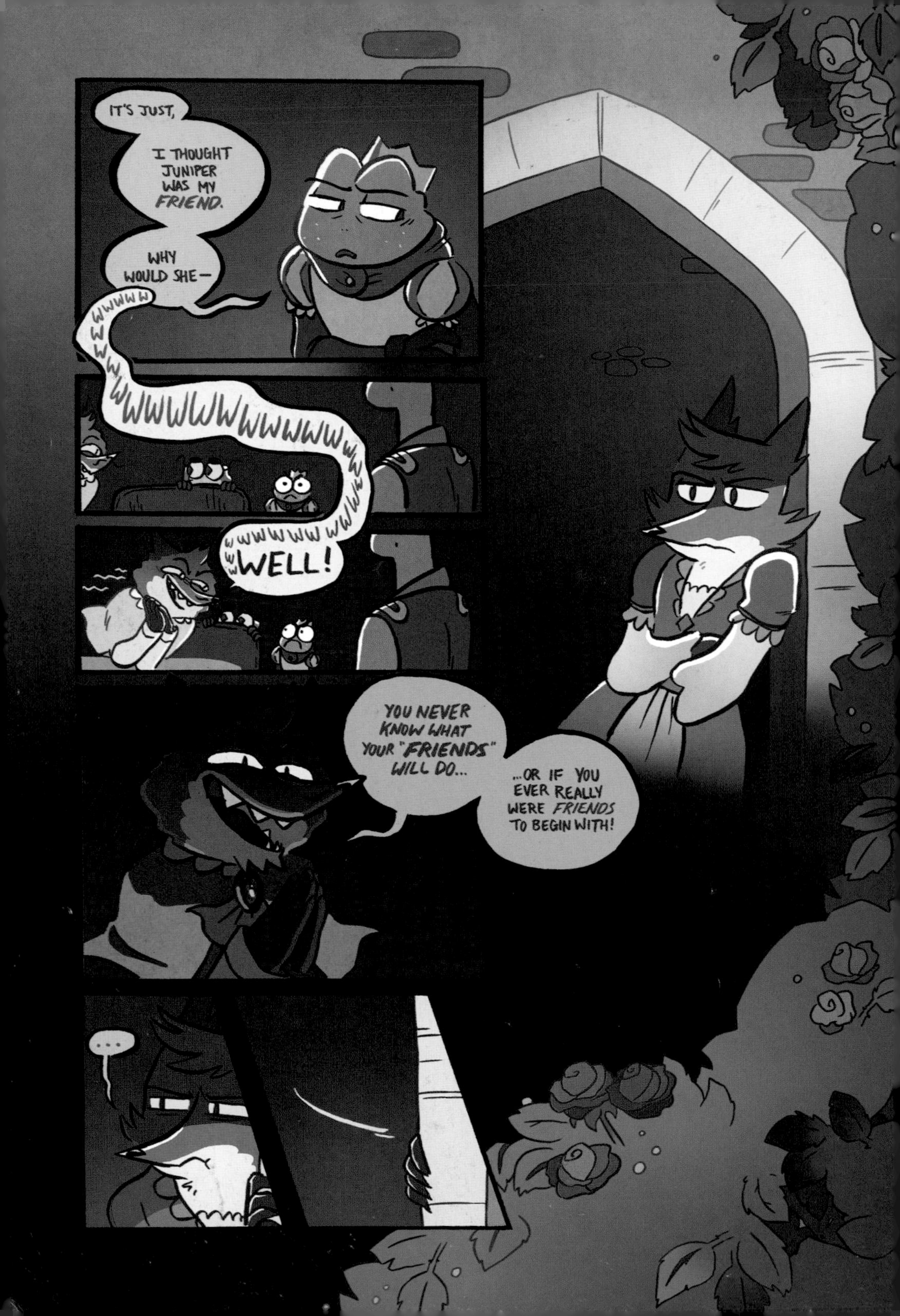

IT'S JUST,
I THOUGHT JUNIPER WAS MY FRIEND.
WHY WOULD SHE—
WWWWWWWWWWWWWWWWWWWWWWWWWWWWWWWWWWWWWWWWWWELL!
YOU NEVER KNOW WHAT YOUR "FRIENDS" WILL DO...
...OR IF YOU EVER REALLY WERE FRIENDS TO BEGIN WITH!
...

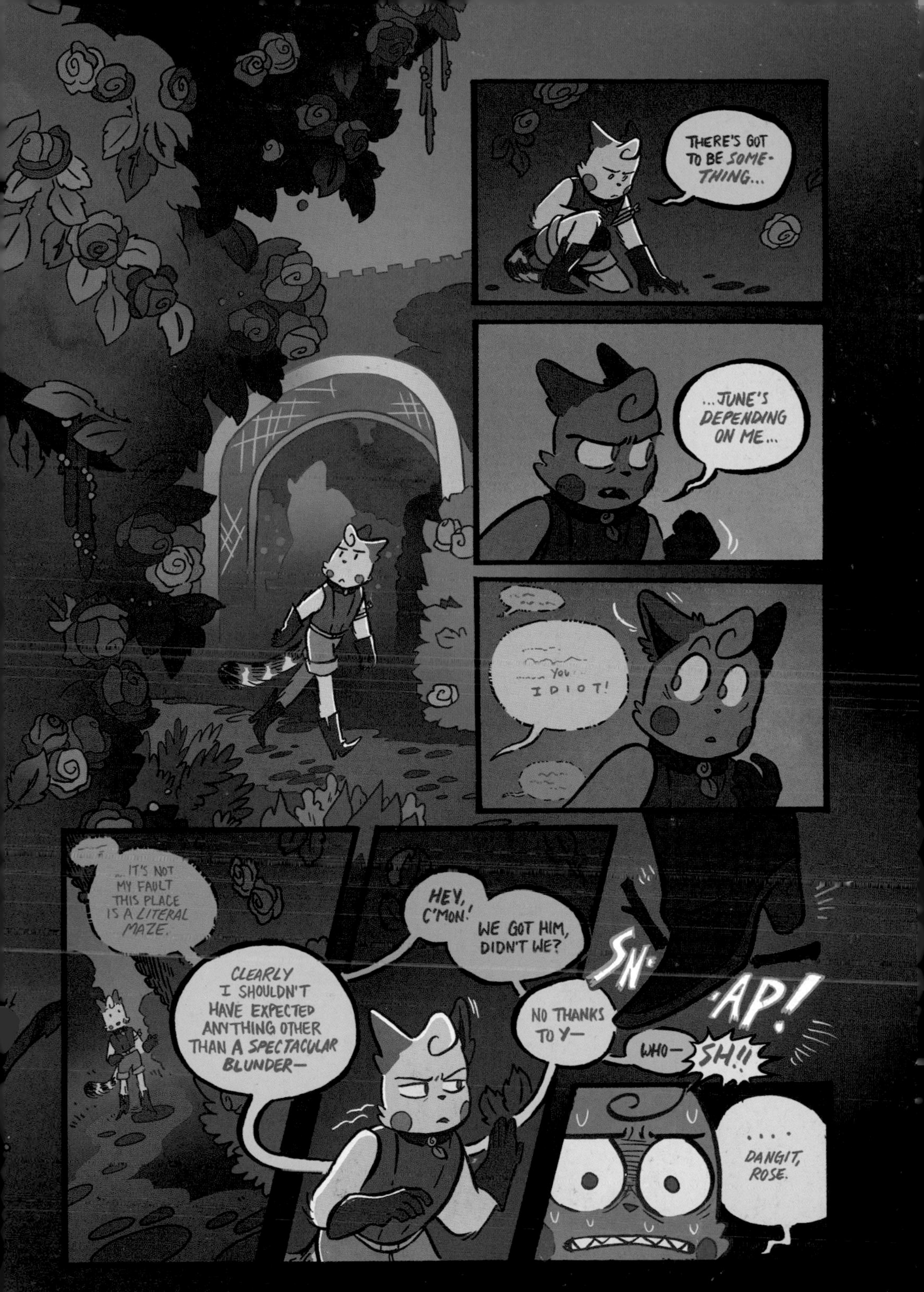
THERE'S GOT TO BE SOME-THING...
...JUNE'S DEPENDING ON ME...
YOU IDIOT!
...IT'S NOT MY FAULT THIS PLACE IS A LITERAL MAZE.
HEY, C'MON!
WE GOT HIM, DIDN'T WE?
CLEARLY I SHOULDN'T HAVE EXPECTED ANYTHING OTHER THAN A SPECTACULAR BLUNDER—
NO THANKS TO Y—
SN-
-AP!
WHO—
SH!!
. . . .
DANGIT, ROSE.

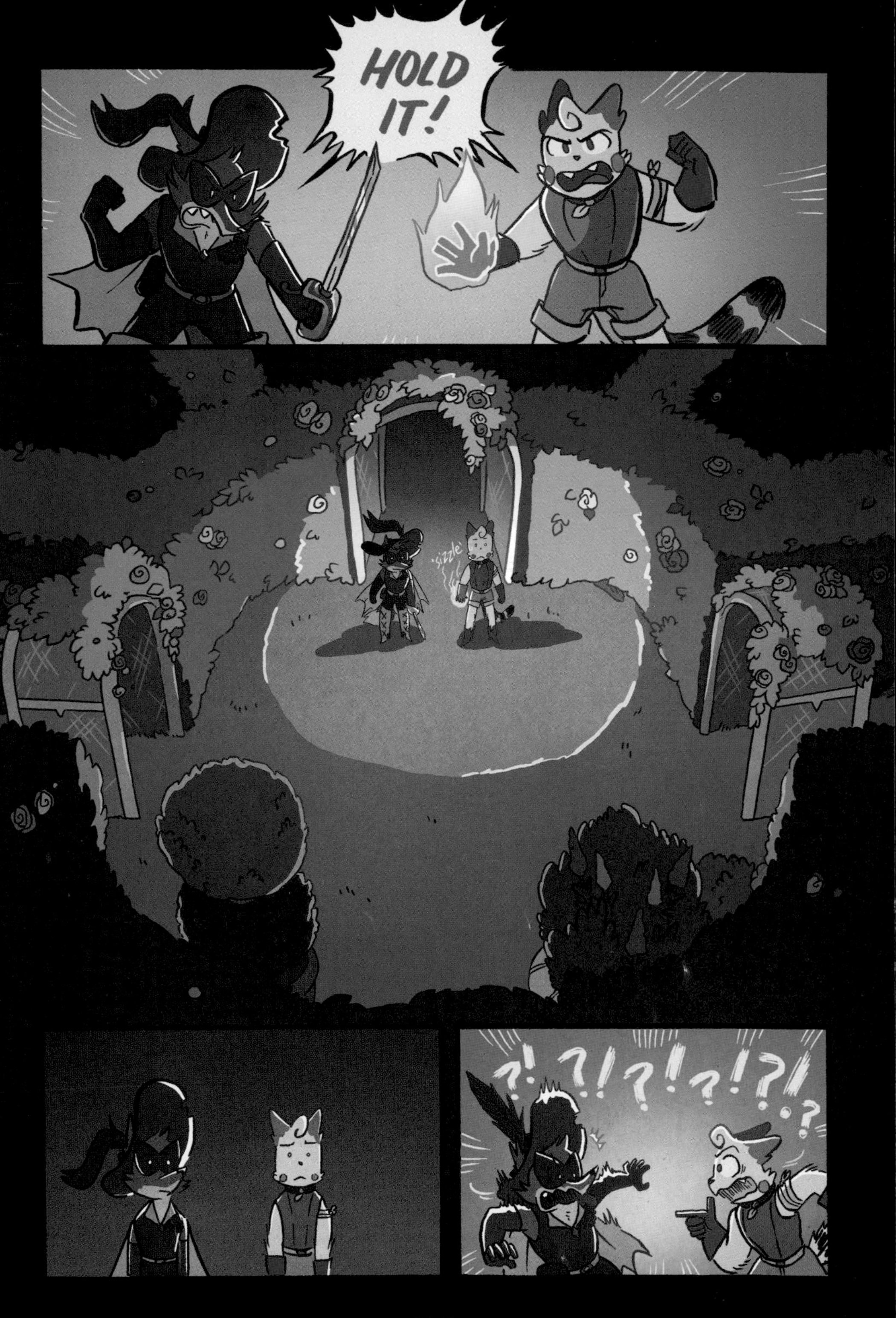
HOLD IT!
sizzle
?!?!?!?!?!?

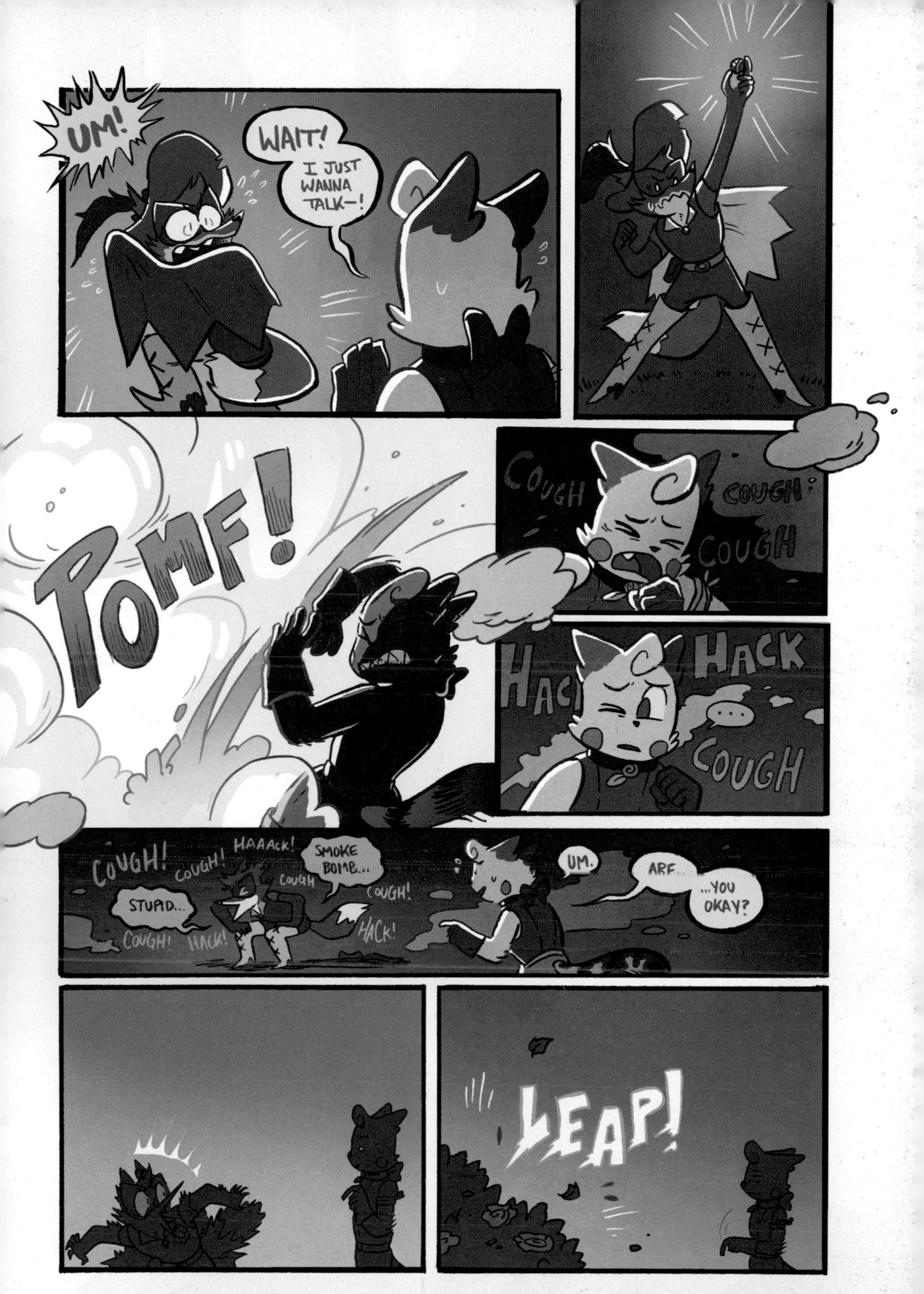

UM!
WAIT!
I JUST WANNA TALK—!
POMF!
COUGH
COUGH
COUGH
HACK
HACK
...
COUGH
COUGH!
COUGH!
HAAACK!
SMOKE BOMB...
COUGH
STUPID...
COUGH!
COUGH! HACK!
HACK!
UM.
ARF...
...YOU OKAY?
LEAP!

164

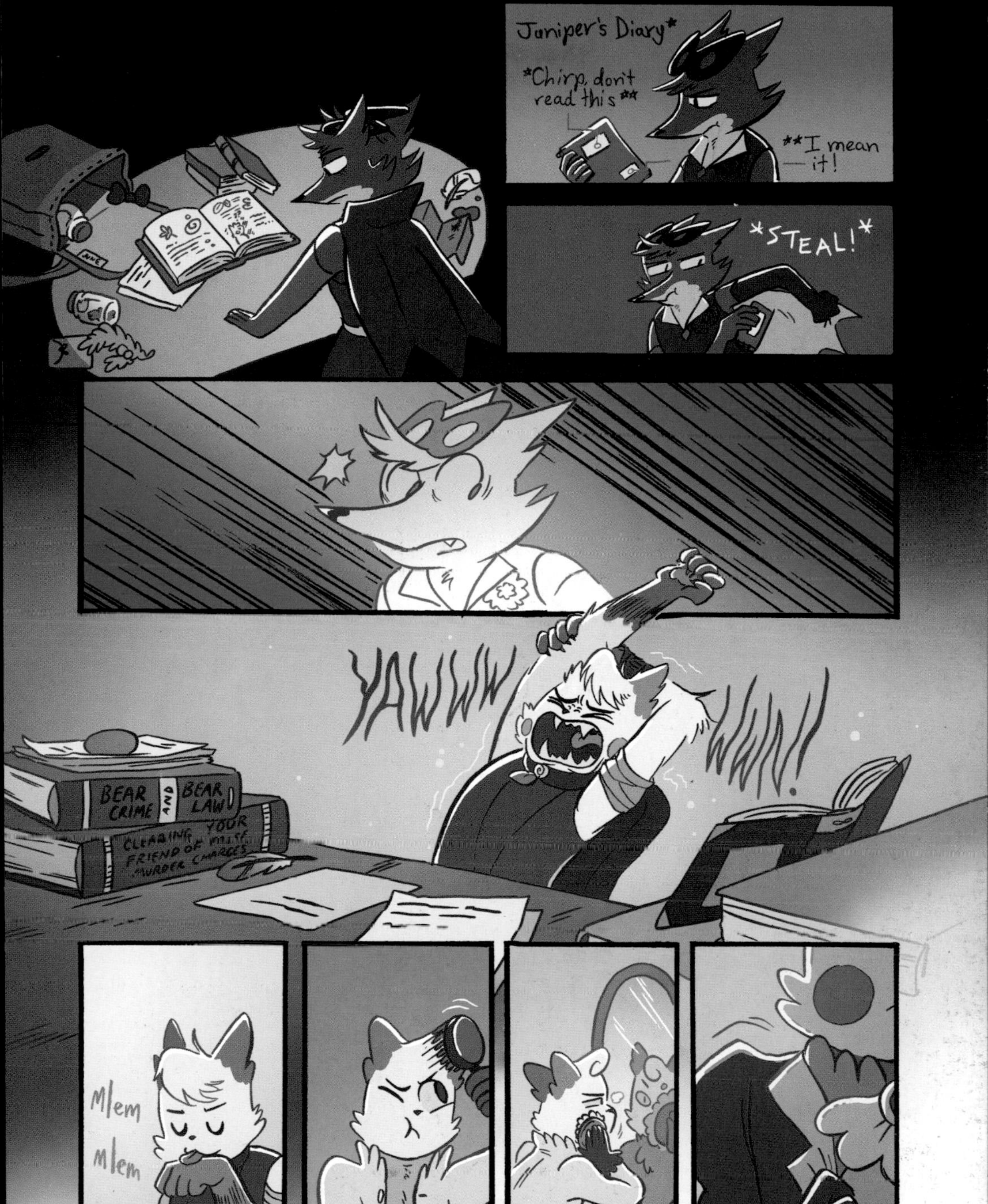
Juniper's Diary*
*Chirp, don't read this**
**I mean it!
STEAL!
YAWWWWN!
BEAR CRIME AND BEAR LAW
CLEARING YOUR FRIEND OF MURDER CHARGES
Mlem
mlem

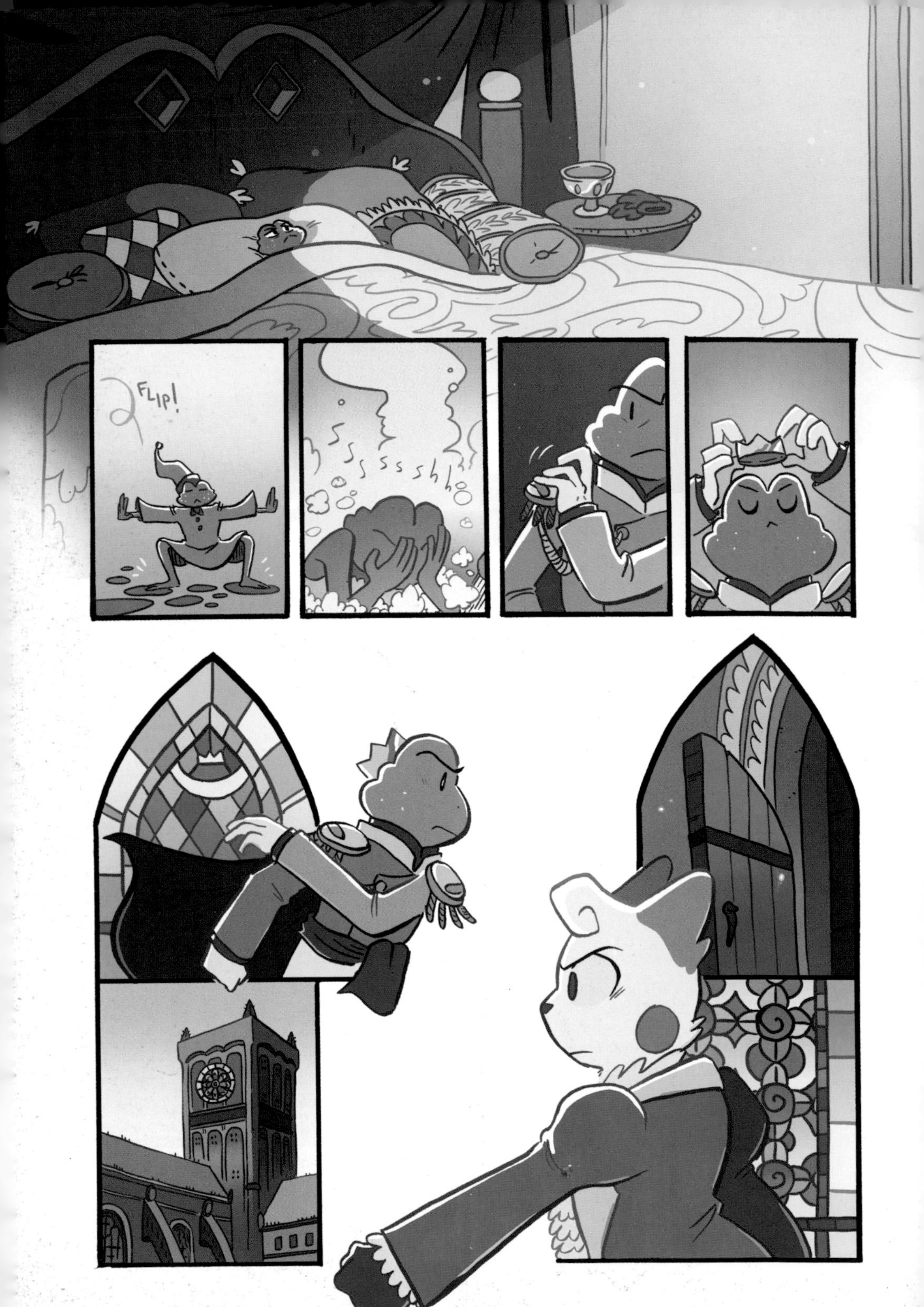
FLIP!
SSSSSshh

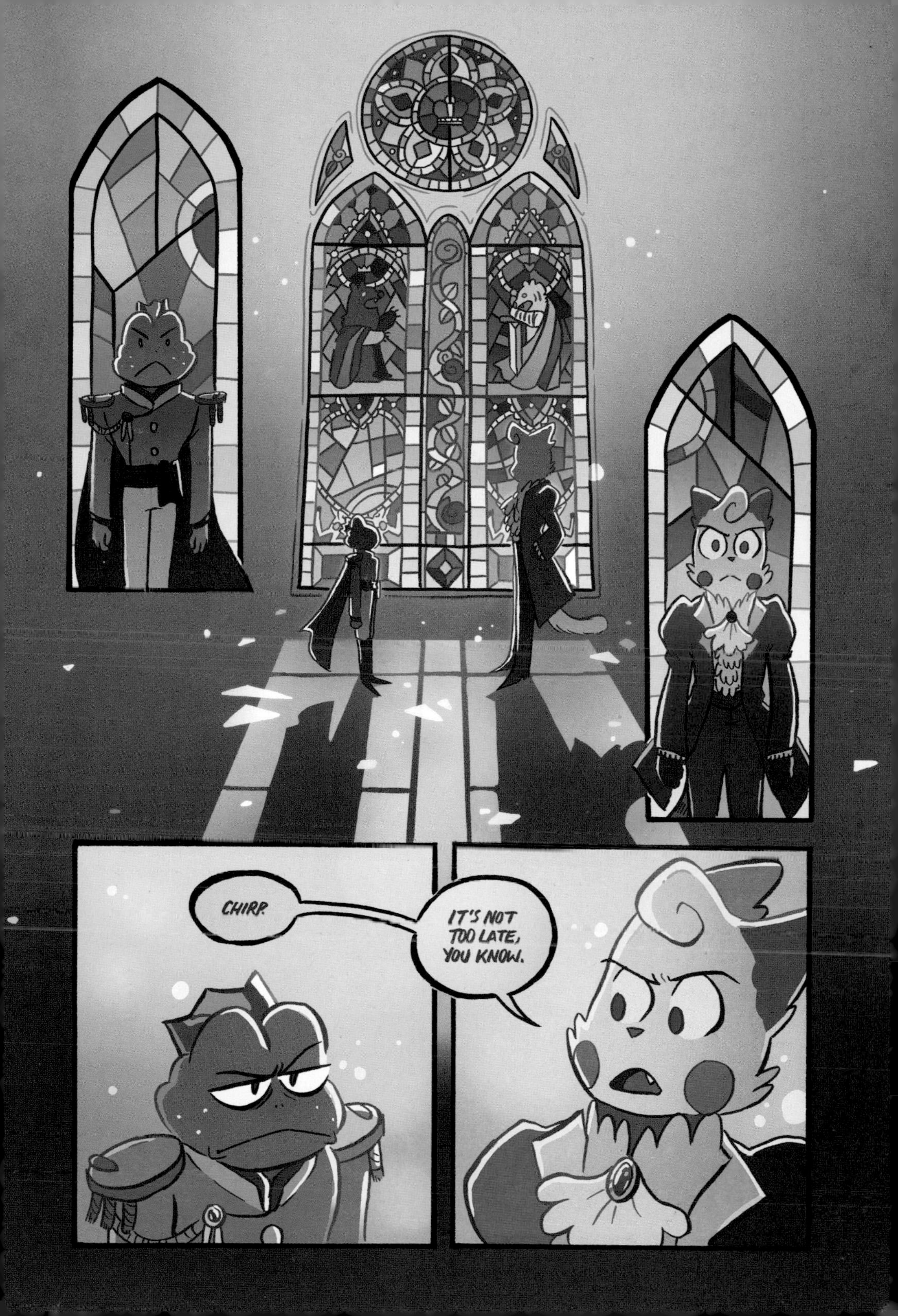
CHIRP.
IT'S NOT TOO LATE, YOU KNOW.

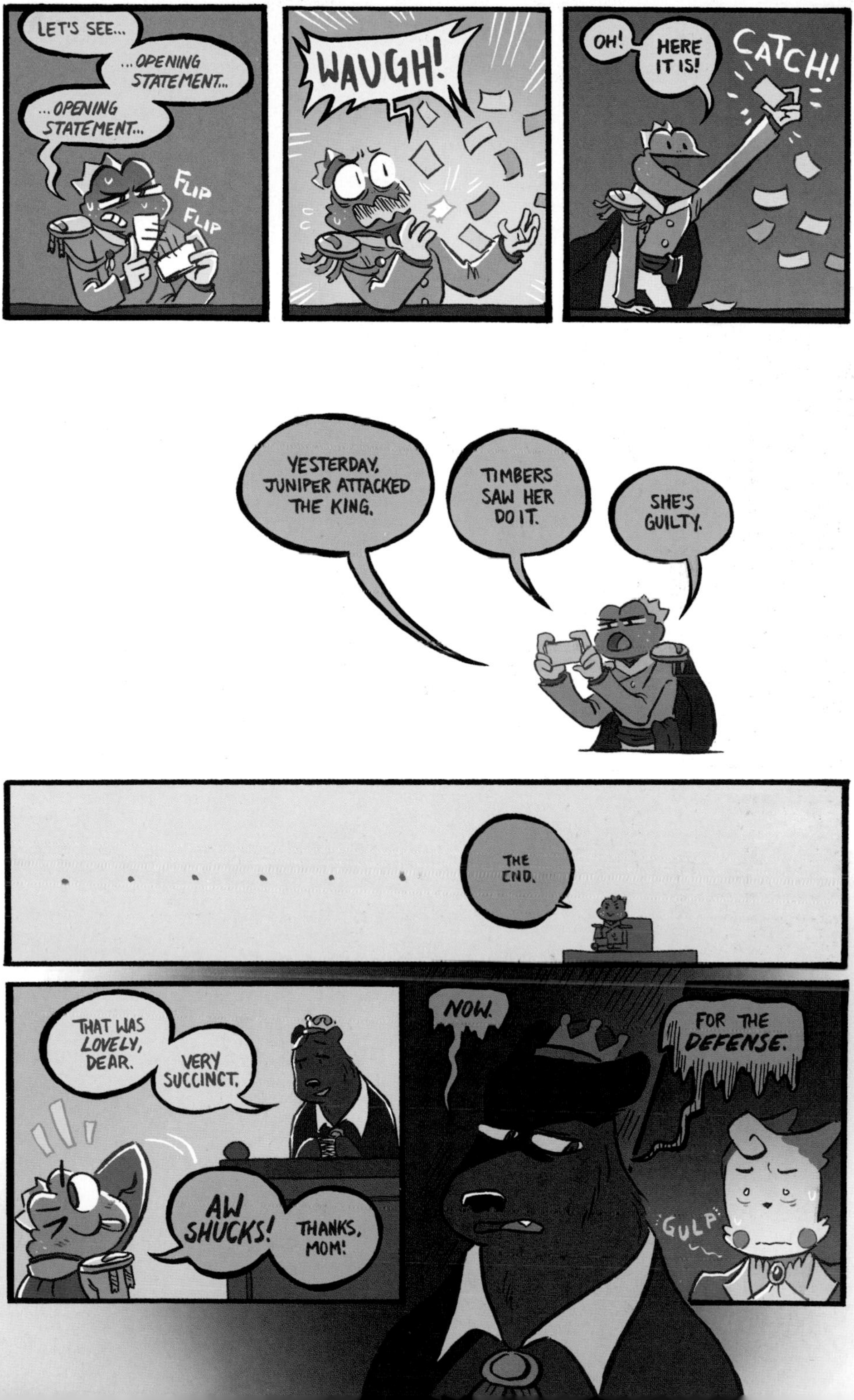
LET'S SEE...
...OPENING STATEMENT...
...OPENING STATEMENT...
FLIP
FLIP
WAUGH!
OH!
HERE IT IS!
CATCH!
YESTERDAY, JUNIPER ATTACKED THE KING.
TIMBERS SAW HER DO IT.
SHE'S GUILTY.
. . . .
THE END.
THAT WAS LOVELY, DEAR.
VERY SUCCINCT.
AW SHUCKS!
THANKS, MOM!
NOW.
FOR THE DEFENSE.
GULP

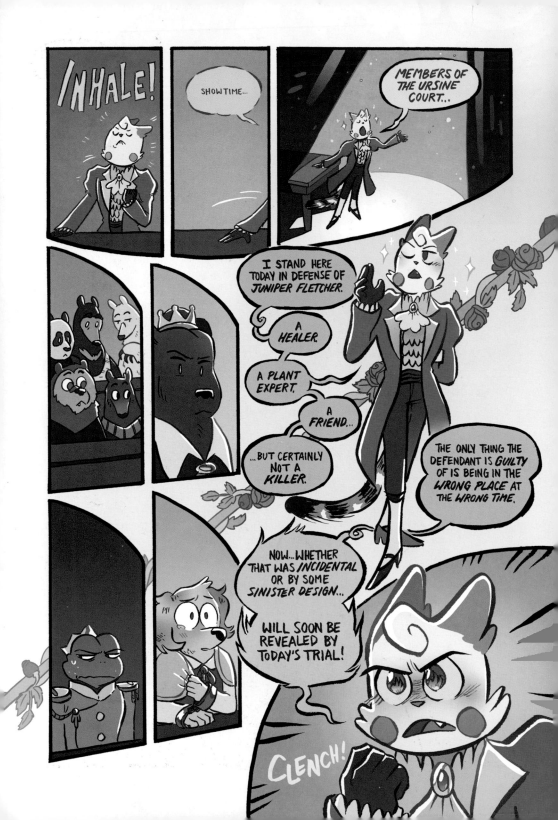

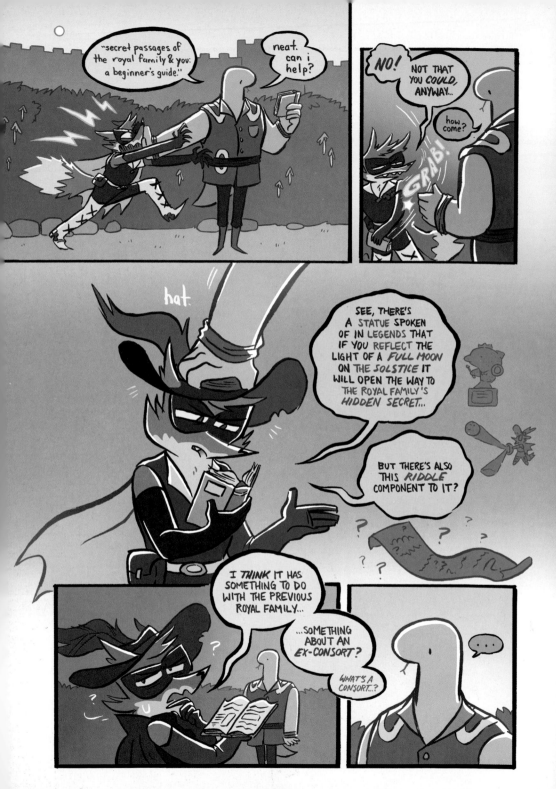

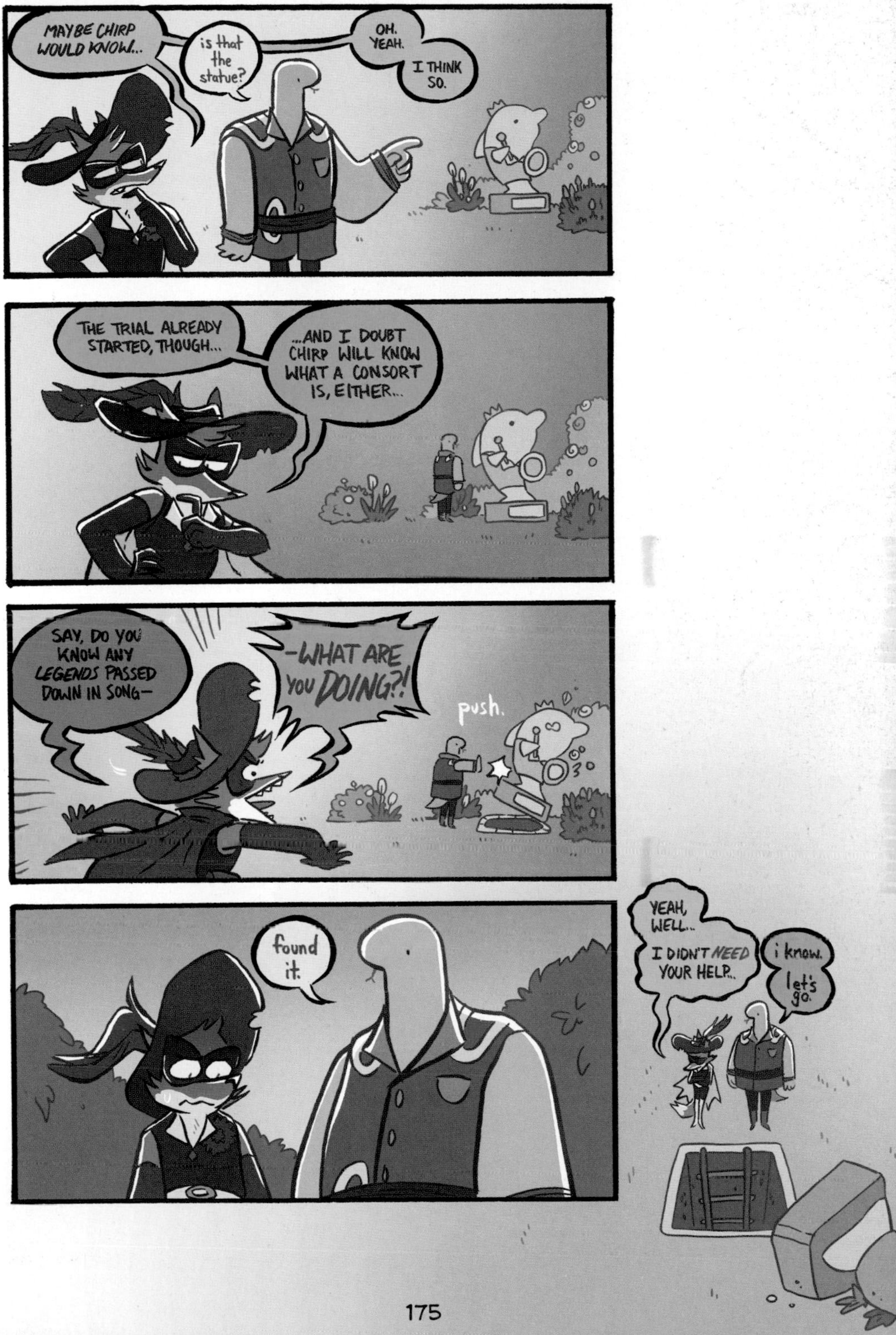
MAYBE CHIRP WOULD KNOW...
is that the statue?
OH. YEAH.
I THINK SO.
THE TRIAL ALREADY STARTED, THOUGH...
...AND I DOUBT CHIRP WILL KNOW WHAT A CONSORT IS, EITHER...
SAY, DO YOU KNOW ANY LEGENDS PASSED DOWN IN SONG—
—WHAT ARE YOU DOING?!
push.
found it.
YEAH, WELL...
I DIDN'T NEED YOUR HELP...
i know.
let's go.

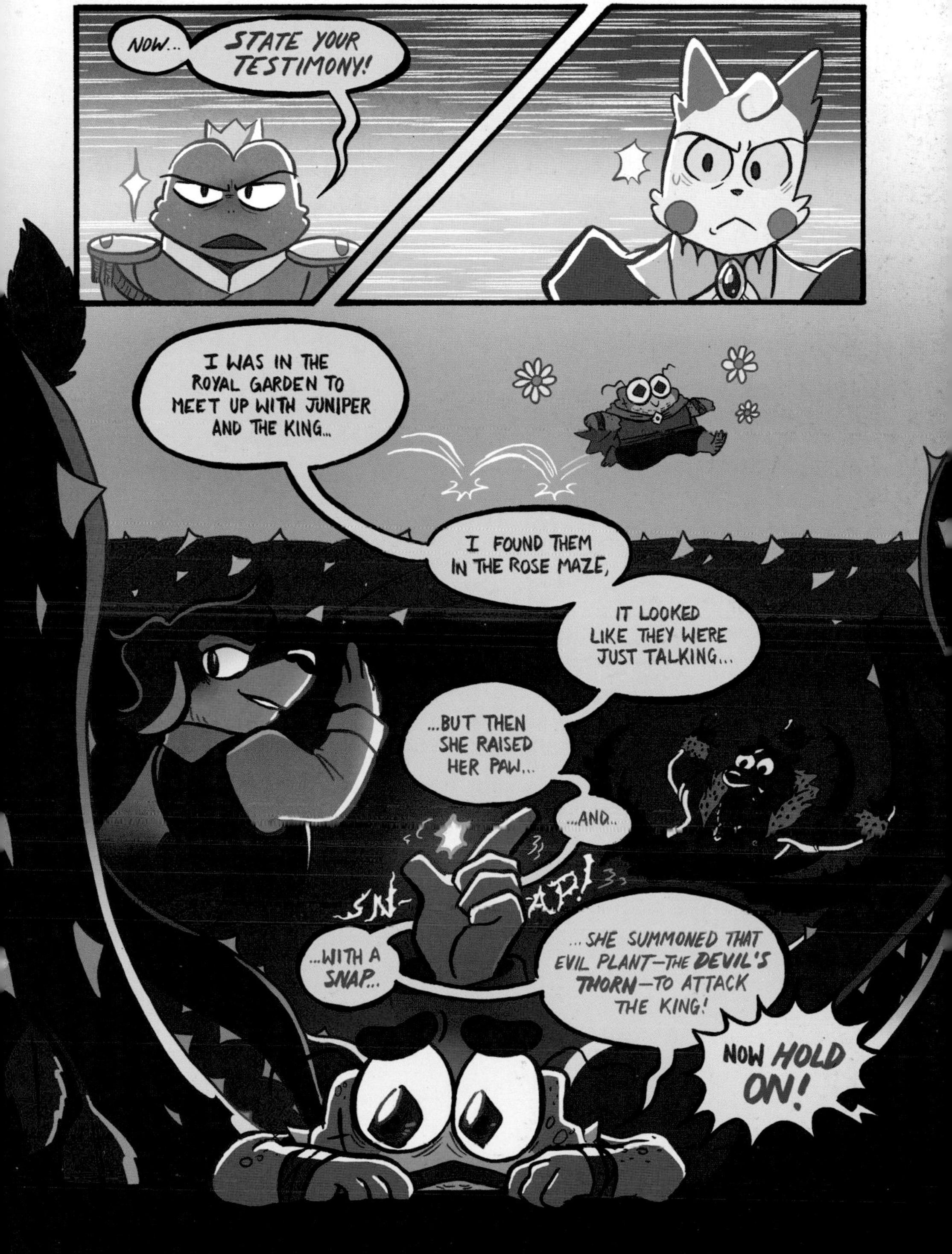
NOW...
STATE YOUR TESTIMONY!
I WAS IN THE ROYAL GARDEN TO MEET UP WITH JUNIPER AND THE KING...
I FOUND THEM IN THE ROSE MAZE,
IT LOOKED LIKE THEY WERE JUST TALKING...
...BUT THEN SHE RAISED HER PAW...
...AND...
SN-AP!
...WITH A SNAP...
...SHE SUMMONED THAT EVIL PLANT—THE DEVIL'S THORN—TO ATTACK THE KING!
NOW HOLD ON!

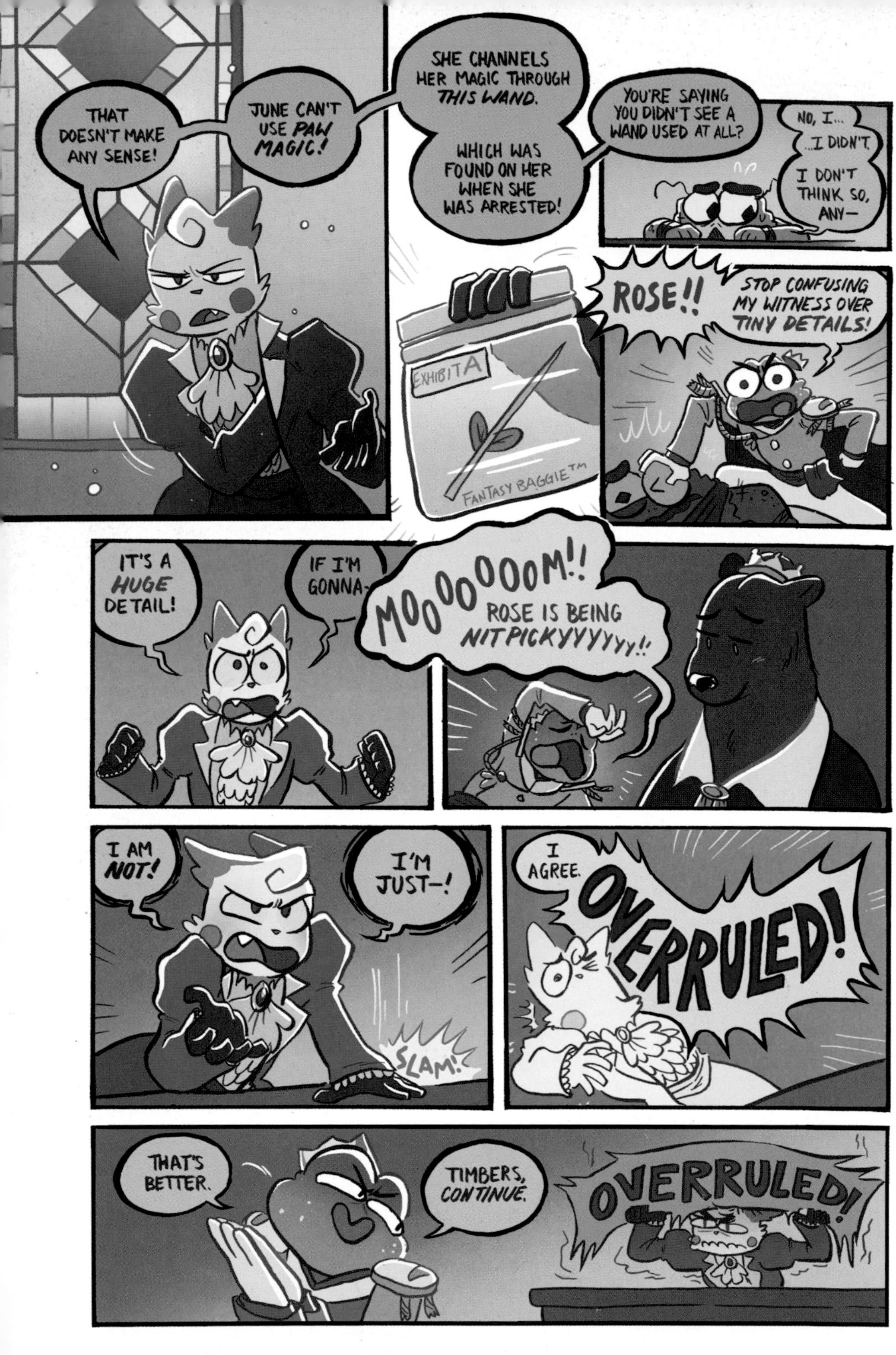
THAT DOESN'T MAKE ANY SENSE!
JUNE CAN'T USE *PAW MAGIC!*
SHE CHANNELS HER MAGIC THROUGH *THIS WAND.*
WHICH WAS FOUND ON HER WHEN SHE WAS ARRESTED!
YOU'RE SAYING YOU DIDN'T SEE A WAND USED AT ALL?
NO, I... ...I DIDN'T.
I DON'T THINK SO, ANY—
EXHIBIT A
FANTASY BAGGIE™
ROSE!!
STOP CONFUSING MY WITNESS OVER *TINY DETAILS!*
IT'S A *HUGE* DETAIL!
IF I'M GONNA-
MOOOOOOOM!!
ROSE IS BEING *NITPICKYYYYyyy!!*
I AM *NOT!*
I'M JUST—!
SLAM!
I AGREE.
OVERRULED!
THAT'S BETTER.
TIMBERS, *CONTINUE.*
OVERRULED!

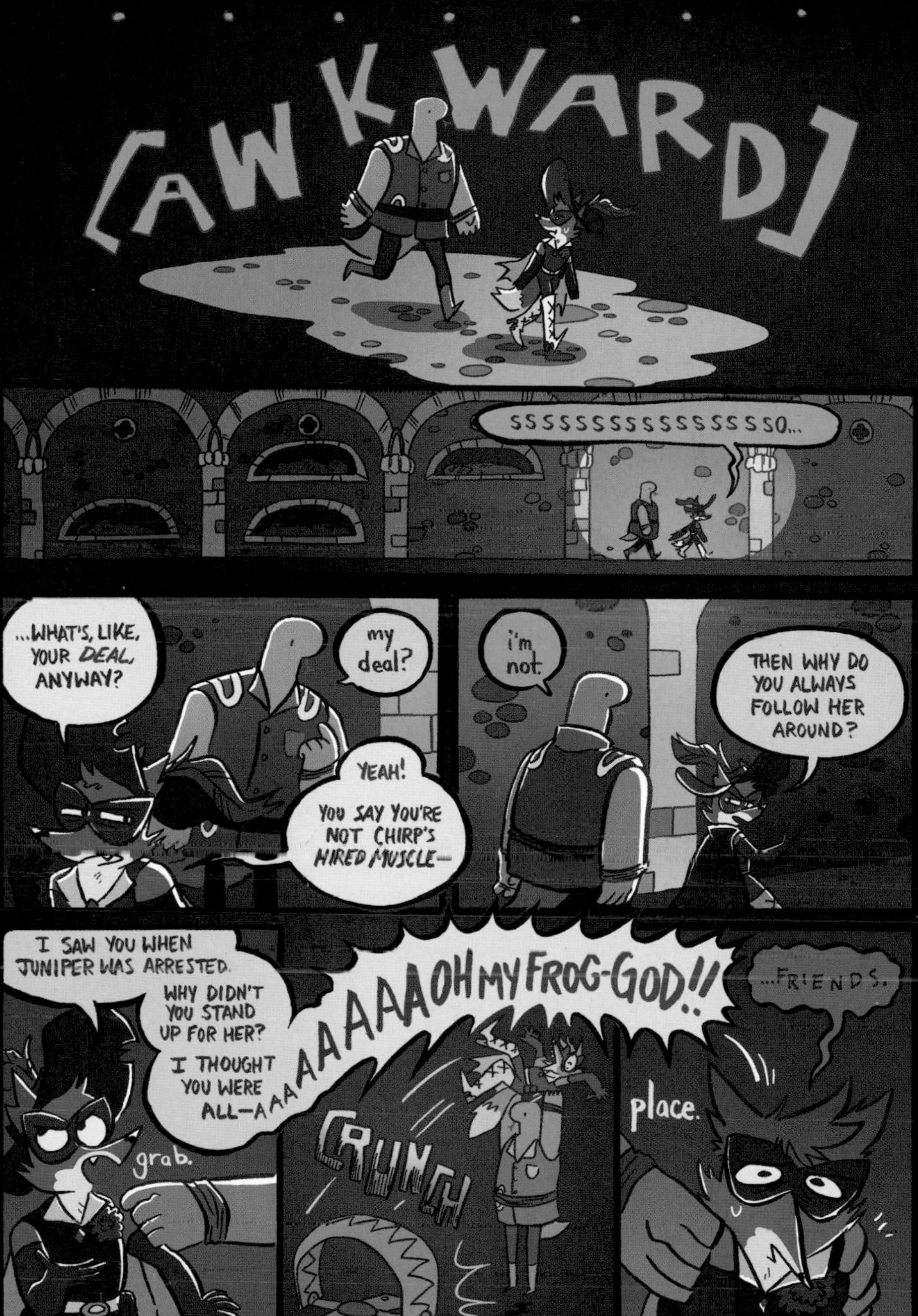
[AWKWARD]
SSSSSSSSSSSSSSSSSO...
...WHAT'S, LIKE, YOUR DEAL, ANYWAY?
my deal?
YEAH!
YOU SAY YOU'RE NOT CHIRP'S HIRED MUSCLE—
i'm not.
THEN WHY DO YOU ALWAYS FOLLOW HER AROUND?
I SAW YOU WHEN JUNIPER WAS ARRESTED.
WHY DIDN'T YOU STAND UP FOR HER?
I THOUGHT YOU WERE ALL-AAAAAAAAAOH MY FROG-GOD!!
grab.
CRUNCH
place.
...FRIENDS.

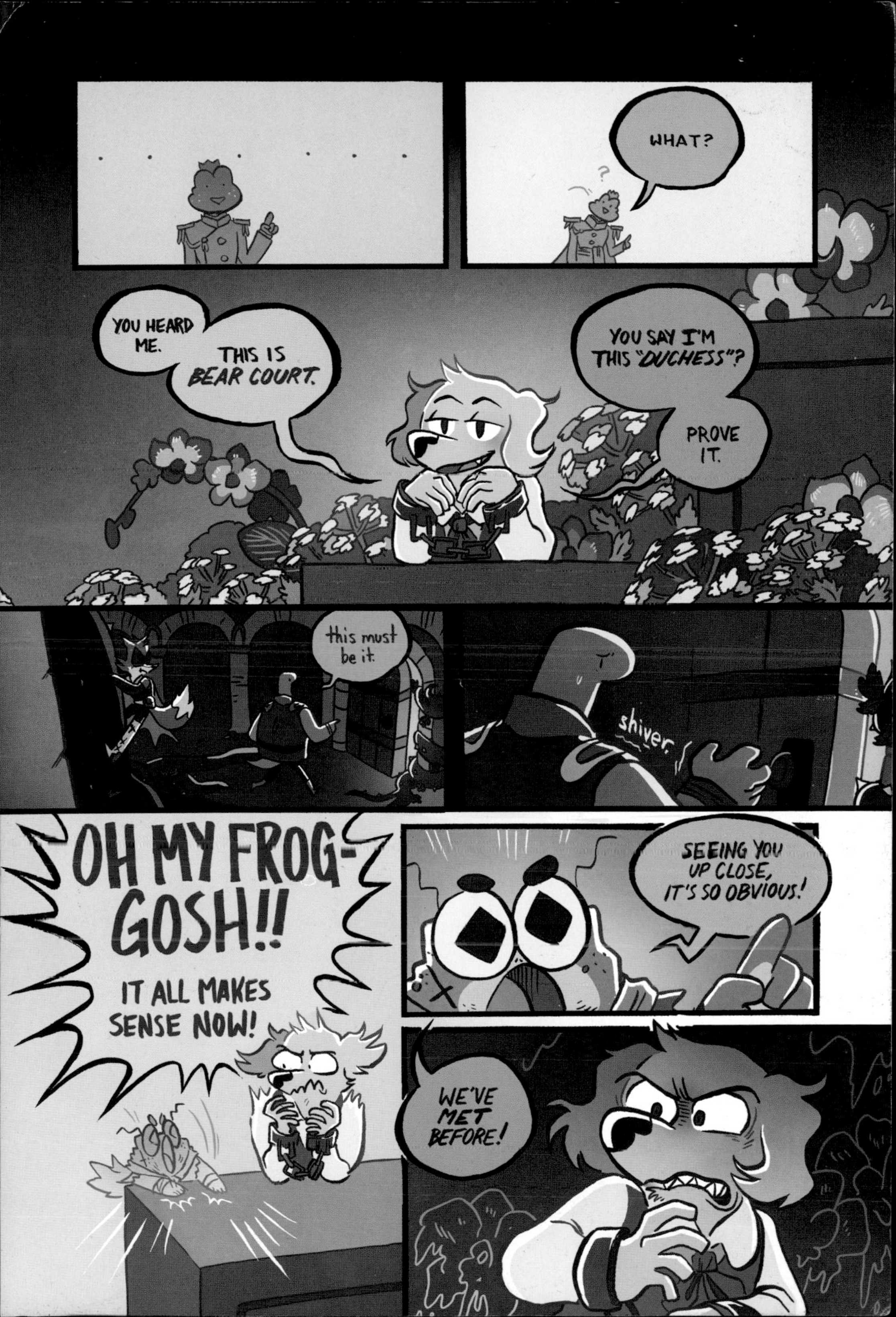
. . . .
WHAT?
?
YOU HEARD ME.
THIS IS BEAR COURT.
YOU SAY I'M THIS "DUCHESS"?
PROVE IT.
this must be it.
shiver.
OH MY FROG-GOSH!!
IT ALL MAKES SENSE NOW!
SEEING YOU UP CLOSE, IT'S SO OBVIOUS!
WE'VE MET BEFORE!

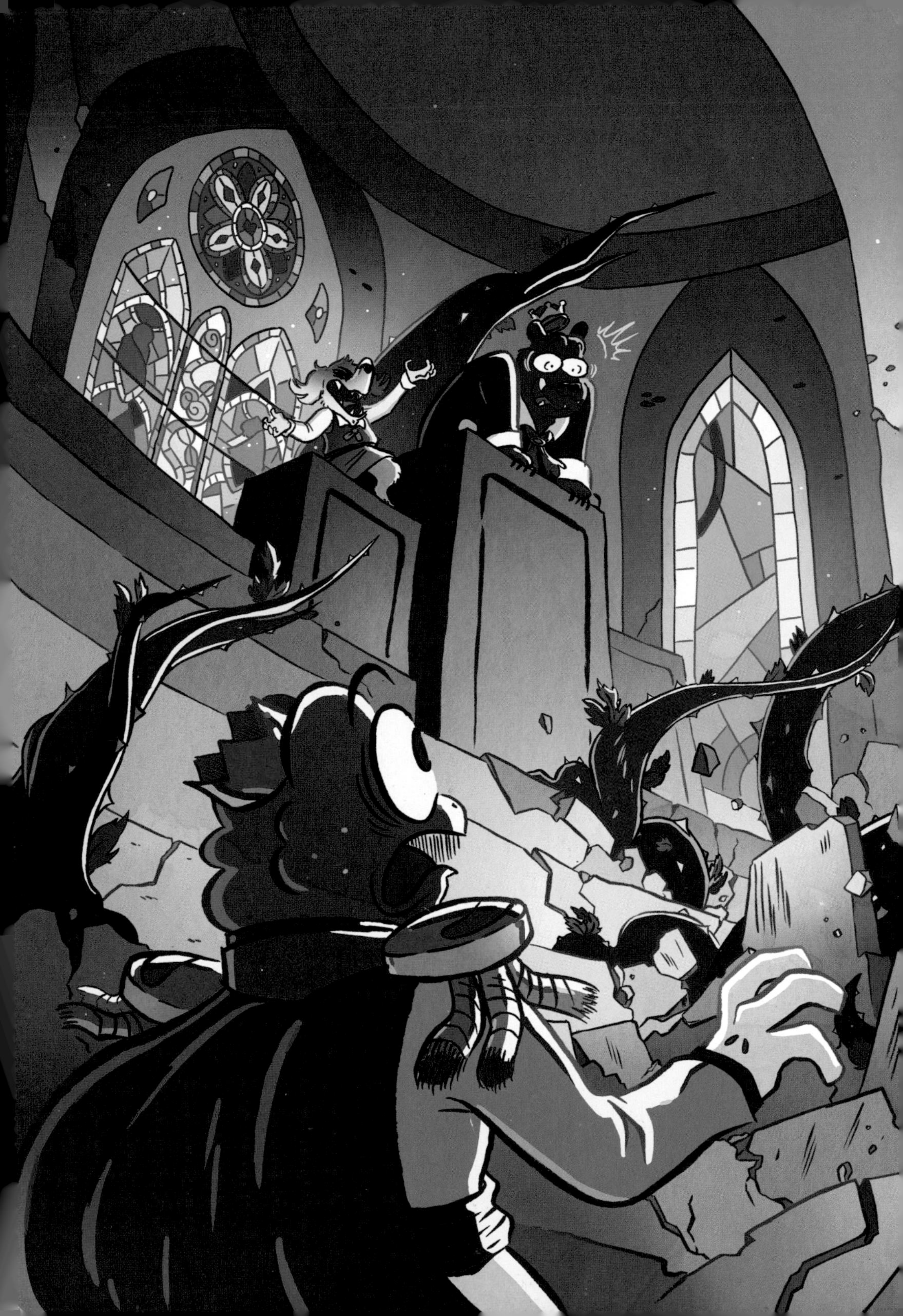

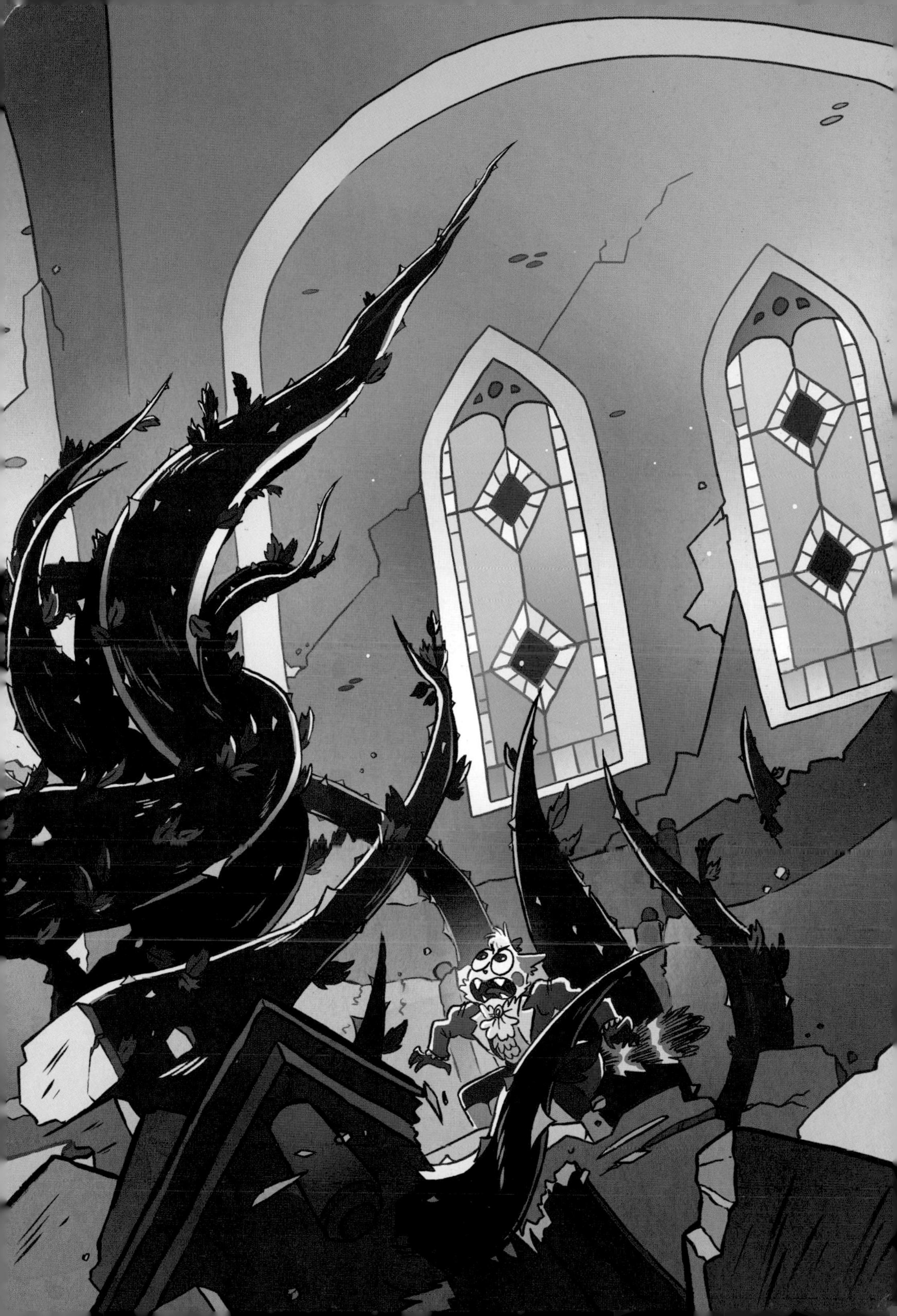

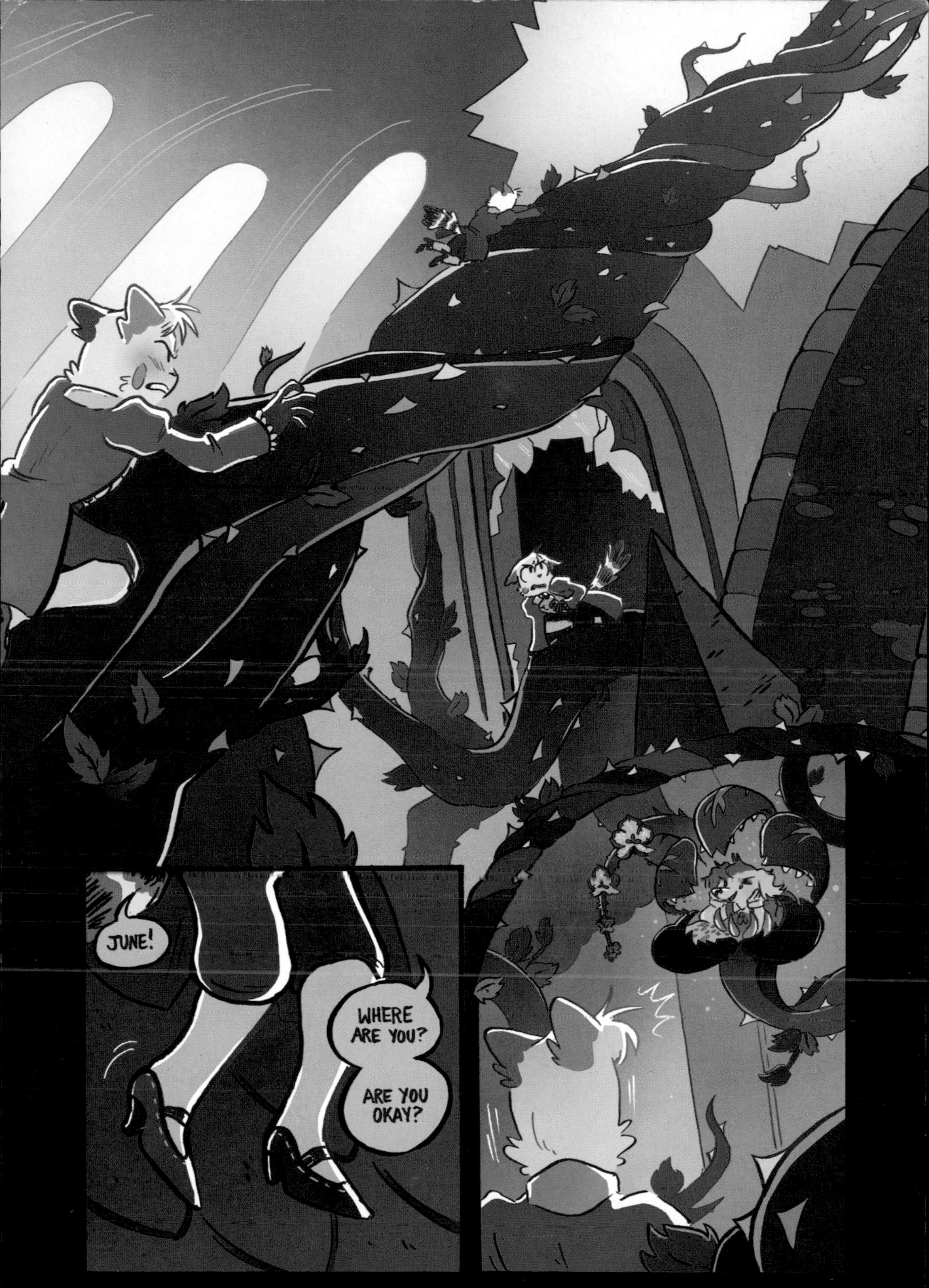
JUNE!
WHERE ARE YOU?
ARE YOU OKAY?

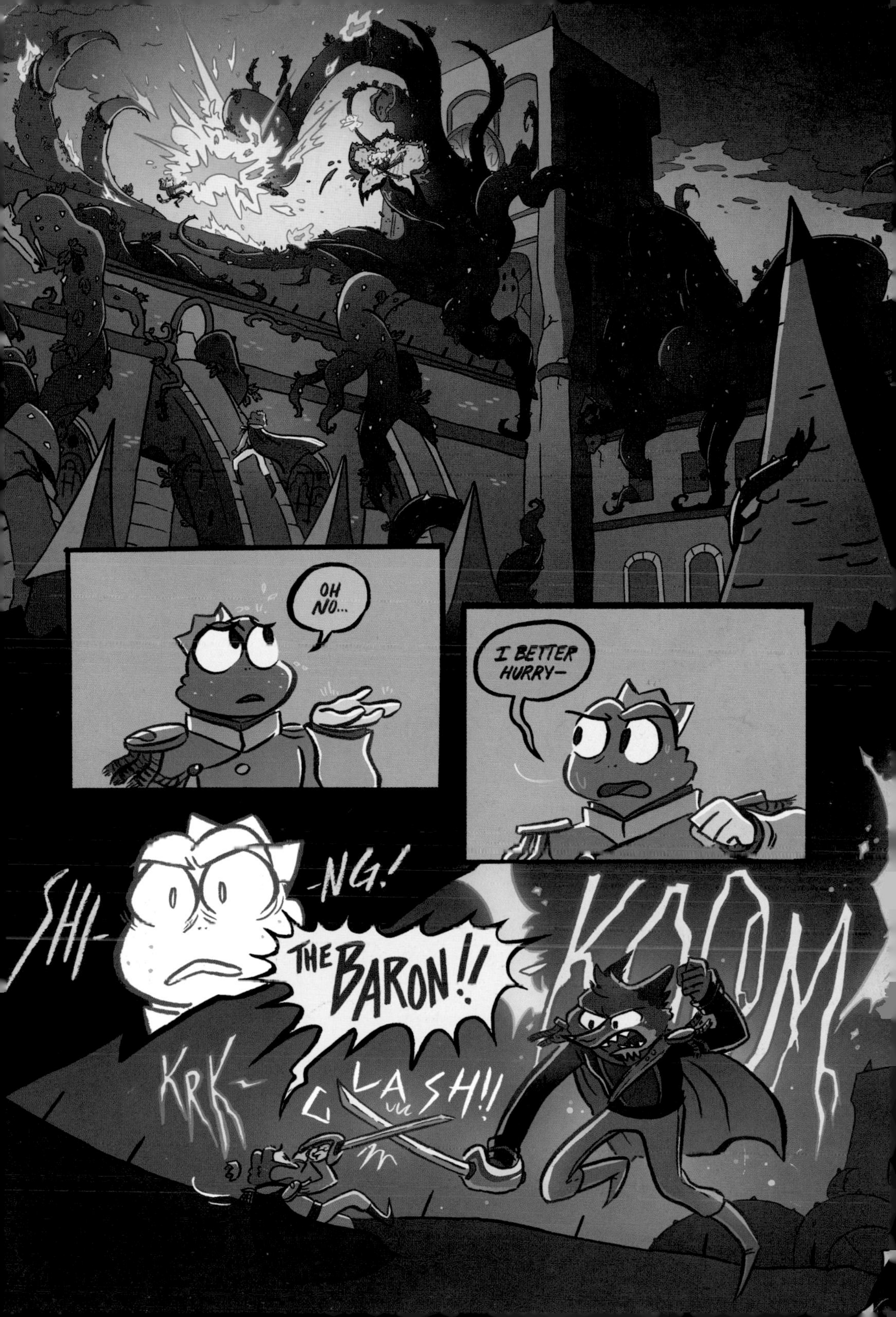
OH NO...
I BETTER HURRY-
SHI-
-NG!
THE BARON!!
KRK-
KOOM
CLASH!!

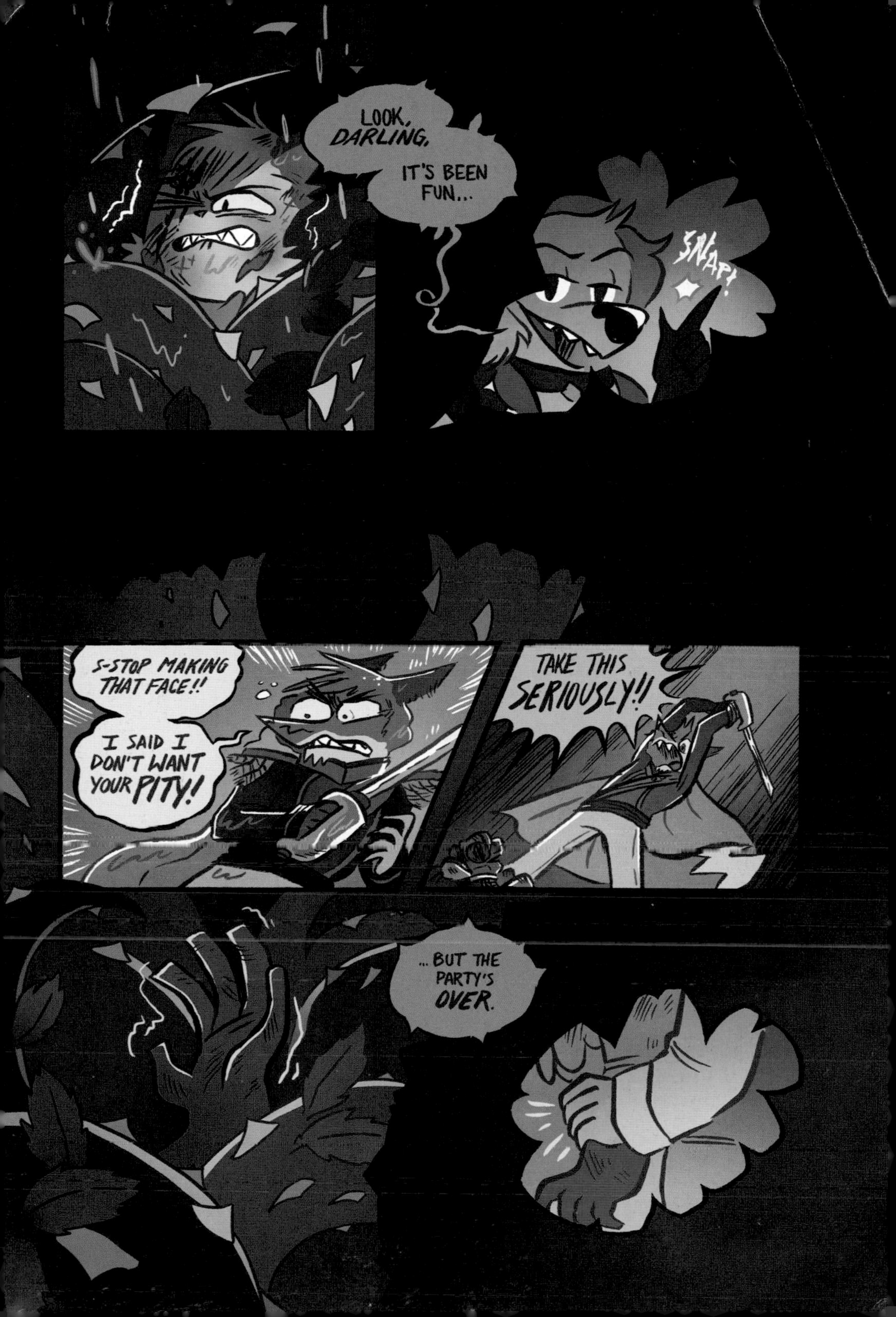
LOOK, DARLING,
IT'S BEEN FUN...
SNAP!
S-STOP MAKING THAT FACE!!
I SAID I DON'T WANT YOUR PITY!
TAKE THIS SERIOUSLY!!
...BUT THE PARTY'S OVER.

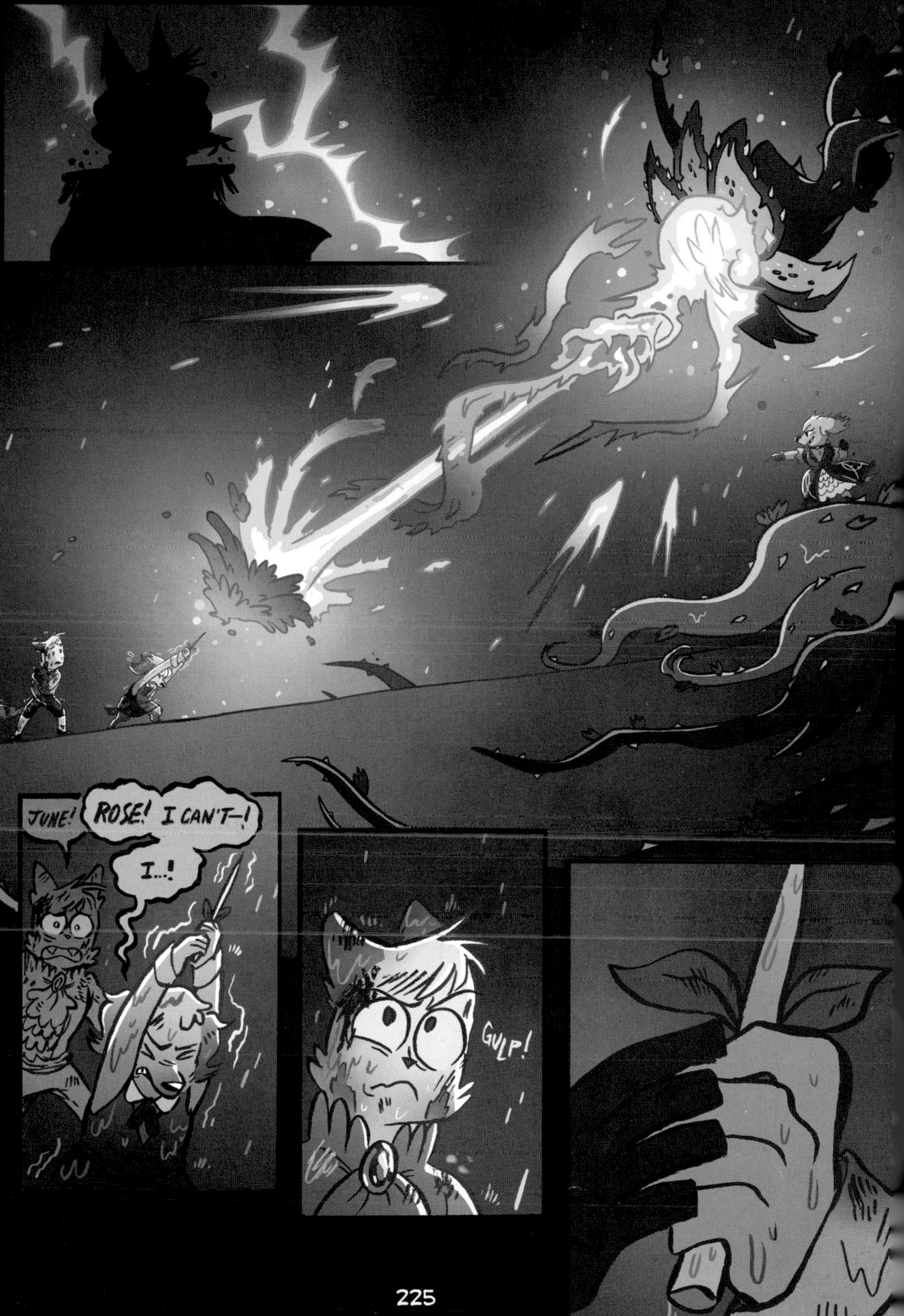
JUNE!
ROSE! I CAN'T-!
I..!
GULP!

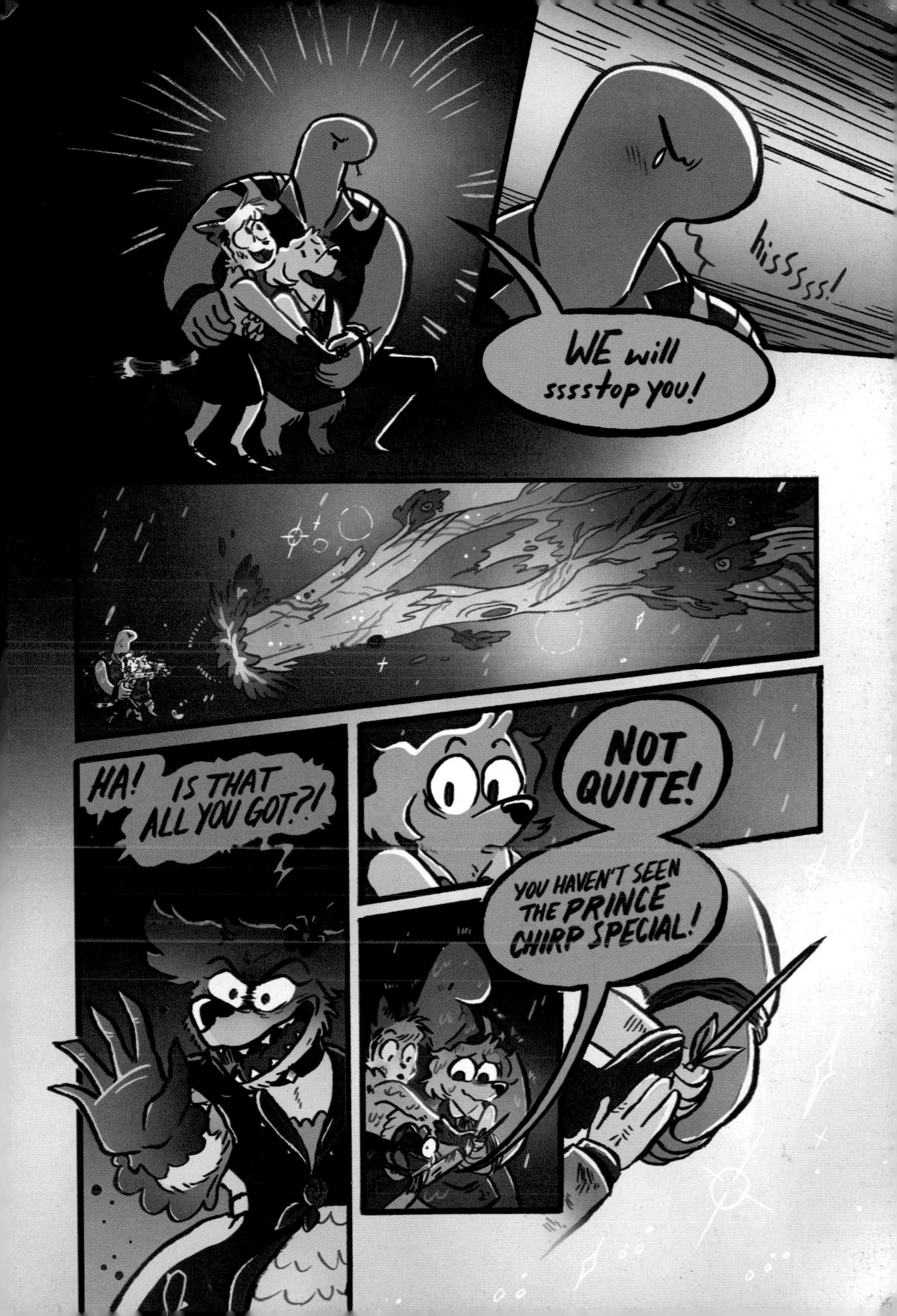
hissssss!
WE will sssstop you!
HA! IS THAT ALL YOU GOT?!
NOT QUITE!
YOU HAVEN'T SEEN THE PRINCE CHIRP SPECIAL!

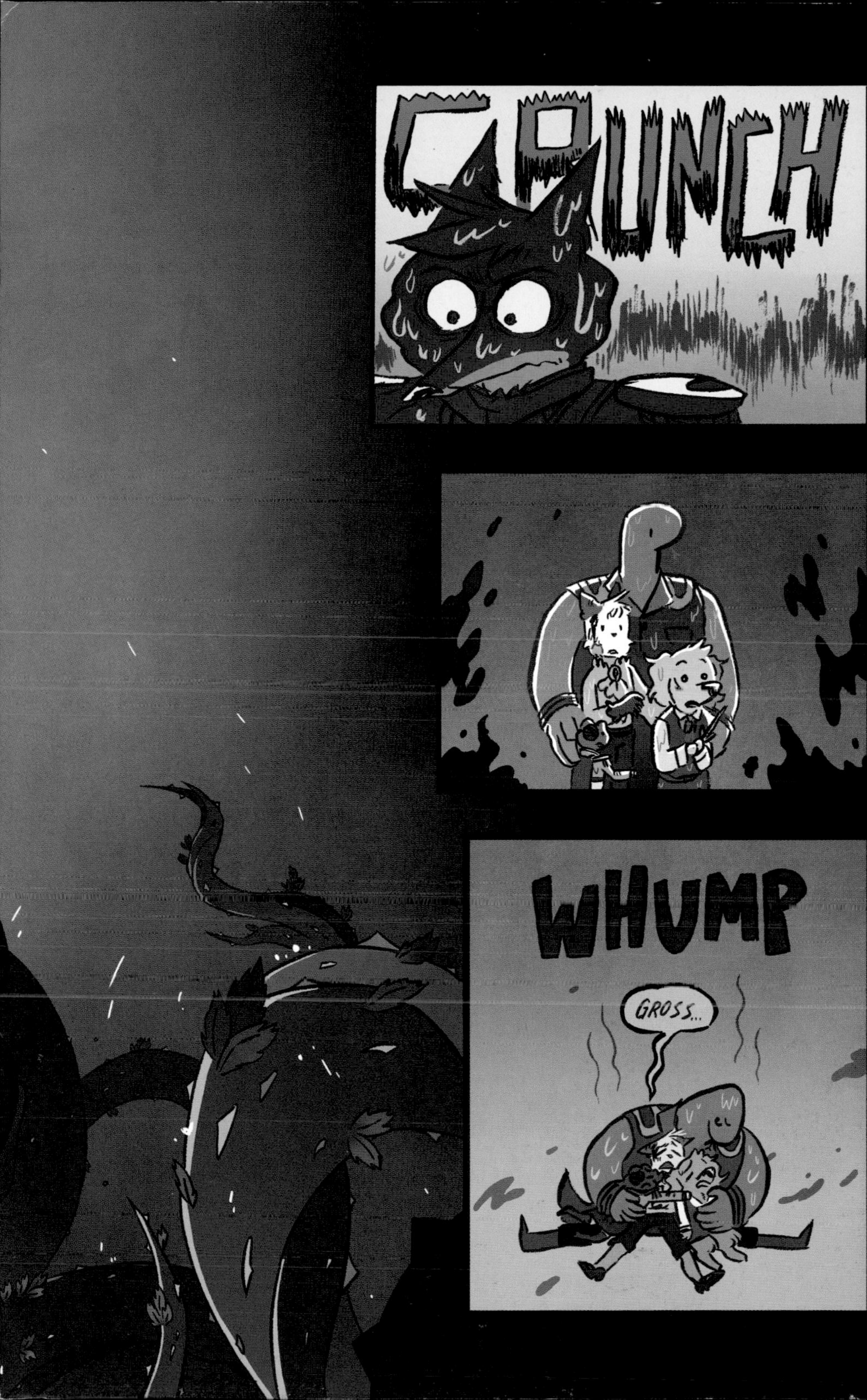
CRUNCH
WHUMP
GROSS...

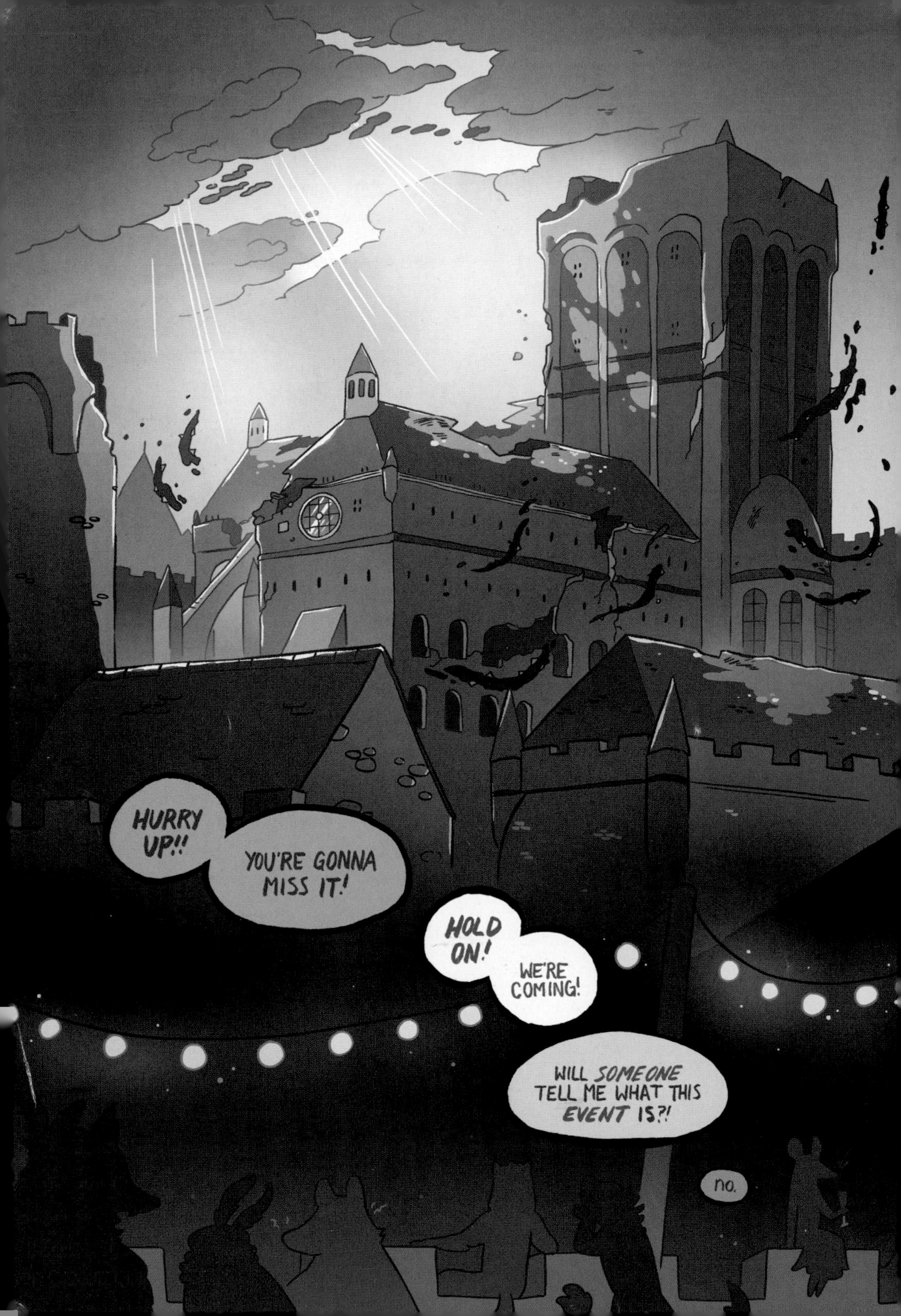
HURRY UP!!
YOU'RE GONNA MISS IT!
HOLD ON!
WE'RE COMING!
WILL SOMEONE TELL ME WHAT THIS EVENT IS?!
no.

oh.
thank you.
dear goro,
i've been kidnapped by eels. i'm being held in the old lighthouse. please come before the full moon.
♡horseboy
OH NO! THE FULL MOON...IS TOMORROW!
WHO'S HORSE-BOY?
. . . . . .
I-I'M KIDDING!
YEESH!
okay.
let's go.
fist pump.
THE END!

Acknowledgments

A lot of people helped get this book made! Thank you to:

Everyone at First Second, but especially our editors Calista and Mariah,
Kirk, for the cover design, and Kiara and Gina
for answering our emails.

Our agent, Steven, and everyone at Curtis Brown for their expertise.

Our cartoonist peers for their constant support, community, friendship,
and advice, because we barely know what we're doing.

Elli, Sin, and Nate for teaching us how to play tabletop games
and sparking this adventure.

Tilly, my cat, who is so beautiful and also small and loves
to scream, for always being there for inspiration.

Last but not at all least, our families, without whom
none of this would be possible.

Thank you for reading our book!

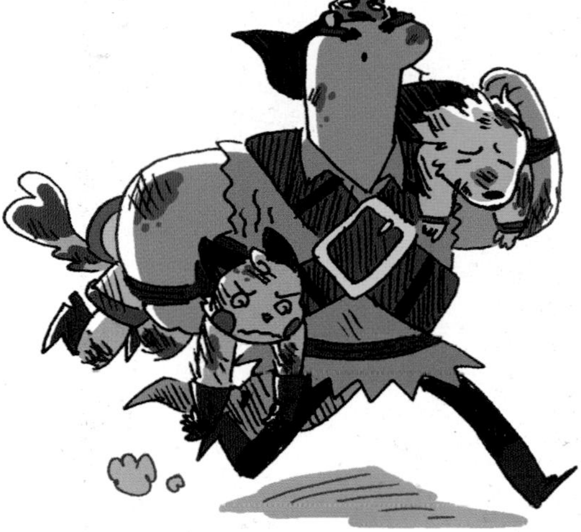

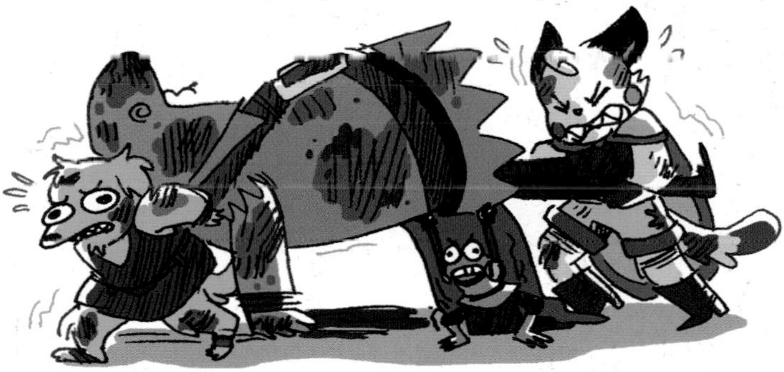

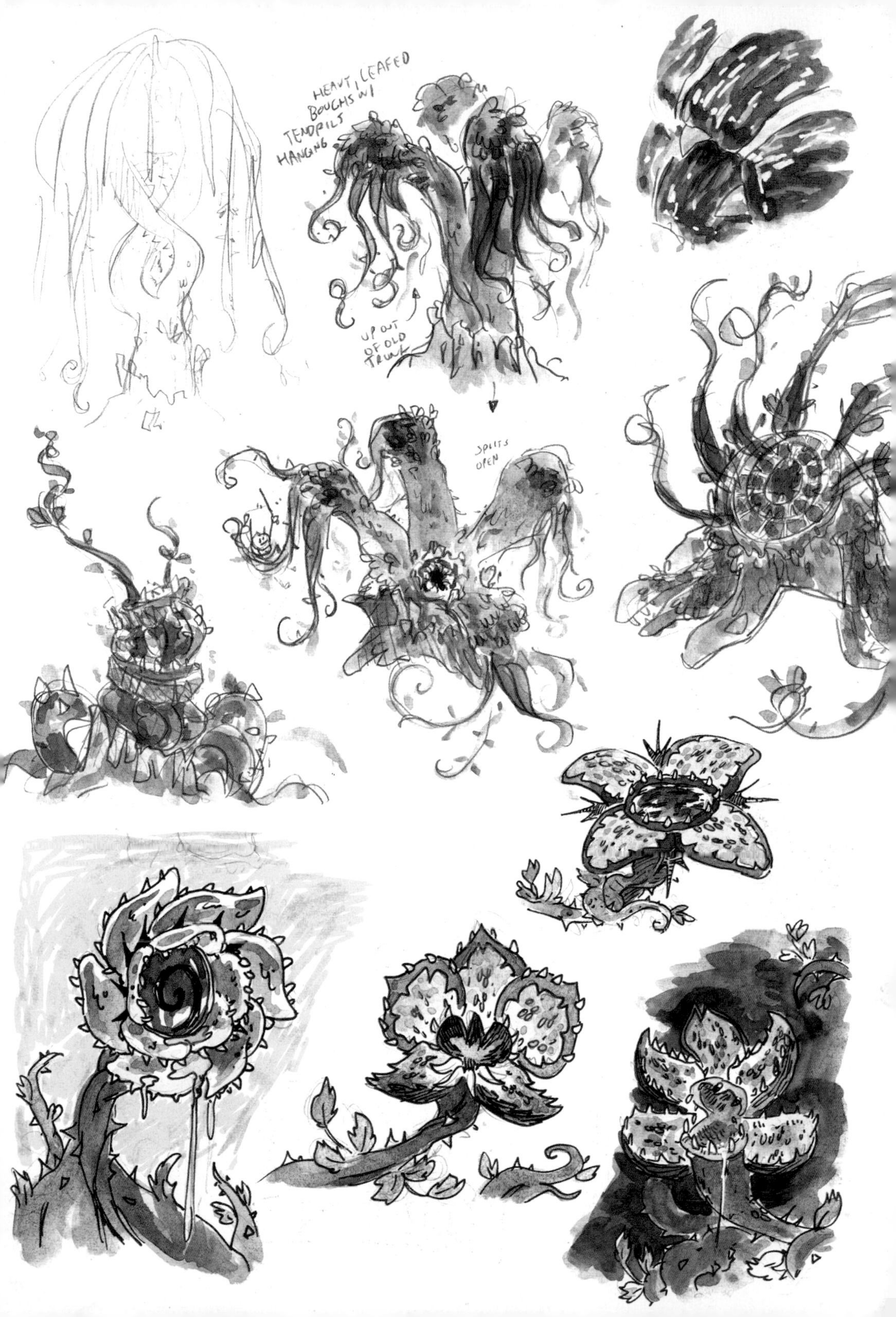
HEAVY, LEAFED BOUGHS W/ TENDRILS HANGING
UP OUT OF OLD TRUNK
SPLITS OPEN

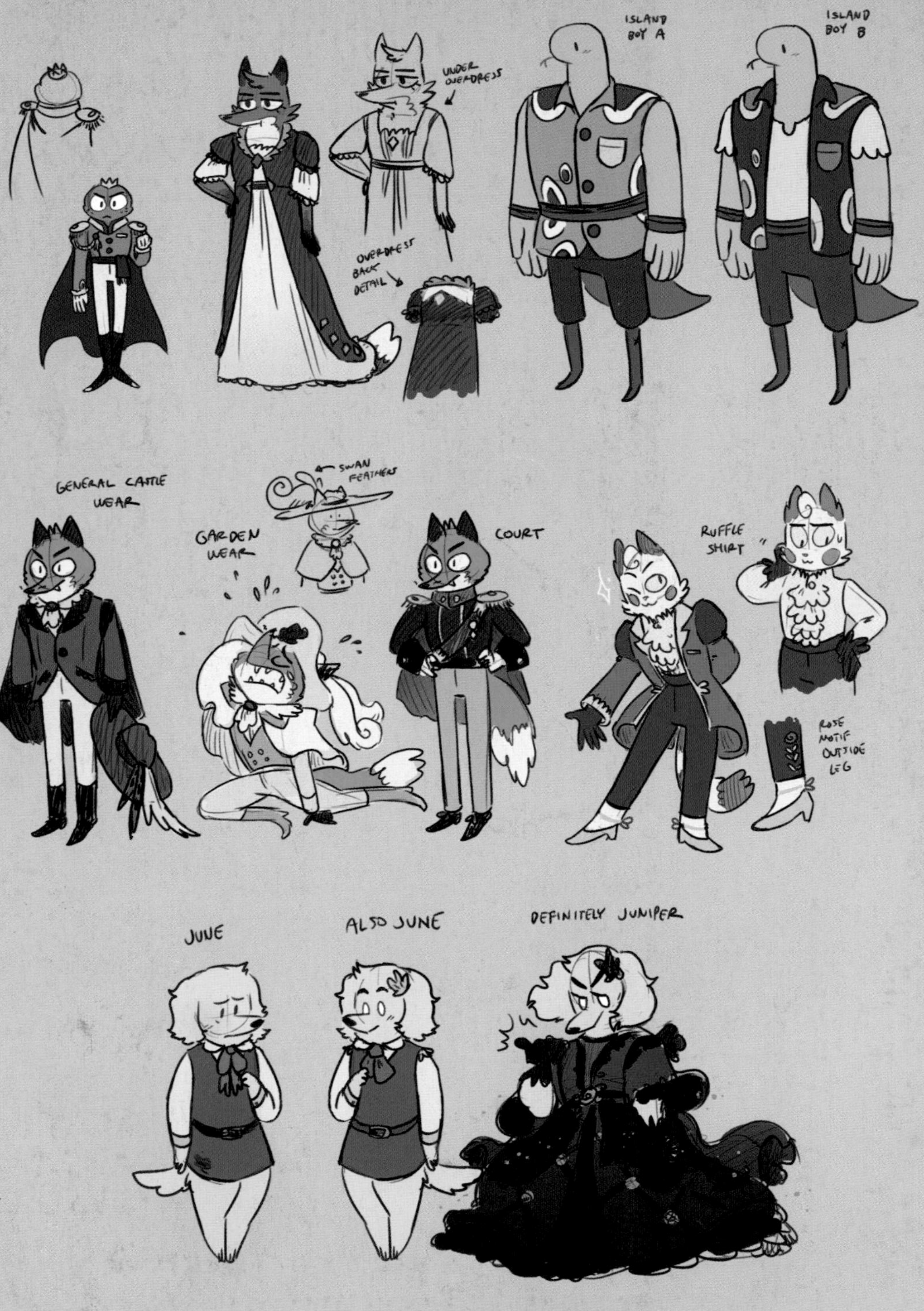

UNDER OVERDRESS
OVERDRESS BACK DETAIL
ISLAND BOY A
ISLAND BOY B
GENERAL CASTLE WEAR
SWAN FEATHERS
GARDEN WEAR
COURT
RUFFLE SHIRT
ROSE MOTIF OUTSIDE LEG
JUNE
ALSO JUNE
DEFINITELY JUNIPER